The
AMERICAN
BOYS

The
AMERICAN BOYS

OLIVIA SPOONER

Published in New Zealand in 2025
by Moa Press
(an imprint of Hachette Aotearoa New Zealand Limited)
Level 2, 23 Victoria Street East, Auckland, New Zealand
www.hachette.co.nz
www.moapress.co.nz

10 9 8 7 6 5 4 3 2 1

A catalogue record for this book is available from the National Library of New Zealand.

ISBN: 978 1 86971 851 0 (paperback)

Cover design by Christa Moffitt
Cover image courtesy of Trevillion Images
Author photo by Samantha Donaldson Photography
Text design by Bookhouse, Sydney
Typeset in Centaur MT Std by Bookhouse, Sydney
Printed and bound in Australia by McPherson's Printing Group

Dedicated to the kind, decent men in this world who give me hope, especially three of the absolute best — my dad, my husband and my son.

'As you marched down Lambton Quay in step with a buddy, your greens sharp and your leather shiny, you saw them turn and smile. The strange smell of foreign cooking and the new and wonderful odors of ale and tobacco; the funny way of talking and the funny money, and the honest merchants who gave baffled Marines a square shake. The beauty of the rolling hills and the gentle summer and the quaintness of the Victorian buildings, matching the slow, uneventful way of life. We were happy in New Zealand. As happy as a man can be six thousand miles away from his home.'

— *Battle Cry* by Leon Uris

PART ONE

WELLINGTON, NEW ZEALAND

JUNE 1942

Chapter I

LORNA

No mathematical equation could fix the situation, thought Lorna. She stepped from the tram, her body tingling with unease as icy drizzle immediately cloaked her coat. Taking a deep breath, Lorna berated herself. *Buck up, don't be silly. Think of your brothers.* What was the point in getting worked up about something that hadn't even happened yet? *Might never happen*, Lorna reminded herself. It was merely a possibility.

But how *much* of a possibility, Lorna wondered. What was the *exact* probability? Lorna loved working out probabilities, or had done when she was at school, but there was no equation she could formulate to give her the answer as to when and if the Japanese might invade her country. Surely there were statisticians working day and night on questions just like these. What did they know that she didn't?

A few months earlier, Lorna had discovered that a boy called Rupert, who'd been in her maths class, was working as a statistician for the Navy. He had been good at maths, but he'd never excelled. He'd never been top of the class three years running.

Pleased her fear had been replaced with a simmering anger, Lorna wrapped her arms around herself and walked briskly, with her head bowed to shield her face from the bitter southerly wind tunnelling down the wide, empty street. It was almost dark. In one week it would be 21 June, the shortest day of the year. Lorna felt as if winter would never end, even though it had scarcely begun. She wished she could snap her fingers and be home.

The blackout siren sounded, eerie and forlorn, and the street lights immediately switched off. Lorna slowed, taking a moment to collect herself and for her eyes to adjust to the gloom. Speeding up again, she hurried down three more blocks before turning onto Ranui Road, relieved to no longer be exposed to the full force of the wind. She glanced at Mrs Fogerty's house on the corner and saw the small gap of light on one side of the front window suddenly disappear as the blackout curtain was quickly pressed back into place. Mrs Fogerty liked to know what was happening. Who was coming and going. She liked to stand at her front gate every morning and give her opinions to those walking past. Lorna wished Mrs Fogerty would mind her own business, but was also reassured knowing someone was keeping watch. Especially now.

Judging by the protest cries of young, high-pitched voices coming from number 5 Ranui Road, the twins were reluctant to have their evening bath. Lorna heard their short, fast footsteps running up and down the hallway. She knew how hard it was to wrangle them into the bathroom, having babysat Lizzie and

Patricia since they were babies. Lorna felt a twinge of sympathy for their mother, Mrs Rowlson, whose husband had been gone for months — he was an engineer on a merchant ship somewhere in the Pacific Ocean. Every time Lorna saw Mrs Rowlson, concern for her husband's safety seemed etched in her forehead, her lips, her tired eyes.

At the next house, the only empty house on their street, the road steepened dramatically and Lorna leant forward for the sharp ascent.

'Lorrie!'

Turning, Lorna spotted her sister-in-law, Penny, waving from across the street as she pulled her gate closed behind her. 'Wait for me.'

Lorna waited until Penny was alongside, then they continued, Lorna on the footpath, Penny on the unpaved road beside her. 'Any news?' Lorna asked.

'Nothing,' Penny replied. 'Did you see the papers?'

Lorna nodded, her chest tight. 'Dad isn't happy.'

'No,' said Penny. 'Neither am I.'

Chester leapt at the fence at number 9, barking, his claws clacking on the wood, and Lorna and Penny shouted at him to *be quiet*. Chester immediately settled down and Lorna leant over the gate to give his ears a rub. 'Good boy,' she whispered. 'Not much longer now.' Mr Bolton worked at Government House in some important role he delighted at being evasive about. He would arrive home at 6.15 pm, then Chester would go inside the house, receive his dinner, and curl up at Mr Bolton's feet while they listened to the radio.

The road widened into a cul-de-sac and soon the two young women reached the last house on the street. Penny unlatched the gate and waited for Lorna to walk through before closing it and following her up the twenty-nine steps to the front door. Lorna could hear the radio in the living room, the clang of dishes from the kitchen. She turned the handle and pushed, immediately hit by the smell of roast mutton and excited nudges from Milly's nose. 'Alright, girl, let us get inside.' Milly was an old Labrador but still managed to drag herself to the door whenever she heard someone coming up the steps.

'That you, Lorrie?' called Lorna's mum, popping her head out of the kitchen door at the end of the hallway. 'Penny too!' she exclaimed happily.

'Hi, Mum,' said Lorna, though she had already disappeared.

'In here,' bellowed Lorna's dad.

Lorna and Penny hung their coats on the rack and entered the living room. In his armchair by the fire, Lorna's dad sat with his legs extended, crossed at the ankles, slippers on. He looked at them over the top of his pipe and raised his eyebrows in greeting. Lorna gave him a kiss on the forehead then moved to stand with her back to the fire, exhaling as the warm air hit her cold, damp trousers. Penny bent to give her father-in-law a peck on the cheek and he grasped her hand. 'Looks like our boys are back in the fray,' he said sternly.

'Yes,' Penny replied, her voice cracking. 'Looks like it.'

Lorna studied the swirling brown-and-yellow pattern on the carpet and tried to think of a way to lift the atmosphere in the room. 'Thought you'd be at the pub, Dad,' she said brightly.

'Not today, love,' he replied. 'Thought I'd best be home early.'

Lorna studied her father, her eyes narrowing. His shoulders were tense and there was an alertness to him, as if he might suddenly leap from his chair.

'Why?' she asked, warily.

Her father glanced at her briefly then stared at the pipe gripped in his hand. 'Jim called—' he coughed. 'He said a Japanese sub was sighted off the coast up near Castlepoint last night.'

Lorna bit her lip and quickly spun to face the fire, her heart racing. A few weeks earlier the Japanese had attacked Sydney. Now they were practically on New Zealand's doorstep. The probability of invasion was clearly higher than ever.

'Our boys should have come home,' snapped Penny, double-checking that the blackouts over the windows were firmly in place. 'They should be here defending their country. Helping *us*.'

'Your mother was reluctant for me to mention it,' said Lorna's dad. 'She doesn't want you worrying, Lorrie.'

Then why did you tell me? thought Lorna.

The front door slammed and Lorna's younger brother, Peter, charged into the room, his nose and cheeks bright red from the cold, his knees muddy below the baggy shorts of his rugby uniform. Lorna was instantly jealous and wished she could have spent the afternoon playing sport too. She loved that burn in her lungs from pushing herself hard, the ache in her muscles.

'I scored a try just before full-time, Dad!' Peter said. 'Right between the posts.'

'Top effort,' said their dad. 'What was the score?'

Peter made a face. 'We lost, but we were up against the first fifteen and they weren't that much better than us. I reckon I've got a chance of making the team next year.'

'They'd be mad not to have you,' said Lorna's dad. 'Who else has your sort of speed, eh?'

Peter grinned and looked at Lorna. 'Did Dad tell you about the Japs?'

Lorna nodded.

'Do you want to come to the lookout later? See if we can spot them?'

'No one leaves this house,' their dad said firmly.

Lorna was relieved. She didn't fancy spending several hours huddled in the lookout she'd built with her brother three years earlier when war had first been declared. Back then, she'd been a quiet girl in school worried about whether or not she would make top of the class. Back then, she would happily go on adventures with her brother after school and on weekends. Lorna was different now. Grown up. School felt like a lifetime ago.

'Tea's ready!' her mum called.

Her dad lowered his voice. 'I don't want any talk of the Japanese at the table,' he said, fixing Peter with a wide stare.

They made their way down the hallway and into the kitchen, then through bevelled glass doors off to one side to take their seats in the dining room. Lorna's mum had set the table with a white linen tablecloth. Fancy napkins were rolled up and tucked inside the silver napkin rings usually reserved for birthdays and Christmas.

'What's the occasion?' Lorna asked, giving her mum a quick hug and waving at her Aunty Jean who was taking a seat opposite. Uncle Jerry must have been on home-guard duty again. Aunty Jean always helped Lorna's mum with dinner and ate with them when he was away. She didn't like being home on her own at night.

'I thought it would be nice,' said her mum, removing her apron, hanging it on the hook behind the kitchen door, and taking her seat at the end of the table. 'Help to . . .' she paused and for a second the happy expression on her face slipped before she could find it again. 'I thought it might perk us up, that's all.'

'It's lovely,' said her dad, taking his seat at the opposite end of the table to his wife. 'And you know how much I love your roast.'

Lorna stayed quiet. They had roast mutton with roast potatoes, carrots, parsnips and peas at least twice a week. She was heartily sick of it and was sure her dad couldn't love her mum's roast quite as much as he said he did.

Milly snuck under the table and settled down in her usual spot at Lorna's feet. Lorna slipped off a shoe and pressed her toes into Milly's fur to warm them up, and to try to ease the knot in her stomach. She wanted to ask what would happen if the Japanese invaded. She wanted to ask if anyone had checked that the bomb shelter they'd dug in the backyard was still in good condition. Perhaps they should put some supplies out there tonight just in case: blankets and food and water and maybe a weapon of some kind. Her dad didn't own a gun. Maybe he should get one tomorrow.

'You'll never guess who the tram conductor was tonight,' Lorna said instead, picking up her knife and fork.

'Who?' asked Aunty Jean, matching Lorna's light tone.

Lorna paused for effect. 'Mrs Waters,' she stated.

Peter snorted and his dad gave him a warning look.

'Mrs Waters from number four?' said her mum, her face incredulous.

'The very one,' said Lorna. 'Who would have thought?'

'Indeed,' said Aunty Jean. 'I have to say I didn't see that one coming.'

'Well I won't be catching the tram again,' mumbled Peter.

'Don't talk with your mouth full,' said their mum automatically. 'I think it's commendable. We all have to find ways to pitch in with so many of our men overseas or called up for war work.'

'Yes, but Mum, this is the same Mrs Waters who wrote to the newspaper to say trams were encouraging idleness,' said Lorna.

'She also told me school children should be banned from using the tram as they're too disruptive,' said Peter.

'She was the friendliest she's ever been,' said Lorna. It had taken her several minutes to realise the conductor was Mrs Waters – she'd looked so different in her uniform. 'I think Mrs Waters was rather proud to be working. And she told me I was doing important work and I'd made the right decision to leave school when I did.'

'We have different opinions there, as you know,' muttered her mum.

Lorna had left school midway through the previous year, and her mother had been bitterly disappointed, though she'd eventually conceded there'd been little choice. The country was desperate for women to work in essential industries and it would have been poor form, not to mention unpatriotic, for Lorna to stay. What was the point in her seeing out the year? Especially when she would have been the only girl from her year left at school.

'Did you ask her about Patrick?' said Peter loudly.

Lorna glared at Peter, knowing he was teasing her. 'No, I did not,' she said, concentrating on slicing her mutton. Patrick was Mrs Waters' son. He was a year older than Lorna and though she'd never been one to take an interest in boys (not like her best friend, Karen), she had always admired Patrick, impressed with the way he was able to speak in front of others with such confidence and clarity. Lorna had been envious when he'd won the speech contest in his final year of school, as she often found it a challenge, her words tumbling out rapidly, as jumbled and rambling as her thoughts. How did he manage to stay so composed?

While they'd grown up on the same street, she'd barely said a word to Patrick, which wasn't unusual by any means. Boys and girls talking to one another was not something parents, teachers, or members of the community encouraged. The last Lorna had heard, Patrick had joined the Air Force and was at a training camp in England.

Lorna's dad cleared his throat and Lorna hesitated, her fork inches from her mouth. When her dad cleared his throat, it meant he had something important to say. 'As you know, I've been overseeing the food stores down at the port,' he said. 'There's been a great deal of talk recently, what with all the comings and goings, not to mention all the building equipment being carted out to the coast. It's all being kept rather secretive, but I believe they've been building a military camp, and judging by the sudden influx of goods and artillery in the last few days I believe something might be about to happen.' He paused. 'Very soon,' he added.

'Military camp,' said Penny. 'Do you think our boys are coming home?' she added hopefully.

Lorna's dad shook his head. 'I don't think so, Pen.'

Lorna glanced at the photo on the sideboard of her two older brothers standing proudly in their army uniforms. She hadn't seen them in over two years. Not since they'd joined the Expeditionary Force and left to fight in the Middle East.

'Then who?' asked Peter, jiggling in his seat. 'What's going on, Dad?'

'I don't know for sure, son. But I've heard rumours.'

'Rumours?' said Lorna's mum. 'What rumours, Frank?'

Lorna's dad placed his knife and fork down, picked up his napkin and dabbed his lips as he looked around the table. Slowly he placed his napkin back on his lap and took a deep breath. 'Americans,' he stated at last.

Lorna saw a look she couldn't interpret pass between her father and mother. 'Why would Americans be coming here, Dad?' she asked carefully.

He gave Lorna a smile that wasn't quite a smile. 'To help us.'

'To help us against the Japanese, you mean?' Lorna felt a piece of mutton stick in her throat.

'Americans!' Peter shouted, leaping out of his chair with excitement.

Looking across the table, Lorna saw tears pooling in Penny's eyes.

Chapter 2

STAN

Not a single Marine on board the *USS Wakefield* had heard of New Zealand. They knew nothing about the place. All they had to go on was the small pocket guide they'd been given the night before, when they'd been informed they would soon be arriving at this small island nation deep in the South Pacific. According to the guide – in bold type on the front cover – New Zealand was a country of great scenic beauty. It was an independent nation within the British Commonwealth. A country where tipping was disliked and actively discouraged, and where the police were unarmed. The guide then told them what they would *not* find in New Zealand. There was no central heating; no nightclubs; little organised entertainment; no hot cakes, donuts, waffles, hot dogs, hamburgers or decent coffee. There was also less money, less to drink, less to wear and less gasoline.

Needless to say, the boys were *less* than enthusiastic that freezing wet winter's morning as their battleship cruised into a narrow harbour surrounded by green hills. The Marines were lined up along the railings in their pressed and impeccably clean uniforms as their ship rounded a headland and the small city and port of Wellington came into view. There wasn't a skyscraper in sight, the tallest building being only five or six storeys high.

'Heck,' said Derek, standing beside Stan.

Stan kept his expression impassive as he scrutinised the clusters of wooden houses clinging to the sides of the hills enclosing the city. The houses were dark, no lights on, no signs of life but for the plumes of smoke coming from chimneys. The wind was brisk and carried with it the smell of coal and fish. It was 0800 hours and yet it was barely light, the sky a washed-out, sepia grey. The few buildings Stan could see surrounding the port looked old-fashioned, Victorian, with a stately air that made him think of England, not that he had ever been. To the far left of the port was a beach covered in barbed wire entanglements.

'Bit different from Chicago, ain't it?' said Derek, nudging Stan in the ribs.

'A bit,' agreed Stan, brushing down his jacket where Derek's elbow had been.

Eventually they berthed at the wharf and the skies decided to open, pelting the thousands of men on board with thick icy droplets. *What a welcome*, thought Stan.

With the rain still coming down, a small crowd of officials gathered beneath them on the wharf and a military band played *The Star-Spangled Banner*, which meant they unfortunately all had to salute – not an easy feat when they were all packed in so tightly on deck. Stan had hoped the wharf would be thronging with New

Zealanders shouting greetings and waving white handkerchiefs. Instead, it looked as if few people knew that the United States Marine Corps — the best of the best, the very emblem of honour, strength and skill, who had travelled hundreds of miles to give these poor islanders the full might and protection of the best military unit in the world — had arrived. Stan brushed away his irritation and reminded himself, as he did regularly ever since his acceptance into the Marine Corps, that he was lucky to be here. Lucky to have a clean uniform, new boots and a purpose.

Three hours later, 6788 members of the 1st Division of the United States Marine Corps disembarked. They stood in formation on the wharf until they were each handed a glass bottle filled with milk from wagons loaded with milk crates. Derek raised his eyebrows at Stan before taking a sip. Then his eyes widened and he immediately began to take huge gulps. Reassured, Stan tried the milk, and his tastebuds exploded. It was the best milk he'd ever tasted, and the freshest thing they'd had since leaving San Diego. Once their bottles had been emptied, the boys placed them in the crates and went to stand with their units on the wharf, rain dripping off their brimless hats as they waited for their gear to be offloaded.

'What's taking them so darn long?' muttered the boy beside Stan. A group of civilians in black oilskin jackets and thick woollen hats were gathered with senior officers from the US Headquarters division. Their voices were raised and they all took turns gesticulating at the *Wakefield* before shaking their heads.

Finally, word spread that the Marines would be required to offload their gear themselves.

'We have unfortunately arrived during an industrial dispute and the dockworkers are on strike,' said their commanding officer.

'What do ya mean, on strike?' asked a Marine in the front row.

'They're unhappy with their current working conditions and are refusing to work in the rain.'

Stan was incredulous. How could you simply refuse to work because it was raining? He'd never heard of anything so ridiculous.

'Let's get on with it,' their commanding officer shouted.

It was a long, slow, painful process. Stan was stunned at the sheer bulk the *Wakefield* had been carrying within its gunnels. How had the ship not sunk with the weight of all their supplies? Within a few hours, the wharves were laden with piles of barrels, rubber tyres, ammunition, food crates and equipment.

Stan was relieved when eventually his unit was instructed to gather up their packs and make their way to the train station. From there, they would be transported to camp.

As they marched down the street from the wharf towards the station, Stan noticed the buildings were charming yet drab. There were few locals around, and the shops were all closed. 'Apparently everything is shut on Sundays by law,' said a Marine marching beside him.

Stan gave a small shake of his head. He actually missed Chicago right now, something he never thought would happen. He missed the scale of it, the hustle and bustle, the pulsing energy. Up ahead an old-fashioned car rounded a corner and headed towards them on the wrong side of the road. The Marines all instinctively began to move further to the right so he might pass, but the car continued to motor towards them before slowing to a stop so that the Marines had to split their lines to march around him. The driver wound down his window, lit a pipe and nodded his head in greeting.

It wasn't until they turned the corner and met with several more cars that Stan realised what was going on. 'They drive on the other side,' he said to himself.

'What's that?' asked another Marine.

'They drive on the left, not the right,' said Stan, louder this time.

A short while later, the train station came into view and Stan felt a rush of excitement. He sensed the other Marines perk up too as they quickened their pace. The station was a magnificent brick building, with a row of circular white columns at the main entrance, above which sat a beautiful clock set within a detailed facade. Before the station was a broad tract of manicured lawn and a road that swept down and around in front of the building.

The rain chose that moment to stop and the clouds broke apart, brightening the view and Stan's mood even further. Marching through the arched main doors and onto the concourse, the boys looked with delight at the grand curved ceiling soaring above them. The kiosks were all closed, and the station grew loud with the sound of thousands of Marines gathered about, waiting for instructions.

Fortunately, they didn't have to wait long before they were directed onto a platform where several trains were lined up, belching black smoke. The carriages looked worn, and when Stan stepped inside, he was disappointed to discover there was no heating and the interiors were shabby. *Worse than the trains in Chicago*, thought Stan, something he hadn't believed possible till now. In yet another exercise in patience, they waited and waited until finally the train blasted its horn and they pulled away from the platform.

All the seats had been taken before he boarded, so Stan was wedged in a corner of the carriage beside the door. He rested on his pack and braced himself against the wall, then pulled out his cigarettes, joining with the other men in lighting up and wondering how on earth he had ended up here, in this strange country so far from America. Briefly he thought of his younger brother and sister. He hoped they were coping alright back in Chicago without him.

The train rattled along at a painful amble, especially when climbing the endless hills they encountered one after another. Derek and Bruno smoked nearby. *His two buddies*, Stan supposed, though Stan knew he was being generous in the use of the word. Stan didn't really have close buddies, though he wasn't a loner either. He was popular in his regiment, well-respected. He joined in with everything and knew exactly the right thing to say and do, but so much of it was an act. A performance. Stan had learnt early on what would garner him the most admiration and praise from his mother — do well at school, excel at sport, look adults in the eye, shake their hands firmly, stand straight, be polite, laugh when others laugh, and show a relaxed confidence you might not necessarily feel. Stan knew how to win people over. He'd been honing those skills for so many years they were effortless, and yet, they didn't make him feel good about himself. If anything, he liked himself less.

After a long, bone-rattling journey, during which Stan smoked six cigarettes, the train stopped. Being by the door, Stan was one of the first to disembark and survey their new home. The Marines had been told they would be based in New Zealand for six months to prepare and train for deployment in the escalating fight against the Japanese. They were in the countryside on low, undulating farmland. In the near distance Stan could make out the coastline, the sea a deep turquoise, and behind him rose steep grassy hills covered with grazing sheep. The wind had dropped off and it felt suspenseful and still. He took a slow breath, inhaling crisp, salty air, and heard an unusual bird call from a clump of bushes nearby. It was as if the place was telling him there was nothing to worry about. That the world couldn't possibly be at war.

Another band stood on the platform to greet them and play tunes as the Marines marched in formation down dusty narrow roads, though the only people lined up to see them were a group of dishevelled school children who smiled and waved. Slowly, their camp came into view: pyramid-shaped canvas tents raised on wooden platforms, as well as a sporadic collection of simple wooden huts. Stan was allocated to a tent with Derek, Bruno and Bruno's cousin, Enzo. The four men had little room for their gear, having to store it beneath their camp stretchers. The tent had no electricity and the only heating was a tiny unlit cast-iron stove in the centre of the tent with a flue disappearing through a hole at the tent's peak. Though the tent was cold, damp and airless, Stan experienced a thrill of childish delight — he'd read about camping adventures in books and heard from his classmates about their family camping trips, but had never been camping himself. He'd always felt as if he'd missed out on something important.

At the clang of the lunch bell, the boys made their way to mess and lined up for their first meal on foreign soil. Derek looked agitated as he searched the room. 'Where in hell is the coffee?'

Stan frowned. He could smell all sorts of aromas, but the familiar scent of coffee wasn't one of them.

'Coffee?' asked Derek, the second he was close enough to the man ladling out food.

'They don't do coffee around here, bud. They love their tea apparently. I did manage to find a coffee in a tearoom in town, but it was dreadful. Tasted like it had been sitting in the urn all darn day, which I suspect it had.'

Derek looked so shocked that Stan wanted to throw an arm around his shoulder and laugh, but he refrained.

'Son of a bitch!' exclaimed Derek. 'How's a man to survive in this country?'

Derek calmed down a little as they ate. The meat, carrot and cabbage stew was rich and flavoursome, the bread doughy and fresh. Plus they were all given another bottle of milk, which Stan finished in several large gulps.

'Mail!' came a shout, and the boys filed outside, eager to hear from loved ones back home. Stan stood at the back of the crowd, wishing for mail from his family almost as much as he dreaded it. When his name was called, two envelopes were passed through several sets of hands until they reached him. He retired to his tent to lie on his bed, light a cigarette and read.

The first letter was from his smother. Stan stared at her loopy, shaky handwriting for several seconds to steel himself before opening the envelope. There was writing on one side of the single sheet of paper, barely more than two paragraphs with a number of words crossed out as his mother tried to correct her mistakes. Inky fingerprints marked the page, and a corner of the paper had been torn. She'd written almost the exact same words as in her previous letter to him – the one he'd received just before he'd left America. She was proud of him, she wrote, and knew he was the only one of her children who would amount to anything. She hoped he was being a good boy, staying out of trouble. Then she asked him to send money – times were tough and a little help would be appreciated. She'd signed off with 'love Mom', and Stan stared at those two words until his eyes blurred.

Stan's mother had been almost permanently drunk since his father disappeared when Stan was twelve years old, and he'd had little choice but to step into the role of the responsible eldest son. He was the smart one, his mother always said, the one the family could rely on, the one who would ensure the bills were paid and his siblings were clothed and fed. Stan had performed his role dutifully, though with mounting desolation.

He'd felt increasingly trapped until the day a man in a smart Marine uniform gave a talk to the school's football team, of which Stan had been the captain. Joining the Marines had been Stan's way out, his salvation, though he could never be entirely free of his past, as his mother's words reminded him.

The second letter was from his brother, Alfie. Younger by three years and a 'loose cannon' as his mother often described him. Alfie was the irresponsible one, the troublemaker, the one who could never be serious about anything, and who Stan was always having to make excuses for. Stan both liked his brother and found him infuriating in equal measure. He hated how their mother was constantly yelling at Alfie, telling him he was useless, asking him over and over again, 'Why can't you be more like your brother?' He saw the way it affected Alfie, made him draw away from them all, yet Stan was envious of Alfie, of his freedom.

Alfie's letter was short too, but the paper was crisp and clean. Stan sat up straight when he read the first line.

I've joined the Marines, Alfie wrote. Can you believe it? They must be pretty desperate if they took me on, right? Or maybe you paved the way. I imagine your records are impeccable. I'm in the 2nd Division and I'm about to start 12 weeks of training before they ship us out. Can't wait to have a go at those Japs. Not sure where we'll end up, but I'm hoping we'll bump into each other. We can have a few drinks, congratulate one another on getting out of shithole Chicago. Prepare yourself, brother, I'm a-coming.

Stan read the letter again. Surely it wasn't possible. Stan had trained and studied and pushed himself to the absolute limits of physical and mental endurance in order to be accepted into the Marines. It had been two years of hard slog, and it had all been worth it because now he got to wear a badge, to be revered, respected. Yet here his brother was, somehow becoming a Marine after only twelve weeks of training. The same brother who had dropped out of school at fourteen and had left Stan to be responsible for everything.

Stan was angry for all of five minutes, until he wasn't.

Derek ducked under the tent flap. 'Good grief, Stan, you're grinning,' he said, feigning shock before collapsing onto his bed. 'What brought that on?'

'My brother, Alfie,' Stan replied. 'He's joined the Marines too. He might be coming here. To New Zealand.'

'Tell him to bring coffee,' muttered Derek, putting his hands behind his head, crossing his legs at the ankles and closing his eyes.

Stan stared at Derek's inert body, his stomach giving a painful lurch, then he folded up both his letters and put them away.

Chapter 3

LORNA

As usual, the Marines were the sole topic of conversation in the lunchroom. The Americans had only been in Wellington for a little over a week but already they had turned the city upside down. Prior to the Americans' arrival, the lunchroom had been a place for subdued mutterings about the war, but now it hummed with female voices, high-pitched with excitement, Karen's voice being the loudest of them all.

'He turned up with flowers and chocolate and a whole carton of cigarettes.' The group of women crowded around their table gave a collective gasp and pressed closer. 'And he had a taxi waiting for us,' finished Karen loudly, her cheeks flushed.

'A taxi!' one of the girls exclaimed. 'Why didn't you take the train?'

'I guess because he could afford a taxi, so why not,' said Karen happily.

'Where did he take you?' asked the same girl, her eyes wide as she hung on Karen's every word.

'We went to a dance at the Town Hall. The ANA Club just moved their weekend dances there and it's such a grand venue in comparison to the little hall in Petone we used to dance at.'

Lorna nodded along with the other girls as if in agreement, though she hadn't attended any of the dances put on by the Army, Navy and Airforce Club yet. She wasn't particularly interested in going either, though she knew she was in the minority.

'All the ladies looked ever so glamorous,' continued Karen. 'Thank goodness I had that dress from my cousin's wedding last year.'

'You haven't even told everyone his name yet, Karnie,' said Lorna, wanting to make sure everyone knew she was privy to more information, being Karen's best friend.

Karen laughed. 'He's called Derek. He kept calling me 'honey' and I could have listened to him talk for hours. Don't you just love their accents?' Karen gushed. 'He was an absolute gentleman and he told me I looked beautiful at least five times.'

One of the girls sitting opposite Karen scoffed. '*Five times*,' she said sarcastically. 'Sounds a little fake to me.'

'No, no.' Karen bounced about on the bench seat making it wobble. 'That's just how they are. They're confident, but ever so polite and very smart-looking.'

'They do dress well,' the girl next to Lorna said, raising her eyebrows suggestively.

'What did Derek think of the dance?' someone asked.

Karen frowned briefly. 'He said it was very sedate. Very British, whatever that means. He said dances back in America are a little more lively.'

'What happened at the end of the dance?' another girl asked from the back of the group.

'Well, Derek had to catch the midnight train back to camp, so we walked to the station and he made sure I was safely on the train to the hostel before he ran to catch his.'

'No taxi home then,' muttered the girl who had spoken with sarcasm earlier. Lorna suddenly remembered her name. It was Linda from Invercargill, who had a husband serving overseas. Linda was staying in the same hostel as Karen. It had been set up after the Manpower Authorities started directing young women to work in essential industries. There were around eighty women living in the hostel, having come from all over the country to help at the munitions plant at the Ford Factory out at Gracefield (after a ban had been placed on making new cars). Lorna could have stayed in the hostel too, but she preferred to catch the train and then the tram home, even though it took her over an hour. Karen, on the other hand, who lived only a twenty-minute walk from Lorna's house, had leapt at the chance to move out of home.

The bell rang, signalling the end of their lunch break, and there was a collective groan as the girls reluctantly peeled away from Karen to return to their duties.

As the lunchroom emptied, Lorna turned to Karen. 'Okay,' she said decisively.

'Okay what?'

'Okay I'll come with you to the next dance, as long as you can find me a date.'

Karen laughed. 'Oh, I won't have to find you a date, Lorrie. All you have to do is walk down Lambton Quay and they'll be clamouring to ask you out. There are hundreds of them. They're simply everywhere you look.'

Lorna wished she could be as excited and confident as her friend. She was still grateful they'd been partnered in a school tennis competition ten years earlier. From the moment Karen had beamed at Lorna and told her to stand at the net and smash every ball that came her way, Lorna had felt herself expand inside. It was first time another girl had looked at her and accepted her, just like that, without a moment's hesitation. Karen seemed to like the fact that Lorna was competitive, that she wore shorts instead of a tennis skirt, that she didn't have a ribbon in her hair, wore thick-rimmed glasses, and talked rapidly, in short, sharp bursts when she was excited about something, or not at all if the topic was of no interest. Karen and Lorna were different to one another in almost every conceivable way, and it made no sense for them to be friends – yet they were. It was one of the few unexplainable things Lorna was happy to accept.

Lorna made her way towards her workstation amongst a long row of girls and arched her back a couple of times in preparation for spending the next few hours bent over metal parts. Their job was highly secretive, and they'd been instructed to keep it hush-hush, but everyone seemed to know they were constructing components for shells. Shells to kill people. Lorna didn't like to dwell on the fact they were putting together weapons, though what choice did they have? She wished for the umpteenth time she could be doing something else to help win the war, rather than this mind-numbing task. Something that didn't make her brain feel heavy and dull.

The day Lorna's two older brothers enlisted in the army, Lorna's mother had announced that Hitler's name was not to be mentioned. He was a person who didn't even deserve to have his name aired in their household. Lorna didn't like any mention of his name either. Hearing it gave her a sense of vertigo, as if she was teetering on the edge of a ledge. Not that anyone was talking about the Germans much at the moment with most of the talk focused on the boys from America.

On the day the Marines had arrived, Lorna had been at church with her family. With lists of casualties appearing in the papers being confirmation that the New Zealand Army was once more fighting on the front line, her mother had insisted they attend service and pray for the safety of her brothers Gordon and Rick. Lorna had almost fallen asleep in her pew, having been awake most of the night convinced that at any second the air-raid siren would sound and Japanese bombs would start to rain down on her street. Yet, tired as she was, she'd noticed there was a restlessness in the congregation, a number of people whispering to one another during the sermon. It wasn't until her family were making their way out of church that an acquaintance of her father's approached and asked if he'd seen the chaos down at the port.

'Chaos?' Lorna had asked, fear making her voice sound more childish than she'd have liked.

'A huge ship has arrived, loaded with thousands of American Marines in their fancy uniforms. By the looks of it, they're here to stay awhile.'

Lorna detected a hint of scorn in the man's voice, but surely he was pleased? The arrival of the Americans couldn't have come at a better time.

Peter clearly thought it was the best news in the world – he gripped Lorna's shoulder and shook it.

'Can I go and see, Dad?' he asked.

'After lunch,' their father replied.

Lorna had feigned nonchalance when she'd offered to bike into town with her brother, though she'd been secretly desperate to see what was going on. Unfortunately, by the time they arrived at the fenced-off area overlooking the port, few Americans were left. Just a handful of men were walking amongst vast piles of supplies that had presumably been off-loaded from the imposing warship. Even though they were quite a distance from Lorna and Peter, they still made an impression in their smart, green, tailored uniforms.

'Look at their badges,' breathed Peter, staring open-mouthed.

Then one of the Americans shouted to someone, leapt into a jeep and sped away, looking and sounding like a Hollywood movie star. Lorna and Peter laughed with delight. Lorna loved watching American movies – the way everything seemed exaggerated for effect.

The following morning, Lorna was nervous catching the tram and train to work, but thankfully she only spotted a handful of Americans on another platform and they'd been so engrossed in their loud conversation they hadn't noticed her. As the week went on, more and more Marines appeared and she began keeping her eyes firmly in the direction she was going, making sure not to make eye contact.

Every single American appeared to smoke, and not roll-your-owns, but proper cigarettes. Lorna wondered how on earth they could afford them.

Word must have spread about a large group of young women staying in the hostel out in Petone because by Wednesday after-noon Marines were hovering around the entrance. Karen had stopped to chat to Derek, and he'd asked her on a date to which she'd agreed without a moment's hesitation, later telling Lorna it was the most exciting moment of her life.

Lorna sighed and lifted up the piece of metal cylinder she was required to screw on to another part. At the end of their shift, she would catch the bus back to the hostel with Karen before walking to the train station. That way she could tell Karen she'd changed her mind about the dance, though she suspected Karen would tell her off for being ridiculous. She just didn't want to go through the whole charade. The dressing up, the make-up, the effortful conversation. She'd rather be home playing cards with her brother and her parents, or listening to the radio, or reading a book, and she didn't care if she was only girl in the room who felt that way – which she suspected she was. Lorna was used to being on the outer, and it only bothered her a little. She certainly had no intention of changing just because a bunch of handsome young Americans had arrived in town.

Chapter 4

STAN

Stan was used to freezing days growing up in Chicago, but the damp cold in Wellington was like nothing he'd experienced before. It sank into his bones and stayed there no matter how many layers he wore. He still couldn't believe the lack of central heating, or heating of any kind. Many of the boys felt the same way, especially those from the South who complained bitterly.

When the reveille sounded, Stan quickly rose from his bed, lit the lantern and dressed. He poked Derek, who responded by groaning and rolling over.

'Come on, Mac,' said Stan. 'We don't want to be late.'

'*You* don't want to be late,' grumbled Derek. 'Knowing you, we'll be damn early.'

Stan frowned and drummed his fingers against his thigh. Derek was always telling him to stop taking everything so seriously. But they were *Marines,* for crying out loud. Stan didn't join the Marines to muck about. He needed to prove himself each and every day. He had to show everyone, including himself, that he belonged in the Marine Corps. That he wasn't there by some sort of fluke, that he'd earned his stripes. He was still coming to terms with the fact that Alfie was going to be a Marine. It made everything Stan had done less significant, his efforts and sacrifices less worthwhile.

Stan yanked the blanket off Derek. 'Get up,' he snapped. 'Or I'll leave you behind.'

At that, Derek did climb out of bed, albeit slowly. It was always partly an act with Derek. He pretended he couldn't care less, but he was as competitive as the rest of them. There was no way Derek was going to turn up late for reveille, and he hated to be left behind in any situation.

After reveille they made their way to mess and joined the chow line for their flapjacks with maple syrup and the revolting coffee they had no choice but to drink. Apparently American coffee was on its way on a liberty ship that would be arriving within a week — it couldn't come soon enough.

Derek sat on the bench next to Stan and slapped him on the back. 'I've just had a message from Karen. I've got you a date for tonight.'

'Didn't know I needed you to find me a date,' said Stan coolly.

'Are you mad?' said Bruno, sitting opposite. 'It's your first liberty and you need to make the most of it.'

Stan realised he ought to show some more enthusiasm. 'Who's the lucky girl then?'

'Didn't catch her name,' said Derek. 'I can't always follow what Karen is saying with her accent.'

'What about you, Enzo?' asked Stan. 'Have you got a date?'

'Sure do. She's a fine-looking sweetie too. Stopped her on the street and told her she had to go out with me, and I thought she was going to faint — she looked so shocked. Barely got a peep out of her but she managed to nod at least. The girls 'round here are timid, aren't they? Not like back home.'

'Not all of them,' said Bruno, winking. Bruno had met a girl the previous weekend in a hotel where she worked. They'd gone for a stroll and ended up in a boatshed down on the harbourfront. Bruno had given more details than Stan wanted to hear or felt was appropriate. This was one of the few things he disliked about being a Marine, hearing how some of the boys talked about girls. The obsession they had with the opposite sex. With sex in general. Maybe Stan was old-fashioned, but he thought the girls deserved a little more respect.

After breakfast, the boys cleaned their gear for inspection before making their way into the city on the rattling old train. Though the carriages were full of men on liberty, Stan was able to nab a window seat this time. He sat on the uncomfortably hard seat and gazed at the passing scenery: farmland, steep hills, valleys and sheep. There were few houses and even fewer people until they descended a final hill and clusters of cream houses came into view. The houses looked as if they could benefit from a paint job, and bizarrely each house was separated by either a tall fence or hedge. Stan wondered if this was a reflection of the people here — closed off and wary of their neighbours.

If someone had put up barriers like that back home, they'd have been considered snobbish or accused of trying to hide something.

Arriving at the train station, Stan followed the other boys across the bustling concourse to outside, where a wind immediately threatened to remove his hat.

'Jesus, Mac,' exclaimed Derek, putting an arm out as Stan went to cross the street and narrowly missed being hit by a car. 'Did you forget they drive on the left?'

Stan stared at the moving cars and took a moment to adjust. He *had* forgotten, and he was annoyed with himself for not remembering something so basic.

As they made their way towards the centre of town, Stan noticed that while there were Marines everywhere, there were very few New Zealanders. Those Stan did spot were in no hurry at all. They ambled along the streets, stopping often to chat to passersby. Stan was used to walking fast and with purpose. There was no way he could have slowed down to chat to people on the busy streets of Chicago. You kept to the right and you kept moving unless you wanted an earful.

The locals were all wearing broad-brimmed felt hats with turned-up brims, the likes of which Stan had never seen before, and he was surprised to notice all the women wore gloves, though their clothes were plain and bland. When Stan happened to catch anyone's eye, they nodded with polite, reserved smiles.

Stan found the streets attractive in an old-fashioned way. There were no glass and concrete high-rises. Most of the buildings were built of brick or wood. Old metal signs hung above shop doors, and he had to step close to the windows to peer inside the dim interiors and see their wares. They gave off a homey feel, so different to the smart, polished, brightly lit stores back home.

The men stopped at a tearoom advertising a 'traditional British high tea' and doffed their hats at the waitress before taking a seat at a table by the window. It had a white linen tablecloth embroidered with pink flowers, and dainty China cups and saucers. The waitress, wearing a frilly apron over a navy-blue dress and with her straight mousy hair tied back with a ribbon, spoke in a quiet, tremulous voice. 'Hello gentlemen, what would you like?'

Derek's voice seemed unusually loud and brash when he announced they were there to sample a traditional British high tea, winking at the waitress and causing her to blush profusely.

Soon the waitress returned with a teapot, something Stan had seen in the movies but never in real life. He watched as she poured their tea with a shaking hand. Then they each added milk from a little jug, a cube of sugar with the dainty tongs provided and clinked their cups before taking a sip.

Derek widened his eyes then pretended to choke, Bruno coughed dramatically and Enzo grimaced. Stan quickly swallowed his first-ever taste of tea and put his cup down with a clatter. It tasted revolting.

'Heck!' said Derek loudly, waving the waitress over. 'Please tell me you have coffee, honey?'

She blushed again. 'Oh no, sorry. Is there something wrong with the tea?'

'It tastes like bathwater I washed my dog in,' said Enzo curtly.

The waitress's eyes filled with tears, and Stan immediately rose to his feet. 'Apologies, ma'am,' he said. 'We are still getting used to the . . . customs here. I'm sure it is a very fine tea.'

The waitress wiped her eyes and mumbled about returning with their food, and Stan sat back down, giving his friends a severe 'behave yourselves' look. He glared at his cup and forced himself to take another sip, the others watching him closely, as if he were doing something dangerous.

'It's not so bad,' Stan lied, carefully returning his cup to the saucer. 'I'm sure we'll get used to it.'

Derek snorted. 'Always trying to please, aren't you, Stan?'

Stan ignored his comment as the waitress placed a three-tiered platter before him. His mouth watered at the sight of small sandwiches with the crusts removed on the bottom tier, various small cakes on the middle tier and something odd-looking on the top.

'Hot diggity dog!' said Derek, leaning forward and pointing. 'What do you call those?'

'Scones,' said the waitress. 'With jam and cream. Hopefully you'll like them more than our tea,' she added with a hint of mockery.

The boys all laughed, Stan included, and he felt a small loosening in the muscles between his shoulder blades. He was about to pass the three-tiered creation around the table when the waitress appeared with another and placed it in front of Derek.

'We get one each?' he asked, his eyes widening. 'Now, *that* is more like it.'

Stan thought of all the times he'd gone hungry. When a pathetically small meal had to be shared around his two siblings and parents. They weren't the only family who couldn't afford to eat in his neighbourhood. It was awash with empty, rumbling bellies (and drunken parents, come to think of it). Pushing thoughts of his family aside, Stan bit into a sandwich and chewed once before shoving the rest of it in his mouth. The bread was soft and chewy, the ham inside full of flavour.

The scones, when he tasted them, were dry and crumbling, not at all sweet as he had expected. But with the fruity jam and freshly whipped cream, they were good. Moorish in fact.

They managed to polish off everything before them, though Stan was the only one who drank any more tea, then they tried to pay using the unusual coins they'd been issued at camp. The waitress had to help point out the differences between pennies and shillings, and when he worked it out in his head, Stan was shocked at the price. It was so cheap he was embarrassed. He wanted to leave a tip but remembered that it wasn't done in this country. He hoped the waitress was being paid well enough.

'So what do you think everyone does for fun around here?' asked Derek, as they spilled back out onto the street.

Stan shrugged. 'Drink tea?'

The boys laughed, and Stan tapped a passing Marine on the shoulder to ask him what there was to do. The Marine took a long time to come up with a response, finally suggesting they catch the cable car up to the Botanic Gardens.

The cable car ride was steep and afforded them fine views over the city and the harbour. Strobes of light burst through the grey clouds and white caps spread across the sea, whipped up by the wind. It was an impressive sight.

After a long walk through the gardens, they caught the cable car back down the hill and Derek suggested they go in search of a drink.

'Sounds good to me,' Stan said, though in truth he didn't much enjoy alcohol. It made him feel less in control of himself, and Stan liked to stay in control.

Pushing through the doors of a bar, they were hit with a welcome wall of warm air and immediately removed their coats, settling into a table by the roaring open fire. Stan glanced at his watch. There were still two more hours until they could meet their dates, and he was glad they had found somewhere to rest and relax beforehand.

Unfortunately, when Stan offered to get the first round and strode up to the bar to order bourbon, he was denied.

'Sorry, old chum,' said the bartender. 'Spirits are rationed 'round here. We only serve them between five and six. Can I tempt you with a beer instead?'

Stan took a moment to process his words. Perhaps the bartender had misunderstood. 'We'll take any kind of whisky, it doesn't have to be bourbon.'

The bartender raised his eyebrows. 'I'd give you a whisky if I could, but as I said, it's rationed. It's beer or nothing.'

Stan returned to the table with four glasses of beer and informed the others.

'This is serious,' said Derek slowly. They sat silently staring at their untouched beers. Stan could feel everyone's good mood evaporating. He snatched up his glass, eager to grasp onto the remnants.

'Cheers,' he said, taking a gulp. Unfortunately his first taste was a disappointment — the beer was warm, flat and bitter.

Derek took a sip and shook his head. 'First the tea, and now this,' he said softly. 'What a country.'

After they'd consumed a couple more beers, with very little enthusiasm, the bar began to fill up. When they'd arrived there had been no more than a handful of Marines in the bar, but now all the tables were taken and a large crowd of locals gathered about the counter. Considering the numbers, Stan was surprised by how quiet it was; put a big group of Americans together and it would have been a louder, far more boisterous affair.

Bruno looked at his watch. 'Almost five o'clock.'

Derek stood abruptly. 'Right,' he said firmly. 'Let's get in line.'

They pressed their way closer to the bar and joined in with the loud cheer that rang out as the barman held up a bottle of bourbon in one hand and a bottle of Scotch in the other. Stan wasn't particularly enjoying being jostled about and told Derek – who had an expression of steely determination as he stood in line – that he'd sit this one out and get the next round.

'Wouldn't do that, chaps,' said an elderly local standing beside him in a creased shirt and crumpled brown pants. 'They only serve one drink at a time.'

'They what?' said Derek, aghast.

The man nodded. 'And the most they'll give you is a double. Usually by the time you get back in line for a second, the whisky's all gone anyway.'

'What do you mean, all gone?' Bruno asked.

'The publican only gets a couple of bottles. As you can imagine, they don't last long.'

Stan tried not to laugh at the expression on Derek's face.

They managed two drinks in the hour, the second only because Derek insisted that the moment they were served their first drink, they returned to the back of the line to queue again.

At exactly six o'clock, the publican shouted 'Time gentleman, please,' and everyone who wasn't wearing an American uniform headed for the door.

Bruno tapped a passerby on the arm. 'What's going on?' he asked.

'Pub's closing,' the man replied.

'But it's six o'clock,' said Derek, frowning. 'Is everyone heading to another bar?'

The man shook his head. 'We're heading home. Everything closes at six.'

'Wait, what?' exclaimed Bruno. 'Everything?'

'Well,' the man placed his palms on the table and leant in as if to confide a secret. 'If you happen to have a room at one of the hotels, they'll let you carry on drinking in the hotel bar, and if you play your cards right, the hotelier might open his back door to let a few extras in.'

'Any particular hotel?' Derek asked, in an equally secretive voice.

The man wrinkled his nose as if deciding whether or not he should reveal such valuable information. 'The St George is maybe your best bet, though I hear you boys are taking over Hotel Cecil so maybe you should try there first.'

Derek rose to his feet. 'Right, Hotel Cecil it is. Would you be so kind as to point us in the right direction, sir?'

'You would have walked right past it. By the train station.'

They retraced their steps, watching the streetcars (or trams, as the locals called them) fill up as locals headed for home and the streets emptied out.

'Oddest country I've ever been to,' murmured Enzo.

Stan silently agreed. He wished they didn't have to wait another half hour to meet their dates. He wished they could board the train and go back to their cold, damp tent.

Chapter 5

LORNA

'Come on,' said Lorna, grabbing Karen's hand and dragging her closer. 'One good thing about being a girl is that they'll let us stand at the front.'

Karen groaned as Lorna pulled her along. 'The game hasn't even started yet.'

'Kick-off is in less than a minute,' Lorna exclaimed, pushing past a tall, narrow man. He turned on them with a furious expression, presumably about to shout, until he saw it was two women and refrained.

'Excuse me,' said Lorna half-heartedly, her words an obvious afterthought.

'Derek won't have a hope of finding us,' said Karen, slowing.

Lorna ignored her and pulled harder, her eyes focused on the perfect spot near the halfway line. With a little more enthusiastic pushing and shoving, Lorna elbowed her way to the barrier and grinned with satisfaction.

'Couldn't get a better view,' she stated, sweeping her hand out across the field.

'Remind me again why we're friends,' said Karen loudly.

Lorna shrugged. 'Who can say, Karnie.'

'I'm freezing,' said Karen, pulling her coat tighter.

Lorna removed her woollen hat and attempted to place it on Karen's head, but her friend shrieked and batted it away. 'I'm not wearing *that*, Lorrie. I'd rather freeze, thank you very much.'

Lorna rammed her father's chunky fishing hat back on her head. 'Suit yourself,' she said, her focus now entirely on the player standing on the halfway line with a ball in his hands. The referee blew his whistle, and the player dropped the ball onto his foot and kicked it lightly up in the air. Lorna joined in with the roar of the crowd as the game began.

'Oohh,' squealed Karen, and Lorna looked at her in shock. She'd never been so excited at a rugby match before.

'There's Derek,' said Karen, waving to someone behind Lorna and jumping up and down. 'He's seen me,' she gasped.

Lorna rolled her eyes and didn't even bother to look at the man Karen had been talking about incessantly. Thank goodness Lorna had decided not to go to the dance and Karen had asked Meg, another girl from the hostel, to go on the double date instead. It was bad enough having to hear about the night, let alone live through it.

'Hello, honey,' drawled a voice, and Lorna half-turned to see a Marine put a hand on Karen's waist and lean in to kiss her on the cheek. The gall! It was far too forward a gesture and Lorna wouldn't have been surprised if one of the locals at the game took offence.

'Lorrie,' said Karen, tapping her on the arm. 'This is Derek.'

'Hi,' said Lorna lightly, keeping her eyes on the game and deciding, rather rudely, to not even shake his hand.

'Don't mind her, she's like this with everyone,' said Karen. 'Hello, Stan. This is my friend, Lorna.'

Lorna had heard all about Stan from Meg and couldn't resist a quick glance in his direction. It was true, he was the spitting image of a Hollywood movie star with his blonde hair, blue eyes, caramel skin and tall, muscular build, but Lorna wasn't impressed. It all looked a bit fake to her.

'Hello, Lorna,' Stan said politely, holding out his hand.

Lorna gave his hand a perfunctory shake and spun back to watch the game. The opposition's winger had the ball and was making a streak down the far sideline.

'Tackle him!' Lorna yelled, slamming her hands on the railing and willing their fullback to run faster. Unfortunately the winger seemed to find another gear and dove across the line, landing heavily on the ball. Lorna threw her hands up in disgust and joined in with the mutterings and head-shakings of those standing around her.

'So this is rugby then,' she heard Derek say. 'Nothing like American football, is it?'

'I have no idea,' said Karen.

'Stan, you're the star footballer, what do you think?' asked Derek.

Lorna hadn't even heard of American football, and since she was interested in learning about any sport, even an American one, turned to hear his reply.

A cigarette dangled between Stan's lips and he ignored them while he lit a match, held it to the tip of his cigarette and inhaled. 'Completely different game as far as I can tell,' he drawled, blowing out smoke as he spoke. 'Not a lot of tactics involved.'

Lorna crossed her arms. 'You've seen all of two minutes, what can you possibly know about the tactics of rugby?'

Stan raised his eyebrows in surprise. 'Not enough, clearly.'

Lorna couldn't tell if he was belittling her or apologising. 'Well,' she said, turning back to the game. 'Maybe you should watch a match before forming a view.'

He didn't respond and she wondered if she'd offended him. As a general rule, boys didn't like Lorna to express her opinions, especially on anything to do with sport, where it seemed only males were the experts and females should keep their mouths firmly shut.

'Why are they in a line?' asked Stan, stepping up beside Lorna but keeping his eyes on the game.

'It's called a line-out,' Lorna replied curtly. 'When one team kicks the ball out, the other team gets to throw it back in. They have the advantage—' She broke off as the ball was thrown above the heads of a line of players from each team. The lock from Lorna's team took the ball cleanly and immediately dropped into a crouching position, others gathering around him.

'What are they doing now?' Stan asked, leaning forward with his hands pressed against the barrier, his eyes intent on the action.

'Now they're in what's called a maul. They'll try to gain a few yards, then probably send the ball wide.' From the edge of her vision, she saw Stan nodding.

'You know a lot about the game,' he said, and Lorna was sure there was admiration in his voice.

'I've been watching it all my life,' Lorna replied. She gave a cheer as her team spun the ball out wide and the centre crashed through to score a try.

Stan joined in with the clapping, and smiled at Lorna, bewildered. 'I have no idea what is going on, but I'm picking that he was meant to dive onto the ground like that?'

Lorna laughed, surprised at the realisation she might actually be enjoying his company.

'Yes, Stan. It's called a try.'

'Would you mind if I kept badgering you with questions?' asked Stan. 'I don't want to irritate you, but I really would love to get a better understanding of the rules.'

'The tactics, you mean?' asked Lorna, raising her eyebrows.

Stan laughed. 'Those too,' he said, his bluest of blue eyes returning to the field.

Lorna decided she had been incorrect in her initial assessment of Stan. While his appearance still seemed somewhat contrived — anyone who was exceptionally good-looking lacked credibility to her — there was something else beneath the surface. A yearning, thought Lorna, as if he desperately needed to know the answer or else he wouldn't be able to rest, something she could well relate to. Even better, Stan hadn't tried to engage in light conversation about mundane things. He'd just jumped straight in with his questions. He'd treated her like an equal, Lorna realised. He wasn't threatened by her demeanour, he didn't sneak furtive glances at her figure, and he didn't look right through her as if she was of no consequence. He had accepted her, ugly hat and all.

On Wednesday, Lorna went back to the hostel after work with Karen to get ready for her first dance.

'Do you think they'll notice?' she asked, biting her lip and staring out of the window at the glimpse of the harbour just visible through Karen's small window. Lorna wished the night was over and she could be home, relieved she had survived the evening. Karen was crouched behind her, drawing a black line down the centre of her leg. They'd already rubbed a pale orange lotion on their legs, which had taken nearly twenty minutes to dry in the cold air.

'Let's hope not,' said Karen, the pen-cap in her mouth distorting her voice. 'There,' she said, standing up. 'Best-looking pair of fake stockings you're ever going to see.'

Lorna tried to twist around to see the backs of her legs. 'Why did I agree to this again?' she asked.

'Because you can't wear trousers to a dance, Lorrie, no matter how much you try to convince me otherwise.'

Lorna wandered across the tiny bedroom and stared at herself in the small mirror hanging on the back of the door. She was aware she had a rounded face and fuller lips compared to most. Karen often said she was jealous of Lorna's 'luscious lips', as she called them, but Lorna felt they were too big, too obvious. Her eyes were nothing special either – a murky green instead of a rich deep blue like Karen's.

Sighing, Lorna turned her head from side to side, studying her hair. She'd barely slept, having spent an uncomfortable night wearing metal rollers. The sacrifice had hardly been worth the effort as the curls in her thick, brown hair had all but fallen out. Why did so many women put themselves through this?

'I'm not sure this is a good idea, Karnie,' she said, still staring at her reflection.

Karen came up behind her and squeezed her waist, causing Lorna to leap away yelping. Lorna was highly ticklish in that area, as Karen knew well.

'Stop worrying, Lorrie,' said Karen. 'You're overthinking it.'

'I'm not overthinking anything, I just don't see how I could possibly enjoy myself.'

'You were the one who agreed to go to the dance, I didn't force you. Besides, it's all about your attitude. If you tell yourself the dance will be a nightmare, then it will.'

Lorna rolled her eyes. 'Now you're sounding like Mum. She lectured me last night on opening myself up to new things.'

'I couldn't have said it better myself,' said Karen, grinning. 'She's a wise woman, your mum.'

They put on their floral cotton dresses, Karen bemoaning the fact they weren't stepping into soft satin gowns cut to the latest design. Then Karen helped Lorna to apply make-up, and they ran for the train to take them into town.

They sat in the carriage shivering, having decided it was best to leave their coats behind. Lorna was pleased, as the shivering helped to disguise her nervousness.

As their train pulled into the station, Karen spotted Derek and Stan from the window. She squealed and gripped Lorna's hands. 'Oh this is going to be grand! Just you wait and see.'

Lorna hung back as Karen stepped off the train and hurried towards the two Marines. When Derek threw his arms around

Karen's waist, picked her up and swung her around, Lorna scanned the platform quickly to see if she recognised anyone. If such a public display got back to Karen's parents, they were likely to lock Karen in her room and throw away the key.

Lorna approached Stan and gave him a brief smile.

'Hello, Lorna,' he said, holding out an orchid corsage. 'You look lovely.'

Lorna's hands trembled as she took it from him and slipped it onto her wrist.

'Thank you, Stan.' She wished she could be relaxed with him, the way they had been at the rugby game a few days earlier. He had peppered her with questions throughout the match, and afterwards at a tearoom with Karen and Derek. Lorna had loved the way he'd listened so intently, and she could have happily spent all evening with Stan, especially as he'd appeared to enjoy her company too.

But now Lorna felt self-conscious in her dress and make-up and her fake stockings. She felt different with Stan, less herself.

There was a moment of awkward silence and then Stan removed his green jacket.

'You're cold,' he said, draping his jacket around her shoulders.

At least he was tall, thought Lorna, looking down at her heels. She had always been the tallest girl in school and had some-times wondered if boys found it threatening when a girl reached a similar height to them.

'Thank you,' she croaked.

His forced smile did little to eliminate the crease lines on his forehead and Lorna got the distinct impression he didn't want to be there either. Rather than make her feel worse, she was relieved. The dance might turn out to be bearable after all.

They followed Karen and Derek from the station, out onto the street and into a misty rain.

'My legs!' Lorna said, before cupping her mouth and hoping no one had heard.

Karen gave her a withering look before hooking her arm in Derek's and increasing her pace.

'What about your legs?' asked Stan under his breath as they fell into step beside one another.

'I'm worried the rain will wash off the pen,' Lorna muttered.

Stan frowned. 'Pen?'

Lorna sighed and pointed to the backs of her legs. 'Silk stockings are rationed and we only get one pair to last three months. I put a ladder in mine a week after I bought them, and Karen put a ladder in her pair last week, so we had to pretend.' Lorna turned back to face him. 'I'm not actually wearing any stockings and my legs are positively freezing.'

Stan widened his eyes and grinned. 'Well, gee whiz,' he said. 'I wasn't expecting that.'

'Gee whiz?' said Lorna, a giggle bursting out before she could stop it. 'I wasn't expecting *that* either.'

⌐∽

The air pulsed with energy as they entered the dance hall. Lorna stopped dead in her tracks at the sight of a mass of bodies whirling about. This wasn't the sedate foxtrot she'd been forced to learn at school. Before her was a flurry of movement, the girls being flung about by Marines, spinning and rocking, clasping hands with their partners and letting them go again.

'This is what I was telling you about, Lorrie!' yelled Karen, gripping Lorna's arm. 'It's the jitterbug, isn't it, Derek?'

Derek laughed. 'It sure is, honey. Fancy giving it a go?'

'Do I ever,' said Karen.

Derek pulled her in amongst the frenetic bodies, gave a quick demonstration and then they were off, dancing as if they'd been doing the boisterous moves for months.

The loud band was playing music unlike anything Lorna had heard before. It was fast and lively, as if the instruments were being pushed to their limits and would break apart at any moment.

Lorna continued to watch in stunned silence. This wasn't dancing, this was something completely different. It was wild and daring and terrifying. There was no way she could ever let herself go like *that*.

'Should we get a drink?' Stan asked. 'I'm not sure I'm up for dancing yet.' His eyes were soft, gentle, as if he could sense her distress.

'Yes, please,' she said, her voice lost in the noisy hall. 'Yes,' she shouted.

They made their way around the edge of the dance floor and when Stan spotted a vacant table, he urged Lorna to sit and wait while he went to the bar. He returned moments later with two glasses in his hand.

'No alcohol being served, which I should have expected.' He shrugged and placed a glass before her. 'I took the liberty of getting you an orangeade,' he said, sitting down opposite.

Lorna thanked him, and then they drank their drinks in silence, their eyes fixed to the dance floor. Karen had convinced

Lorna to leave her spectacles at home so her vision was blurry, which for once she didn't mind. It meant she was able to treat everyone in the room as separate from her, like they were dancing on the other side of an opaque wall. Occasionally, Lorna risked a quick glance at Stan, and at some point she realised he wasn't focused on the dancing at all. His face was blank, his fixed smile like a mask.

'Have you done the jitterbug before?' Lorna asked, during the brief lull at the end of a song.

Stan nodded. 'Sure have.' He seemed to drag himself back to the moment. 'What about you?'

Lorna laughed. 'I've never even seen it till tonight.'

Stan considered her reply, then pushed back his chair and stood. 'Let's give it a go,' he said firmly.

Lorna shook her head. 'Oh no, I couldn't.'

Stan stood there waiting without speaking and Lorna felt something build inside her. Why couldn't she? Her brothers were in a desert thousands of miles away, fighting to stay alive, and she was worried about a bit of dancing? She was being ridiculous.

'Alright,' she said, standing so fast Stan blinked and took a quick step back. 'Let's dance,' said Lorna, holding out her hand.

He grinned and led her onto the dance floor.

Chapter 6

STAN

The dance had been more bearable than Stan had anticipated. He'd found Lorna's wide-eyed innocence mixed with her forth-right manner easy to be around, as if he didn't need to be on his guard. She lacked sophistication and refinement — a refreshing change from the confident, well-groomed girls from home, some of whom had a predatory air about them, as if they wanted to devour him.

He'd always found dancing difficult, not because the moves were challenging, but because it required you to let yourself go, to release yourself in a way he wasn't comfortable with. But he'd managed to dance with Lorna, maintain his composure and still enjoy himself. It gave him hope.

Stan had waited with Lorna for her father to pick her up after the dance. He'd greeted Lorna's father politely and knew he'd been convincing when her father had invited Stan to their place for tea that weekend. Stan had accepted, liking Lorna's father immediately — the way he'd been reserved, yet friendly; the way he'd slapped Stan on the shoulder and told him he was a 'good joker', whatever that meant. Stan had waved goodbye and then walked slowly through the quiet streets of Wellington back to the train station, enjoying the solitude and reflecting on a night well done.

He woke early the next day filled with energy and had a long walk on the deserted beach before being first in the chow line for breakfast. It was a relief to no longer feel as if there was a fist pressing on his chest. Derek noticed, of course, announcing Stan must have had a good night with his new girl. Stan didn't correct him and tell him Lorna wasn't 'his girl' just because they'd been to one dance together. He punched Derek light-heartedly on the arm and told him to shut up.

A few days later, Stan stepped off the tram, glanced again at the directions he'd written on the piece of paper in his hand, and walked several blocks until he turned on to Ranui Road. After a steep climb, he reached the gate of number 11 and gazed up the steps to the front door of Lorna's house. Taking a deep breath, Stan began to climb, but before he reached the top, the door was flung wide and a skinny boy in shorts and a jersey grinned down at him. A dog immediately pressed past the boy, barrelling into Stan's legs.

'Stan the American,' the boy announced loudly, as Stan steadied himself and bent down to pat the dog. He'd never been around a dog before, but this one seemed friendly enough.

Lorna pushed past the boy, rolling her eyes. She was wearing a blouse with a cardigan and trousers that were at least an inch too short. Her hair was messier than he'd ever seen on a woman, and it pleased him for some odd reason.

'I told Peter not to do that,' she said apologetically.

Stan straightened and held out his hand to the boy. 'Hello there, I am indeed Stan the American.'

They shook hands and Stan was taken aback at how cold and small the boy's hand felt. He was reminded of when he'd taken Alfie to a Cubs game and had reached for his hand to cross the busy street. Alfie had snatched his hand back, appalled, and insisted on walking behind Stan the rest of the way to the ballpark.

'I'm Peter,' the boy said. 'Lorna's brother. And that's Milly, our dog.'

Stan nodded, while wondering how to greet Lorna. He felt as if shaking her hand would be awkward for them both. Thankfully, she didn't give him time to consider his best approach as she stepped back and waved him inside.

The hallway was narrow and dark, with cream-patterned wallpaper, brown carpet and dim lights. Stan was disappointed to discover, as he followed Lorna, Peter and Milly down the hallway, that inside was barely any warmer than outdoors. He entered a kitchen, and a woman turned from where she was stirring something on the stovetop. She wiped her hands on her apron and clasped his hand. 'Hello, Stan,' she said warmly. 'Welcome to our home. I'm Lorna's mother, Mrs Baxter.'

Stan retrieved the package he'd been holding under one arm and held it out. 'Thank you for having me, ma'am.'

Lorna's mother looked embarrassed as she opened the package, then her face grew bright. 'Oh, I love chocolate,' she said.

'And the fancy cigarettes you love too, Mum,' said Lorna, holding up a carton of Chesterfields.

Stan pulled out another smaller package from his pocket. 'These are for you, Lorna,' he said gruffly.

Lorna opened the brown paper bag and laughed. 'Stockings!' she said, hugging them to her chest. 'Oh my goodness, thank you, Stan. Now I won't have to draw pen on my legs.'

Stan was pleased with himself. Pleased he could make these people he barely knew happy. 'It's nothing,' he said truthfully. The store at camp was packed with items that Lorna had told him were rationed. He couldn't understand why the goods were so cheap and easy for the Marines to get hold of, yet the local people went without.

'Right,' said Mrs Baxter, shepherding them out of the kitchen. 'Go see Father.'

Mr Baxter was sitting in an armchair beside an attractive fireplace with a carved wooden mantle. The fire provided some blessed warmth and an inviting glow, while an old-fashioned standing lamp with a green-tasselled lampshade cast a golden light on the bald patch on Mr Baxter's head. He closed his newspaper with a loud rustle, reached out to turn down the radio, and stood, holding out a hand. 'Stan, old chum, lovely to see you. Come in, come in. Would you like a beer?'

'Hello sir, a beer would be swell, thanks.'

Peter had been hovering at Stan's heels. Now, as his father left the room, Peter pointed to the armchair opposite the one Mr Baxter had just vacated. 'That's for you,' he said firmly.

Stan glanced at Lorna, who was biting her bottom lip in an effort not to laugh. Stan sat stiffly in the armchair and looked about the room. It had a nice, homey feel. A deck of well-handled cards lay splayed on the dark wooden side table; the bookcase, though messy with a jumble of books leaning in all directions, gleamed with polish; and the armchairs and couch in a faded floral fabric looked inviting and lived-in. Lorna stood with her back to the fire and stared at the carpet, while Peter continued to jiggle about beside Stan's chair. Stan felt as if he was an object on display, and the evening stretched before him.

Mr Baxter returned with two glasses of beer. 'Cheers,' he said, clinking his glass with Stan's. 'I hope you're being made to feel welcome.'

Before Stan could reply, there were noises in the hallway and Mrs Baxter walked in with a younger woman behind her. Stan immediately rose to his feet, but the young woman scowled at him before turning on her heel and leaving.

'Excuse her,' said Mrs Baxter, looking torn between following the woman and staying. 'Penny is . . . she has . . .' her voice faded.

Lorna cleared her throat. 'My two older brothers, Rick and Gordon, are in the army. They're in the Middle East right now and, Penny, well she's married to Gordon, and he's been gone an awfully long time, and Penny was hoping — we all were hoping actually — that our boys might come home to help defend us from the Japanese, but . . .'

Lorna paused. Stan knew she was about to say the Americans had turned up instead.

Mrs Baxter clapped her hands. 'Let's have tea!' she said brightly, ushering Stan down the hallway and back into the kitchen.

Penny was standing in the centre of the room as if waiting for him and immediately stuck out her hand. 'Hello,' she said, politely. 'I'm Penny, I hope you are settling in.'

'Yes, thank you ma'am,' he replied.

Mr Baxter guided Stan into the dining room. 'Why don't you take a seat, old chum,' he said, pointing to a chair.

'Actually,' said Stan, shuffling his feet. 'I wondered if I might use your washroom?'

They all looked at him blankly. 'You don't need to wash,' said Peter, his face confused.

'I think he means the bathroom,' said Penny with a slight smile.

They all laughed, except Stan, and Mrs Baxter pointed back down the hallway, telling him to take the second door on the left.

Stan opened the door to what he hoped was the washroom and searched for a light switch. Unfortunately when he spotted the switch it appeared to already be on, and Stan wondered if the bulb had blown. He flicked the switch down and was surprised to see the light come on. Stan flicked the switch up, and the light went off, then down and the light came on again. He realised that in this country, as well as driving on the left, their light switches were opposite too.

Stan relieved himself quickly, then went to wash his hands, discovering with some amusement that the hot and cold faucets were around the wrong way too.

Returning to the dining room, Stan took a seat and smiled politely at his plate loaded with stew, potatoes, carrots and cabbage. He opened his mouth to speak, then closed it again.

'Please,' said Mrs Baxter. 'Do start.'

Stan placed his napkin on his lap, then picked up his knife and fork. He had eaten a large meal at a tearoom near the train station before he'd caught the tram out to Lorna's house. He'd assumed, as her father had suggested, that he was here to drink tea. Lorna had repeated it too, during their conversation when she'd given him directions to her house. He specifically recalled she had used the word 'tea'. Yet there wasn't any tea in sight, for which Stan was somewhat grateful, though he wasn't relishing the thought of eating another large meal.

'So, Lorna tells me you're from Chicago,' said Mr Baxter, nodding his head. 'Quite a large city compared to here. Population of more than three million people, I believe.'

'Yes, sir,' said Stan.

'By a large lake. Lake Michigan, is it?'

Stan glanced across at Lorna who was looking amused.

'Yes, sir,' said Stan again, slicing a piece of carrot while also attempting to keep a straight face.

Lorna giggled. 'We were studying the Britannica earlier this afternoon,' she said, 'in preparation.'

'Better to be informed than ignorant,' said Mr Baxter firmly.

'Absolutely,' agreed Stan, placing down his knife, swapping his fork to his other hand, and raising his carrot to his mouth.

'Why are you eating like that?' asked Peter.

Stan lowered his fork. 'I'm sorry?'

'You're eating rather oddly,' Peter announced.

Stan looked around the table, then across at Lorna who, as if to demonstrate, kept her fork in her left hand and used it to pierce a piece of meat, which she sliced with the knife in her other hand, before lifting her forkful of food to her mouth.

Stan moved his fork back to his left hand. 'I guess we do things a little strangely in America,' he said, raising his fork and being struck by how odd it felt. 'You'll have to forgive me.'

'Not at all,' said Mrs Baxter, smiling. 'You'll catch on in no time, Stan.'

Chapter 7

LORNA

Stan and Derek were waiting for them in the foyer of the movie theatre. Lorna was pleased to see Stan again, though it had only been a few days since he'd been for tea.

'We haven't bought tickets yet,' Lorna said, omitting the fact that Karen had insisted they wait so that the boys could pay.

Stan looked about. 'Right,' he said. 'Where do we get tickets from? Outside?'

'Of course not!' exclaimed Karen, pointing to the ticket counter.

Stan nodded and went to buy tickets. When he returned, he waved the tickets in the air. 'We have actual seats,' he announced, as if it were a surprise.

'Well, that makes for a nice change,' said Derek. The usherette showed them to their seats, with the two girls choosing to be in the middle and the boys on either side.

'We don't have ushers in America,' said Stan, as he settled beside Lorna. 'Or allocated seats.'

'Really?' Lorna replied, swivelling to give him her full attention.

'And it's swell to see everyone's made a real effort to dress up. Back home, it's a completely different affair. You sit anywhere and the movies run continuously. Often people just turn up not even knowing when the movie started, and they're coming and going and getting in the way. Usually there's a bunch of noisy kids in the front row calling out and throwing popcorn boxes.'

'Gosh, that wouldn't be allowed here.'

'No, I imagine it wouldn't. This is much nicer. More civil.'

Derek leant across, having caught the end of their conversation. 'Far more your style, eh, Stan?'

Lorna didn't like the way Derek spoke to Stan sometimes. His teasing had an underlying bitter edge to it that she didn't understand. Lorna wondered why they were friends; they seemed so different to one another. Then again, she was vastly different to Karen and they were as close as sisters.

After two short features and a newsreel, they returned to the foyer for refreshments before taking their seats again for the feature film. When the curtains closed at the end, they all rose to their feet as 'God Save the King' played through the speakers. Lorna sang quietly, conscious of Stan standing silently beside her.

As they filed out of the theatre, Stan gave a short laugh.

'What?' asked Lorna.

'I was about to start singing, "My Country, 'Tis of Thee". It's practically the same tune as "God Save the King". Thank goodness I didn't.'

'Should we go to the Green Parrot?' suggested Karen, hooking an arm through Derek's.

'Lead the way, honey,' Derek drawled.

Lorna had only been to the Green Parrot twice with her family. Once, for a treat on her fifteenth birthday, and the second time in the week before her brothers left for Egypt. Tonight the restaurant was packed with Marines, many with their dates — several of whom were girls Lorna recognised from her old school. A haze of cigarette smoke filled the air, and the room was awash with the din of American voices.

The four of them were lucky to find a table, and Derek immediately waved over the waitress. 'I've a strong hankering for steak and chips, having seen Mac's plate over there. Stan, fancy a steak?'

Stan nodded. 'Sure.'

Lorna and Karen ordered the soup, and the waitress took their order to the kitchen before returning moments later with a jug of milk and four glasses. 'Milk is free,' she said. 'Just so you know.'

Stan and Derek looked pleased and immediately downed a glassful each.

A sudden loud bang caused the room to vibrate. It sounded as if a truck had slammed into the building. Lorna braced herself during the split second of eerie silence, knowing what was coming. Then the room came alive like a giant angry beast shaking something in its jaw. Glasses and plates smashed to the floor and lightshades swung wildly. There were shouts as Marines leapt to their feet in shock and confusion.

Lorna's chair clattered to the floor as she jumped up and snatched Stan's hand. 'Get under the table,' she hissed, pointing beneath the tablecloth and tugging his arm.

He stumbled to his knees, hitting his head as he ducked beneath the table to curl up as best he could in the small space.

Lorna crawled in next to him, noticing Karen and Derek were already sheltering there.

Lorna had let go of Stan's hand but now she reached for it again and squeezed. 'It's an earthquake, Stan, but we'll be okay. It will be over soon.'

'We should get out,' he said, his voice short and clipped, his face white.

Lorna shook her head. 'Just hold tight.' She firmly gripped his hand as the room roiled and rocked.

Then, in an instant, the earthquake stopped.

Their milk jug had slid off the table and shattered on the floor next to Stan. His trouser legs were soaked in the white liquid and Lorna shifted slightly to avoid the milk reaching her skirt.

'Are you alright?' she asked Stan.

Stan nodded and put his hand on the floor by his side to steady himself, then winced and quickly lifted it back up. A shard of glass was sticking out from his palm and a bead of blood trickled down his wrist. 'Son of a bitch,' he muttered. 'Watch for broken glass.'

They carefully scrambled out from beneath the table and looked around. Others were getting to their feet and speaking in low voices, as if afraid to wake the beast again. The room was a shambles.

'Let's get out of here,' said Derek.

'Shouldn't we stay and help clean up?' said Stan, trying to catch the drops of blood running down his wrist with his other hand.

'Reckon we're better to leave them to it,' Derek replied, placing a hand on Karen's lower back and guiding her towards the door.

They joined the other dazed patrons of the Green Parrot out on the street. It was dark, all the buildings now without power. In the glow of a car's headlights, Lorna could see the front facades of several buildings further down the street had collapsed, strewing chunks of brick and plasterwork across the street and onto parked cars.

A group gathered around someone lying on the ground, groaning, their legs disappearing beneath a curved row of bricks, which presumably had been surrounding the shopfront window.

'That's why you never run outside,' whispered Lorna. Then she grasped Stan's hand firmly, pulled out the shard of glass and pressed her handkerchief to the wound.

'Ouch,' said Stan. 'Thanks for the warning.'

A Marine standing nearby slapped Stan on the back. 'Well, Mac, reckon that's gotta have been worse than Pearl Harbour, don't you?'

Stan took a step away from the Marine. 'No, I don't *reckon*,' he said, turning and colliding with Karen and Derek, who were locked in a deep embrace.

'For fuck's sake,' barked Stan, shoving Derek's shoulder and striding a few steps down the street before turning back to glance at Lorna. 'Will you be okay?' he asked curtly.

Lorna was taken aback at the sudden change in Stan's behaviour. 'Yes,' she replied. 'Where are you going?'

'Back to camp,' Stan said. 'Sorry,' he added.

Lorna watched him walk away. She wasn't hurt by his odd behaviour; instead she was concerned. The earthquake must have shaken Stan more than she realised. Then Lorna thought of her family and forgot about Stan completely. She needed to get home, to check everyone was okay.

Chapter 8

STAN

It had been over a week since the earthquake and Stan still winced every time he thought of his behaviour. Thankfully, his regiment had been training hard with little opportunity to rest. Long marches through dense bush, relentless practices of amphibious landings on the beach. Countless drills in camp as their sergeant barked instructions and told them they were useless pieces of crap.

Stan was pleased to be exhausted each night when he fell into bed. Though this didn't stop him from waking at odd hours, sweating with embarrassment as he replayed his outburst over and over in his head.

The worst part had been Stan's appalling treatment of Lorna. How could he have just left her standing there? He'd called her the next morning to apologise and she'd brushed him off as if it was of no concern. She'd even invited him for tea again when he next had liberty to town.

Stan stared at his palm now. At the wound that kept losing its scab and bleeding, refusing to heal. He sighed loudly and glanced along the sidewalk, his heart skipping a beat when he sighted Lorna walking towards him. He'd phoned her the night before to let her know he would be free for tea the next day and asked if she might like to meet in town beforehand — perhaps they could have a stroll along the waterfront? Stan wanted to have a moment alone with Lorna, so he could apologise again.

When Lorna waved, Stan stood up from the bench seat where they had agreed to meet.

'Hello, Stan the American,' said Lorna warmly. She gave him a light, somewhat awkward hug before she carried on walking. 'Come on,' she called over her shoulder. 'I need some proper exercise.'

'I really am so sorry, Lorna,' Stan began, catching her up.

'No,' said Lorna holding up a hand while maintaining her rapid march. 'There's simply no need to apologise. Besides, you had every right to be mad at that man. Fancy suggesting a little earthquake was worse than the bombing of Pearl Harbour. What stupidity!'

Stan had mentioned being put out at the man's comment, but he hadn't explained that it wasn't the entire reason for his awful behaviour. 'Where are you taking me?' he asked, surprised at her pace. Stan liked the way she hadn't tried to make herself all pretty for his benefit. She wore a tatty, out-of-shape sweater, a pair of trousers, chunky socks and extremely ugly black boots. It made him want to grab her hand and kiss it.

'Top of Mount Victoria,' Lorna replied. 'Have you ever been fishing?' she added without a pause.

Stan shook his head. 'You want to go fishing from the top of a mountain?'

Lorna looked confused for a second then burst out laughing, which made him laugh too. Stan had never been one for genuine laughter. He was used to laughing without really meaning it, more out of politeness and because it was expected.

'Sorry,' said Lorna. 'Dad says my words have a hard time keeping up with my thoughts. He was wondering if you'd like to go out on the boat with him sometime? Dad loves fishing. He used to always go with my brother Rick, who is fishing *obsessed*, but he . . . well, he's not here.'

There was a change in the tone of Lorna's voice at the mention of Rick's name.

'Sure,' Stan said brightly, 'sounds swell.'

They were heading up a steep hill with small wooden houses on either side. The houses had neat gardens, painted front doors and identical windows either side. He thought of his family's tiny apartment back in Chicago and had a sudden, aching desire to never go back. To never see the neediness in his brother and sister's eyes again. To avoid the pressure he felt to shield them, to care for them, to perform.

'Your parents are very nice,' he said, as they reached the end of the street and started up a path surrounded by trees and shrubs. The path was too narrow for them to walk side by side, so Stan dropped back behind Lorna.

'Yes, I can't complain,' said Lorna. 'What about you? I bet your parents miss you. Mum and Dad talk about Gordon and Rick often, but I'm sure they're thinking about them practically nonstop.' Lorna's pace slowed a fraction. 'I know I am.'

Stan didn't reply. He was having too nice a time to let his parents spoil it. 'What was it like growing up in a houseful of brothers?' he asked.

Lorna laughed. 'Well, as you've probably noticed, it's not helped to make me . . . what's the word,' she waved her hand in the air. 'Feminine? Womanly? Heaven forbid.'

Stan was smiling again. Just listening to Lorna talk had that effect. It baffled him, the way he felt so comfortable in her presence. How she made him feel safe. *Safe from what?* Stan wondered as the path steepened further and they scrambled towards the top. Lungs bursting, Stan followed Lorna onto a plateau of grass, the harbour stretching out below them.

Lorna stood with her hands on her hips, puffing loudly, her cheeks red and her eyes glinting. 'Dad reckons you Americans have scared the Japanese off,' she said. 'There's no chance of them invading us now.'

'I'm not sure they would have invaded anyway,' Stan replied.

'Really?'

Stan shrugged. 'The Japanese took a big hit at Midway, and their focus isn't really down this way.'

Lorna looked thoughtful. 'That's what it said in *The Dominion* last week.'

'Well there you go.'

'But *we* don't know, do we? The strength of the Japanese, what capabilities they have, where they might attack next.'

'I suspect those higher up have some idea.'

'Do you like maths?' Lorna asked.

Stan blinked, trying to follow Lorna's train of thought. 'You mean math?' he said, confused. 'I suppose so. Why?'

Lorna turned away from him, crossed her arms, and looked down at the port where two American supply ships were docked. 'I love maths,' she said quietly. 'Which I realise is strange for a girl to say, but, well, I always thought I'd go on to study it at university. Mum was dead keen for me to go, Dad too, but then the war came along, and suddenly maths wasn't a priority. Only I keep thinking that if I were a few years older, and ideally if I were male,' Lorna added under her breath, 'then I could be helping, because I bet they're using maths all the time, for all sorts of reasons. Predicting, plotting, planning – statisticians must be working around the clock.' She stopped, out of breath. 'Sorry, I don't know why I'm telling you this.'

Stan went and stood beside her, facing out to sea, and crossed his arms too. 'They would have been lucky to have you.'

'Really?' asked Lorna, spinning to face him.

He wanted to take her into his arms, this strange girl who was unlike anyone he had ever met. He wanted to hold her tight and tell her she was remarkable. She made him feel for the first time in his life that it was okay that not all people fitted into the mould they were supposed to. Not only was it okay, it was admirable.

'Race you back down?' Lorna asked, uncrossing her arms and crouching as if she was about to start a race. 'Ready, set, go!' she said, taking off.

'Hey,' he called, starting to run. 'Unfair advantage.'

When her caught up with her at the bottom of the grassy plateau, they were both out of breath and laughing.

Chapter 9

LORNA

'Has he kissed you yet?' Karen asked.

Lorna swatted Karen lightly with her gloves before putting them on. 'No! Not that it's any of your business.'

'For goodness sakes, Lorrie, what's taking you so long? You've seen him how many times this past week? Three? Four?'

'Three, if you count this afternoon. But they weren't exactly dates.' On Sunday, they'd gone for a long walk around the coast from Island Bay to Rongotai. The waves had been so wild that by the time they'd reached the end of their walk they were soaked from the sea spray. Then after work on Thursday they'd visited the new public library on Mercer Street. Lorna missed the old library, though she had to admit the newly designed building was striking. They'd wandered up and down the rows of shelves for over an hour, barely talking, just pulling out a book when it caught their eye and showing it to one another. Earlier that day, Stan had been to watch Peter's school rugby game with Lorna and her parents. He'd returned to camp only a short while ago to get ready for the dance.

Lorna enjoyed Stan's company, and she'd wondered once or twice what it would be like for them to kiss, but she didn't feel silly or giddy about him. Not like the girls at work who talked incessantly about whichever Marine they were swooning over. Lorna figured it was just another way she was different.

Her brother and her parents had been completely won over by Stan's charms, and insisted he was to visit them whenever he had leave. Even Penny, who had been reluctant to have anything to do with the Marines, had warmed to him. And Lorna knew he was handsome – enough people had mentioned it – but that wasn't why Lorna enjoyed his company. She just felt comfortable when she was around him. Accepted.

'Can you believe someone congratulated me yesterday on making a good catch,' said Lorna, shaking her head. 'They looked rather surprised that I could draw the attention of Stan.'

'They were probably jealous.' Karen inspected her face in Lorna's mirror and nodded as if satisfied. 'Right, let's go,' she said, opening the bedroom door.

Lorna followed her down the hallway. 'Bye, Mum,' she called.

Her mother's head popped out of the kitchen. 'Have fun,' she said, smiling. 'Say hello to Stan.'

The sun had been stuck behind ominous low-hanging cloud all day, and it was a cold, bleak night as they stepped outside.

'At least it isn't raining,' said Lorna, wishing she were wearing her brother Rick's old black boots – which she'd found in his wardrobe the week after he'd left for Egypt – instead of the uncomfortable pumps currently on her feet.

On the tram, they huddled onto a seat together for warmth, and Karen leant close to whisper in Lorna's ear. 'Derek and I kissed after he took me to the movies on Wednesday.'

Lorna's eyes widened. 'Why didn't you tell me?'

'I'm telling you now.'

'What was it like?' Lorna was surprised Karen had let Derek kiss her after the way she'd been talking about him recently.

Karen grimaced. 'Sloppy.'

'What happened to him being insufferable?'

Karen tipped her head to one side in thought. 'I guess I just wanted to know what it would be like.'

'Well, it can't have been that bad if you've agreed to go to the dance with him tonight.'

Karen studied Lorna silently as if waiting for her to understand something.

'What?' Lorna asked.

'I agreed because I wanted to get you to another dance, and you wouldn't have gone with Stan unless I went too.'

'Why did you want me to go to another dance? You know it's not really my sort of thing.'

'Because I saw how much fun you had learning the jitterbug, even though you keep pretending it was all done under sufferance. You are *allowed* to like girlish things, Lorrie.'

Lorna opened her mouth to argue, then closed it again. She *had* enjoyed dancing far more than she had anticipated, and getting ready for the dance with Karen tonight had been surprisingly fun too. Perhaps her friend had a point. Maybe Lorna had been trying so hard to be a certain way that she hadn't considered she could allow herself to change.

When the tram stopped outside the train station, they clambered off and made their way onto the platform, where more than thirty other girls waited in their dresses and coats for the train that would take them to the Paekākāriki town hall where the American Red Cross had organised a dance.

'I love your hair,' said a girl Lorna recognised from work. Normally Lorna would have scoffed and turned away, but she was secretly pleased with how Karen had styled her hair, pinning it into elegant folds around her neck, so she smiled instead.

'Thanks,' she said, lightly touching her hair.

When their train arrived, its wheels screeching, all the girls on the platform emitted high-pitched, irritating cries of excitement. Lorna raised her eyebrows at Karen, who was practically keening, but didn't join in. She might allow herself a certain leeway when it came to 'girlish things', but there were definite limits, and squealing like a piglet was one of them.

The hall was crammed, Marines outnumbering the girls by quite a margin. Lorna squeezed into the hall behind Karen and was overpowered by the smell of men's cologne. Her eyes watered and she coughed quietly.

Stan and Derek appeared, as if they'd been watching the door, and Derek immediately pulled Karen towards the dance floor.

'You look nice,' said Stan politely, giving the red skirt and cream blouse she'd borrowed from Penny a brief glance. Lorna frowned. His face was strained and he looked ill at ease.

'Thank you, so do you,' she said brightly.

Stan shrugged, her comment appearing to make him even more uncomfortable. 'Do you want to dance or should we grab a drink first?' he said.

'Are you okay?' blurted Lorna. She hadn't expected him to be this tense when they'd been so relaxed in each other's company all week.

Stan nodded. 'Why wouldn't I be?' he said, his weak smile doing little to reassure her.

'I'm happy to dance if you'd like?' she said hesitantly. Was she imagining it, or was he deliberately avoiding looking at her?

Without a word, Stan clasped her hand and strode purposefully onto the dance floor. Then they were dancing, but it didn't feel like last time. Stan was going through the motions, but he didn't smile, never even looked up from a spot on the floor that appeared to have him mesmerised.

After four songs, Lorna had had enough. She stopped and put her hands on her hips. 'Stan, what on earth is going on?' she demanded loudly.

Before Stan could respond, Derek, still dancing with Karen, bumped into Stan's shoulder. 'This looks interesting,' he said, pausing to look back and forth between Stan and Lorna. 'Not getting too forward with you, is he, Lorna?' he said, giving her a suggestive wink. 'Don't rush the girl, Stan, plenty of time for that after the dance, eh?' He nudged Stan's shoulder again, laughing as he resumed dancing.

Stan was frozen in place, his cheeks flushed red. 'Lorna, I . . .' he trailed off. 'I'm sorry, but I'm not very well. I think I might have caught a stomach bug.'

'Well, why didn't you say something earlier?' said Lorna, relieved she wasn't the reason he had been so out of sorts. 'You shouldn't have come to the dance, Stan. I would have understood.'

'I'm terribly sorry, Lorna,' he said, beads of sweat on his upper lip adding to his obvious discomfort. 'I don't . . . I didn't want to let you down.'

'I'll be perfectly fine here, Stan. You head back to camp. There's hardly a shortage of young men for me to dance with, now is there?' she said, waving her hand around the room and trying her best to hide her disappointment.

Stan left quickly then, and Lorna forced herself to dance with several men, all of whom were chatty and attentive. But whatever excitement she'd had for the evening had disappeared. It felt like an interminable wait for the train that would return her home.

Chapter 10

STAN

Enzo ducked into the tent. 'Mail,' he said, dropping an envelope on Stan's chest before collapsing onto his own bed and closing his eyes. 'Nothing for me,' he muttered. 'Not that I'm surprised.'

Enzo was an only child and his parents had been so furious when he'd joined the Marines they'd refused to write. Stan knew it upset Enzo more than he let on.

Derek and Bruno were on liberty in town. Stan and Enzo had also been granted leave, but when Enzo had said he was exhausted and preferred to stay and sleep all day instead, Stan had opted to remain in camp too.

'Useless buggers,' Derek had said as he'd left, a box of chocolates under his arm for the new girl he was seeing.

Stan lifted the envelope to his face and immediately recognised the writing. It was another letter from Alfie. Stan should have replied to his brother's previous two letters, but he hadn't had a chance. That was a lie. Stan could have easily written to Alfie, and to his mother, had he been inclined. But what was he supposed to write about? He wasn't able to tell them where he was or what he was doing, so what was left to say?

Tearing open the envelope, Stan pulled out a thin slip of paper.

Stan, have you killed any Japs yet? Training is shit, but you knew that. Not sure why I joined to be honest. At least there's food and a uniform right? Anyway, signing off so I can get some shut eye. Keep your head down and make sure you leave some of those Japs for us. Alfie.

Stan sat up and slid the letter under his pillow. Enzo was already snoring and the noise was irritating. Sliding on his boots, Stan left the tent and made his way towards the latrines.

'Did you hear?' said a Marine, crouched outside his tent, smoking.

'Hear what?' Stan asked.

'We're shipping out in the next day or two.'

Stan frowned. 'I thought we were here for a few more months.'

The man shook his head. 'They need us to deal with the Japs now.'

'Right,' said Stan, glancing at his watch. He had almost eight hours of liberty left. Plenty of time to get changed, catch the train to town and visit Lorna. It didn't feel right to leave without seeing her one final time.

Signs of damage from the earthquake were still evident as Stan made his way through the city. Parts of Manners Street were closed and there were several cordons in place. Twice Stan was stopped by eager schoolboys offering to shine his shoes. He shook his head but tossed them a few coins anyway.

Passing the St George, Stan had a sudden urge for alcohol and nipped inside for a quick bourbon. He'd called Lorna before leaving camp to check she would be home, and to let her know the news. She'd sounded disappointed to hear they were leaving so soon.

At six o'clock, Stan left the St George and jogged down the street to catch the tram. He leapt on as it started to move and smiled politely at the tram conductor, who narrowed her eyes at him warily.

Stan was halfway up the steps to Lorna's front door when it swung open and Lorna appeared. 'I heard there was a suspicious-looking Marine headed this way,' she said, putting her hands on her hips.

Stan stopped. 'How?'

'Mrs Fogerty,' said Lorna. 'From the house on the corner. She just phoned.'

'Gosh,' said Stan. 'That was impressive.'

'Annoying old busybody,' said Lorna, opening the door wider for him to enter.

Mr Baxter was in his usual chair by the fire. 'Stan, old chum,' he said, rising. 'Come in, come in, can I get you a beer?'

Stan shook his hand. 'Thanks, Mr Baxter, that would be swell.'

As Mr Baxter left the room, Peter came tearing through the door. 'Stan!' he yelled. 'You're here.'

'Mum insists you stay for tea,' said Lorna, shrugging apologetically. 'I think it's roast mutton though, so I wouldn't agree too readily.'

'I heard that,' said Mrs Baxter, bustling into the room in her apron. She gave Stan a quick hug. 'There's plenty if you'd like to stay,' she said, already heading back out the door.

'Thank you, ma'am,' Stan replied.

Lorna wrinkled her nose, as if in thought. 'What about a walk?' she said. 'I've barely left the house all day. I could do with stretching my legs.'

'Sure,' Stan replied, following Lorna to the front door.

'We'll be back shortly,' called Lorna.

'Right you are, love,' replied Mr Baxter, appearing in the kitchen doorway with two glasses of beer in his hand. 'I'll drink yours if it starts to get too warm,' he told Stan with a wink.

Lorna put on her coat, and they walked in silence to the corner of Ranui Road, falling into step with each other as they turned the corner.

'How's Penny?' Stan asked.

'She's okay. Gordon is out of hospital which is a relief. And Rick's name wasn't on the casualty list this morning so we're keeping our fingers crossed.'

The Kiwis had been having a difficult time and the news in the papers had been sobering enough for the Marines, let alone the New Zealand families who had loved ones fighting overseas.

'We think your boys are very brave,' said Stan. The Marines talked often about the battles the Kiwis were facing seemingly one after another in the Middle East. How tough they had to be to cope in those conditions.

'Dad said it's chaotic down at the port,' said Lorna. 'Do you have any idea where you will be going?'

'No. They're keeping it quiet.'

'How are you feeling? I imagine you're nervous, I know I would be.'

'I can't wait to finally fight,' said Stan. 'I'm excited more than anything.'

'Please keep yourself safe, Stan; don't try to do anything heroic.'

Stan put a hand on Lorna's arm so she would stop walking.

'Lorna, I wanted to . . .' he hesitated. 'I'm sorry about the dance the other night.'

'You've already apologised enough, Stan. Have you fully recovered?'

Stan took a deep breath. He wished he could tell her that it wasn't his stomach that had been bothering him that night, but something else. 'Lorna, you're a wonderful girl, really the very best, but I'm about to head off to war and I don't want to give you . . . that is, I'm not . . . I can't . . . I don't want to make any promises . . . it wouldn't be fair . . .'

Lorna put a hand on Stan's chest. 'You don't have to say anything, Stan, I understand.'

The way she looked at him made Stan feel she did understand in a way that no one else did. 'I'm sorry,' he whispered.

'There's nothing to be sorry for, Stan. Just focus on taking care of yourself. Maybe you could write? Send a postcard from Chicago when this war finally ends. Let me know you're safe.'

Stan hugged her and she hugged him back so tightly he could barely breathe. He'd never been held that way before in his life.

The following morning, the 1st Division of the United States Marine Corps stood to attention as they were informed they would be leaving the next day. They were given the afternoon to pack up and get any final mail in the post.

Stan left the camp and wandered over the undulating hills to the beach. It was overcast, and a low mist hung over the island he could see in the distance. The sea was loud, giving off a constant roar, and bits of yellow-tinged sea foam danced along the sand. Stan sat on a piece of driftwood and finally wrote to his brother. The wind whipped at the sheet of paper on his knee as he told Alfie that he'd met a girl called Lorna. He wrote of Lorna's brother Peter and her parents, of their hospitality and kindness. He didn't mention Wellington, or New Zealand, knowing it would be censored. He didn't tell his brother that he was about to go to war. He told Alfie that he was proud of him for stepping up, that he would make a great Marine. He told Alfie he'd deal with most of the Japs, but that he'd leave a few behind. *Don't want you missing out on all the action,* he wrote. Then he signed his name and folded up the piece of paper.

Stan continued to sit on the beach for another half hour, watching the waves crash and roll to shore. Days like today he felt that being a Marine was all he had to cling to. There was no one he could be his true self around. Except perhaps Lorna.

Stan unfolded his letter and added a postscript.

P.S. Lorna's the only one, Alfie. If circumstances were different, I would have asked her to marry me.

GUADALCANAL, FOUR WEEKS LATER

Stan was so exhausted he fell asleep standing up in his foxhole. Even the drone of 'washing machine Charlie', as they named the Japanese bomber who circled above the Marines each night, keeping them on edge, toying with them until he finally decided to drop his bombs, wasn't enough to keep Stan's steel helmet from flopping forward to land on the wall of the foxhole and him from sinking into welcome oblivion.

He no longer dreamed in the hour or two of sleep he snatched each night in this baking-hot jungle. Sleep brought blessed, utter blankness.

Ten minutes later, Stan startled awake to find Bruno screaming in his face, but he couldn't hear a word coming from Bruno's mouth. Instead, there was a strange humming in his ears, like a bee was trapped inside. Stan touched the side of his face, and his hand came away covered in blood.

Bruno was still yelling as he shoved Stan's rifle into his chest then grabbed at his own cartridge belt, his face determined and unafraid as he loaded his ammo.

Not again, thought Stan. *I can't do this again.*

Yesterday Stan had shot fifteen Japanese soldiers, and shoved his bayonet through four. He'd also seen Derek's body blown into pieces, then been ordered to gather up those pieces to bury in the ever-growing grave by the airstrip.

Bruno was clambering up out of their foxhole and Stan automatically followed, his head thumping painfully from his wound. His tongue felt fat and dry. He'd emptied his canteen hours ago and there would be no more water till the morning. Assuming, this time, supply ships could get through.

Out of the foxhole, Stan stumbled as his already wet, stinking boots sunk into the mud. He glared at the dark jungle, which hid all sorts of horrors, then raised his rifle as Japanese soldiers emerged, running, their snarling faces shouting words Stan still couldn't hear. Their bodies began to shudder and drop as bullets tore into them from the machine gun Stan knew must be firing from nearby, yet all he could hear was the bee, trapped in his ear, tunnelling deeper into his skull.

Bruno was further in front of Stan, running at the Japanese, firing from the hip, and Stan knew he was filled with rage so potent that he wouldn't stop until he had killed every last enemy soldier on this godforsaken island, or died trying. Bruno had seen what they'd done to Enzo's body. He would never forgive or forget that.

Stan sensed movement near his right shoulder and turned to see a Japanese soldier only a few steps away. The enemy raised his sabre above his head with two hands, a demented smile on his face.

It was as if, in that moment, the entire world froze. Stan knew that he was about to die. He would be buried with the other Marines on this island in the middle of the Pacific, hundreds of miles from America. He thought of Alfie and wished he could somehow send him a message. He wished he could tell his brother to get out. To leave the Marines, to go back to Chicago and to be damn grateful for every little thing he had. Stan realised, as he watched the sword arc slowly through the air, that his time in New Zealand had been preparation. A glimpse of heaven, before being sent into hell.

PART TWO

WELLINGTON, NEW ZEALAND

NOVEMBER 1942

Chapter II

LORNA

They'd been lying on the concrete floor of the munitions factory for over three hours and Lorna wanted to scream with boredom. Her hip bones hurt from rolling side to side in an effort to get comfortable. She knew they were doing this for a good cause but sincerely hoped they wouldn't have to stay there much longer. She was starting to wonder if their refusal to work had been in vain.

'Hang in there, girls,' called Jane, the one who'd convinced everyone to strike. Jane was at least ten years older than Lorna and filled with conviction, energy and righteousness – traits Lorna normally admired, especially in a woman, though she currently found them trying.

The female workers were on strike because the red paint on the shell casings was making them sick. All the girls complained of a metallic taste in their mouths and while Lorna hadn't experienced many other untoward effects, she often had a low-lying unexplained nauseousness, which had only developed after she'd started working there. Jane had been adamant the strange tingling in Lorna's hands and feet were another side effect too.

Those who'd worked at the factory longest were in worse shape, suffering from headaches, stomach pains, vomiting and diarrhoea. They were unable to concentrate, slurred their words and had tremendous difficulty getting a proper night's sleep.

The girls weren't just protesting about the paint — though it was by far the biggest issue — they were also fed up with having to work with the sun beating down on their backs as the windows had no curtains. It was bearable in the winter months — when the sun was mostly stuck behind rain clouds — but now that it was November, the days were heating up. The girls were determined not to have a repeat of last summer when everyone's clothes had stuck to their sweaty bodies and several had fainted in the heat.

Lorna was desperate to use the bathroom. The *washroom*, Lorna thought suddenly, remembering Stan and his funny American sayings. Her throat tightened. According to the casualty list in the paper, Stan had been killed four weeks after leaving Wellington, while fighting at a place called Guadalcanal. Lorna couldn't quite believe he was dead and often woke in the night utterly convinced the lists in the paper weren't real, none of it was, the whole war was one giant made-up horror story that everyone stupidly believed.

After reading of Stan's death, Lorna had cried for hours, surprising herself with the extent of her grief. She'd barely even known him, yet he had filled some void in her life she hadn't realised was there. Wanting to learn more about where he had died, Lorna's father helped her to look up Guadalcanal in their well-thumbed atlas. It was a tiny dot of land in the middle of the Pacific. Seemingly insignificant, and yet the Americans and Japanese were still fighting over it now, three months later. Mr Baxter had explained it was something to do with a strategic location and an airstrip, but it still didn't make sense to Lorna.

Peter had been furious when he'd found out Stan had been killed. He'd stomped around the house for days, and spent hours up at their lookout, even though the threat of a Japanese invasion seemed to have passed. Mrs Baxter had been eerily silent, barely speaking a word. It was silly in a way, how the news had shaken Lorna's family. There was something about Stan having been in their home that made it more personal.

Derek had been killed too, along with a long list of other Marines Lorna had probably seen on the streets of Wellington, or who would have been at the dances, or at the rugby, or at other places she'd been to with Stan.

Karen had felt guilty when she'd learnt of Derek's death, having spent several days after his departure expressing relief he was gone. When Lorna asked her why she'd dated Derek in the first place, she said she'd been using the experience as a learning tool – having never kissed a boy before – in preparation for when she met a Marine she actually liked.

Thank goodness Lorna's brothers were still alive. Gordon had been injured during the fighting at El Alamein, but according to the last letter they had received he was out of hospital now and on recuperation leave in Alexandria. Rick was fine too, he'd written, though fed up with the desert and ready to come home. He'd sent Lorna a silk scarf for her nineteenth birthday, which had taken everyone by surprise; Rick not being known for remembering birthdays.

Lorna released a loud breath of frustration and closed her eyes, willing herself to fall asleep like her friend lying beside her.

'That sigh was so loud it woke me up,' grumbled Karen, rolling over to face Lorna. 'What time does your mum want us at the Cecil?' she asked.

'Six o'clock,' Lorna replied. 'We'll have to be quick leaving here if we want to make the five-fifteen train.'

The week after learning of Stan's death, Lorna's mother had signed up to volunteer for the American Red Cross. She now worked at the Hotel Cecil, which had been turned into a recreational club for the Marines. Lorna's mum was responsible for organising and serving food for the Wednesday evening dances. She took her new role seriously, spending many hours rounding up neighbours to bake cakes and provide sandwiches, as well as baking a pile of cakes of her own. No easy feat with a shortage of eggs and butter.

A few days earlier, another large group of Marines had arrived in Wellington, adding to the ever-increasing numbers of Americans filling the city, and the Cecil was expected to be overrun at this evening's dance. Lorna and Karen had offered to lend a hand, having volunteered a couple of times already — Karen happily dancing with one Marine after another, while Lorna busied herself serving food and clearing away glasses. She didn't refuse to dance if one of the boys happened to ask her, she just made sure she always looked so busy there was less chance of them doing so.

Lorna was starting to get used to the American presence in Wellington now — the way they doffed their hats and opened doors with a flourish. How they relished the opportunity to give away coins to children, and spent money on frivolous things. Lorna no longer squirmed when they fixed her with their steady gazes, or called her 'sweetheart', or asked if she was married.

Every week the city changed to meet the needs of its visitors. Florists and laundromats appeared everywhere. Schoolboys roamed about selling corsages from home-made trays slung around their neck. There were new restaurants, clubs, milk bars and popcorn stands. Lorna hadn't even known what a milk bar was until Peter insisted they visit one. They'd sat on high stools and drunk milkshakes through straws, and Peter had chatted to a couple of Marines who'd given him lollies, or 'candy' as they called it. Jewellers had queues out their doors of Marines wanting to buy watches, greenstone necklaces and chunky rings they referred to as knuckledusters. Everywhere they went, the Marines smoked fancy cigarettes and paid to have their shoes shined and their uniforms pressed. They spoke loudly, walked confidently and smiled as if they knew some secret the New Zealanders didn't.

Lorna wasn't sure what to make of it all. Some days she found the presence of the Americans exciting, other times she wished they'd never arrived. There was no doubting Karen's view, however. She loved everything about the Americans: everything they did, everything they said, everything they ate and everything they wore. She was in love, she told Lorna, with the American way of life.

'I've heard the new Marines from the Second Division are a wild bunch,' whispered Karen, stretching her arms over her head and yawning. 'Should make for an interesting night,' she added with a grin.

Lorna shook her head and was about to comment when she heard a door open and turned to see her boss, Mr Postlewaite, emerge from his office. He was a short man with a thick, bushy moustache, and permanently crumpled shirt. While Lorna had yet to see him smile, she hadn't seen him frown either, and she respected his calm unflappability. Karen was more critical, calling him Mr Plank and claiming he showed as much excitement as a piece of wood.

Mr Postlewaite called Jane over and they spoke quietly for a few minutes. Then Mr Postlewaite nodded and indicated with the slow raise of his palm that the girls should stand. 'On your feet, girls,' Jane exclaimed. 'Mr Postlewaite has listened to our demands.'

As they gathered themselves off the floor, Mr Postlewaite announced in his soothing monotone that he would have someone in to measure the windows for curtains the following week. 'And I have arranged for an inspector to come tomorrow to examine the casings.'

Everyone clapped, and there were a couple of faint cheers before the girls began to return to their workstations.

Lorna sighed loudly again, as she finally headed towards the bathroom. She was pleased with their small victory, but it didn't change the fact her job was tedious. She wanted to be part of the war effort and she had no qualms about working long hours, but she wished she could be doing something a little more rewarding. Something that didn't make her stare at the clock on the wall, willing it to speed up.

She wished they were at the Hotel Cecil already. Even if it was going to be overrun with American boys, at least it was bound to be more interesting than this.

Chapter 12

ALFIE

Alfie drained the last of his Budweiser and threw the bottle on the grass beside him. He reached for another bottle, opened it and took a big gulp.

'Your turn, Alf,' said Curtis with a smirk.

Alfie glanced at his cards, picked up a coin — a shilling, he reminded himself — and tossed it into the upturned steel wheel rim lying in the centre of the group. 'Better watch out, my luck's changin', I can feel it.'

The two other Marines in the circle laughed as Curtis handed Alfie a card. Alfie looked at it and immediately threw his cards to the ground in disgust. 'You're riggin' it, Curt, you must be.'

'No riggin' involved, bud, it's just not your day.'

Alfie stretched out his legs, propped himself up on one elbow and drank his beer as he half-watched the rest of the game, and half-watched the sheep grazing on the hills in the distance. He couldn't believe this was how he was spending his afternoon. Losing at poker and watching damn sheep.

They'd been at camp for five days and Alfie was restless and bored. From what he'd seen so far, this country was the dullest place he'd ever been. Alfie reached for the booklet resting on Jethro's leg and began to thumb through it. They'd been issued the booklets, written by the New Zealand Department of Internal Affairs, when they'd arrived at camp. They were supposed to help the Marines understand the people and culture, but as far as Alfie could tell, they were just reinforcing what he already knew — this country was small and backward.

Alfie snorted. 'Listen to this: 'cow' may just mean cow but may also mean unpleasant man or woman or situation.'

'So they insult someone by calling them a cow,' said Jethro, laughing. 'Makes sense.'

Alfie turned the page and shook his head. 'Apparently the ratio of sheep to people is eighteen to one. Can you believe it?'

'Do you think they're proud of that fact?' asked Curtis.

'Who knows,' said Alfie, losing interest in the booklet and laying it aside. 'This country is a damn joke.'

'It's not that bad,' said Curtis, dealing a card to Martin on his left and blatantly glancing at the cards in his hand as he did so. 'I think you should fold, Marsh, your cards are crap.'

Martin, or Marsh as he was called on account of him being a 'soft, squishy marshmallow' both in looks and personality, pressed his cards to his chest. 'That's cheatin', I demand a re-deal.'

'Suits me,' Alfie replied. 'Though I've only got this left.' Alfie held up a small coin and squinted at the engravings. 'A *florin*.

What the hell kind of word is that? What's wrong with just calling it a dollar or a quarter?'

The chow bell sounded and Curtis stopped shuffling the cards. 'About darn time,' he said, slipping the cards into his pocket and immediately getting to his feet. 'Let's go,' he said, reaching down to pull Alfie up.

'Wait on,' said Jethro, 'they ain't gonna run out.'

Alfie sensed Curtis's anxiety and put a steadying hand on his arm. 'Alright Curt, we're going.'

Like Curtis, Alfie knew what it was like to be hungry. When they'd first met, aged fourteen, they'd been skinny boys with hollowed cheeks and no shoes. They'd been scrappers, eating everything on their plates and anything they could scrounge up, fighting for it if necessary. It stayed with you, the desperation, even when you weren't starving, even four years later when you were in the Marines and you had more money than you could have dreamed of, when you could buy all the food you wanted. You still remembered. Curtis most of all.

Alfie had met Curtis on a farm in the middle of nowhere Texas. Alfie's mum had sent him there, hoping to straighten him out, she'd said, and to reduce the number of mouths she had to try to feed. Alfie had never been anywhere outside of Chicago before and had felt lightheaded getting off the train at Fort Stockton. All that wide-open empty space.

Roosevelt was the one who'd come up with the idea: A way to help all those families who couldn't feed their kids. *The Civilian Conservation Corps*, the president called it. For six months, teenagers were sent to the country to work on irrigation or drainage schemes. Housed in barracks, the boys wouldn't be paid, but they would be fed and clothed. They'd ease the pressure on families back home.

Curtis was on the bunk above Alfie, and they became friends on day one. Curtis loved being out there in the middle of nowhere and dreaded going back to his hometown, Seattle. He loved the hard work, being outdoors. It became his dream to own a farm one day. A dream he was saving up for with every pay-check.

Curtis had been the one to convince Alfie to join the Marines. 'It's our ticket,' he kept saying. 'Our ticket to a better life.'

Curtis wouldn't have even considered joining the Marines if Alfie hadn't mentioned his older brother, Stan. He'd told Curtis that Stan joined the Marines and never came back. Instead Stan sent short letters and money. Alfie didn't tell Curtis that he was angry at Stan every time another envelope arrived. Angry because he knew the money was Stan's excuse, his reason for not coming home.

Curtis had written to Alfie the day he turned eighteen to say he was joining the Marines and to urge Alfie to join too. They'd met in San Diego the following week, signed up together, and Alfie hadn't seen his mom or sister since.

As they sat in the mess hut and ate their plates piled high with chilli and potato, Alfie tried not to think about Stan, and failed.

Apparently the 1st Marine Division had stayed in Camp Mackay, the same camp Alfie was in now. Stan would have eaten right here in this building, would have slept in one of the tents, walked the same paths, seen the same sheep grazing on the hills. Alfie couldn't believe his brother was dead. That he hadn't had a chance to see him. Alfie had wanted to stand next to his brother in his Marines uniform and prove that he had become some-thing, that he could get out of Chicago and never look back too.

After eating, the boys shaved, showered and dressed. They applied deodorant, shaving lotion and cologne. They put on their cufflinks, tie-clasps and rings. They hung their keychains around their necks and combed their hair. Then they made their way to the platform and stood waiting for the four o'clock train that would take them into town.

Two hours later, the pubs closed, and Alfie and his friends found themselves out on the streets. 'Son of a bitch,' Alfie exclaimed. 'This place is the damn pits!' He'd managed to down three bourbons in the meagre hour spirits had been available, the third a gift from Marsh who wasn't much of a drinker.

'Come on,' said Curtis, striding off around the corner. 'We can see if they'll let us in at the Cecil.'

They made their way to the hotel near the train station and Curtis knocked on a door at the rear of the building. An older man in a three-piece suit that had seen better days opened the door. 'Bar's closed to the public,' he said.

'I understand,' said Curtis, handing over a paper bag containing three cartons of cigarettes. 'We're staying in one of the rooms, aren't we buds?'

'Absolutely,' said Alfie.

Jethro nodded and Marsh stood frozen, unable to go along with their story.

The man looked inside the bag and stepped back, opening the door wider. 'Well, come on in then, you jokers, before anyone catches sight of you.'

Alfie raised his eyebrows at Curtis, who stifled a laugh. Then they followed the man inside and settled themselves at a table. The barman who had let them in approached. 'What can I get you?' he asked.

Alfie grinned. 'A bourbon please, sir.'

The barman nodded. 'You going to the dance next door then?'

'What dance?' asked Jethro.

'The Red Cross organises a dance at the club every Wednesday night. Very popular, it is.'

'A dance,' said Curtis. 'Count me in.'

Alfie nodded. 'Me too. Assuming there will be some pretty girls.'

'There'll be some nice girls, I'm sure.'

Alfie waited for the barman to leave. '*Nice* girls,' he said, grumpily, 'are not exactly what I had in mind.'

Three hours later, they were all dancing the jitterbug and trying to look sober. Alfie's head spun and he wanted to sit down but thought that might make him feel worse. The girl he was dancing with was called Mary. She had frizzy brown hair and thin lips, and she wore a dress Alfie would have expected an old lady to wear.

When the song ended, Alfie excused himself and went to the washroom to splash water on his face. Returning to the dance hall, he spied Curtis standing by a table of sandwiches and cakes and went to join him.

'Alfie, this is Karen,' said Curtis, gesturing to the pretty girl standing beside him. She had a wide smile and flushed cheeks.

'Pleasure,' said Alfie, shaking her hand.

'Where are you from then, Alfie?' she asked in the oddly appealing Kiwi accent.

'Chicago,' he replied.

'Really?' Karen replied. 'I knew a Marine from Chicago. Stan someone.'

Alfie held himself very still as if protecting himself from a blow he knew was coming.

'Alfie's brother was called Stan,' said Curtis.

Karen bit her lip and frowned. 'Gosh, I'm so sorry.' Then she looked around the room, frantically searching for someone.

'Lorrie!' she called, waving to a rather tall girl who had her arms full of empty glasses. Karen beckoned her over.

'This is Alfie, Stan's brother,' she said.

The girl looked at him and colour drained from her face. She opened her mouth to speak, then closed it again, tears welling in her eyes. 'I'm very sorry for your loss,' she mumbled.

'Thank you,' Alfie replied, studying the awkward girl whose spectacles were sliding down her nose. 'Did you know him?'

The girl nodded. 'Yes . . . though not very well.'

Alfie thought of the last letter he had received from his brother. The one declaring love for a girl he'd met in Wellington. A girl he would have married if he hadn't been heading off to get himself killed.

'Lorna,' Alfie stated abruptly, making the girl jump.

'Yes,' she replied, her voice cracking and her cheeks turning red. 'That's me.'

Chapter 13

LORNA

Stan had never mentioned a brother. A brother who was also a Marine but looked nothing like Stan. Though now she knew they were related she could see Alfie had the same nose, the same slight peak in the middle of his eyebrows. Alfie was shorter and slimmer though, with curly, dark brown hair. And he had a look in his eye she didn't like; as if he had assessed her and found her lacking.

'So you're the girl,' said Alfie, tapping out a cigarette and lighting it. 'I'll be damned.' He blew smoke into the air above her head, his eyes on the dance floor behind her.

Lorna decided she didn't like this Alfie character, and while she was sorry he had lost his brother, she didn't have any obligation to spend time with him. 'Excuse me,' she said, indicating the glasses in her arms. 'I need to carry on.'

'Fine by me,' muttered Alfie, his eyes remaining on the dancers.

Lorna looked at Karen, hoping for sympathy, but Karen was engrossed in a conversation with the Marine standing beside her.

Lorna weaved her way towards the kitchen where she offloaded the glasses then stood for several seconds working up the courage to go back out. It had been a long day and she was tired. Tired and annoyed. The way that boy Alfie had looked at her. It was as if he couldn't believe any man, let alone his brother, could be interested in her.

Well, hopefully she could avoid him for the rest of the night, and with a bit of luck, for his remaining time in Wellington too.

'Lorrie,' said her mum, racing through the door in her grey uniform. 'I just met Stan's brother! What a surprise. I've invited him for tea tomorrow.'

'Oh Mum,' Lorna exclaimed, throwing up her hands. 'Why?'

'What do you mean, why? It's the very least we can do for the poor boy.'

Lorna wondered if she could come up with some excuse so she wouldn't have to be home the following evening. Maybe she could arrange a last-minute game of tennis with a friend or go back out onto the dance floor and try to get one of the Marines to take her on a date.

Lorna shook her head. As if she could ever be that bold.

The following evening at 6.30pm, there was a knock on the front door. Peter raced to answer it, while Lorna stayed in her bedroom reading her book. It was the latest in the detective series by Ngaio Marsh and she was at an exciting part. At least that's what she told herself.

Eventually she heard her father calling her name, so she closed her book and headed for the living room.

Alfie was standing with his back to the fire and barely gave her a second's glance when she entered. Milly was sitting at his side looking up at him adoringly.

'I understand you've met Lorna already,' Mr Baxter said from his armchair before tucking his pipe back between his lips.

'Yes, I have,' said Alfie without acknowledging her.

Lorna felt a ball of heat inside her.

'Look what Alfie gave me,' said Peter, holding up his hands stuffed full of packets of chewing gum.

'I heard all the kids are real keen on gum,' said Alfie with a smug smile.

'Chewing gum is banned in New Zealand,' said Lorna crisply.

'What on earth for?' asked Alfie, laughing. 'Worried they're going to choke on it?'

'Because it's full of sugar,' Lorna retorted. 'Bad for your health.'

Still laughing, Alfie raised his eyebrows and met her gaze as if to challenge her. 'I've been chewing gum all my life and I couldn't be healthier.'

Lorna attempted to smile politely, then turned away. 'Excuse me, I'll go and see if Mum needs help.'

Alfie barely stopped talking throughout the entire meal. Everyone else in Lorna's family seemed to find him funny and interesting, and didn't appear to mind that he was dominating the conversation. Even Penny, who had walked up to join them, laughed at his poor-taste jokes. As for Milly, the traitor hadn't left his side since his arrival. Couldn't her family see how cocky and conceited he was? Stan would never have acted in such a way.

'You're nothing like your brother,' said Lorna, interrupting his story about a snake.

For a split second there was a flash of anger on Alfie's face. 'So I've been told,' he said.

'Did you get on?' she asked.

'We barely saw each other,' said Alfie, his eyes narrowing. 'He left home when I was a kid.'

'He was a lovely young man,' said Lorna's mum quietly. 'We are very sad he's no longer with us.'

'Did you always want to be a Marine, Alfie?' Peter asked. 'Like Stan?'

'Not really,' he replied. 'It's a recent thing. Because of the war.' Alfie sat up straighter, puffing out his chest as if he was the most important person in the room. 'I wanted to do my part,' he drawled.

Lorna bit back a retort.

'Very commendable,' said her dad.

'And brave,' said her mum, lifting the bowl of mashed potatoes from the middle of the table and passing it towards him. 'Have another helping, Alfie, we want to make sure you're well fed.'

'Thank you, Mrs Baxter, that would be swell.'

Alfie's voice dripped with kindness and Lorna knew it was an act. She could see right through him. He may have pulled the wool over her family's eyes, but not hers.

'Lorna, pass Alfie the carrots,' said her mother.

Lorna glared at the bowl of carrots but didn't move.

'Oh, I'd love some more carrots!' Alfie said brightly. He held out a hand and waited as Lorna snatched up the bowl and gave it to him. 'Thank you,' he replied, smirking.

Lorna wanted to pick up her plate and tip the remaining contents over his head.

'He's not that bad, Lorrie,' said Karen, giving Lorna's shoulder a nudge. 'And it's not like you have to date him or anything.'

'Heaven forbid,' said Lorna, following Karen into the foyer of the Majestic Cabaret. 'Why do you have to go and date his friend, Curtis?' she asked grumpily. 'There are plenty of other Marines you could choose.'

Karen turned and gripped one of Lorna's hands. 'That's just it, Lorrie. I don't want to date anyone else. Ever!'

Lorna rolled her eyes. 'Please don't start going on about him again.'

'Oh, be in a bad mood if you want to, but look where we are, Lorrie. You've been wanting to come here for months. Can't you try to forget about Alfie and enjoy it?'

'Gladly,' said Lorna, following Karen down the stairs. 'Consider him forgotten.'

It was true that Lorna had wanted to come to a dance at the Majestic. Not because she had developed a love of dancing — though she had come to enjoy it more than she was letting on to herself or anyone else — but because she wanted to see what all the fuss was about. A night at the Majestic was all the girls at work talked about and Lorna had been surprised at how envious she'd felt listening to their conversations. She'd never been concerned about missing out before.

Now she found herself scanning the dresses and hair styles of the other girls in the foyer, comparing them to her own. *What have I become*, she thought, disgusted with herself.

As they entered the grand ballroom, loud with the din of voices, dancing, and music, Curtis leapt at them from where he had presumably been waiting beside the main doors. 'Honey,' he said, giving Karen a kiss on the cheek. 'You look just swell in that dress.'

Alfie was leaning against the wall behind Curtis and slowly peeled himself off to come and see them. His head was bald, but for a short spiky fuzz. 'Hello ladies,' he said, giving them both a perfunctory glance.

'Hello Alfie,' said Karen gaily. 'I hear you spent some time in the brig recently.'

Lorna bit her lip to stop from smiling.

'He's going to be on his best behaviour tonight, aren't you Mac,' said Curtis, slapping Alfie on the back.

Alfie had been caught sneaking into camp after curfew and rather than apologise, he'd apparently told the guard to lighten up. As a result, Karen informed Lorna, they'd shaved Alfie's head and he'd spent three days whitewashing the walls of the brig with a toothbrush.

Lorna could smell alcohol on Alfie's breath, even though he was standing a reasonable distance away. 'I take it that doesn't actually contain lemonade,' she said, looking pointedly at his lemonade bottle.

He peered inside. 'It seems not. Fancy a mouthful?' he asked, holding out the bottle and fixing her with the challenging look she had come to recognise. 'Though I should warn you, they call it shell shock for a reason.'

'No thank you,' she replied politely, before adding sarcastically, 'But it's very kind of you to offer.'

Alfie shrugged and took a large gulp. 'Suit yourself,' he said, wiping his lips. He was watching a girl on the dance floor, her skirt swirling high as she spun around.

'Excuse me,' said Alfie, as the song came to an end. He strode up to the girl, stepped in front of her as if her dance partner didn't exist and leant in close to murmur in her ear. Then he gently brushed a strand of hair from her cheek and she giggled pathetically.

Gritting her teeth, Lorna charged over to a Marine who had been looking in her direction, clasped him by the hand and dragged him out onto the dance floor.

Chapter 14

ALFIE

The six weeks he'd been in New Zealand had turned out alright, Alfie supposed, though he was glad to be leaving. Most of the time had been spent on training drills and twice weekly liberty to town, where he alternated between drinking too much and not drinking enough. Either way, Alfie was always happy to get the rattler back to camp at midnight, neither the dances nor the girls lively enough to make him wish he could stay out for longer. Plus, if he was honest, he didn't fancy another trip to the brig.

The Marines had boarded their warship in Wellington Harbour on Christmas Eve and had spent Christmas morning settling into their compartments, polishing their shoes and buckles, and opening parcels and cards from home. Alfie had received a card from his sister, Alice, containing a token message of Merry Christmas and hope you are well, and nothing from his mother. Alfie hadn't been hurt — at least that was what he kept telling himself.

Alfie had been sending half his pay-check home ever since he'd starting receiving one, and it hadn't cramped his style much, since he was used to having no money at all. But he hadn't managed to save any money either, not like some of the other boys. He liked the idea of savings – the opportunities it could give.

At midday, the Marines gathered on the mess decks for a festive Christmas lunch of roast turkey with stuffing and all the trimmings. It felt strange eating a turkey when the day was hot and bright instead of cold and dark. While most of the boys were cheerful, it seemed effortful, and Alfie could tell they were thinking of their families back home.

Alfie and Curtis were pleased when they were allowed to queue for seconds. Then Alfie spent the rest of the afternoon trying to snooze on his bunk. He kept thinking about the fact that they were heading off to fight. Soon he would confront the Japanese, face the possibility of death, just as his brother Stan had done.

'Come on, Mac, I'm not gonna miss our boat 'cause of you,' said Curtis, who had spent the past hour showering and making himself smart.

'Then go without me,' said Alfie grumpily.

Curtis slapped him on the leg. 'I'm not leaving you moping about on the ship. It's Christmas! Come on, it'll be fun.'

Alfie rolled his eyes. 'Just 'cause you have a good-lookin' girl who worships the ground you walk on.'

Curtis stood taller. 'You think so, Alf? That she's keen on me, I mean? 'Cause I'm mad about her, honest to God.'

'Yeah, I can see that,' said Alfie. 'You've got it bad, Curt.'

'If I wasn't so keen to bag me some of those Japs I'd be considering going AWOL just so's I can stay and be with her.'

Alfie leapt off his bunk and reached for his pressed shirt. 'Well we can't have that happening,' he said firmly. Alfie knew Curtis was joking but hated the mere thought of going off to war without his best friend.

'I managed to borrow a gramophone and some records from Todd across the way.' Curtis dipped his head at the opposite compartment. 'Thought it might liven things up a little.'

Alfie sighed. 'Why does it have to be at that girl's house? Why can't we go to Karen's place instead? Or the Cecil, Basil will happily let us in.' Basil, the proprietor of the bar at the Hotel Cecil had come to know Alfie and his buddies well by now.

Curtis frowned and shook his head. 'Karnie's parents are terrifying. They had a complete fit when someone from their church told them they'd seen us holding hands. No wonder Karnie wanted to go live at the hostel. She's been spending Christmas dinner with Lorna's family for years and she reckons we'll love it.'

Alfie made a face at the mention of Lorna's name. He hadn't seen her since the night he'd been to her house for 'tea' as they liked to call it, and he was in no rush to see her again. She was seemingly harmless, and decidedly dull, yet he found he was unsettled and irritated when he was around her, as if she were silently judging him. As for her family, they were all so nice and eager to please it was unnatural somehow, fake even. Surely a family couldn't be *that* damn nice.

At least Jethro and Marsh were coming to Christmas dinner at Lorna's house too, since Curtis was bound to be fully preoccupied with impressing Karen.

'I still think it's strange we have to take a plate,' said Alfie, sitting on his bunk to tie his laces.

'Karnie said we don't have to, just that it's what people tend to do. She said if it was going to be too hard, she'd organise a plate for us, but I want us to fit in, you know.' Curtis had purchased four China plates a few days earlier and had wrapped them heavily in newspaper. They were in his bulging duffel bag, presumably along with cartons of cigarettes and chocolates.

Alfie put on his jacket and slid a packet of cigarettes and matches into his pocket. 'Well, let's get this over with,' he said, smiling to show he was joking.

'That's the spirit,' Curtis replied, slapping Alfie on the back as they filed out of the door.

Curtis dashed through the door opposite and reappeared a second later holding a large wooden box with metal clasps. Alfie grinned despite himself. 'Good luck carrying that up Lorna's stairs,' he said. 'Seriously, Curt, a gramophone?'

'Barely weighs a thing,' Curtis said. 'Though since you're empty-handed—'

Curtis shoved the box at Alfie's chest and Alfie quickly grabbed it by the handle before it fell to the floor. 'It weighs a damn ton,' he exclaimed, but he didn't try to give the gramophone back. Secretly Alfie felt guilty arriving without a gift for their hosts. This way he wouldn't look as if he had turned up with nothing.

Alfie felt sweat dripping down his back as they stood waiting. They'd been knocking at Lorna's door for several minutes with no response. 'Maybe they cancelled,' muttered Alfie.

'You don't cancel Christmas,' said Jethro, peering through a window. 'Maybe you need to bang harder.'

Alfie raised his fist and beat it hard three times against the door. 'Jesus, Alf,' said Marsh. 'He didn't say break the damn door down.'

They heard fast footsteps and then the door opened to a red-faced Mrs Baxter. 'Oh boys,' she said, wiping her hands on her apron. 'I hope you haven't been here long? I don't hear the door well from the kitchen. Good heavens,' she uttered, her eyes alighting on the box at Alfie's feet. 'What on earth have you got there, Alfie?'

It pleased him, for some reason, hearing her say his name. 'It's a gramophone, Mrs Baxter,' said Alfie, holding out his hand. 'Lovely to see you again, Mom.'

Lorna's mum laughed as they shook hands. 'Oh, such polite manners.' She greeted Curtis, who she had met a couple of times already, then Jethro and Marsh, before ushering them into the living room. 'Everyone's gone down to the field to play cricket,' she said. 'Bit of a Christmas tradition. Karnie offered to wait for you, but I said I'd be here anyway. Leave your things and you can head on down. It's not far.'

Alfie had stopped at a sports field the previous week to watch a group of local schoolboys play this sport called cricket. He'd had to ask a passerby what they were doing and why the players seemed to spend a great deal of time standing around doing nothing.

'That's cricket for you,' the passerby had said with a grin. 'But it's not a bad way to while away a few hours.' Alfie had lasted all of twenty minutes and had marvelled that someone had created a sport so dull and unexciting.

'Perhaps we can just wait here until they return,' said Alfie hopefully.

Curtis, already heading for the door, ignored him. 'Point us in the right direction, Mom,' he said, his eagerness to see Karen obvious.

They followed the directions they were given and arrived at a park with grass so bright green it glowed in the early evening light.

'There,' said Curtis, pointing. He stepped over a low wooden fence and strode across the grassy field, leaving the others to trail behind. As they approached, Milly spotted them and trotted over. She headed straight for Alfie, and he felt a rush of satisfaction at being singled out. He crouched to rub her ears, thinking of all the years he had wished desperately for a dog, and knowing, even as he wished it, that it would never happen, that he would never even ask.

Straightening, Alfie saw Mr Baxter trying to balance something between three sticks poking out of the ground, the daughter-in-law, Penny, several feet behind him with her arms crossed looking bored, and Peter, who waved a bat and shouted a greeting. Karen jogged towards Curtis, while Lorna, who had a small red ball in one hand, watched with barely concealed disgust as Karen gave Curtis a hug.

Alfie suppressed a smile. It was nice to know he wasn't the only one who found the romance between Karen and Curtis a bit much.

Lorna greeted the approaching Marines with a faint wave of her hand, before turning away to repeatedly toss the ball into the air and catch it again. She was barefoot, and wore long shorts and a tatty shirt. Alfie couldn't believe a girl would be seen in such an unflattering outfit.

While Peter and his father took turns explaining the rules, Alfie removed his jacket and rolled up his sleeves. He had always enjoyed sport of any kind and he was prepared to give this cricket a go, even if it was a vastly inferior version of baseball.

'How about you take a turn with the bat there, Alfie,' said Mr Baxter, handing over a heavy wooden bat with a flat surface on one side and a ridge on the other. Alfie stood in front of the wickets, as he now knew they were called, and faced Lorna, who apparently was going to 'bowl' at him.

'You start with the bat resting on the ground, old chap,' called Mr Baxter, and Alfie lowered the bat from where it had been hovering by his shoulder.

Lorna, a good fifty feet away, started to run towards him, the ball in her right hand, then she suddenly rolled her arm around and over her head, sending the ball in his direction. She looked ridiculous, her arm spinning, her body tipping to one side, her back leg stuck out, pointing like a ballerina. Alfie was laughing before the ball left her hand.

The ball flew towards Alfie faster than he had expected from a girl, and he quickly swung his bat as the ball bounced at his feet and spun inwards, travelling between his legs. He heard it connect with the wickets, and everyone leapt about, shouting 'out'.

'Lucky our rule is you can't be out first ball,' said Peter, grinning.

Jethro, standing in the outfield, clapped loudly. 'She got you there, bud,' he yelled.

Lorna stood, flushed, her eyes wide with glee. 'You might need to keep a closer eye on the ball there, Alfie,' she said lightly, before catching the ball her father threw to her lightly in one hand.

Mr Baxter came up close behind Alfie. 'She's been practising her spin for years. Don't worry, you're not the first she's done that to.'

Alfie watched Lorna's back as she returned to her starting position. He gripped his bat tightly in both hands and banged it on the ground a couple of times, determined that this time he would knock the ball clean over her head.

'Ready?' Lorna called, holding up the ball and raising her eyebrows.

Alfie narrowed his eyes. 'Send it down,' he yelled.

As Lorna began her run towards him, he narrowed his eyes and focused. This time when the ball bounced, he anticipated it would change direction after it bounced, so he adjusted his position. But the ball didn't curve at all. It drove at him straight and he jabbed at it, the edge of the bat sending the ball straight into Penny's waiting hands.

'Out!' Peter and Lorna shouted in unison.

'Great catch,' cried Mr Baxter, running towards Penny and giving her a resounding pat on the back.

Curtis fell to the ground and rolled about laughing. 'Bud, this is turning out to be the best Christmas ever,' he said between gasps.

Alfie avoided looking in Lorna's direction and forced himself to smile. So this was Christmas in New Zealand. Being upstaged and humiliated by a girl the night before you headed off to war.

Chapter 15

LORNA

Lorna could tell Alfie was embarrassed, but then, boys often were when they realised a girl could play sport well. She was secretly pleased she'd managed to wipe the proud smirk off his face.

To be fair, he had recovered from his early humiliation and they had gone on to play a fun game of cricket, each person being given a chance to bat and bowl. Alfie had of course asked if he could bowl, or 'pitch' as he kept calling it, when it had been Lorna's turn to bat, and while his technique had been questionable, looking more like he was playing softball than cricket, he had bowled rather well and she'd been lucky to score even a handful of runs. Not that she was going to tell him he'd played well anytime soon.

They returned to the house and sat in the welcome breeze in the backyard, some perching on the low brick wall surrounding the vegetable garden, and others on the chairs they'd carried outside. The men drank cold beers while the women were given a glass of sparkling wine – something Lorna's dad had saved up for Christmas Day. Milly lay at Alfie's feet in an exhausted sleep, her head resting on one of his shoes.

Lorna's mum had been hard at work in the kitchen preparing the special Christmas menu and she finally took a break, sitting beside Lorna with a sigh of relief. 'How was the cricket?' she asked, taking a sip from her glass.

Lorna glanced at Alfie and was surprised to find him looking at her. She raised her eyebrows and smiled.

'Your daughter is very good,' said Alfie, returning Lorna's smile before looking at her mum. 'I have to say, it took me by surprise. Girls back in America tend to talk about sport a lot, and they sure know about all the players, but they don't really play much.'

'It's true,' said Jethro. 'They prefer to cheer from the sidelines in their pretty dresses and make-up.'

Lorna scoffed, then quickly covered her mouth, hoping no one had noticed her reaction.

'Lorrie certainly wouldn't like America then,' said Karen. 'Though I would be very happy to stand on the sideline in a pretty dress.'

'You played well too,' said Curtis, and this time it was Alfie who suppressed a snort. Karen was not a natural cricketer, to put it politely.

'Lorna's grown up playing sport,' her dad said proudly. 'You should see her play basketball, or tennis for that matter.'

Peter, who had been absent since their return home, raced towards Alfie with a shoebox. 'Do you want to see my collection?' he asked, taking off the lid.

Peter was very proud of the badges, American coins, matchboxes with flip lids, buckles and other bits and pieces he had been given by Marines over the past few months. Lorna had to admit, somewhat begrudgingly, that Alfie politely showed more interest than anyone in Lorna's family had managed to muster, though she was disappointed, and unsure why, when he dug a dime out of his pocket and threw it in the box.

'How does it feel being here at Christmas?' asked Penny, directing her question at Jethro. 'I imagine this is very different from back home.'

'Yes, ma'am,' said Jethro. 'It's still light out for starters. I'm not used to sitting outside like this, not that I'm complaining.'

'My two eldest boys, Gordon and Rick, are in the Middle East,' said Lorna's mum, a wobble in her voice. 'Rick says it is very strange being so far from home at Christmas.'

Lorna reached over and squeezed her mum's leg.

'I have a great deal of admiration for them, ma'am,' said Marsh.

'We hope we can show the same fighting qualities,' added Alfie.

Lorna saw Penny brush a hand across her eyes.

'Yes, well.' Her mum cleared her throat and stood up. 'Let's eat, shall we?'

'Oh, I nearly forgot, we brought plates,' said Curtis, racing off and returning with four China dinner plates. Lorna looked at Karen and they burst out laughing.

'Girls,' reprimanded Mr Baxter, trying to look serious. 'These chaps weren't to know.'

'Know what?' asked Curtis.

Karen was still laughing as she explained that 'bring a plate' meant to bring a plate of food to share.

Curtis widened his eyes and his cheeks turned pink. 'Well now, that's embarrassing then,' he said, joining in as everyone laughed.

They moved to the dining room where the table had been laid with all the family's best China. A bunch of blue hydrangeas from Penny's garden had been placed in a vase in the centre. Then Lorna saw the awful papier-mâché decorations she'd made in school when she was six years old sitting in the middle of each place setting. 'Mum!' she exclaimed, as she quickly gathered them up.

'They're adorable,' said her mum.

Before Lorna could pick up the misshapen bauble in front of Alfie, he grabbed it and started to inspect her terrible drawing. 'Is that a Christmas tree?' he asked, pointing to a brown line with green triangular swirls.

'I was six,' said Lorna, snatching it out of his hand, her cheeks hot.

Alfie opened his mouth to say something else, then closed it again and handed over the offending bauble with a teasing smile. She was sorely tempted to whack him on the arm.

Thankfully her dad walked in with a silver tray containing a huge golden-skinned turkey, and everyone began to clap and cheer as Lorna retrieved the remaining baubles and stuffed them into a basket of newspapers nearby.

'There's ham too,' said Lorna's mum, as Penny appeared with another tray. 'And plenty of potatoes and vegetables.'

'It's a feast,' said Curtis. 'Thank you for inviting us.'

'Yes,' said Marsh. 'You've been very generous.'

'It's the least we can do,' said Mrs Baxter, flustered at their words. 'I'm sure your parents would have done the same if our boys had been in your situation.'

'I doubt it,' muttered Alfie as Lorna took her seat beside him. She was surprised at the sharpness in his tone.

'Why do you say that?' she asked quietly.

His eyes flashed at her. 'Not everyone has been blessed with a family like yours.'

Lorna sat back, unsettled by the vehemence in his voice. She reached for her glass and took a big gulp, then choked as the bubbles erupted in her throat.

'You alright?' said Penny, patting her on the back.

Lorna nodded, her eyes watering as she tried not to cough. Alfie shouldn't have been so rude, and she wished she hadn't sat beside him. She'd thought things had improved between them. If she was honest, she'd thought he might have even been flirting with her when they were sitting outside.

'Well, good luck,' said her dad, standing at the head of the table and raising his glass of beer. 'You jokers are our boys now, and just like our sons, we'll be sending you our prayers too.'

'Make sure you stay safe,' said Karen, looking at Curtis sitting across from her.

He pressed a hand to his lips and blew her a kiss. 'Those Japs won't know what hit them.'

As plates were piled high with food, Lorna joined in with the chatter and laughter, while doing her best to ignore Alfie.

'I thought it was Stan who ate funny, but you all eat that way,' said Peter, watching Jethro switch his fork to his other hand to eat.

Lorna felt Alfie tense beside her. 'Perhaps we think your way of eating is funny,' he said, sharply. He folded his napkin in half and laid it beside his plate. 'Excuse me,' he said, pushing back his chair and standing. 'I need to visit the washroom.'

There was an awkward silence as Alfie left the room.

'Make sure you all leave some room for my pavlova,' said Lorna's mum brightly.

'Now that sounds intriguing,' said Curtis. 'What's a pavlova?'

As her mum explained, Lorna wished more than anything in the world that her brothers were home. She wanted to be celebrating Christmas with them, not these strangers. She wanted Gordon and Rick to be here at the family table. Safe.

Once the pavlova had been devoured, the men all moved to the living room, while the women cleaned up. In the kitchen, Penny opened another bottle of sparkling wine, and the women chatted and laughed, Lorna far more comfortable and relaxed now the Marines were elsewhere. Then, once the dishes were washed, dried and put away, and the leftovers stored, they joined the others.

The couch and two armchairs had been pushed to the edge of the room, and the men hovered around the card table newly placed under the window.

'Ooohhh,' squealed Karen, rushing closer. 'You brought a gramophone!'

'Sure did,' said Curtis, holding up a record.

'Who is it?' asked Lorna.

'The one and only Frank Sinatra,' Curtis replied.

'Who?' asked Lorna, examining the record.

The four Marines all looked at her in shock.

'Unbelievable,' said Alfie, rolling his eyes.

'Please tell me you're joking,' said Jethro.

Lorna shook her head and tried not to react when Jethro suddenly reached for her hand and dragged her into the middle of the room. 'Until you've danced to Frank Sinatra, you haven't lived,' he said as he bowed to kiss her hand. 'May I have this dance?' he asked in a posh voice.

Lorna giggled as the sound of brass instruments filled the room. Then, rather surprisingly, everyone started to dance.

Lorna wondered what had come over her family. It wasn't like them to behave with such enthusiasm. As Jethro spun her around, she knocked into Alfie, who let go of Penny and grabbed Lorna by the waist to stop her falling. Then Jethro took Penny by the hand and suddenly Lorna was dancing with Alfie.

She felt awkward all of a sudden and wondered why she felt so unsettled around Stan's younger brother. 'The first time I ever danced the jitterbug was with Stan,' she said.

Alfie's smiled dropped. 'Is that right?'

'He was a wonderful person. He always made me feel . . .' she searched for the right word. 'It was like even though we hadn't spent much time together, we connected.'

Alfie didn't respond, and Lorna got the impression he wished he was dancing with someone else.

'What do you think of Sinatra?' he asked, his voice polite.

'He's alright.'

Alfie frowned and stopped dancing. 'Heaven forbid you actually like anything from America, right?'

Lorna took a step back. Just when she had shaken off his blunt tone with her at tea, he was back trying to make her feel horrible again.

'I need a glass of water,' she muttered, quickly walking away.

In the kitchen, she filled a glass with water and drank it slowly, willing herself not to cry.

'I'm sorry,' came Alfie's voice. 'I didn't mean to be rude.'

She spun to look at him standing in the doorway. 'Yes you did,' she stated.

He immediately switched from looking contrite to looking annoyed. 'Maybe you're a little too quick to judge,' he snapped.

They continued to stare at one another for several seconds, Lorna refusing to be the first to look away. His eyes were bigger than Stan's, his lashes dark and thick. There was an intensity in his gaze that made her palms feel odd, as if she'd clapped too hard and it had left a residual aching tingle.

Alfie looked down and cleared his throat as he brushed a hand over the dark stubble on his head. 'I think it's time to leave,' he said quietly.

Lorna felt her glass starting to slip from her sweating hand and turned to place it down in the sink with a clatter. 'Then leave,' she said, keeping her back to him. 'I certainly won't be stopping you.'

She waited for him to respond, but he didn't speak or move. So, with her head high, Lorna brushed past him, strode back into the living room, took her little brother's hand and started to teach him the jitterbug.

When the song ended, Alfie appeared in the living room doorway and began to thank everyone for the evening. Amidst disappointed cries, he left, taking a protesting Curtis, Marsh, Jethro and the gramophone with him.

The moment the front door closed behind them, Karen ran to Lorna's room and flung herself onto the bed. 'What if I never see him again?' she cried.

Lorna sat next to her and patted her arm sympathetically. 'In a few weeks you'll forget all about him.'

'No I won't!'

'Yes,' said Lorna, thinking of Alfie. 'Of course we will.'

Chapter 16

ALFIE

The water was calm and clear, small ripples glinting in the early morning light. Alfie stood on deck with his fellow Marines of the 2nd Division, watching the city of Wellington grow small as they pulled further away from the wharf. Seagulls swooped back and forth above their heads in the cloudless sky, cawing loudly and aggressively as if to say good riddance.

Alfie was pleased to be leaving. Relieved he would soon enter the war so many other men had faced. If he could be courageous, he'd have earnt his place. For the rest of his life he could say he was a Marine who had fought for his country.

He tried to imagine Stan leaving Wellington only six months earlier. Did he stand proudly on deck with the same fizz of excitement in his chest? Had it crossed his mind that he might die? Had he been sad leaving Lorna behind? The girl he might have asked to marry, if he hadn't been heading off to fight.

Alfie wished he hadn't spent Christmas with Lorna's family. He would have preferred to have gone to the Cecil for a few drinks, maybe played some cards and grabbed a late night hot dog from the new pie cart by the train station.

Curtis, Jethro and Marsh had gone on at length about how much they'd enjoyed themselves, and they couldn't understand why Alfie wasn't positive about the experience too. It had felt wrong, like everyone was playing a game. It was as if the more Lorna's family tried to include him and make him feel welcome, the more he felt like an intruder. Stan had probably been perfectly at home with Lorna's family, and they had clearly all adored him. Alfie had lost count of the number of times they'd brought Stan up in conversation. Stan would have said and done the right thing, just as he always did. Lorna and her family had probably been wishing it had been Stan joining them for Christmas, rather than his inferior younger brother.

Alfie knew it wasn't right to think so harshly of his dead brother, but the truth was they had never got on very well. Stan had always taken his role as the eldest so seriously, bossing Alfie around and telling him off. All adults, especially teachers, had liked Stan, complimenting him on how handsome he was, how clever, how capable. Their mother used to proudly tell visitors that Stan was the man of the house, and once Stan was accepted into the Marines, his status rose even further. When Stan left, their mother drank and complained even more. Every day she reminded Alfie and Alice that Stan was the only one of her kids who would amount to anything.

When Alfie told his mum he was joining the Marines, she laughed, as if she didn't believe for one second he would succeed.

Alfie had overheard her telling their neighbour the next day that the Marines must have been desperate to accept her Alf.

'There she is!' yelled Curtis, gripping Alfie's arm. He pointed and waved, leaping about and knocking into several other Marines standing nearby. Alfie squinted at the headland where he could just make out someone standing in a gap between the trees waving frantically, a yellow piece of cloth in their hand.

It was Karen, having promised to see them off.

Curtis stopped leaping about and his hands stayed suspended in the air as if he'd been turned to stone. 'Feels wrong,' he muttered. 'Feels all kinds of wrong leaving my girl.'

'Jesus, Curt,' said Alfie, turning away in disgust. 'You barely even knew her.'

'We better be coming back here,' said Curtis, resuming his waving and jumping. 'After we've dealt with the Japs.'

'I hope not,' Alfie said.

Curtis ignored him. 'If we do come back, the first thing I'm gonna do is ask Karnie to marry me.'

'Damn, how's that gonna work?' asked Alfie, sticking a cigarette between his teeth and lighting it. 'It's a long way from here to America.'

'Well, she's gotta agree to marry me yet,' Curtis replied.

As their ship left the shelter of the harbour and turned towards the open sea, most of the Marines headed below deck but Alfie stayed at the railing watching the land recede. *Goodbye New Zealand*, he thought.

Alfie hoped he wouldn't be returning as there was nothing he would miss about Wellington. Plus, if they came back, there was a good chance Curtis would do something foolish. Something he'd most likely live to regret. An image suddenly popped into Alfie's head of Lorna holding the cricket ball up in the air and calling, 'Ready?', her cheeks flushed and her eyes mocking him as if to say he was a disappointment and would never measure up to Stan.

It was an ugly truth, and Alfie knew it made him a terrible person, but he was determined to survive the war and return home to America, not because he wanted to be a hero, but because he would finally, finally, have achieved something his perfect brother had not.

WELLINGTON, NEW ZEALAND

FEBRUARY 1943

Chapter 17

LORNA

Lorna rattled the bolts on the big rear doors of the truck to check they were secure, then strode around to the driver's door and pulled herself up into the cab. She checked in her wing mirrors, gave a brief wave at the soldier stationed at the open roller door, and started the engine. As the truck rumbled into life, she felt a familiar thrill run through her.

Easing out of the huge warehouse, she drove slowly to the exit where a pair of guards waved her through and out onto the road. She glanced down at her new navy skirt and was dismayed to see a black mark. She took one hand off the big steering wheel and brushed at the mark, relieved when it lifted away, staining her fingers. Probably coal dust, she thought, returning her hand quickly to the wheel as she approached a corner. For the rest of the drive, Lorna focused intently on the road.

After Christmas, she'd made an abrupt decision to leave her work at the munitions factory and join the Women's Auxiliary

Army Corps. Her father had been the one to mention the WAAC were searching for drivers, and Lorna had leapt at the chance to change jobs. She'd learnt to drive at the age of fifteen, resolving to drive as well as, if not better than, her older brothers. During her summer holidays, she'd helped her father by driving small trucks between the port stores and various farms in the Wairarapa, and she was self-assured behind the wheel. Her WAAC driving instructor, Sergeant Decker, had been impressed with her skills from day one. He'd immediately put her name forward to the United States Marine Corps when they asked for more drivers. Lorna was secretly thrilled to have been singled out to work for the Americans, and she enjoyed wearing the smart blue Marine Corps uniform. Karen had told Lorna it made her look five years older and ten times more attractive. Lorna had scoffed and rolled her eyes, but she had to admit she'd since replayed Karen's words several times with pleasure.

Wellingtonians had become used to the Americans, whose presence had grown and solidified even further. Several more camps had been built both out at the coast and in the city parks, and a great number of buildings in the city centre had been requisitioned by the Marines for various uses, from officer accommodation, to recreation clubs, to administration offices. It was clear the Americans wouldn't be leaving anytime soon, and Lorna was happy for them to stay for the duration of the war, however long that would be, if it meant she could continue to drive trucks.

Lorna completed her delivery of vegetables to the camps at Paekākāriki before returning to the stores on the wharf. It was her fourth delivery of the day, having started at 5 am, and she was looking forward to her shift coming to an end. She was meeting Karen at the beach for a swim, before they both headed to Lorna's place for tea.

'Lorna!' shouted Karen, waving from a spot halfway along the beach, her fashionable wide-brimmed hat hiding her face. Lorna noticed Karen was wearing her new swimming costume and felt oddly envious as she wrapped her towel tighter around her faded baggy swimsuit.

Karen rushed towards Lorna, her face lit with joy. 'He's back,' she squealed, 'Curtis arrived yesterday, he phoned me from camp this morning.'

Lorna was pleased to hear Curtis had returned from what had sounded like a terrible battle at Guadalcanal. Karen had been on edge ever since he'd left, reading the casualty list every day and worrying about him constantly. They'd been sad when they'd recognised Marsh's name on the list.

'That's great news,' said Lorna, giving Karen a hug.

'It's the best news in the world,' said Karen. 'Honestly, I feel like I can finally breathe properly again. He's hoping to get liberty tomorrow to come and see me.'

Lorna wondered if Alfie was back in Wellington too, since his name hadn't been on the casualty lists either.

'Alfie's at Silverstream Hospital,' said Karen, as if reading Lorna's mind. 'With malaria.'

'Oh, that's no good,' said Lorna mechanically. 'I mean, it's no good he's got malaria, but at least he's returned in one piece.'

'Curtis said he's in a frightful state. Perhaps you should go and visit him? Cheer him up a bit?'

'Me? Why would I go and see him? I hardly know him, and as you know, I didn't exactly warm to him.'

Karen shrugged. 'Up to you,' she said. 'Come on, let's go have a swim, I'm sweltering.'

Lorna should have known the second her parents heard Alfie was at Silverstream they would insist she pay him a visit. 'Of course you must go and see him,' her mother said. 'I'll bake some biscuits for you to take.'

'Why don't you go instead?' said Lorna, grumpily.

Her father studied her across the dinner table for a few seconds. 'That young boy has been fighting a war to protect our country, Lorna. Don't you remember last year, when the Japanese were close to our shores? We owe a great deal to these Marines — the least you can do is go and visit Alfie, don't you think?'

Lorna immediately felt guilty. 'You're right, sorry. I'm just exhausted. I'll go and see him after work one day this week.'

'That's my girl,' said her mum, reaching to pat her on the arm.

'Can I come too?' asked Peter.

'No,' their parents replied in unison.

Peter pouted. 'Why not?'

'Because it is not the place for young boys,' said Mrs Baxter firmly.

Lorna knew the real reason. She'd overheard her mum talking to her friend, Barbara, who'd popped in for a cup of tea that morning. Barbara was a volunteer nurse at Silverstream and had been describing some of the wounds she'd been dealing with. 'It's from being in those wet, hot conditions for so long, I suppose,' said Barbara. 'Ulcerating sores filled with pus, terrible cases of dermatitis from the knee down. The *smell*,' Barbara said, wincing. 'It's just awful. It's not a pretty sight, I must say, and I've been nursing for twenty years.'

'How was your game yesterday, Peter?' Lorna asked, wanting to change the subject.

Peter narrowed his eyes. 'Don't ask, I got caught behind on the first ball.'

'It happens,' said their dad supportively. 'You more than made up for it with your bowling though. He took three wickets.'

'That's great!' said Lorna. 'I wish I could have seen it.'

Peter sat up taller, grinning. 'Guess who I bowled with only five runs on the board.'

'Who?'

'Greg Porter.'

'Really?' Lorna laughed. 'Now I really wish I could have seen *that*.'

Greg Porter believed he was God's gift to the world, but in reality no one liked him much at all. He was far too full of himself, and had once accused Peter of bowling like a girl. Peter hadn't taken the comment well at all and ever since, Lorna's family had placed a black mark against Greg's name.

'I completely forgot,' their mum said, pushing back her chair and standing. 'I made a sponge cake for dessert.'

Peter and Lorna cheered, and Lorna tried her best not to think about her impending visit to Alfie.

Chapter 18

ALFIE

Six weeks. It had only taken six weeks for Alfie to leave New Zealand as one person, and return as someone else. He didn't like this new version of himself, but it wasn't like he could leave his body or turn back the clock. He should be grateful he was alive, though at times he wasn't. At times, he remembered his brother, Stan, who didn't have to return from war. And Marsh, who had been killed a week before they'd left Guadalcanal. At least when you died you didn't have to come to terms with what you'd seen. Live with what you'd done.

The hospital was a shithole in every sense of the word. Everyone either had the shits, was recovering from the shits or felt like shit. It certainly smelt of shit, though the nurses tried their best to cover up the smell by applying disinfectant so liberally it made his eyes water.

Alfie wasn't sure he would ever live down the shame of having a middle-aged woman give him a sponge bath. She was good about it: brisk, efficient, no-nonsense, but he saw the way she flinched when she removed the dressings on his feet and lower legs. The smell was enough to make him gag and he had to look away from the mushy, disgusting flesh. At least it had improved quickly in the space of five days, now that his skin finally had a chance to dry out.

Alfie stopped his brain from going where it was trying to go by counting the number of leaves on the tree outside the window opposite. He refused to think of those never-ending nights he had spent in the baking-hot trenches where you could never escape the relentless rain, the mud, or worse, the fear. The darkness was the worst part. They weren't allowed lights as they crouched in knee-high mud, listening to the insects, inhaling the sickening stench of Japanese corpses hidden within the dense jungle, and trying not to flinch as large, fat rats scuttled past.

Alfie wonders now what he had been expecting. What they had all been expecting. Once they'd learnt they were on their way to Guadalcanal, they still hadn't really processed what would be involved. They thought they would saunter in, kill some Japs and leave as heroes. Well, that was what Alfie had thought anyway.

Alfie sighed and gave up on counting leaves. He didn't recognise the tree. It wasn't one he would have seen in America, that's for sure, not that he looked at a lot of trees growing up. But he knew enough to know this tree was foreign, that it was there to remind him he was miles from his country.

Curtis and Jethro had been to visit that morning, delivered a carton of cigarettes and several packets of Baby Ruths, knowing they were Alfie's favourite. They'd been in good spirits, Curtis especially, and were happy to be back at Camp Mackay out in

Paekākāriki. In a newly built wooden hut this time, they were pleased to report, rather than a tent. They told Alfie that even more camps had been erected out on the coast and that it was turning into quite a community. The Marines had successfully 'taken over', Jethro said.

Curtis told Alfie that he was taking Karen to a dance that evening. He wanted to ask her to marry him, but felt he should wait a week so she would know he wasn't rushing into it. Plus, he was nervous her parents wouldn't give consent. There had been a crackdown recently on marriages between Marines and the local girls, concerns that it was not ideal for either party. Senior officials felt during times of war it was possible that rationality made way for impulsivity.

Alfie suggested Curtis wait longer. He could spend more time with Karen's parents, 'work on buttering them up', Alfie said, when what he really wanted to say was, 'hopefully after a month you'll come to your senses and realise that proposing to this girl is madness'.

Jethro told Alfie he was looking good, and that he'd be heading to the Cecil with them in no time. They both spoke about the newly opened Allied Services' Club, and said they were sure Alfie would love it once he was out. Alfie found their enthusiasm exhausting and was pleased when they left. He wanted to sit in his misery for as long as possible.

'Alf, check it out,' whispered the Marine in the bed beside him.

Alfie turned his head to watch a tall, slim woman in Marine Corps uniform make her way confidently down the ward. He decided he'd try to catch her attention, which wasn't going to be easy since every pair of eyes on the ward were watching her too.

As the woman drew closer, Alfie narrowed his eyes. She looked familiar, in fact she was the near spitting image of that girl, Lorna, only far prettier and with small attractive spectacles making her cheekbones stand out. It was uncanny, the resemblance.

'Hello, Alfie,' said the woman, stopping at the end of his bed. 'Karen told me you were here.'

Holy heck, it *was* Lorna. 'What are you doing in that uniform?' he blurted.

Lorna smiled, held out her arms and did a slow twirl. 'Do you like it?'

Alfie shook his head. He'd been in and out of a delirious state for days, though he thought he'd been getting better. Maybe the malarial fever was back. 'Lorna?' he asked, uncertainly. 'Is that actually you?'

Lorna's arms dropped to her side and her smile was replaced with a scowl. Now he could recognise her more clearly.

'Yes, it is me, Alfie. You don't have to look quite so shocked, you know.'

At her harsh tone, Alfie felt a lightness he hadn't experi-enced for weeks. He almost smiled, but managed to stop himself just in time. 'You're the last person I thought would pose as an American.'

Lorna's eyes widened. 'I'm not *posing* as an American, thank you very much. I am a proper member of the United States Marine Corps. They recruited me to drive trucks, and I'm very good at it too.'

'What happened to your job at the munitions factory?'

'I quit,' she announced, perching on the edge of his bed as far from him as possible. 'I couldn't face going back after Christmas, so I joined the Auxiliary Army. I only had to do a couple of weeks of training before I passed the driving test. Dad taught me to drive trucks when I was fifteen.'

Alfie was still trying to come to terms with this attractive woman being the Lorna he remembered. He may have changed in six weeks, but he clearly wasn't the only one.

'It suits you,' he said at last. 'Well done.'

Lorna looked surprised. 'Thank you,' she said. 'You look terrible, by the way.'

'Thank you,' Alfie said, smiling. 'I feel like shit too.'

'I'm sure you do.' Lorna looked around the ward and wrinkled her nose. 'It's fairly unpleasant here, isn't it? Are you bedridden or do you think you could go for a walk with me?'

Alfie gave her what he hoped was a 'do you think I'm stupid' look. The head matron – a bossy, terrifying woman, who had been hounding him to get out of bed all day – must have spoken to Lorna, because there was no way the Lorna he knew would be wanting them to go for a walk together.

When Lorna laughed, Alfie couldn't believe how good he felt. 'Okay, I would never have suggested a walk, but that woman who accosted me when I came in made me promise to try to get you out of bed because you haven't wanted to do *anything* apparently.'

'I'm just enjoying the rest, that's all,' said Alfie. 'I have been busy fighting a war, you know.'

Lorna looked about the ward then back at him. 'Alfie, if you'd rather be in here than out there, then there is something quite wrong with you. It's a gorgeous day. Not a breath of wind. Come on, let's walk barefoot on the grass. As my dad would say, the fresh air will do you the world of good.'

Alfie shook his head. Who was this girl? 'I can picture your dad saying that, actually.'

Lorna studied him, her expression a mix of concern and irritation. She leant down to retrieve her handbag off the floor, pulled out a round tin and held it out to him. 'Mum made you biscuits, or what you call *cookies*.'

Alfie took the tin and opened the lid. They looked and smelt delicious. For the first time since leaving Guadalcanal, he actually felt like eating.

'Don't you think it's strange that to Americans, a biscuit is something savoury,' said Lorna. 'Shouldn't a biscuit be the same thing wherever you're from?'

Alfie was too busy chewing to reply. The oaty cookie (he refused to think of it as a biscuit) was crunchy on the edges and chewy in the middle.

Lorna sat in silence as Alfie finished eating. Rather than stare at her, which was what he wanted to do, he looked off into the distance, trying to pretend she wasn't there.

'Well,' said Lorna, getting to her feet. 'If you don't want to go for a walk, I'll be off.'

He could tell he'd upset her, and he was annoyed with himself. He wasn't sure what to make of her visit. 'Did you want to come visit or did your parents tell you to?' he asked abruptly.

Lorna's cheeks flushed and he knew the answer before she spoke. 'They asked me to visit, but I'm sure . . . well, I probably would have come to see you anyway.'

When she met his eye, they both laughed.

'Okay,' said Alfie. 'Since you wanted to come and see me so much, let's go for a walk.'

Lorna nodded. 'I'll wait for you outside,' she said, already striding away.

It had taken Alfie almost fifteen minutes to get his stiff, weak body out of bed and dressed in his trousers and shirt. A nurse insisted he wear shoes, even though his swollen, raw feet screamed with agony as she forced them on, and he hobbled like an old man towards the door. Lorna was leaning against the outside of the wooden building, smoking a cigarette. She glanced at him, then kept her eyes fixed on the green field ahead of them while Alfie slowly and painfully navigated the two small steps.

'That was pathetic,' he said.

Lorna threw away her cigarette stub and tucked an arm through his, causing goosebumps to rise on his arm.

'What did you expect?' she said lightly. 'You made it outside, that's a start.'

They began to walk slowly, Alfie gritting his teeth to stop crying out in pain. Lorna led him towards a bench on the edge of the grass. 'Should we sit?' she asked.

Alfie nodded and lowered himself onto the seat.

'Is it the shoes?' Lorna asked, sitting beside him.

'Mostly,' Alfie replied, staring ahead.

Lorna leant forward, undid her shoelaces and removed her shoes, exposing her stockinged feet.

'If I could I'd whip off my stockings too, but—' Lorna made an exaggerated pout, then leant across and started to undo Alfie's laces too. He jerked backwards, knocking her hands away.

Lorna slowly sat up and turned to face him. 'Alfie, do you want those shoes off or not?'

'I'm not sure,' he said. 'But I *am* sure I don't want you to do it.'

'Fine,' said Lorna, throwing up her hands. 'Only trying to help.'

Alfie really wanted to walk barefoot in the soft grass with Lorna. He wanted it more than anything.

'If I take them off, you have to swear not to look,' he said.

'At your feet?' said Lorna. 'With pleasure, Alfie. I've heard all about how revolting the boys' feet are.'

'Thanks for your concern,' said Alfie sarcastically.

Lorna smiled and stood. She walked over to the tree Alfie had been counting leaves off earlier and remained facing it. 'Let me know when I can turn around,' she said loudly.

Alfie bit his lip as he carefully removed his shoes and peeled off his socks.

'Okay,' said Alfie, getting to his feet. 'Eyes front and centre.'

'Yes, sir,' said Lorna returning to his side. This time she didn't tuck her arm through his. 'Once around the green?' she asked.

Alfie looked at the field stretching wider than a football field before him.

'Twice,' he replied, setting out. It was easier now the shoes were off, and the cool grass felt magnificent. Lorna's father was right, the fresh air was doing him the world of good.

Chapter 19

LORNA

Lorna knew the handful of Marines smoking nearby were judging her performance as she backed the ten-wheeler between two pillars, and she sighed with relief as she reversed towards the warehouse doors without a hitch.

As she stepped down from the truck, the group of men clapped, one whistling in appreciation. 'Nice one, honey,' another called.

'Thanks,' Lorna called back, taking a bow. It was funny how being in the uniform made her bolder. It was almost like, because she was wearing an American uniform, she became more American herself. More talkative, less timid, more willing to engage with strangers like these. It was why, she realised, she'd been able to act differently with Alfie when she'd been to visit him. She had wanted to show him that she was a confident young woman now, not the gawky girl she'd been when he left.

'Come on, boy,' said Lorna, looking over to the passenger seat and pulling her door wider. 'Time for a break while they load up.'

Her 'driving partner', as she liked to call him, immediately bounded across the seats and down from the truck. Chester tried to heel by her side as she commanded, but his tail wagged so frantically his backside kept shifting about.

Lorna rubbed between his ears. He was always so ready, eager for her next instruction. It had been her dad who'd asked their neighbour, Mr Bolton, if Chester might like to spend his days with Lorna, travelling around in a truck, seeing the sights, having some company instead of sitting at home waiting for Mr Bolton to return from work. Mr Bolton had been unsure, until her father mentioned the 'incident', then Mr Bolton had urged Lorna to take Chester with her.

Lorna had been equal parts embarrassed and pleased. Pleased to know Chester would be keeping her company but embarrassed that it had taken her father bringing up the 'incident' to make Mr Bolton agree.

The 'incident', as it would seemingly always be referred to, occurred during Lorna's second month driving for the Marines. She was transferring her load to the new Camp Russell, and had been asked if she could give an officer a lift. She'd agreed of course, since it really hadn't been a question in the first place, plus she'd given lifts to Marines several times already. But the second this man had sat in the cab and turned to face her, she'd felt uncomfortable. He'd run his eyes up and down her body then raised his eyebrows suggestively. 'Wasn't expecting such attractive company,' he'd said. Lorna had ignored him and started the engine. For the first five minutes, they'd driven in silence.

'Let me guess, you're from California?' the man had asked. Then before she could answer, he'd announced he was from

Texas and was married with two young boys. He then went on to complain about New Zealand. 'Don't you find this just the most sad little place? The people are mighty reserved and the lack of entertainment's downright criminal if you ask me. What do you get up to in the evenings, little lady?'

Again, he hadn't waited for her to respond. Instead, he'd launched into talk of the war, the fact that there were so many kids in the 2nd Marine Division who shouldn't have been there. 'It's the basics, isn't it, that are lacking in those boys.'

Lorna had never disliked a person more, and she'd deliberately taken a corner too fast so his shoulder banged against the door.

'Ease up there, honey,' he'd said, putting a hand on her knee and giving it a squeeze. 'Maybe I should take over the driving, eh?'

Lorna had jerked her leg away and he'd lifted his hand, only to bring it down on her forearm. 'You're not like those uptight Kiwi girls, I hope. How about we pull over and go for a little walk?'

Lorna had changed gear abruptly and the truck had roared. 'I don't think I *will* pull over. And I would ask you to remove your hand from my arm, please,' she'd said firmly. She'd felt his eyes on her but kept looking straight ahead.

Slowly he'd lifted his hand. 'You're not American,' he'd snapped. 'Why didn't you damn well tell me? And why in hell do you get to wear that uniform?'

Lorna hadn't answered and had sagged with relief when they reached the camp. As she'd pulled to a stop, the officer had sworn at her, jumped out and slammed the door.

⌒

Lorna returned from a walk along the waterfront with Chester to find her last load of the day ready for transport. 'Short trip this time, Lorna,' said her supervisor. 'Silverstream Hospital. Lucky buggers get a full truckload of pork. Though I guess they're not really lucky buggers,' he added. 'Since they're in hospital and all.'

For months, the sale of pork in local shops had been banned so farmers could carry pigs to greater bacon weights — bacon being so popular with the visiting troops. Only hospitals, foreign forces and ship suppliers could get pork, though Lorna's father had mentioned it was being sold on the black market.

There was a certain amount of resentment from locals that the pork their country was producing wasn't available for them to eat and instead was being given to the Americans. Lorna loved roast pork and was unhappy with the ban too.

The drive to Silverstream took less than an hour and Lorna decided she would pay Alfie a quick visit while her delivery was being offloaded. She tied Chester up beneath a tree, much to his disappointment, and headed into the hospital. When she reached Alfie's bed, she was pleased to find he wasn't there — instead a nurse directed her to the recreation building.

It was a big, lively space, Lorna discovered as she stepped through the doors, filled with loud American voices. There was a long counter doing a busy trade in food and drinks, several games of table tennis in action, round tables where people were playing cards or board games, and a quieter corner where several patients in wheelchairs were parked.

Eventually Lorna spotted Alfie leaning against the counter at the far end. He was smoking and chatting to a ridiculously attractive woman in an American Red Cross uniform. Lorna hesitated, unsure if she should approach him or leave him be. Then Alfie glanced towards the door and spotted her. His expression went from surprise to something she couldn't read, and she gave him a tentative wave. He waved back, then leant close to whisper to the girl he was with, planting a kiss on her cheek. As the girl walked off, she looked briefly in Lorna's direction, her expression unfriendly.

Alfie stubbed out his cigarette and wove his way towards her. 'This is a surprise,' he said.

'I had a delivery to the hospital,' said Lorna. 'Thought it would be the polite thing to stop by.'

Alfie tipped his head back and laughed. 'That's the response I was looking for.'

Lorna heard Chester's distinctive bark, then winced. 'That's my new companion,' she said, pointing out the door at Chester pulling at his rope in a desperate desire to get to her.

Alfie raised his eyebrows. 'How's that working out?'

'Very well.'

'He appears to be mighty protective of you.'

'He just doesn't like to be tied up.' Chester gave another loud bark. 'Actually, do you think we could move a little? Once I'm out of sight, he'll calm down.'

Alfie shrugged. 'How about a drink?'

They made their way to the counter where Lorna ordered a milkshake and Alfie a coffee. 'You look better,' said Lorna. 'Less like every step is torture.'

'I'm going back to camp tomorrow,' Alfie replied. 'Can't wait.'

Lorna lowered her voice. 'Is it just me, or do all the patients look very yellow?' It was something she'd been noticing more and more, not just now, but with many of the Marines she saw around the city too.

Alfie grimaced. 'It's a side effect from the medicine we're supposed to be taking to prevent malaria.'

'Surely it can't be good for you?'

'Trust me, malaria is a whole lot worse than your skin being an odd colour.'

Alfie finished his drink in one big gulp and slammed the mug on the bar. 'How about some ping pong?'

Lorna choked on her milkshake. 'Sorry?'

Alfie pointed across the room. 'Ping pong,' he stated.

Lorna grinned. 'You call table tennis — what did you say? — *ping pong?*'

'We do,' said Alfie gruffly, crossing his arms. 'I'm not sure why you find it so amusing.'

'I'm not really sure either,' said Lorna. 'But, yes, I'll play some *ping pong*, Alfie. Though I can't stay long.'

They wandered over to a now empty table and stood at each end. Alfie picked up his bat. 'Have you played much before?' he asked.

Lorna shrugged. 'A bit. How about you?'

'Sure have. Even won the competition we held here last night.'

'Impressive.' Lorna decided she wouldn't tell him she'd been playing table tennis since she was seven and had been the star player at school.

Alfie served and Lorna returned the ball easily but with little power or speed. They batted the ball back and forth politely until

Alfie hit the ball to Lorna's end, where it clipped the edge of the table and flew down at a sharp angle, impossible for Lorna to reach.

'My luck,' called Alfie.

Lorna retrieved the ball and prepared to serve it back.

'You're pretty good at this,' called Alfie. 'Which I should have expected after your cricket performance last Christmas.'

'I've just been warming up,' she said.

'Really?' said Alfie. 'Well then, let's see what you've got.'

Irritated by his cocky manner, Lorna served a short, fast ball. Alfie had only just managed to return it when she pounced on the ball, sending it smacking onto the table and careering past his shoulder before he had a chance to lift his bat.

A couple of Marines watching from nearby cheered and moved closer to watch. 'Looks like you've got some competition there, Mac,' one said.

Alfie didn't look at Lorna as he gathered the ball and sent it across the net with so much power that it missed the table entirely and hit Lorna in the stomach.

Alfie dropped his bat on the table and ran around to her side. 'Ah shit, Lorna, I'm sorry.' He threw an arm around Lorna, who was doubled over, gripping her stomach and laughing so hard it hurt.

'Alfie, you are just so easy to rile,' she said, her voice wobbling. Straightening up, she was about to rib him further when she froze. His face had turned pale, and beads of sweat were on his forehead and his nose. His body was shaking, and he had let go of Lorna to grip the table.

'Alfie, what's wrong?' Lorna asked, taking his arm.

'Nothing,' he muttered, shaking her off.

The woman Alfie had been standing with when Lorna arrived brushed past and stood in front of Alfie, blocking him from Lorna's view.

'I did warn you, Alfie,' she said gently, her American accent soft and soothing. 'Come on.' Glaring briefly over her shoulder at Lorna, she led Alfie to a chair.

'I'm fine,' Alfie muttered.

'I don't understand,' said Lorna, moving closer. 'What happened?'

The woman tossed her head and glared at Lorna again. 'Malarial fever isn't something you know much about, is it?'

Lorna took a step back. 'No,' she stammered. 'I suppose it isn't.'

Alfie had his head between his hands, and his body was shaking so hard she was worried he would topple off his chair.

'Is there anything I can do?' she asked awkwardly.

'You've done enough,' muttered the woman, wiping a handkerchief tenderly over Alfie's brow.

'Lissa,' said Alfie quietly. 'Be nice.'

Lorna was grateful when Chester chose that moment to let out a bark. 'I'd better go,' she said. 'Chester is getting fed up and I should take the truck back to the depot.'

Alfie lifted his head and attempted a weak smile. 'Rematch another time, Lorna.'

'Absolutely,' Lorna replied. 'I'll give you a few weeks to get in some more practice first.'

When she reached Chester and let him off his lead, he raced over the grass, running in a wide arc before returning eagerly to her side. Lorna rubbed between his ears and thought of how

Alfie had changed in the six weeks he'd been away fighting. Her brothers had been gone far longer. She wondered where Gordon and Rick were, and what they were doing at this very moment. How changed they might be when, God willing, they returned.

Chapter 20

ALFIE

Alfie and Jethro joined the crowds leaving the train station, swept along with the locals and fellow Marines who were heading to the races too. Alfie liked being amongst the well-dressed, chatty crowd, though they were sedate in comparison to the boisterous crowds heading to a Cubs game in Chicago. Alfie had been to a few games with his father and Stan, before his father walked out on them. Alfie couldn't remember much, but he did recall being carried on his father's shoulders as they approached the stadium, the mass of shouting people below him both electrifying and alarming at the same time.

Stan had taken Alfie to a couple of games when he was around ten years old, Stan buying their tickets with money he'd earnt from his part-time job at the local newsagent. They'd kept their trips to the games secret from their mom, knowing she would be upset that Stan had spent money without her approval. Their mother didn't like baseball, mostly, Alfie suspected, because their father had loved it. It was one of the few times Alfie saw Stan genuinely happy; sitting in the stadium eating hot dogs and drinking Coca-Cola, yelling encouragement or shaking his fist. Stan was always checking on his little brother, asking him if he was enjoying himself.

Trentham Racecourse was only a few yards from the train station and within minutes they were gathered outside the tall stands heaving with people.

'Heck, they must take their racing seriously,' said Jethro. 'This has gotta be most of Wellington right here.'

There were queues leading up to the betting windows — lots of men examining their newspapers and discussing the horses.

'Alf!' came a voice, and Alfie turned to see Curtis weaving through the crowds towards them, pulling Karen along behind him.

'There they are,' said Jethro, reaching to shake Karen's hand. 'Congratulations.'

'Yes,' said Alfie, following Jethro's lead and shaking Karen's hand with as much enthusiasm as he could muster. 'Wonderful news.'

'Thanks.' Karen's eyes were bright with joy. She was in a lovely dress with matching hat, and Alfie had to admit she looked very much like a glowing bride-to-be.

'I hear Curtis was a true gentleman,' said Alfie, grinning. 'Even braved talking to your father.'

Curtis groaned as Karen laughed. 'I think my parents were so shocked they didn't know how to respond.'

'They agreed because they couldn't resist my charms,' said Curtis, putting an arm around Karen's waist and kissing her on the cheek.

'Now starts the fun part of convincing the powers that be to let us marry,' sighed Karen.

Curtis had explained the process the previous evening as they'd been enjoying a drink at the Cecil. It had been the first touch of alcohol Alfie had consumed since returning to camp, and he'd enjoyed the warmth that had spread through his body, a relaxed, mellow feeling he hadn't felt since before he left for Guadalcanal.

There had been concern amongst both the New Zealand and United States governments that marriage between Kiwi girls and American boys was not something that should be encouraged. Measures should be enacted to ensure any marriages that did take place would have longevity. There were a lot of hoops to jump through, according to Curtis.

'We're sitting with Lorna's family up in the stands,' said Karen, pointing to the curved stairs leading up to a covered stand filled with people. 'Come on, let's go join them and we can come back to place a bet when the queue is shorter.'

Alfie trailed behind the others as they climbed the steep stairs. He hadn't seen Lorna since the embarrassing episode at the recreation centre and had spent several sleepless nights recalling the way he had whacked the ping-pong ball at Lorna like a grumpy child.

'Alfie!' called Lorna's mum as they approached. 'How wonderful.'

She raced over and enveloped him in a hug. 'I'm sorry I didn't manage to visit while you were in hospital. How are you?'

'Much better, thank you, Mom,' Alfie said politely.

He shook hands with Mr Baxter and said hello to Peter and Penny, then he finally looked at Lorna.

'Hi,' he said, as lightly as he could. She was in a green floral dress and brown hat, and her hair had been cut to her shoulders. If he'd thought she was attractive in her uniform, it was nothing compared to how striking she looked today. His stomach flipped and he clenched a fist to calm himself.

'Hi,' she replied, matching his light tone, before turning to greet Jethro.

'It's quite the occasion,' said Jethro. 'Nothing like this at home.'

'Have you placed a bet yet?' Mr Baxter asked.

Alfie and Jethro shook their heads. 'No, sir.'

'Well, you've got a few minutes to study the lineup.' Mr Baxter held up the newspaper and Alfie moved to stand beside him, while Jethro squeezed in next to Lorna to study the paper in her hand.

'Got any hot tips?' Jethro asked Lorna, his face close to hers.

'I'm afraid not,' Lorna replied. 'Usually I'd have spent some time looking into the horses' form, but I've been too busy.'

'Poor dear worked nearly eighty hours this week,' said Mrs Baxter, reaching down to open the lid of a basket tucked beneath her feet. 'How would you boys like a sandwich?'

'That would be swell thanks, Mom,' said Curtis, already holding out a hand.

A hush came over the crowd as the announcer started to introduce the horses in the upcoming race. Alfie risked a quick glance at Lorna. She was scrutinising the horses parading below with intense concentration, and Alfie made a split decision. Whichever horse Lorna bet on, he would bet on the horse numbered immediately after it.

'Well, I'm going to have to bet on Florida clearly,' said Jethro, after the announcer had finished.

'You and most of the Marines here, I suspect,' said Mr Baxter.

'Well, it is the only one that sounds remotely American,' said Curtis. 'So I think I'll do the same.'

'My shilling is on number five,' said Lorna decisively.

'What about you, Alfie?' said Curtis.

'Number six,' stated Alfie confidently.

He thought he might have heard Lorna snort, but he ignored her and looked the other way.

A few hours later, Alfie had lost twice as much money as anyone else in their group. He wondered if he should change his tactic for the final race, since it clearly wasn't working out for him, but since he'd come this far, he felt he might as well see it through to the end.

Lorna and Mr Baxter had been the most successful, but since they only bet a shilling at the most, their wins were more about backing the right horse than making any money.

Alfie had enjoyed the afternoon and viewed the scant amount of money he had lost as a small price to pay. He loved that the locals were so excited, yet humble. They were quick to congratulate the winners in their group and there was friendly rivalry but no aggression.

As Alfie stood in the queue to place his final bet, he decided to throw caution to the wind and put a full five pounds on his horse to win. 'Number eleven,' he said, sliding the money beneath the grill. He retrieved his ticket and turned to find Lorna staring at him, her hands on her hips.

'Unbelievable,' she said.

'What?' said Alfie innocently.

'You knew I was betting on ten.'

'So?'

'So you're betting on whichever horse comes after mine.'

Alfie considered denying it, but chose to tell the truth. 'It's as good a strategy as any.'

'Is it?' said Lorna with a laugh. 'It certainly hasn't helped you so far.'

Alfie held his ticket aloft. 'Ahh, but I have a feeling about this one.'

They walked back to the stands together, the fading sun casting a purple glow over the ranges in the distance. Alfie was pleased they had a moment alone.

'I'm sorry about the other day,' he said, focusing on the steps as they climbed.

'So am I,' Lorna said quickly. 'I had no idea you were still sick. You seemed fine.'

'I *was* fine,' said Alfie, tersely. 'That's not what I was referring to. I was apologising for hitting you with the ball.'

Lorna stopped walking and faced him. 'How's the practice going?' she asked with a raise of her eyebrows. 'Ready for round two?'

Alfie laughed and they kept moving, not wanting to hold up the people behind them. 'Name the place and the time,' said Alfie, but Lorna was distracted, having moved to one side to stare down at the track, her eyes fixed on the horses below. 'Bugger,' she muttered, and Alfie was taken aback at her swearing.

She looked at him with narrowed eyes. 'Number eleven looks good,' she said reluctantly.

Lorna was right, number eleven was good. So good he came in first.

Chapter 21

LORNA

Karen was clearing tables when Lorna arrived at the Allied Services' Club. She was thrilled to no longer be working at the munitions factory, though moving back to her parents' house a few weeks ago had proven to be a challenge. Lorna was pleased her friend was now within walking distance of home again, though they had little spare time to catch up.

Having just finished a ten-hour shift, Lorna sank gratefully onto a stool at the milkshake counter and waved as Karen caught sight of her.

Karen rushed over, a stack of plates in her arms. 'You made it,' she said brightly. 'I'm off in twenty minutes — it's been so busy they asked me to work an extra hour. Wait for me?' Karen called, already heading to the kitchens.

Lorna ordered a passionfruit milkshake and sipped it appreciatively. The lounge was packed with Marines and young women who were presumably their dates for the evening. Lorna recognised a few faces, but none well enough to walk up to and join in their conversation.

'Hello, honey,' said a Marine, sliding on to the stool beside her.

'Hi,' said Lorna, smiling politely and trying to work out if they had met before. He was handsome, and Lorna was pleased he'd approached her. She'd decided just that afternoon on her long drive back from the Wairarapa that she needed to get out more, to not let work be her sole occupation. There were so many Kiwi girls having a grand time going to dances and on day trips, yet she hadn't been out once since she'd started driving.

'I'm Dan,' the Marine said, holding out his hand. 'I hope you don't mind me bowling over here like this.'

They shook hands and he fixed her with an intense look that made her heart leap. 'I don't mind,' she croaked. 'I'm Lorna.'

'Are you going to the dance downstairs later, Lorna?' he asked.

'Yes, I am,' she replied, though she'd had no intention of going until now.

'Excellent!' Dan said. 'I hope you'll save me a dance?'

They chatted for a few more minutes and then Dan excused himself to return to his group of friends.

'Who was that?' asked Karen, appearing from the staff room.

'Dan,' replied Lorna, wishing she wasn't blushing.

Karen raised her eyebrows. 'Well, you certainly made an impression.'

'Actually he asked if I was going to the dance downstairs tonight.'

'I hope you said yes. Curtis and I are going, you can come with us.'

'Okay,' said Lorna, sipping her milkshake.

'Lorrie, that's great. Come on—' Karen pulled her off her stool. 'Let's go and get ready at your house.'

Lorna glanced over her shoulder at Dan and was pleased to see him watching her. They waved goodbye to each other as Lorna and Karen headed for the door.

Everyone was sitting at the dining table when Lorna and Karen arrived home. At her mother's insistence, they sat down and had a quick bite to eat.

'It's good you're going out,' said Mrs Baxter, though she had that worried look that meant she wasn't entirely sure.

'She'll be fine,' said Karen, who knew Lorna's mum well. 'I'll take care of her. Curtis too.'

'What are you going to wear?' Penny asked, reaching for the bowl of peas.

'No idea. Apparently fancy evening gowns are expected.'

'I grabbed a spare dress from home on my way here,' said Karen. 'It's formal enough for the occasion and Lorna might fit into it,' she said hopefully, though everyone at the table knew the chances of anything of Karen's fitting Lorna was unlikely, considering Lorna was almost a head taller.

'I've a nice dress you can borrow,' said Penny. 'It's the one I wore to the first dance Gordon and I went to together.' There was a pause at the table as everyone thought of Gordon. Penny cleared her throat. 'I'll nip down and get it as soon as we've finished. It was always a tad too long for me, so it should be just right.'

Lorna's stomach was too tied in knots for her to eat much. She was nervous about the dance but also looking forward to it. More specifically, she was looking forward to seeing Dan again.

'That would be lovely, thanks, Pen,' said Lorna, realising somewhat belatedly she hadn't responded to her sister-in-law's offer.

'Do you want to come, Penny?' Karen asked. 'There are quite a few married girls at these dances.'

'Yes, I know,' said Penny quickly. 'And I'm not interested.'

There had been murmurings about married girls being swept up by the attention they received from the Marines, and concern that their thoughts were not so much on their husbands serving overseas, but on the Americans — specifically on the gifts the Marines tended to lavish on them. Tensions were rife, particularly when a married girl was seen having too much fun.

Lorna wasn't sure how she felt about it. On the one hand, wives should be allowed to go out and enjoy themselves rather than sit at home, but on the other, she couldn't shake the view it was a tad disrespectful. Lorna was secretly pleased Penny had declined Karen's invitation, and yet she would have loved to see Penny out enjoying herself.

Penny's dress was beautiful and reached all the way to Lorna's ankles. It was slim-fitting, a pale blue satin bodice with a drop waist that flared out to a floaty chiffon skirt which swirled about her legs as she moved. With her hair pinned up, she spent several seconds staring at herself in the mirror, surprised at how well she looked.

Her father whistled when she walked into the lounge to show her family. 'Look at you,' he said. 'Very nice, Lorrie.'

'Beautiful,' said Penny.

'You look ridiculous,' said Peter, shaking his head.

Her mum rushed over to adjust the sash at Lorna's waist. 'Make sure you are careful,' she whispered, leaning close to Lorna's ear.

Her dad put down his pipe and stood. 'Well, I can't let you both catch the tram. I'll give you a lift.'

Lorna protested, knowing how precious their petrol was. They barely used the car and yet managed to run out of their ration every two months.

'I insist,' he said, picking up his keys.

Twenty minutes later, he pulled up outside the Club, and Karen and Lorna climbed out of the car. The crowd of Marines milling about the doors all turned to stare.

'Come on,' said Karen, taking Lorna's hand. 'Shoulders back, head up.'

Lorna took a deep breath and did as Karen said, her heart thumping loudly. 'I don't know why I'm so nervous,' she whispered, as the men stepped aside to let them through.

'Because you don't like being the centre of attention, and right now none of these boys can keep their eyes off you,' said Karen.

Lorna realised it was true. She'd gone through life expecting boys to barely notice her. It was odd to be seen and admired.

The music was loud and fast as they stepped into the room. It wasn't as big or as glamorous as the Majestic, and for some reason this helped Lorna to relax a little.

Curtis appeared, throwing his arm around Karen. 'Hello, my beautiful fiancée,' he said, then he did a double take when he realised it was Lorna standing beside her.

'Well, honey, don't you look lovely?' he said warmly, before dragging Karen towards the dance floor.

'You okay?' Karen mouthed, looking back.

Lorna smiled and nodded, then moved to the side of the room, searching for Dan. She had to squint without her glasses on but eventually spotted him dancing with an attractive redhead and was instantly jealous, not that she had any right to be. Chances are he'd forgotten all about asking her to save him a dance.

Lorna ducked behind a pillar and wondered what to do next. Why did she always have to feel so ill-at-ease in these sorts of situations? She couldn't stay behind the pillar all night. She needed to show confidence she didn't feel.

'Lorna? By God, is that you?' Jethro was leaning against the wall a few feet away, smoking. He pushed himself off the wall and came towards her. 'I barely recognised you. Great dress!'

'Thanks,' said Lorna. 'How are you?'

Jethro shrugged. 'They're training us pretty hard but I'm not complaining. Wanna dance?'

They found a spot on the dance floor, and Lorna tried to tune out everyone around her and let herself move to the music. She was doing well, even enjoying herself, until a woman bumped into her.

'Excuse me,' said Lorna, faltering. It was the girl Alfie had been chatting to at the recreation centre out at Silverstream. The one who had come to Alfie's aid when he'd become ill.

'Watch your step,' the girl said, before pulling her partner towards the centre of the room. Her partner looked back over his shoulder at Lorna and stopped dancing. It was Alfie.

'Holy shit, is that you, Lorna?' he said loudly. He looked confused, as if he couldn't work out why she was there.

'Don't look so shocked,' Lorna called back.

He blinked a few times, his expression strangely neutral, before spinning his dance partner in a neat twirl as they were absorbed amongst the other moving bodies.

Lorna put a hand on Jethro's shoulder and leant in. 'Do you think we could take a break?' she asked.

'Good idea, let's get a drink.'

They made their way to the bar where Jethro ordered them each a Coca-Cola, then they stood by an open window. Lorna enjoyed the cooler air on her flushed cheeks.

'There you are,' said Karen, pushing past Lorna to stand by the window and flap her arms up and down. 'Gosh, it is hot in here.'

Curtis arrived with a couple of drinks, and they chatted as best they could over the music.

'Who's that stunning girl Alfie's dancing with?' said Karen, pointing.

Jethro rolled his eyes. 'Lissa. They've been dating ever since Alfie came out of hospital.'

'Why did you roll your eyes?' asked Karen.

'She's demanding,' said Curtis. 'Keeps Alfie on a tight rope.'

Lorna laughed. 'I'd like to see that.'

'Trust me, you would not,' said Jethro. 'We're hoping he gets tired of her soon.'

Karen shuffled closer to Lorna. 'Don't look now, but Dan is headed this way.'

Lorna widened her eyes and tried to act calm.

'Lorna,' Dan said, arriving at her side. 'What a sight for sore eyes. I hope you've remembered to save me a dance?'

'Of course,' said Lorna, before introducing him to the others.

'Can we dance now?' asked Dan, the moment polite greetings were over.

She shivered as he took her hand and led her away.

They danced the rest of the night together and even when Lorna excused herself to go to the ladies' room, he hovered outside the door, waiting for her return.

As it drew close to midnight, the tempo of the music slowed, the lights dimmed and couples moved close, pressing their bodies together for the last dance of the night. Dan slipped his arm around Lorna, and she put her head on his shoulder. It was the closest she'd ever been to a man, and she was thrilled yet petrified.

'You really are so beautiful,' murmured Dan.

Bravely, Lorna tilted her head so that her lips were inches from his. She thought – hoped – he might kiss her, because she would like him to be the first, this man who seemed to have eyes only for her.

She held her breath as Dan lightly brushed his warm lips against hers. For a second she wasn't sure how to react, before she kissed him in return. Then the music stopped, the lights grew bright and Lorna took a hasty step back.

'Can I walk you out?' said Dan.

'Okay,' said Lorna, breathlessly.

They joined the stream of others heading towards the door and Lorna glanced about, hoping to spot Karen. Instead she caught Alfie's eye. He was staring at her with such ferocity she wondered if he might be angry. Before she could react, Lissa pulled him away, speaking intently to him.

Descending the outside steps, Lorna inhaled the cool, crisp air. There appeared to be some sort of commotion on the footpath below and Lorna heard raised voices. Suddenly there was a surge of movement, and she gasped as a plain-clothed man punched a Marine in the stomach. The Marines on the steps behind Lorna shouted and pushed past her, running to join in.

'Stay here,' said Dan, heading into the fray.

Within seconds, there were more than fifty men throwing punches and pushing each other.

'Hey!' yelled a girl Lorna recognised. Kaia had been in Lorna's year at school, and they'd been in the same netball team.

Lorna watched horrified as Kaia ran into the mass of angry men and yanked at a Marine's jacket. Lorna realised he'd been punching Kaia's brother, Wiremu, in the stomach. Wiremu had his arms pinned behind him by another Marine. 'Get off him,' Kaia screamed.

The Marine Kaia was pulling at gave her a shove and she fell heavily to the ground. Lorna ran to her aid but just as she reached the edge of the mob, she felt someone grab her arm and pull her backwards. 'Let me go!' yelled Lorna, turning to confront whoever was preventing her from going to help.

'Don't be an idiot,' said Alfie gruffly, still grasping her arm tightly.

'Let me go!' snapped Lorna. Suddenly she was elbowed hard from behind and Alfie caught her as she stumbled.

'Get out of here, Lorna,' he said, pushing her behind him.

Tears smarted in her eyes as she stumbled away a few steps and tried to compose herself. Alfie pushed his way towards Kaia and lifted her off the ground.

'You bastards!' Kaia cried, looking towards her brother.

Wiremu still had his arms pinned behind his back and a stream of blood was gushing from his nose. One eye was red and swollen.

'My turn,' said a Marine, stepping forward, and Lorna had a sickening realisation it was Dan. She watched as he grinned, then punched Wiremu in the jaw, sending his head ricocheting sideways and globules of blood flying off his face.

'That's enough,' said Alfie, grabbing Dan by his collar.

Dan cursed. 'Whose side are you on, Mac?' he said, spitting in Wiremu's direction.

'Clearly not yours right now,' growled Alfie.

Jethro and Curtis ran past Lorna towards Alfie, but he didn't see them coming as he'd turned his back on Dan and was telling the Marine holding Wiremu to let him go.

'Hey,' yelled a civilian charging at Alfie. 'You bleeding thug.'

Alfie held up his hands. 'I'm trying to—' He was cut off as another civilian bore down on him and punched him in the face.

'Hey!' yelled Jethro. He and Curtis stepped in front of Alfie, who was shaking his head as if to clear it.

More and more Marines and plain-clothed men kept pushing in around Lorna, and she found she was struggling to see what was happening.

'Lorrie!' Karen ran up to her. 'What on earth are you doing in this circus? Come on.' She dragged Lorna off the road, onto the footpath and down the block.

The street was filling rapidly. Hundreds of Marines and civilians were facing off against each other.

'Stupid boys,' said Karen, shaking her head with wry amusement.

Lorna stood on tiptoes, trying to spot Alfie and the others without success. Then she saw Kaia with her arm around her brother, sitting on the ground with their backs against a building. Lorna raced over.

'Oh gosh, how awful, are you both okay?' she asked, crouching down.

Wiremu held a handkerchief soaked in blood to his nose and removed it briefly to speak. 'They called me a nigger.'

Lorna frowned. 'Why would they call you that?'

'Why do you *think*, Lorrie,' said Kaia angrily. 'It happens all the time, surely you must have noticed?'

Lorna had heard there was negativity from some of the Marines towards the Māori, especially those Americans from the South, where her father had told her segregation still occurred. But Lorna hadn't witnessed anything untoward herself. Perhaps it had been happening right under her nose and she'd been blind to it.

'Yesterday I was told to get off a tram by a couple of Marines because they didn't think it was right for me to be there,' said Kaia. 'And last week I was barred when I tried to enter a milk bar.'

Karen handed Wiremu a clean handkerchief. 'Sometimes I don't even think they realise what they're doing. I told Curtis off the other day for being rude to my neighbour, Mr Te Hira.'

Lorna thought of Alfie. 'They're not all like that,' she said quietly.

'Enough are,' said Wiremu, resting his head back against the building and closing the eye that wasn't swollen shut already.

'You should go to the hospital,' said Lorna.

Sirens began to scream from every direction as Military and local police appeared.

'We should go,' said Wiremu, wincing as he slowly rose to his feet. 'Trouble has a way of finding me.'

Kaia shook her head with resignation and stood too. 'Thanks,' she said, glancing at Lorna briefly, 'for trying.'

Lorna felt as if the comment was both a compliment and a criticism, and she felt guilty as she watched them disappear around the corner.

Karen sighed. 'I suppose we should go too.'

'What about Curtis?' asked Lorna. 'Aren't you worried about him?'

Karen raised her eyebrows. 'Serves him right if he gets arrested.'

The crowd was thinning, and some had gone from yelling at one another to slapping each other on the backs and laughing. There was little tension or aggression now, mostly men standing around chatting.

'For goodness sake,' muttered Lorna.

'There they are,' said Karen, waving a hand.

Curtis, Jethro and Alfie wandered over, all three of them grinning.

'Well, that was a good bit of excitement to end the evening,' said Curtis.

'Says the man who didn't get a fist in his face,' said Alfie, holding a hand to his jaw.

'Come on,' said Jethro, giving Alfie a light punch on the arm. 'A second ago, you said you barely felt it.'

'I hope you all feel better now that's out of your system,' said Karen, crossing her arms. 'For the record, neither of us are impressed.'

Lorna avoided looking at anyone. She was embarrassed and kept seeing the awful smile on Dan's face when he'd said he was next: As if there was nothing that would please him more than hitting a man purely because of the colour of his skin.

'Well Lorna,' said Jethro. 'I think your man, Dan, has turned out to be not quite the gentleman he seemed.'

Lorna didn't reply. She stared at the ground, tears welling unhelpfully in her eyes. Dan had made her feel special. Dan had been the first man she'd kissed. She'd been swept up in his charms like a gullible, silly girl. She was sick to the stomach and disappointed in herself.

'Come on,' said Karen, hooking her arm through Lorna's. 'I think it's time to call it a night.'

'We'll grab you a taxi home,' said Alfie. 'But we'll have to get a bit further away from here to find one, I suspect.'

'Fine,' said Karen, as she guided Lorna along the street, the boys following behind.

Lorna glanced behind her and caught Alfie's eye.

'You okay?' he mouthed.

She knew then, as she read the expression on his face, that something had changed between them, something she couldn't put into words. Her heart thumped painfully in her chest as she nodded and quickly looked away.

Chapter 22

ALFIE

Too exhausted to remove his pack, Alfie sank to the ground and flopped backwards, his pack acting as a backrest. Every part of him hurt; his feet most of all. He knew if he were to remove his boots, he'd never be able to get them back on. Around him, Marines were collapsing with loud groans.

'I hate my life,' said Jethro, lying prone beside him.

They had just completed a forced march from camp to Foxton and back, a distance of 140 gruelling miles.

Curtis, lying curled up beneath one of the willow trees, looked to have already fallen asleep, as had many others.

Alfie was too exhausted to sleep, too exhausted to drink water, even though he knew he needed to. He was so exhausted he couldn't focus, his eyes blurry and his head swaying about as if he were drunk.

They had been training harder and harder for the past two months and Alfie was by far the fittest he'd ever been. Up until twenty-four hours ago he'd felt strong and powerful, as if he could take on anything thrown his way. He shouldn't have been so cocky.

With agonising difficulty, Alfie edged his heavy pack off his back. Immediately his back and shoulders seized up, creating waves of cramping pain that made him gasp for breath.

They were at Mackays Crossing, a short distance from their camp, and most of them had sought out shade beneath the trees on the side of the road. Occasionally, a truck or a jeep would motor past, the driver slowing down to stare. Briefly, Alfie wondered if Lorna might drive by on her way to deliver supplies. He wondered what she would say if she were to spot him. Probably she would make some clever remark with that deadpan expression he couldn't read. Did it mean she found him annoying or was it her way of being friendly? The girls in America were so much easier to understand. They said what they meant and asked for what they wanted. Kiwi girls kept everything, especially the way they felt, closer to their chests.

Alfie groaned again and lay down, fully stretched out on his back. He hadn't been able to shake the image of Lorna at the dance on the night of the brawl from his head. What was she doing wearing a dress like that? He'd kept looking at her all night, to the point that Lissa had told him off. Then that bastard Dan had kissed her, right there in the middle of the dance floor, and she had kissed him back, and Alfie had felt a fever sweep over him as if he was in those early malaria days again. He had realised then, with a shock, that he felt something for Lorna, something he couldn't and shouldn't feel, because she was Stan's girl. She always would be. More so, because if Stan were alive, he would have been the one dancing with Lorna, kissing her on her full lips, and Alfie would have never considered Lorna in any other way.

That evening, Alfie lay on his bed, freshly showered, his blistered feet throbbing, and read Stan's letter again. He forced himself to reread the postscript, until he could recite it word for word. *Lorna's the only one, Alfie. If circumstances were different, I would have asked her to marry me.*

Alfie needed to forget about Lorna. Starting right now. 'What time are you getting the train to town?' he asked Jethro, who was doing up the buttons of his shirt.

'In about twenty minutes, why?' Jethro sat on his bed and made groaning noises as he bent down to put on his socks. 'You gonna come along after all?'

Alfie shoved Stan's letter back in its envelope and placed it under his pillow. 'Yep, a drink or two is just what I need.'

***

Two weeks later, Alfie was wandering along Lambton Quay when he heard his name being called and saw Mrs Baxter waving at him from across the street.

She hurried over to his side. 'I was hoping to bump into you.'

'Hello, Mom,' he said, removing his hat.

'We've missed you, Alfie. Everyone's been wondering what you've been up to, though I hear you've been training very hard. Frank has been wondering if you'd like to go fishing with him. Are you free this weekend?'

'Fishing?' Alfie said, stalling for time. He wasn't sure if spending time with Lorna's family was such a good idea.

'Yes, a boys' trip. You, Peter and Frank. The forecast is supposedly excellent.'

Alfie had been wondering what to do for the weekend. He'd been granted a 72 for the first time since his arrival back in New Zealand, and he should have a planned a trip away to Rotorua or the South Island, as many of the other Marines had done, but he hadn't been able to muster the enthusiasm. A day of fishing — something he'd never done before — sounded appealing.

'It just so happens I have seventy-two hours' leave this weekend, Mom, so yes, I'd love to go fishing.'

'Wonderful! You must stay with us. Frank likes to leave bright and early while the sea is calm, and of course, fingers crossed you'll catch us enough that we can have fish for tea.'

'Oh, that's not necessary,' said Alfie quickly. 'I can stay in town.'

'No, I insist. I'll have Rick's room all ready for you.'

Alfie smiled politely. 'Well then, that would be swell.' It wasn't as if he could say no and risk offending her, and if he was honest, Alfie had missed seeing Lorna's family. He'd missed seeing Lorna too.

Leaves swirled in mini tornadoes as Alfie stepped off the tram and began the walk towards Lorna's house. He zipped up his jacket as the strong wind sent a chill through his body. When he turned into the shelter of Ranui Road, he breathed a sigh of relief. The front door of number 1 opened, and an elderly woman stepped out.

'Are you Alfie?' she called as she hobbled towards him.

'Yes, ma'am,' he replied.

'I thought so. Haven't seen you for a while. Thought you might have shipped out.' She spoke as if she knew him, when he had no memory of meeting her before.

Reaching her gate, the woman stared at him for several uncomfortable seconds. He wasn't sure what he was supposed to say. Did the woman want something from him? Perhaps he should offer her a carton of cigarettes from the paper bag he was carrying.

'Off you go, then,' said the lady, as if he'd passed some kind of test. 'Tell Peter next time he wants to take one of my apples, he'd better knock on my door and ask.'

Alfie doffed his hat. 'Yes, ma'am.' Confused, he continued on his way.

'Lizzie,' screamed a woman, as a young girl in her pyjamas tore out of the gate at number 5. 'Get back here and brush your teeth.'

The girl ducked behind Alfie's legs. 'Hide me,' she whispered, her thin arms gripping him around the legs.

A frazzled woman appeared, carrying another girl who looked remarkably similar to the one currently wrapped around Alfie's legs.

'I'm sorry,' she said, flustered. 'You must be Alfie.'

Alfie frowned. How did these strangers all seem to know who he was?

The girl let him go and came around to stare up at him. '*You're* Alfie,' she said, assessing him. 'Lorna didn't tell me you were handsome.'

Alfie laughed. 'I'm sure she didn't.'

'Did you bring me a treat?' she asked. 'Americans are always giving out treats.'

'Well now,' Alfie dug around in his bag and pulled out a Baby Ruth. 'If you're good for your mom, I might be willing to give you this.'

The girl's eyes widened as she fixated on the packet.

Her mother laughed. 'Well, that ought to do it,' she said, taking the girl by the hand. 'Say thank you, Lizzie.'

'Thank you, Mr Alfie,' she said solemnly as she reached her other hand out for the chocolate bar.

'Enjoy your stay,' said the girl's mother, taking Lizzie back through their gate.

Shaking his head, Alfie continued on until he arrived at the bottom of the stairs leading to number 11. He stared up at the house in shadow, the late afternoon sun having dropped below the hill behind. It looked quiet, calm and solid, as if its sole purpose was to protect the family living within its walls. Alfie had never known a place like it. A house which was also a home.

Alfie hadn't thought about his mother and sister in a while. In the last letter he'd received from them, his sister had talked about them moving into another apartment. It only had one bedroom, Alice had written, so she was sleeping on a mattress on the floor behind the settee. Alice had decided to leave school, although she'd only just turned fifteen. Alfie wondered now if he should send her a belated birthday present, something other than money.

'Are you going to stand there creepily and look at my house all night?'

Alfie spun around to see Lorna. She opened the gate at number 9, let Chester through and closed it again.

'I was thinking how lucky you are,' said Alfie, wondering why he hadn't noticed her beauty the first time they met.

'Why is that?' Lorna stopped beside him, and he had to look away from her lips.

'You have a home,' he said, his voice short and clipped.

'That's a rather astute observation.'

She had that infuriating tone again, the one he couldn't work out.

'When you say things like that, are you trying to be funny or are you making fun of me?' snapped Alfie, taking a step back to try to gain some distance.

Lorna blinked, and he knew he'd hurt her with his outburst.

'Sorry,' said Alfie as she started up the stairs. 'Should I even be here?'

'Only if you want to be,' said Lorna, reaching the front door.

'Do you want me here?' he asked, taking the stairs two at a time.

Lorna paused, her hand on the door handle. 'Alfie, what has gotten into you?'

He wanted to tell her then. Tell her that he couldn't stop thinking about her. That even though he was dating Lissa, it was Lorna who made his heart thud and his palms ache.

'Nothing,' he muttered instead.

'Peter has been talking about going fishing with you ever since Mum told him you were going,' Lorna said, opening the door. 'Alfie's here,' she called.

As Peter raced out of the living room, Lorna walked down the hallway into her bedroom, and closed her door.

By 8 am the following morning, Alfie had caught his first fish. Feeling that initial tug on the line, he'd felt as excited as he did at a Cubs game with his brother. Then short, rapid tugs had him standing up and shouting, 'I've got one, I've got one.'

Lorna's father had slapped him on the back, grinning. 'Better reel it in there, old chum. Keep the line tight like I told you.'

Alfie wound in the line and Peter started pointing, 'I see it, Alfie, it's a good size too.' Then Mr Baxter had leant over the side of the boat to scoop the fish into a net, and Alfie had officially landed his catch.

'Wait till you taste it,' said Peter. 'Snapper is my favourite fish, Lorna's too.'

Alfie looked at his snapper, lying dead in the steel bucket beside him. He'd barely slept the night before, lying in Rick's bed. The evening had been pleasant enough, and he'd tried to relax and chat the best he could during dinner (or tea as they called it), and as they'd played cards afterwards. Lorna had excused herself early to go to bed, saying she was tired after a busy week of work. Which was probably true, but also, Alfie wondered, was she aware of a tension between them? Maybe it was just him. Maybe she simply found him annoying.

'One of my favourite places in the world right here,' said Mr Baxter contentedly, crossing his legs and lighting his pipe. Alfie looked at the glassy sea, the streaks of sunlight cutting through the water making tiny particles glisten. He leant over and trailed his hand in the water, relishing the cold on his skin and enjoying the sound of water slapping against the side of the boat.

Peter gave an excited yelp. 'I've got one,' he said, winding his reel frantically. Alfie smiled and reached for the net.

'You'll have to come with us next time, Curtis,' said Mr Baxter, leaning back in his armchair.

'I'd like that, sir,' Curtis replied, sipping on his beer.

When they'd returned from their fishing trip, Mrs Baxter had announced that Curtis and Karen would be joining them for tea.

'How are the wedding plans coming along?' asked Mrs Baxter.

Karen gave an exaggerated sigh. 'It's a nightmare. Why should I have to prove myself? I even had to submit a medical report.'

At the sound of the front door, Alfie stopped listening to Karen. He assumed it was Lorna, finally home from work. He'd been worrying about her, as it had been dark for almost an hour. Plus, it was freezing. He had been hoping that someone might light the fire, but it seemed it wasn't quite cold enough yet.

Lorna's head poked through the door. 'Hello, everyone.'

'Well about time,' said Karen. 'They really are making you work too hard, Lorrie.'

Lorna shrugged. 'Be right back. I'm dying to get out of this uniform.'

When Lorna returned, wearing trousers, a cardigan over a shirt and thick socks, she sat cross-legged on the carpet in front of the fire.

'I was hoping the fire would be going,' she said. 'Is no one else cold?'

'Alfie caught three snapper,' said Peter. 'Big ones too.'

'Really?' said Lorna, though she didn't look at Alfie as she spoke. 'How exciting.'

'I had a great time,' said Alfie.

'Well, while you boys were out fishing, I had a day from hell.' Lorna stretched out one leg, exposing her ankle and bent forward to rub her toes. Alfie tore his eyes away.

'What happened?' asked Karen.

'I was detailed to pick up some dehydrated potato from up in Levin, and I came across an army boy who was hitchhiking, so I offered him a lift.'

'Lorna, we've talked about this,' said her father, a warning in his voice.

'He was fine, Dad. A very nice boy actually. Gosh, he looked young. He said he was eighteen, but he looked younger than Peter. Anyway, Chester loved him, and we had a lovely chat, but when I dropped him off at the depot, I got told off by my supervisor for giving a dogface a lift. Then as punishment, I was put on loading out meat from the freezing chambers, which everyone knows is the worst possible job. It's no wonder I'm still cold.'

'What's a dogface?' asked Peter.

'Anyone in the army,' said Curtis. 'We don't have anything to do with them.'

'Oh, I've heard the way you Marines talk about those poor boys,' said Karen. 'You're not *that* special, you know.'

'We're a hell of a lot better than them,' muttered Curtis.

'Well, he was a nice boy, so I don't regret giving him a lift, regardless,' said Lorna, getting up. 'I'm going to see if Mum needs some help in the kitchen.'

Alfie leapt to his feet. 'Perhaps I could light the fire,' he blurted. 'If that would be okay with you, Mr Baxter?'

'Of course. If you don't mind getting some wood. Lorna—' Mr Baxter called, 'show Alfie where the woodshed is so he can light you a fire.'

Still in her socks, Lorna led Alfie out the back door and around the corner of the house. 'In there,' she said, pointing to a tin shed.

'Thanks,' said Alfie.

'You don't have to light the fire, you know.'

Alfie ignored her and headed towards the shed.

'Not if it's just for me,' she called.

Alfie turned to look at her. 'It's not,' he said flatly. 'You're just a good excuse. The house is damn freezing.'

They stared at one another, and Alfie suddenly knew. He knew from the way her eyes flared and her lips twitched. He knew, and it was both the very best and the very worst moment of his life.

'Good to know it wasn't just me then,' said Lorna, her voice nothing but a whisper.

'It wasn't,' Alfie replied.

Lorna bit her lip and hurried back into the house, leaving Alfie with a yearning he knew would keep him tossing and turning in Rick's bed throughout the night.

Chapter 23

LORNA

She hadn't planned on entering the running race. In fact, Lorna had every reason to boycott it on principle. The whole addition of a women's event was clearly a token gesture and Lorna felt offended on behalf of all females. Why couldn't they have competed in the hurdles and high jump, and all the other track events? Why did they only get to enter one short sprint race which clearly wasn't being taken seriously? If anything, Lorna thought the race was an excuse for men to ogle the women.

'Go on, Lorrie,' said Cathy. 'We need you to represent all of us.'

Lorna was at the Basin Reserve to watch the athletics meet with a handful of other female drivers she'd gotten to know since joining the Marine Reserves. The girls were all American, apart from Betty, a fellow Kiwi who had been recruited from New Plymouth and who drove trucks better than anyone Lorna had met, men included.

Cathy was the undisputed leader of their group with her loud, bossy tone and take-no-prisoners approach. She had been the one to convince them to attend the athletics day as part of a 'bonding opportunity'. Lorna didn't mind Cathy's enthusiasm, as it was good for her to get to know the others better. For the first time in her life, Lorna was interested in making friends. She'd always been content spending time with her family and Karen. She hadn't needed anyone else. But with Gordon and Rick hundreds of miles away, and Karen preoccupied with her fiancé, Lorna was lonely. She wanted to keep busy, to get out and about, to find distractions, to *not* think about Alfie.

'Okay, I'll do it,' Lorna said. 'Enter me in the race before I change my mind.'

The girls hooted and took turns hugging Lorna, then Cathy ran off to put her name down. Unfortunately, Cathy informed Lorna as they gathered in the stands to watch the first sprint, her race wouldn't be happening until the afternoon, which gave Lorna far too much time to regret her decision.

'Check it out, Lorrie,' said Betty, a cigarette dangling from her mouth as she dipped her head in the direction of the high jump. Betty was taller than Lorna, and not overweight by any means, but she took up space and didn't seem self-conscious or concerned about the fact. Her husband had been killed in Africa a year ago, and she'd told Lorna that since then, she didn't much give a damn about anything. 'Those are rather tight-fitting shorts for a grown man, don't you think?'

Lorna snorted when she looked at the tall, slim man wearing what appeared to be his underwear, prancing towards the high jump bar. 'Doesn't leave much to the imagination.'

They had a good time cheering on various boys they recognised, before heading to the cafeteria for tea and scones.

'What are you going to wear for the race, Lorrie?' Cathy asked. 'You can't run in that skirt.'

Lorna shrugged, her cheeks growing warm. 'I might have put shorts in my handbag just in case.'

'Attagirl,' said Betty, slapping Lorna on the back.

'Hello, ladies,' came a voice Lorna recognised. She glanced up to see Alfie and Jethro looking suave in their leather jackets, with shirts unbuttoned at the neck, and sunglasses on.

'Alfie,' said Cathy, leaping out of her chair eagerly. 'I thought you might have entered one of the events?'

Why was it, Lorna wondered, that everyone knew Alfie?

'Nope,' said Alfie, giving Lorna a fleeting look. 'Not really my thing.'

'Have you met?' asked Cathy, looking from Alfie to Lorna.

'Sure,' said Alfie, offhandedly. 'Lorna's family have been very hospitable.'

'They have,' said Jethro, moving closer to Lorna. 'Good to see you, Lorrie.'

'Hi, Jethro,' said Lorna, stiffening as Jethro bent to give her a kiss on the cheek. 'This is Betty,' she added, leaning away from Jethro and noticing Alfie's scowl. Her heart thudded in her chest. Did this mean he was jealous? Did he have feelings for her as she had hoped?

'Lorna is entered in the sprint race later,' said Betty. 'I've got money on her to win.'

'No you don't,' said Lorna, her voice high-pitched and squeaky.

'No,' laughed Betty. 'But I would if I could.'

'What time?' asked Alfie.

'Oh, you don't have to watch,' said Lorna quickly. 'It's embarrassing enough as it is.'

'Of course we'll watch,' said Jethro. 'Won't we, Alf?'

Lorna met Alfie's eyes and found she couldn't look away.

'Course we'll watch,' he said softly, his eyes searching hers.

Thankfully, Lorna was so nervous when her race was called that she barely noticed the crowd. She'd removed her jacket and rolled up her shirtsleeves. As she stepped up to the starting line and crouched, she was alarmed to discover her shorts had somehow shrunk and were shorter and tighter than she remembered. When the firing gun sounded, Lorna launched herself down the grassy lane, her legs and arms pumping. There were only another six girls in the race, and she was determined to win.

As Lorna surged across the finish line in first place, she could hear her friends shouting her name. She grinned and waved as they jumped up and down, yelling congratulations. It wasn't until she was leaving the track that Jethro came charging towards her, Alfie trailing behind.

'That was fantastic!' Jethro said, picking her up and swirling her around before putting her down.

'Thanks,' said Lorna, grinning.

'Well done,' said Alfie, gruffly, tucking his hands into the pockets of his jacket. 'I was confident you'd win.'

'Why is that?'

'Because I figured you'd be good at running, just as you're good at every other sport.'

Lorna wasn't sure from his tone if he was paying her a compliment or not.

'Thanks,' she said crisply.

Alfie put a hand on her arm. 'I didn't mean . . .'

'Forget it,' said Lorna, shaking him off.

'Are you still coming to the dance out at Camp Mackay tonight?' asked Jethro, seemingly oblivious to the tension between her and Alfie.

Lorna had promised Karen she would go, but now wished she hadn't.

'I am, yes,' she said reluctantly.

'Save me a dance?' Jethro asked.

Lorna made sure she didn't so much as look in Alfie's direction.

'Absolutely,' she replied, before turning and walking away.

'It's an act of defiance,' said Lorna, sitting next to Karen on the bus.

'How on earth is looking like a frumpy old maid an act of defiance?' cried Karen, throwing up her hands in disgust.

Lorna had decided she wouldn't make any effort on her appearance for the dance. She'd gone years without caring about what she wore or how she looked, and she was annoyed knowing it had become important to her now.

'I'm not looking to impress anyone, Karnie,' said Lorna, tossing her head. 'And besides, shouldn't a man like me for who I am, not what I wear?'

'I guarantee they'd like you a whole lot more if you weren't wearing your everyday shoes and socks,' muttered Karen. 'And my mother has that exact same top. Trust me when I say that is not a commendation.'

Lorna had changed into the button-down knitted collared top at the last minute. It was more comfortable than the blouse she'd been wearing and a better match for her knee-length tartan skirt.

'It looks like I'm going to school, doesn't it?' said Lorna, realising too late that she might have taken her act of so-called defiance a little too far.

'Worse,' Karen replied. 'You look like you're going to church.'

Arriving at Camp Mackay, the women who had been invited to the dance filed off the bus and into the hall. It was filled with Marines, who immediately flocked over to ask them to dance. Karen hadn't even made it through the door before Curtis had whisked her away, and Lorna was starting to worry about finding a dance partner when Alfie appeared at her side.

'Nice of you to dress up for the occasion,' he said, eyeing her outfit.

Lorna felt a sharp stab of pain in her ribs. 'Nice of you to come over and say that, Alfie,' she retorted. 'Most gentlemanly of you.'

Alfie paused. He seemed about to say something more before deciding against it. 'Jethro sends his regards,' he said finally, his expression neutral. 'He couldn't make it.'

'Oh no,' said Lorna, hoping she sounded disappointed, though in truth she was relieved. 'I hope he's okay?'

'Bad headache. He gets them from time to time. Hasn't stopped throwing up for the last hour.'

Lorna wished she could dislike Alfie, especially considering the way he'd just spoken to her. Instead, she felt a thrill of excitement having him close. She'd never ached for a man this way before. Hadn't even known it was possible to feel such a fierce pull of desire.

Alfie cleared his throat and stepped back. 'Don't,' he muttered.

Lorna blinked. 'What?' she asked. *Oh god*, she wondered, had he seen something of her longing in her expression?

Alfie ran a hand across his chin and sighed heavily. 'Nothing,' he said. 'Do you want to dance?'

His tone seemed to imply that having to dance with her would be a terrible chore.

'Don't feel obliged. I know there are plenty of other women in this room you would rather dance with.'

Alfie shook his head angrily. 'You really have no idea, do you?'

He grabbed her hand and pulled her towards the dance floor. A shiver ran down her spine as he placed a hand on her waist. The band was playing a jazz-style piece with an uneven rhythm, and Lorna wasn't sure what kind of moves were required.

'I don't know what to do,' she said, her voice cracking.

'Neither do I,' muttered Alfie, pulling her fractionally closer.

Lorna's body burned and she held her breath as they started to dance, their movements jerky and awkward. She looked determinedly over his shoulder, but her eyes kept flicking to his chin, his neck, the corner of his mouth. She inhaled his scent of soap and musk and tobacco, and it made her feel lightheaded, woozy.

I'm swooning, she thought, disgusted with herself. How could she have got to this? With *Alfie* of all people.

Lorna stumbled and Alfie hauled her up so that her head rested against his shoulder. Their bodies stilled and they made no attempt to dance.

'Lorna,' Alfie murmured.

She tipped her head up and willed him to kiss her.

'Alfie,' she whispered, her lips almost, almost on his.

Suddenly, Alfie leapt back, staring at her in horror.

'What is it?' Lorna asked, shakily. 'There's nothing going on with Jethro, Alfie. With me and Jethro, I mean. I like him, but not . . . not in that way.' Flustered, Lorna put a hand to her cheek. She didn't understand what was going on. One second, she thought he had feelings for her, the next she wondered if it was all in her imagination.

'Thank you for the dance,' said Alfie stiffly. Then he strode towards the door and disappeared outside.

Bewildered, Lorna looked around the hall.

'May I have the next dance?' said a Marine, appearing before her.

Lorna stared at him, taking several seconds to process his words. 'Excuse me? Oh, sorry, what did you say?'

The man frowned. 'I asked if you would like to dance.'

'Dance?' Lorna needed a minute to think, to get her breath back under control.

Why was this stranger standing before her looking at her oddly? *He asked you to dance*, Lorna reminded herself. *You need to respond.*

'Yes,' she said, glancing at the door. 'Yes, we should dance,' she said, trying to clear her head.

Come back, she thought, looking at the door again. *Alfie, why did you have to leave?*

Chapter 24

ALFIE

Dusk was turning Kāpiti Island a deep unsettling mauve as three giant warships hovered in its shadows.

Alfie shivered with cold and anticipation. He was crouched low in a Higgins boat, crammed in with the other boys. They wore full combat kit, packs on, rifles slung across their shoulders. Surrounding them in the choppy seas were at least twenty other boats loaded with Marines, all motoring towards the shore.

Up ahead, tank lighters were fighting their way through the surf, delivering tanks and jeeps to the beach. Planes flew low above their heads, and Alfie gulped as a mine exploded, sending sand flying high into the sky like a fireworks display.

'Get ready!' Barked their sergeant, standing at the front of the boat. Alfie felt the surge as they rode a wave closer, then the slack as they were sucked backwards. Glancing behind, Alfie saw a wave rise behind them and crash over the hull, covering them in the freezing spray.

'Shit,' muttered Curtis, wiping the salt water from his face. 'This is going to be damn nasty, isn't it?'

Alfie slapped him on the back. 'Just jump off and keep running, alright?'

The second their boat hit the sand, the ramp was lowered and they started to disembark, their gaits ungainly as the boat rocked about. Curtis was in front of Alfie and charged down the ramp, leaping into the shallows and soaking his boots. Then he took a couple more steps and gave a sharp cry as he sank up to his waist. Alfie grabbed the back of Curtis's pack and helped to haul him out, and they negotiated the hollows and sandbars side by side until, soaked through, they finally made it out.

Alfie scanned the scrub covering the sand dunes ahead, knowing there were men camouflaged, lying in wait.

'Come on,' said Alfie, his boots laden with water as he ran. 'Get to cover.'

Another mine exploded nearby and a tank roared past, gun booming, the noise reverberating in Alfie's ear.

Arriving at the base of the sand dunes, Alfie and Curtis grabbed a crate of ammo from the stash that had been deposited moments earlier and followed the other men in their unit up into the dunes. They crashed through the scrub until they reached the group of men who were rapidly constructing a howitzer. Alfie and Curtis dumped their ammo and packs, pulled their rifles off their shoulders and stood guard, training their weapons on their surroundings.

'Over there,' muttered Alfie, dipping his head towards a cluster of weather-beaten trees where he'd seen movement. He crept slowly closer, inching his way around the edge of the trees.

'Jeepers!' he exclaimed. 'What are you doing?'

A family of four looked up from their picnic dinner and grinned.

'Exciting show, chaps,' said the father, climbing to his feet.

The smallest of the two little girls leapt up. 'Can I see your gun, mister?'

'Now, Clara,' said her mother, smiling at Alfie. 'He's busy with his training exercise. Let him get on with it.'

Alfie shook his head but couldn't help smiling back. It was first time he'd smiled since running out on Lorna at the dance, and the memory of that made the smile slip from his face.

'You do realise you're in the middle of a fairly dangerous drill right now,' he said gruffly.

The father nodded vigorously. 'Oh yes, don't worry, we'll stay out of your way. Pretend we aren't even here.'

'Alf, what's going on?' Curtis came charging up behind Alfie, then stared in disbelief at the picture before him. 'You're kidding me?'

Alfie shouldered his rifle. 'Good evening, sir,' he said, shaking the father's hand. Then he and Curtis returned to battle.

⌒

'I'll get it takeaway,' said Jethro, dipping through the doors of the Hasty Tasty.

'Order me a bacon sandwich, will you, bud?' said Curtis, lighting a cigarette.

'And I'll have a hamburger,' Alfie called, leaning against a post and shoving his hands in the pockets of his heavy, woollen coat.

He'd been unable to warm up all morning and was grateful for the weak winter sun on his face.

It was a Saturday afternoon, and the city was bustling with locals and Americans on liberty, most of whom were waiting for a baseball game, due to start in a couple of hours.

'What time are we meeting the Baxters?' Curtis asked.

Alfie watched a boy across the street who was doing his best to convince a Marine to let him shine his shoes.

'Two o'clock,' he replied, hoping he sounded nonchalant. Alfie had spent the past two weeks trying not to think of the dance, and of Lorna in particular. He kept replaying the night in his head. Lorna walking into the hall in her terrible outfit. The way he'd teased her about it, but he'd botched the compliment – he liked her rebellious side, just as he'd admired her for running in that race. He'd admired her shapely legs and fitted shorts during the race too, though he'd been disgusted with himself for noticing.

Then he'd stupidly asked her to dance, and it was the very worst thing he could have done because holding her had been glorious, and for a second he'd let himself get carried away. He'd almost gone and kissed the damn girl.

If only Lissa had been able to attend the dance, instead of working a night shift. Then Alfie wouldn't have dared dance with Lorna. Lissa was jealous whenever he so much as looked at another woman, and she'd already accused him of being sweet on Lorna. Something he had vehemently denied.

Shaking his head to clear it, Alfie headed into the coffee bar and joined Jethro standing at the counter.

'Decided I needed coffee too,' Alfie said, placing an order. Once he'd downed his coffee, they headed back outside to wait for their food.

'So?' said Curtis, throwing his cigarette butt on the ground and grinding it with his heel. 'How did the date go last night, Jethro?'

Alfie held his breath. He'd wanted to ask Jethro about his trip to the movies with Lorna too, but hadn't been able to bring it up.

Jethro shrugged. 'It was okay,' he muttered, staring at the ground.

Alfie's heart thumped. 'That bad, eh?'

Jethro looked at him sharply. 'Did she meet someone at the dance?'

'No,' Alfie replied quickly. 'Not that I know of.'

'It's true,' said Curtis, giving Alfie a strange look.

Jethro sighed. 'Well, she made it pretty clear she's not looking for romance, at least not with me. I tried. Slid my arm around her and leant in for a kiss, you know, but she shrugged me off, said she really liked me but as a friend.'

'That's too bad,' said Curtis, shaking his head and glancing at Alfie again.

Thankfully, someone yelled out to tell them their food was ready, and Alfie hurried to retrieve it. They ate as they walked, joining in with the large crowd heading to the game, and briefly nipped into a milk bar for a Coca-Cola to wash down their meal.

Alfie glanced at his watch. 'We'd better get a move on,' he said, quickening his pace. As they approached Athletic Park, he spied Mr Baxter and Peter waiting on the corner where they had agreed to meet, but there was no sign of Lorna.

'Hello, chaps,' said Mr Baxter warmly. 'Lorrie couldn't make it, unfortunately. Had to work again.'

'She told me I have to explain all the rules when I get home,' said Peter, jumpy with excitement. As they entered the stadium, Curtis tapped Alfie's arm and indicated he should hang back.

'I think I know why Lorna brushed off Jethro,' he said in a secretive whisper.

'Why?' said Alfie, staring straight ahead.

'Karen told me she's keen on someone else.'

Alfie tripped and knocked into the man beside him. 'Sorry,' he said, flustered.

'Any idea who?' Curtis asked.

'No.' Speeding up, Alfie pressed ahead to join the others.

Chapter 25

LORNA

Someone knocked loudly on the front door but before Lorna could muster the energy to rise from the couch, Karen burst into the house, sending the door slamming against the wall.

'Lorrie!' she shouted.

'In here,' Lorna called.

Karen appeared, out of breath, her cheeks red. 'You'd think after so many years climbing those stairs it would get easier,' she puffed.

'What's going on?' Lorna had been enjoying a rare moment of having the house to herself. Everyone else had gone to church but her mother had let her sleep in, as she'd worked so hard all week.

'We got it,' said Karen, dancing about the room. 'We finally have permission to marry.'

Lorna sat up. 'That's fantastic!'

'I know,' squealed Karen. 'I was starting to wonder if it would ever happen. I went to St Paul's with Mum and Dad first thing this morning, and we spoke to the priest and he can marry us Saturday after next.'

'But that's so soon.' Lorna hoped Karen couldn't hear the panic in her voice.

'Curtis might leave at any moment, and we don't want to wait any longer. It's just going to be a small ceremony, but I'm hoping your family will all come. And you'll have to ask for the day off work. What a relief your mum has nearly finished sewing the wedding dress — when will they be home by the way? I'm bursting to tell them.'

Lorna shrugged. 'Soon enough, I suspect.'

Karen perched on the edge of the couch, then leapt back up again. 'I'm too excited to sit. Come on, let's go to town.'

'It's Sunday,' Lorna reminded her. 'Almost everything's closed.'

Karen pouted and sat down again. 'Why are you lying here moping?'

'I'm not moping. I'm resting.'

'Curtis said Alfie was here again yesterday.' There was a question in Karen's voice that Lorna chose to ignore.

'Yes, he's been here a few times now. Not because of me,' Lorna added. 'He goes fishing with Dad or plays rugby with Peter. The only time I see him is at teatime and maybe afterwards if we're playing cards or listening to the radio.'

'Nothing going on between you two then?' Karen asked, edging closer on the couch.

'No.'

Karen raised her eyebrows. 'Just thought, now you're seeing more of him . . .' Karen left her sentence unfinished.

Lorna stood up and walked across to the window overlooking the street. 'I regret saying anything to you now,' she said, keeping her back to Karen.

'Look, I know you said not to say anything, but I might have let slip to Curtis that you might have mentioned you rather liked Alfie.'

Lorna spun around. 'Karen, you *didn't*.'

Karen held up her hands in mock surrender. 'He swore he wouldn't say anything to Alfie, but he's convinced Alfie is keen on you too. He says that when he and Alfie were 'round here last week chopping firewood for your dad, Alfie kept looking at you, and his face lit up when you brought them out a drink.'

'I don't think so,' said Lorna faintly. Alfie hadn't been unfriendly to Lorna since the dance, but he'd been guarded. Lorna was sure it was because she'd made it obvious she had feelings for him, and he didn't feel the same way. He was doing his best to show her he wasn't interested without embarrassing them both by saying it out loud.

Lorna spied her family coming up the stairs.

'Here they come,' she said, grateful for the interruption.

Penny was with them too, and she was smiling again. She'd been smiling almost permanently since receiving the telegram telling her that Gordon would be arriving shortly from overseas. With the war in Africa at an end, he was coming home on furlough, along with the other married men plus those single men who had been lucky enough to have their names drawn in the ballot. Rick hadn't been successful, and Lorna felt a strange mix of joy and sadness. It didn't seem right that one brother was able to finally come home while the other had to stay behind.

It wasn't clear yet when Gordon would arrive, as the authorities needed to keep the movements of a ship full of troops a secret, but there was to be a radio broadcast in the next few days which would let them know when he was expected. Their mum was permanently agitated, waiting for news.

Karen ran out to meet Lorna's family at the top of the stairs and they all cheered loudly at her news. Lorna was happy for her friend but unable to shake her worry. Her best friend was marrying an American who was only here because he was training to go and fight a war where he might be injured or killed. This was terrifying enough, but what worried Lorna even more was what would happen after the war. Assuming Curtis did survive, Karen would go to America to be with her husband. They might never see one another again.

It was a day of the wedding was wet and bitterly cold. It reminded Lorna of when the Marines had first appeared in Wellington. So much had changed in little more than a year that it was hard to imagine life before their arrival. She thought of the awkward girl she'd been, of meeting Stan, how handsome and foreign he had seemed. She remembered her first attempt at dancing the jitterbug, the first time a Marine had whistled at her across the street, the changes that had happened to her city.

Lorna spent the morning helping her mother prepare food for the reception, then she headed to Karen's house so they could get ready together.

'Hello, Mrs Robotham,' said Lorna, when Karen's mother opened their door.

'Hello, Lorna, don't forget your shoes.'

Whenever Lorna visited, Mrs Robotham made the same request, even when Lorna was already bending down to remove her shoes. Karen joked it was the equivalent of any normal person saying, 'Lovely to see you, please come in'.

Lorna stepped inside the immaculate house, where she'd learnt to never touch a thing, and hurried towards Karen's room. She found her friend standing at the open window in her coat, smoking.

Karen quickly hid her cigarette behind her back. 'Jesus, I thought you were my mother,' she gasped, before coughing and laughing at the same time.

'It's freezing in here,' said Lorna, joining Karen and reaching for the packet of Chesterfields on the windowsill. 'Can I?'

'Help yourself. Curtis gives me a carton every week.'

Lorna smiled as she lit a cigarette. 'Today's the day.'

'It is.'

'Tonight you'll be a married woman.'

'Finally.'

'Are you nervous?'

'Heavens no, I can't wait. I wish this war would hurry up and end so I can go to America. I can't wait to be somewhere other than New Zealand.'

'I'll miss you,' Lorna said quietly.

'Oh, Lorrie.' Karen pulled her into a hug. 'We'll write, and it's not too late, you could fall in love with a dashing Marine tonight for all we know. Then you can come to America too. I know it's a big place but surely it can't be *that* big. Ooh, Curtis is so excited about the concert, he hasn't stopped talking about it. He reckons Artie Shaw is putting on a show just for us, as a wedding present.'

There had been a buzz about the city all week with news that Artie Shaw and his big band were in town. Lorna had never heard of him, but he was obviously a big deal to the Americans. He was playing at the Majestic that evening, and they were going after the wedding reception.

Karen pulled a folded piece of tinfoil from her coat pocket, opening it so they could stub out their butts, before wrapping them up and putting it back in her pocket.

'Let's get ready,' she said eagerly.

Karen stripped rapidly and stepped into her wedding dress. It was a long-waisted ivory satin gown with a fitted bodice, heart-shaped neckline, a train and long sleeves pointed over the hands. Lorna did up the row of pearl buttons her mother had painstakingly sewed down the back, the girls strangely quiet.

'There, you're in,' she said at last.

Karen did a quick twirl. 'What do you think? Will Curtis love it?'

Lorna blinked back tears. Karen looked so beautiful and grown-up it was almost as if she'd turned into someone else.

'Extraordinary,' Lorna murmured.

Together they swept Karen's hair into an elegant chignon, then Lorna dressed in her full-length powder-blue dress — a surprise gift from her parents — and they took turns doing one another's make-up.

As they were preparing to leave, Karen sat down suddenly on the edge of her bed. She took a deep breath in and let it out slowly and loudly. 'I should have told you this sooner, Lorrie.'

'Told me what?'

Karen avoided looking at her. 'I'm pregnant,' she whispered.

Lorna stared at her friend. 'You're what?' she breathed, even though she'd heard Karen clearly.

Karen gave Lorna a brief apologetic smile. 'Why do you think we've been in such a damn rush to get married?'

'So Curtis knows?' Lorna tried to keep the hurt from her voice. She couldn't believe her friend had been having sex, had gotten pregnant, had been through these momentous things and not shared them with her.

'I almost told you a few times, Lorrie, but I was . . . I didn't want you to think badly of me.'

'I just can't believe that you . . . I mean . . . when?'

'We've spent a few nights at a hotel when he's had overnight leave. I told my parents I was staying with you. And remember when we took that holiday up to Rotorua?'

Lorna nodded.

'We stayed in a room together.'

They both turned as they heard footsteps coming down the hallway.

'Mum and Dad don't know,' whispered Karen, fearfully. 'Can you even imagine how they would react?'

Lorna had heard of other girls who'd reportedly fallen pregnant to Americans. The previous year, a girl they had known at school had gone to stay with her aunt for six months. When she'd returned, her parents had barely let her leave the house. Lorna had heard the aunt was bringing up the baby, but she'd also heard the baby had been adopted out.

There was a knock on the door.

'Ready?' called Mrs Robotham. 'The taxi is outside.'

'Coming.' At the look of uncertainty and vulnerability on Karen's face, Lorna threw her arms around her friend and gave her a hug.

'We didn't exactly plan it,' said Karen, her voice cracking. 'But Curtis is happy and . . .' Karen gulped. 'I am too,' she whispered.

'At least you're not showing,' said Lorna, pulling back and grinning.

They both burst out laughing, gripping onto one another.

'Don't make me cry,' gasped Karen. 'It will ruin my make-up.'

They took a moment to compose themselves, and Lorna attached the tulle veil to Karen's head, along with a coronet of fresh orange blossoms. Karen in turn attached a coronet of red sweet peas to Lorna's hair. Then Lorna handed Karen her trailing bouquet of orange blossoms and carnations, and picked up her posy of red sweet peas and carnations.

'Okay,' said Karen, taking a deep breath. 'Let's get on with it.'

Lorna opened the door and raised her voice. 'It's high time you and Curtis were married, don't you think?'

'Oh absolutely,' said Karen, giggling. 'This wedding couldn't come soon enough.'

The rain and wind seemed to increase in strength during the taxi ride to St Paul's. Lorna sat in the middle of the back seat between the bride and bride's mother, while Karen's father sat in front. Pulling up outside the church, Lorna saw Alfie and Peter sheltering under the portico at the entrance. They put up umbrellas and ran to the taxi to greet them.

'Can't have the bridal party getting wet,' Alfie said, opening the door.

'Thanks, Alfie,' said Karen as she and her father climbed out and sheltered under his umbrella. Lorna and Karen's mother huddled beneath Peter's umbrella as they walked quickly up the path.

They hovered in the small entrance foyer and Lorna peeped through the doors. Curtis was standing at the front of the church beside Jethro, looking nervous. When he saw Lorna, he widened his eyes in a question, and she nodded and gave him a thumbs up. He grinned widely.

'I'd better get back in there,' said Alfie. Lorna jumped at his suddenly being so close behind her and quickly stepped back so he could move past. Peter and Karen's mother followed to find their seats, leaving just Lorna, Karen and Karen's father.

Lorna felt goosebumps on her arms and legs as she checked that Karen's dress and hair were in good shape. 'Ready?' she asked her friend.

'Ready,' Karen whispered.

Mr Robotham opened the door wide, and Lorna stepped through. As she walked nervously down the aisle, Karen and her father following a short distance behind, everyone turned in their seats to stare.

Jethro and Alfie stood next to Curtis and the priest at the front of the church and Lorna kept her eyes trained on the shoes of the priest, a smile fixed on her face as she walked. She knew everyone was more interested in Karen, but she hated being the first one down the aisle.

After what seemed like an age, Lorna reached the spot where she was to stand and looked at her parents in the front pew, who smiled back warmly. Then Lorna watched her best friend complete the final section of her walk down the aisle. Karen was smiling at Curtis with tears in her eyes, and Lorna instantly started crying too. She was annoyed with herself, not just for tearing up, but because she didn't have a handkerchief. Sniffing and blinking, Lorna tried to stop the tears from spilling down her face.

Jethro leant across and tapped Lorna on the arm, then pulled a handkerchief from his pocket and pressed it into her hand. Lorna smiled gratefully. 'Thanks,' she whispered, dabbing her eyes.

She caught Alfie's eye briefly and immediately turned away.

Chapter 26

ALFIE

Alfie was relieved when the official wedding ceremony was over. He'd found it difficult with Lorna standing opposite and had done his best not to look at her: at the blue dress clinging to her body, at the red flowers in her hair, her crimson lips, the small constellation of freckles on her cheeks, her exposed lily-white neck. He hadn't noticed she was crying until after Jethro had stepped forward like a gentleman and given her his handkerchief.

Alfie was no gentleman. He was only a Marine because the military were desperate for men. His mother was right, he was useless, he wouldn't amount to anything. He didn't measure up, and Lorna would be better off with someone else.

Alfie wanted to leave. Following the newly married couple back down the aisle, he wished he could escape to the Cecil and have a few drinks before meeting Lissa at the Majestic. He couldn't wait to see Artie Shaw perform, especially as he'd missed the concert the performer had put on a couple of nights earlier out at camp. Alfie had been in town with Lissa — she'd wanted him to take her to a movie, which he'd found dreadfully boring. To be honest, he often found himself bored when he was with Lissa. Her two favourite topics of conversation, in fact the only two things she seemed to talk about, were the lack of decent shops in Wellington and the fact that he didn't pay her enough attention. But she was a distraction for him. A distraction he needed now more than anything.

Outside the church, the rain had eased and everyone gathered in front of the attractive entryway as the photographer took photos. Alfie could tell Lorna didn't like being in front of the camera. She kept trying to move away, only to have Karen grab her and pull her back to her side. 'No sneaking off just yet, Lorrie,' Karen exclaimed. Lorna smiled awkwardly for the camera and Alfie wished he could tell her she had no need to feel uncomfortable, that she was utterly beautiful.

'Alfie, get in here,' called Karen, waving him over. 'The best man needs to be in the photos too. Stand next to Lorna.'

Alfie stepped forward and stood stiffly beside Lorna.

'Bit closer there, chum,' said the photographer. 'Don't be shy.'

Alfie brushed against Lorna, and he felt her stiffen.

'I won't bite,' he snapped under his breath. Why did he have to be like this with her?

Karen must have heard his comment too as she spun around and glared at him.

'Put an arm around her Alfie,' she hissed, 'and stop acting like you don't care when we can all see that you do.'

Alfie stepped back. 'Think I'll sit this one out.'

'Get in the damn photo and stop acting like an idiot, Alf,' Curtis said loudly.

Alfie shouldn't have come to the wedding, he told himself. No one wanted him there, even his best friend.

Putting a feather-light arm around Lorna's shoulder, he forced a smile, then as soon as the pictures were taken, he charged off around the corner of the church for a smoke.

He was halfway through his cigarette when Lorna strode towards him, having put on her coat. 'Can I have one?' she asked, looking at the cigarette in his hand. He retrieved his packet, tapped one out and handed it over, then lit a match. When she leant close to light her cigarette, he held his breath.

'Do you want to tell me what that was all about?' she asked, blowing out smoke and fixing her eyes on him.

'What?' he asked.

'I realise I made a bit of a show of myself at the dance, Alfie, and it's made things awkward between us.'

'I don't know what—'

'I'm embarrassed bringing it up, but I think it's best to just get it out in the open.'

'Lorna, I really don't know what you are referring to.'

Lorna rolled her eyes. 'I *swooned* Alfie,' she said, her voice full of disgust. 'It was pathetic, truly. I promise it won't happen again.'

Alfie looked at the ground and shuffled his feet. He wished he could tell her that he had wanted to kiss her at the dance more than anything he had ever wanted in the world; that having her close to him had been an exquisite agony.

Lorna sighed. 'Look, Alfie, our best friends have just got married and I'd like them to have a special day.'

'Do you ever think about Stan?' Alfie asked abruptly.

'Your brother?' she said, surprised.

Alfie nodded.

'Yes, I do. I was thinking about him earlier this morning for some reason. Are you thinking about him?'

'I've had him on my mind a lot lately.'

Lorna waited, giving him space to say more, but he didn't know what else to say.

'You must miss him,' she said eventually.

Alfie wished he'd never brought up his brother.

'Did you get on?' Lorna continued.

Alfie shrugged. 'It's like you said, we were different. He was a much better man than me.'

'What makes you say that?' Lorna appeared genuinely shocked.

Alfie didn't know how to reply and was relieved when Lorna's father appeared.

'Okay you two,' Mr Baxter said, slapping Alfie on the back. 'We're heading to the reception. Are you happy to walk now the rain has let up?'

'Of course,' said Lorna quickly. 'We'll be right behind you.'

'Righto,' said her father brightly, and they both watched him leave.

'Can you handle walking to the hall with me?' Lorna asked with an apprehensive smile. The tight knot of tension Alfie had been carrying all day eased.

'I can handle it.'

They walked for a short while before Lorna spoke. 'Why do you think Stan was better than you?'

'Come on, he was every girl's dream, wasn't he? Smart, good-looking, always did and said exactly the right thing, never offended anyone, never failed at anything. He was always going to amount to something, while I never was and now . . . and now he's gone.'

Lorna put a gloved hand on Alfie's sleeve. He turned to face her, his heart thumping so loudly he was sure she could hear it.

'It's horrible to hear you talk this way, Alfie. What's this really about?' she asked softly.

They stared at one another and Alfie wanted to tell her about Stan's letter. He wanted to explain that he had developed feelings for Lorna but that it wasn't right. He was no match for his dead brother.

'Nothing,' he said, flatly.

Lorna lifted her hand. 'Okay,' she replied, matching his tone. They walked the remaining distance to the hall in silence.

The reception was a far more elaborate and formal affair than Alfie had been expecting. Weddings were obviously taken more seriously in New Zealand. Tables had been laid with attractive table settings and there were speeches from the father of the bride — a dull, monotonous ramble where he spoke more of God than of his daughter — and the groom, who went on at length about how lucky he was. Then an array of dishes was laid out on long trestle tables before the bride and groom cut the cake. Alfie sat in his designated spot next to Curtis at the head table and was relieved he wasn't able to look at Lorna, as she was seated further along next to Karen.

Once the meal was over, Curtis led Karen into the centre of the room for a waltz. As best man, Alfie knew he was expected to lead the maid of honour out onto the dance floor to join them. When he stood, Lorna pushed back her chair and strode ahead of Alfie to the dance floor. She looked away from him as she planted a hand on his shoulder. Then they began to dance, their bodies rigid as they maintained a gap between them.

The moment the waltz ended, Lorna let him go and went to ask her father to dance. Alfie slunk to the corner of the room and lit a cigarette. He wished he could stop acting like a grumpy child. Everyone else was enjoying themselves, why couldn't he?

Who was he kidding? Alfie knew exactly why.

'Mind if I join you?' asked Penny, coming to stand beside him.

He offered her a cigarette and Penny took it gratefully.

'I should be enjoying this occasion instead of wishing it was over,' she said in a low voice.

Alfie thought she'd been having a wonderful time.

'I hear your husband is coming home on furlough,' he said.

'Yes.' Penny studied her cigarette. 'I worry he'll be different,' she muttered.

They stood and watched the dancing for a few seconds, Alfie unable to stop himself from tracking Lorna as she made her way over to the table for a glass of water.

'Beautiful, isn't she,' stated Penny.

'Yes,' said Alfie mechanically, glancing at Karen.

'I wasn't talking about the bride,' said Penny, giving Alfie a pointed look. 'Lorna has changed so much in the past year. She's all grown-up and sure of herself. Well, she acts that way at least.'

Alfie didn't know how to reply.

'She's like a sister to me,' said Penny, her voice firmer.

Alfie knew there was a warning behind Penny's words, and he wondered if she had somehow picked up on the feelings he was trying so desperately to hide.

'Should we dance?' asked Penny, stubbing out her cigarette in a nearby ashtray.

Alfie knew he had no choice but to agree.

It was a relief to arrive at the Majestic an hour later. Alfie had caught a taxi with Jethro and Lorna, and had thankfully been able to sit in the front, leaving them to chat in the back. Alfie marvelled at the way Jethro had been able to simply accept his role as a friend to Lorna, seemingly without any bitterness. Karen and Curtis were following in a separate taxi, Karen still wearing her wedding dress as she'd decided it would be fun to wear it at the show.

Inside, the Majestic was packed with barely any space to move. Alfie left Lorna and Jethro standing at the door and pushed his way through the crowd, trying to find Lissa. Eventually, she found him, calling out his name from several feet away with her loud, high-pitched voice.

'You made it at last,' Lissa said, tucking her hand through his arm.

'Thought I'd never get away,' said Alfie. 'I was worried the show might have started without me.' The large band was warming up on stage and the crowd buzzed with anticipation.

'Ooh, here he is,' squealed Lissa, gripping Alfie to her side.

A roar of excitement filled the room as Artie Shaw came bounding onto the stage. Then the band struck up and Artie began to play. Alfie clasped Lissa by the hand and they joined in with the others jiving and shaking around them. He made sure he didn't look around, didn't even try to see where Lorna was. Or who she might be dancing with.

Chapter 27

LORNA

Lorna opened the gate and ran up the stairs to her house. She flung open the door and raced into the living room. 'Is he still here?' she gasped.

Her father grinned as he removed the pipe from between his lips and sat forward in his chair.

'You've just missed him, but he's coming back up for tea.'

Tears pricked Lorna's eyes. 'I can't believe they made me work late today of all days,' she moaned, collapsing onto the couch. 'How did he seem?' she asked, immediately sitting back up.

'Good,' her father replied quickly. 'Very good.'

Getting to her feet, Lorna walked to the window and looked down the street to number 6.

'I could nip down there now, just to say hello.'

'Let Penny have some time with him, love,' said Mrs Baxter, coming into the room. 'They need a chance to become reacquainted. It's been a long time apart.'

Lorna threw her arms around her mother and hugged her tightly. 'Did he seem okay?' she asked again.

Her mum squeezed her back. 'He's fine, Lorrie, don't you worry.'

Lorna didn't know why she felt out of sorts. She was so relieved to have Gordon back home, but she worried she wouldn't recognise him, that he would be different.

'Did he have any news of Rick?' Lorna asked, wishing for the hundredth time her other brother had been granted furlough too.

'He did,' her mother smiled bravely. 'Rick is in good spirits, though disappointed he wasn't in the ballot to come home. He's on leave in Palestine.'

Lorna glanced at her father. 'We have one of our boys home,' he said, stoically. 'Both would have been great, but one is better than none.'

'Absolutely,' her mother said with conviction. 'Give me a hand with tea, Lorrie, once you've changed out of your uniform.'

'Sure,' said Lorna, heading to her bedroom. She glanced at her maid of honour dress as she opened her wardrobe door. The newlyweds were away on honeymoon in the South Island, and Lorna keenly felt the absence of her friend. She still couldn't believe Karen was pregnant, and the secret weighed on her. Karen's plan was to announce her pregnancy in a few weeks – hoping everyone would assume she had fallen pregnant on her wedding night.

Lorna had tried hard to enjoy the reception and the show afterwards, but it had been a struggle. She should have had a great time, and she would have if Alfie hadn't gone and spoiled it. He obviously found her nothing more than a nuisance, and she wished she didn't like him. In fact, she had made a decision, standing in the packed Majestic watching Alfie dance with Lissa, that she would force her silly infatuation away by sheer will, starting right there and then.

Lorna sighed and threw herself down on the bed. She'd agreed to go on a date with a Marine from Idaho and their trip to the movies had been lovely. He'd given her flowers, and held open the door, and hadn't attempted anything amorous. In fact, his manners had been impeccable – boringly so.

Rolling onto her back, Lorna stared at the ceiling. She was nervous about seeing her brother again. Three years ago, she'd been at school. Three years ago, her brother had never held a gun, never been to another country, never been to war.

Lorna was setting the table when she heard the front door open. She stepped into the hallway and watched Penny, then her brother, enter the house. Penny grinned as she let go of her husband's hand and moved to one side so Gordon and Lorna could see one another.

'Lorrie!' exclaimed Gordon loudly. 'I heard you'd gone and grown up on me.'

He strode towards her and gave her a hug so strong he lifted her off the ground. Lorna wanted to speak, but she was too choked up. He had a rich, caramel tan and he'd lost weight, but otherwise he was unchanged. There was still that one eyebrow raised as if he was permanently asking a question, and the dimple on his left cheek. He didn't appear damaged or scarred in any way. If anything, he looked more relaxed than when he'd left. Lorna remembered the three months from when Gordon enlisted to when he finally shipped out to Egypt. He'd been permanently on edge, anxious and aloof.

Gordon let Lorna go. 'Now what's this I hear about you cavorting with the Yanks? The chaps were not impressed when they heard you'd joined their ranks.'

'I even wear an American Marine Corps uniform,' said Lorna, pleased to hear his familiar teasing tone.

'She looks jolly good in it too,' said Penny kindly.

'Just so long as you don't get involved with one of them,' said Gordon sternly. 'We're not impressed with that sort of carry-on, I can assure you. As for Karen . . .' Gordon shook his head. 'I'm disappointed in her, that's all I can say.'

'Yes, well, I'm not exactly thrilled with her marrying an American either,' said Lorna.

Mrs Baxter wandered out of the kitchen to join them.

'Curtis is a lovely young man. Alfie too. In fact, I won't have a bad word said about those American boys.'

Gordon shook his head. 'Mum, I'd keep your views to your-self if I were you. Those so-called lovely American boys have been having a gay old time here with our girls while we've been having a helluva time over there.'

For a moment, there was a heavy pause, then they all moved to the living room and Gordon told them about his experiences — the pyramids in Cairo; visiting Palestine, Syria and Alexandria. He showed them a few photographs he had taken with a borrowed camera. When Lorna saw her brother posing in front of a pyramid, she found it hard to believe that the photograph was real, that he had been all those miles away and seen such amazing sights. They didn't talk about the fighting, though there was mention of their cousin Brian, who had been killed. Gordon said he'd seen Brian the week before he'd lost his life – they'd chatted over a beer at the New Zealand Forces Club in Cairo, and Brian had been full of cheer.

When Aunty Jean and Uncle Jerry arrived, they all squeezed in around the dining table and celebrated Gordon's homecoming with a rabbit stew.

Every time Gordon put down his knife and fork between mouthfuls, he would reach for Penny's hand and grip it tightly. No one commented on the way his fork shook as he raised it to his mouth, or how he jumped when the bathroom door banged shut in the wind. Everyone was happy and determined it would stay that way.

'There's a dance tomorrow night for all the furlough boys,' said Penny, her face flushed and her eyes alight with enthusiasm. 'Would you like to come with us, Lorrie?'

Gordon looked quickly at Penny then away again. 'This is the first I've heard of any dance,' he said, staring at his plate.

Penny looked crestfallen. 'I only found out about it a few hours ago. My friend Becky called and asked if we were going. I told her we'd be there, but if you don't want to . . .' Penny trailed off as Gordon continued to glare at his plate.

'I think it's a wonderful idea,' said Lorna brightly, thinking of all the times Penny had stayed home. In fact, Penny had avoided having any fun, any interaction with the Americans, out of respect for her husband. 'It's high time you got to dance the jitterbug, Penny,' she added.

'Yes,' her mother said. 'Gordon, your wife deserves a night out, don't you think?'

Gordon sighed loudly. 'Well, it sounds like the decision has been made for me,' he replied.

The following evening, Lorna wandered down the hill with her coat over her arm and knocked on the door at number 6. Gordon answered, a cigarette hanging from his mouth.

'Still can't get used to seeing my little sister all grown up,' he said, shaking his head and giving a wry smile. 'Come in, Pen is still getting ready.'

Lorna followed Gordon into the living room and watched him sit stiffly in the chair by the window. He stared outside, as if on guard.

'Penny has missed out on a lot,' blurted Lorna. 'She refused to go to any of the dances.'

Gordon raised his eyebrows. 'I should think so.'

Lorna stood in front of him and crossed her arms. 'Plenty of other married girls haven't done the same, and I for one am going to make sure Penny enjoys the night.'

Gordon appeared to weigh up her comment.

'You're right,' he said at last, getting to his feet. 'I shall endeavour to buck up my act.'

'I'm ready,' gasped Penny, dashing into the room. 'Gosh, it's been such a long time since I had to do my hair and make-up.'

'You look lovely,' said Lorna. 'Where did your beautiful dress come from?'

Penny's cheeks grew pink. 'I made it,' she said softly. 'From some fabric I found on sale.'

'Well, Lorrie's right, my dear, you look simply gorgeous.' Gordon put an arm around Penny's shoulder and kissed her on the forehead. 'Let's hope I can get the hang of this jitterbug everyone keeps talking about.'

They donned their coats and wandered down the road in the fading twilight to catch the tram. Onboard they were met by several other furloughed soldiers heading into town. It was a jovial trip and Lorna thought how nice it would be to go to a dance where the men would all be Kiwis. Hopefully there wouldn't be an American in sight.

The town hall was heaving, and they had to push their way inside past the mass of men gathered at the door smoking.

'Goodness me,' said Gordon, his arm tight around Penny's shoulders. 'This is almost as busy as the Lowry Hut.'

'The what?' asked Lorna loudly above the music.

'It's a recreation hut at Maadi Camp. They put on a few shows for us there.'

'Gordie, my lad.' A tall, dark-haired man with a bushy moustache slapped Lorna's brother on the back. 'This is better than lying in a slit trench and trying to keep the flies at bay.'

Gordon grinned. 'It is, Eddie, it is.' He held out a hand to present his wife. 'This is Penny.'

'Well, it's lovely to meet you, Penny. Gordon has talked about you often, and he's shown me your photo about a hundred times.'

'It's true,' said Gordon, laughing. 'And this is my sister,' he said, waving in Lorna's direction.

'Ahh, the lovely Lorna,' said Eddie, giving a slight bow. 'Another young lady I have heard about.'

'Really?' said Lorna, surprised, yet pleased.

'Absolutely. Now, if you don't already have a dance partner lined up, would you consider joining me?' he said. 'Though I may need a brief lesson. What is this?' he said, gesturing at the dance floor.

Lorna laughed. 'It's very popular. Something the Americans introduced.'

Eddie scowled. 'So I understand. Perhaps we should refuse to dance in protest.'

'Protest?' asked Penny.

'I wish the damn Yankees had never turned up here. Better yet, I wish they'd damn well leave.' He said the words with such venom that Lorna stepped back in shock.

'They are helping to protect us,' she said hesitantly. 'If they hadn't turned up when they did, things could have turned out quite badly. Plenty are giving up their lives in the Pacific as we speak.'

'Yes, well, I still think it should have been us coming home to protect you ladies, not a bunch of overpaid, oversexed Americans.'

'Alright, alright, Eddie,' said Gordon. 'I agree, but it's done now, so let's dance, shall we?'

Chapter 28

ALFIE

Every single Marine had come to dread their regular march up Little Burma Road, as it was unaffectionately known. Even though they had tackled the fifteen-mile route countless times, it never got any easier. Its real name was Paekākāriki Hill, and Alfie suspected they'd also given the dreaded march another name as they found Paekākāriki a difficult word to pronounce. Alfie quite enjoyed trying to say some of the Māori words, especially place names, although he knew his attempts were poor. He'd become friendly with a group of school children who were often hanging around near Mackays Crossing in the hopes of being given some candy or coins – which they invariably were. Most of the children were Māori and they laughed when Alfie practised the language with them. They'd started to recognise him now, which was why as the long line of Marines marched past on a cold, grey morning, Alfie heard them calling out to him from where they hung off the fences beside the road.

'Alfie, say Paraparaumu,' a young boy with thick, wavy dark hair yelled, grinning.

Alfie shook his head and smiled back. 'Not a chance,' he called.

'Ah, go on, Alf,' said Jethro, nudging him. 'Give them a laugh, why don't you?'

Alfie ignored them and reached behind to adjust his pack. It always felt the heaviest and the most uncomfortable at the start of their march, digging into his shoulders and his hips. Today it felt extra heavy, as if it contained not just his gear, but several bricks as well.

The cloud was low, covering the top of the offending hill. Alfie felt a smattering of misty rain on his face and sighed. It had rained so much during the past two months, and he was heartily sick of it. Camp was a challenging place to be when your hut was damp, your boots were permanently wet, and your feet remained cold throughout the night, no matter how many pairs of socks you wore.

With the bad winter weather came ever-increasing bouts of homesickness amongst the Marines. It was made worse by thinking that if they were back home in America, it would be sunny and warm and they wouldn't be forced to march up a damn hill that seemed to go on and on without end.

Alfie didn't feel as homesick as the others. He didn't miss Chicago and he'd grown used to the open expanses of New Zealand. He couldn't imagine going back to a city that hemmed him in on every side. A city full of people and noise and busyness. Here, there was so much space everywhere. So much land and sea and sky. It made him feel both humbled and filled with awe.

The sea in particular had captured him. He'd gotten into the habit of walking down to the shore early in the morning. He loved to watch the waves crash, to gather up handfuls of seafoam and let it blow away from his outstretched palms. He would look out at Kāpiti Island and feel a peaceful stillness he had never experienced before.

More recently Alfie had developed a wariness of the sea, a respect. Especially since the tragedy a few weeks earlier.

He hadn't known the men who had drowned during the landing exercise, but he had been nearby, in another Higgins boat. He'd been so focused on getting their own boat safely to shore, he hadn't noticed when the boat a few metres away started to get into trouble. The landing should never have been attempted in those conditions, at least in Alfie's opinion. The sea had been wild and angry, the storm fierce. Alfie knew that Marines were killed at war, but to drown during a training exercise, without even having a chance to fight in battle, was downright wrong.

'Going to the match tomorrow, Alf?' asked Curtis, marching behind him.

'Sure am,' Alfie said over his shoulder. 'Should be interesting.'

There was a rugby match to be played between the New Zealand Army and the Marines, and a huge crowd was expected to attend.

Alfie hadn't been to town much recently. Instead, whenever he was given liberty, he would hitch a ride with a friendly local and go exploring. Often whoever picked him up would offer him a bed for the night or happily drop him somewhere far removed from their destination. The New Zealanders were big-hearted but in a nonchalant way, not expecting to be recognised or congratulated for their generosity.

It helped that Alfie no longer had to spend his liberty time with Lissa, as he'd decided to put an end to their relationship. He thought it was only fair to admit to her he wasn't looking for anything serious and saw no marriage proposal in their future. Lissa had taken it poorly, and Alfie had felt awful at the time, but also relieved. He was enjoying his travels alone, although he wasn't ever really alone, always being welcomed by locals wherever he went.

There was another reason Alfie had avoided going to town. Since the New Zealand soldiers had returned on furlough, the mood in the city had altered. Marines no longer had the run of the place, and both parties felt threatened. Alfie could see why the returned soldiers might be unhappy with the Americans being in their country, but it wasn't like the Americans had a choice. Many families back in America were questioning why their boys had to be in New Zealand too — miles from home, fighting and dying on small, seemingly insignificant islands in the Pacific.

The Marines who did go to town came home angry, not just at the rude attitude of the New Zealand soldiers, but at their lack of inhibition when it came to drinking. Marines would be embarrassed to appear drunk in public, but the Kiwis seemed to see it as a badge of honour.

Perhaps that was why the rugby match had been proposed — in the hopes that the two sides would bond together over good old sporting rivalry.

It was tough on the girls who were seen with Marines too — Curtis said Karen had been subjected to dirty looks and demeaning words when they found out she was not only married to an American but also pregnant.

Alfie still couldn't believe Curtis was going to be a dad. He'd congratulated his friend, of course, but privately the news made him angry. What was Curtis thinking, getting his wife pregnant when at any moment he could be heading off to war?

A huge crowd turned up to watch the rugby match, and Alfie was a long way back on the grassy slope with a poor view of the field. Curtis and Jethro had given up watching altogether and had retreated to huddle by a shed and shelter from the chill wind.

Alfie found himself scanning the crowd for Lorna, knowing how much she enjoyed the sport. Perhaps she was here now, with her brother and her parents. Maybe they would catch sight of Alfie and wave him over. 'Come join us,' they would call out, as if it was the most natural thing in the world. As if nothing would please them more.

The Kiwis were winning by a slim margin, and Alfie could feel tension building in the crowd as the minutes ticked down. The strained atmosphere made the Americans shout louder and the Kiwis grow quiet. There appeared to be no hostility, though that could turn on a dime.

Alfie wished he understood the rules a little better. Whenever the referee blew his whistle, Alfie was at a loss as to what either team had done wrong. When the game ended, the crowd cheered and a man standing next to Alfie slapped him on the back.

'Hard luck there, son,' he said. 'Your boys put in a good effort, I'll give 'em that.'

It was a mostly happy crowd that filed their way out of the stadium and headed towards the centre of town.

Curtis walked fast, keen to get to the Allied Services' Club to see his wife. She was serving at the soda counter and waved enthusiastically as they entered. Alfie gave a cursory glance around the room and realised he was looking for Lorna again. For weeks he had been making an effort not to let her into his thoughts and had been proud of how well he had succeeded. Until today.

While Curtis raced over to talk to Karen, Jethro and Alfie found a seat at a nearby table.

'What's on the cards tonight then, Alf?' asked Jethro, leaning back in his chair. 'We haven't visited the old Cecil in a while.'

Alfie winced. 'Not sure that's such a good idea. Chances are Lissa will be there.'

Jethro nodded. 'True. Perhaps we should try somewhere else. The Midland?'

They were discussing various options, including being lazy and just catching the train back to camp, when Curtis slunk into the empty chair next to Jethro.

'I hope you haven't got any plans for tonight because I said we'd go to Lorrie's house. Her brother is back on furlough, and he wants to give me the once-over. He's pretty put out about Karen marrying a Yank.'

'Hell,' said Alfie. 'Don't drag us into it, Curt.'

'I'm not going without you, so don't even think of wheedling your way out of it.'

'You made your bed there, Curt,' said Jethro, backing Alfie up.

'Come on,' Curtis pleaded. 'Lorna will be there with her new boyfriend – you can check him out.'

Neither Jethro nor Alfie responded.

'I already said you were coming,' said Curtis. 'And Karen rang Lorna's mom to let her know too. You can't back out and let down dear Mrs Baxter now, can you?' Curtis grinned, pleased with himself.

'Low blow,' muttered Alfie. Then he stood quickly. 'Come on, I need a bourbon. It's nearing 5 o'clock, let's get to the nearest pub.'

'Right behind you,' said Jethro, getting to his feet.

It was warm and cosy in Lorna's living room, the light soft and golden. Alfie felt a comforting familiarity flood through him. He shook Mr Baxter's hand and moved to stand with his back to the fire, Milly coming to flop onto the floor at his side. 'Cold night, sir,' he said politely.

'I've had the fire going since 4 pm,' said Lorna's father. 'Most extravagant of me.'

Alfie laughed, though he knew Mr Baxter wasn't making a joke. If there was one word Alfie found summed up the Kiwi way of life, it was *frugal*.

'We'd be happy to hunt for firewood to fill the woodshed anytime you like,' he said.

'Absolutely,' piped up Jethro from an armchair.

'You're good chaps,' said Mr Baxter, tapping his pipe. 'But I know you're busy. I hear the training has cranked up another notch.'

'They're trying to make sure we're too tired to get into any trouble,' said Jethro.

Mr Baxter chuckled. 'That so?'

'How's Peter?' Alfie had been anticipating Peter racing to greet them the moment they arrived, but he wasn't home. Lorna, Karen, and Peter were down at Penny's house, and Mr Baxter had sent Curtis down to tell them to come back up.

The front door opened and there was a burst of voices and footsteps before everyone entered the room. First Penny, then two men, one of whom Alfie recognised from the photo on the mantlepiece.

'Well hello, here's more of them,' said Penny's husband, stepping forward. Alfie shook his hand.

'Pleased to meet you, Gordon, I'm Alfie. Welcome home.'

'Alfie!' Peter exclaimed, rushing through the door. 'You haven't been to see us in an age.'

Alfie thought for a moment the boy might give him a hug, but Peter paused, clearly thinking better of it. Alfie felt a surge of affection — he wouldn't have minded a hug.

'Hey Peter, how's the rugby season going? Were you at the game earlier?'

'Of course we were at the game,' snapped the man Alfie took to be Lorna's boyfriend. 'I knew you Yanks wouldn't be any match for us.'

'Alright, alright, let's not talk about the damn rugby before we've even finished introductions,' said Karen, entering with Curtis close behind her. Alfie expected Lorna to follow but she didn't appear.

'Alfie,' said Gordon, 'This is my mate, Eddie. We're in the Second Division together.'

Alfie forced a smile as he shook Eddie's hand. 'We've been following news of you boys in the Middle East, and I have to say we've a great deal of respect for you all.'

'Sure do,' added Jethro, approaching to introduce himself.

Alfie studied Eddie. He was tall and slim, and perhaps it was the thick moustache, but he seemed much older than Gordon, and far older than Lorna.

'I hear you've been enjoying the fishing, Alfie,' said Gordon, coming to stand beside him in front of the fire.

'I have,' Alfie replied. 'Your family has been most welcoming.'

'It seems everyone has gone out of their way 'round here to accommodate you boys,' said Eddie, sitting in the armchair Jethro had recently vacated.

'Think I'll go and help Lorna and her mum,' said Karen, an edge to her voice.

'I'll join you,' said Curtis, giving Eddie a pointed look of irritation.

'Gordon, my boy,' said Mr Baxter. 'How about you get everyone a beer?'

Now that Alfie knew Lorna was in the house, he wanted to charge out of the room and down the hallway into the kitchen. He had such an urge to just *see* her that it made his mouth dry.

The next ten minutes passed painfully as everyone tried their best to engage in polite conversation and drink their beer. Jethro asked about the pyramids in Egypt and Eddie gave a detailed description, while Alfie found himself involved in a conversation with Gordon and his father about the exorbitant price of beef. Alfie was relieved when Peter came over and they were able to talk about rugby. When Alfie promised to watch Peter's next game, the boy blushed with pleasure.

'Tea's ready!'

Lorna strode into the room and Alfie held his breath waiting for her to look in his direction. She glanced around and her eyes barely landed on Alfie before they moved on. It was as if his being there meant nothing to her at all, and his heart gave a painful lurch.

Everyone made their way to the dining room and squeezed in around the table. Alfie found himself in a seat between Karen and Peter, while Lorna was at the other end of the table beside Eddie and her father. They didn't say a word to one another all evening. And when Alfie and Jethro said their goodbyes and made a hasty exit as soon as they were able, Lorna waved politely as she stood by the window, Eddie's arm draped across her shoulder.

Chapter 29

LORNA

'It was the one time I wished we were both still working at the munitions factory. Imagine how exciting it must have been for the girls,' said Karen, stepping to the side of the footpath and bending down to re-tie her shoelace. Lorna suspected that soon Karen would struggle to perform this mundane task. She had quite a bump, though she was doing her best to disguise it.

'Even getting to meet Eleanor Roosevelt would not have been enough of an incentive to get me back there,' Lorna replied. The president's wife had made a surprise visit to New Zealand a few weeks ago and had been particularly keen to see and speak to women involved in the war effort. Her visit to the Ford Factory had been splashed all over the papers.

'At least we caught a glimpse of her,' said Lorna. During her brief stay in Wellington, First Lady Roosevelt had also appeared at an all-women event held at the Majestic, which Lorna and Karen had been lucky enough to attend.

'There were so many girls vying for her attention she didn't even look in our direction,' Karen said, straightening. 'Oof, that was tricky.'

'Imagine how hard it will be in a couple more months,' said Lorna.

Karen grimaced. 'I had thought I might make it to America before I had the baby, but Curtis reckons this war is going to last a fair while longer.'

'Have you discussed where you will go?' Lorna asked, with a lump in her throat.

'Curtis says he wants to buy a small farm. He's talking about Texas or Tennessee. Wherever he can get a cheap bit of land.'

'At least you won't be going to one of those big cities like New York,' said Lorna.

'Actually, I think I would have preferred New York, not that I'd tell Curtis.'

Lorna waved at a Marine she recognised across the street, then quickly lowered her hand hoping that no Kiwi boy on furlough had spotted her. It was bad enough she was wearing an American uniform, which Eddie continued to be upset about. It was a constant, exhausting struggle trying to make sure she didn't offend anyone. Though of course her loyalties lay with Eddie and Gordon, Lorna quickly reminded herself.

Lorna sighed loudly and Karen gave her a questioning look.

''Fess up,' Karen said, hooking her arm through Lorna's. 'I know when something is bothering you.'

They were walking along the waterfront, the afternoon sunshine warming their backs on a still, sunny Sunday afternoon; the improved weather a sign that winter was finally behind them. Lorna was pleased to have some private time with Karen. Recently they had either been working or Karen had been with her husband.

'It's nothing really,' said Lorna, wanting to share her troubles with Karen but also not wanting to air them out loud.

'Tell me about *nothing* then.' Karen knocked her shoulder against Lorna's. 'Go on, I won't judge.'

'Yes, you will,' Lorna replied.

'So it's about Eddie then,' said Karen briskly. She had made it clear from the start that she didn't like Eddie, and Lorna knew it was another reason she hadn't seen much of her friend lately. Karen and Curtis had so far declined any invitation to socialise with Lorna and Eddie, not that it would have worked out anyway. Eddie had said numerous times he had no desire to spend any time with the Yanks.

'I know you don't like him very much, Karnie, but that's because you only see him when he's bent out of shape.'

'Because he can't handle the fact that I married an American,' said Karen flatly. 'He's made that very obvious.'

Lorna winced at the hurt she could detect in Karen's voice. 'I'm sorry, it's just hard for him, Karnie, for all of the boys who've come home to find their whole world tipped upside down. They're unsettled.'

'They're more than just unsettled,' said Karen bitterly.

'Eddie is angry,' said Lorna. 'He's angry because he doesn't think he should have to go back to war. He says they've done their duty and it's time for others to step up. All those men who are in forestry or farming, it should be their turn. Eddie says he'd be very happy to cut down some trees or shear a few sheep if it meant he was able to stay home, and who can blame him? It seems frightfully unfair.'

'Hmmm.' Karen looked unconvinced. 'I don't see how that has anything to do with his attitude to the Americans, or to me for that matter.'

'I'm sorry, I know he's been rude to you, Karnie, and I've told him to stop. He's going to make an effort, he promised.'

Karen walked to a nearby bench and sat.

'Let's hope so,' she replied, resting her hands on her belly. 'Do you know, I think these strange fluttering sensations might be the baby moving? But then again it could just be gas.'

Lorna laughed as she sat down beside Karen. They looked at the ships in the harbour, the busy docks, the light reflecting off the water.

'He's talking about refusing,' Lorna said softly, still staring out to sea.

Neither of them spoke for several seconds.

'Deserting?' Karen whispered. 'Is he serious?'

Lorna sighed again. 'He says there's quite a few of the boys who feel the same. There's talk of some kind of mutiny.'

'Have you told anyone?'

'No! I can't do that to him, Karnie, I just can't.'

'How do you feel about it?'

Lorna shook her head. 'I don't know. I feel as if I should respect his decision, but Karnie,' Lorna lowered her voice as an elderly couple wandered past. 'If he gets caught, he'll go to jail. He'll be . . . he'll be . . .' Lorna couldn't finish her sentence.

'He'll be shamed,' finished Karen softly. She swivelled to face Lorna. 'Are you in love with him, Lorrie?' she asked.

Lorna hesitated. 'I *think* so,' she finally replied.

Karen nodded, her expression stern. 'That's what I thought.'

—⁓

'The Italians have declared war on Germany!' Lorna's father strode into the kitchen, grabbed his wife by the waist and gave her a loud kiss on the lips. Lorna widened her eyes in surprise. Clearly the demonstrative ways of the Americans were rubbing off on everyone.

'That's wonderful,' her mum said, her cheeks flushed. 'Does this mean the war will end soon?'

Mr Baxter's expression grew sober. 'There's still a way to go, love. But it's a good sign. Especially with our boys now in Italy.'

Rick had recently transferred to Italy with the rest of the army's 2nd Division, and it was understood the men on furlough would soon be re-joining them there. The previous evening, Lorna and Eddie had gone to the movies and out for a meal with Gordon and Penny. It had been an enjoyable evening, but Lorna had found she was on edge the whole time, worrying Eddie might say something about his increasing obsession with not going back.

Thankfully, he'd been calm and happy, and when they decided to take a walk along the waterfront rather than heading straight home, Lorna had very much enjoyed the way he'd kissed her with a passion and urgency that left her breathless and wanting more.

'I've asked Alfie to come fishing with me the next time we get a good day for it,' her dad said, as Lorna was turning to leave the kitchen.

She stopped. 'That's nice,' she said steadily.

'I did ask Eddie beforehand, but he says he gets terrible seasickness.' Her father sounded defensive, and she felt herself grow angry.

'It doesn't bother me, Dad,' she said. 'I know you like Alfie's company more than Eddie's.'

'Now that's not fair,' her mum said quickly. 'We both like Eddie. He's been a jolly good friend of Gordon's.'

'Yes, quite,' added her father.

Lorna wished she hadn't said anything. She felt as if everyone was against her these days, as if nothing she did was quite right or measured up.

'I can't wait for Peter any longer,' she said. 'I'll be late for work.'

'I'm ready!' Peter yelled, tearing out of his room in his school uniform. 'Let's go.'

'You haven't eaten breakfast,' said Mrs Baxter.

Peter grabbed a piece of freshly sliced bread off the breadboard and stuck it in his mouth. 'I'll eat this on the way,' he muttered through his mouthful.

Mr Baxter gave a stern shake of his head.

Walking quickly, Lorna retrieved Chester from number 9, and they headed down the hill.

'In another year, I'll be able to join up,' Peter said eagerly.

Lorna froze. 'What?'

'I'll be eighteen next September. I can sign up. I'm thinking about joining the Navy.'

Lorna tried to maintain a level of calm she didn't feel. 'The war will be over by then.'

'Alfie says I might still get there if I'm lucky.'

Lorna spun to look at him. 'What a thing to say! When did you see him anyway?'

'He came to watch my rugby game last weekend. You were going to come but you went to church with Eddie instead.'

Lorna had felt bad when she'd said at the last minute she couldn't go to watch Peter's game. It was an important match. If Peter's team won — which thankfully they did — they would be in the regional final. Eddie had asked Lorna to go to a memorial service with him for one of his cousins who had died from a blood infection he'd picked up while fighting in the Middle East. Attending the memorial had been the right thing to do, but it hadn't stopped Lorna from sitting through the whole service wishing she was at the game and berating herself for having such thoughts.

'Well,' said Lorna, quickening her stride. 'I suspect the war will be well and truly over by then, so I wouldn't count on it.'

When she arrived at the depot, her truck was loaded with supplies for Camp Mackay. She opened her door, Chester leapt up into the passenger seat, and they set off.

Peter's talk of joining the services had rattled her. He was too young, too immature. Surely eighteen wasn't anywhere near old enough to be going off to war. He was her little brother, for crying out loud.

Wiping tears from her eyes, Lorna gripped the wheel tightly and told herself there was no point in worrying. After pulling into camp, she climbed out of her cab and wandered over to the mess hut for a coffee while she waited for the supplies to be unloaded. She'd started drinking coffee a few months earlier and the taste had grown on her, especially the American coffee, which had a lovely burnt-toffee smell.

'Hello, Lorna.'

Lorna turned to see Alfie walking towards her in his dungarees. She hadn't seen him out of his dress uniform before, and she was momentarily distracted by the muscles in his forearms below his rolled-up sleeves.

'Hello, Alfie,' she said shortly. 'I don't think it's really your place to be encouraging Peter to go to war.'

Alfie stopped walking towards her and gave a good show of looking confused. 'Sorry?'

'It's hard enough my two older brothers have to be a part of it, but Peter is—' Lorna gulped, unable to say more in case she started crying.

Alfie stepped closer. 'Lorna, I would never encourage Peter to join up. It would kill me if he . . . I doubt the war will still be going a year from now.'

'You told him he'd be lucky if he went to war,' Lorna's voice grew louder. 'Like it's something to be excited about.'

Alfie shook his head. 'That isn't what I said, Lorrie. At least, it wasn't what I meant.'

Lorna slammed her empty coffee cup on the table and strode past him towards her truck.

'Lorna!' Alfie called.

She could hear his footsteps coming closer and quickly started opening her door.

'Lorna, stop.' He reached past her and stopped her door from opening further. 'Please,' he whispered, close to her ear. She was trembling, tears running down her face.

'You're right, you know,' said Lorna, wanting to hurt him the way he was hurting her. 'Stan was a better person than you will ever be.'

Chapter 30

ALFIE

Lorna was engaged. Ever since finding out a week earlier, Alfie had wanted to punch someone or something, from the second he woke till the second he finally managed to fall asleep. Their brutal training wasn't enough to tire him out anymore. While others collapsed on their beds exhausted, Alfie would head out of camp again, up into the hills, walking, running, shooting at rabbits, behaving like a lovesick fool. But nothing he did stopped him from replaying her words. He could never be good enough for Lorna; he would always be second best to Stan.

Alfie returned to camp each night when his legs could barely hold him up. Then he drank beer until he couldn't walk, Jethro and Curtis taking turns to half-carry him to bed.

As for Eddie, he wasn't worthy of Lorna. He wasn't even a very nice person, as far as Alfie was concerned, and yet she'd accepted his proposal. A date had been set, and Alfie and Jethro had been invited. That was the part that hurt him the most. To be invited to Lorna's wedding by her family meant that he was complicit, that he had to accept the whole damn situation.

Alfie wished the Marines were packing up and shipping out. He wished he'd never come to this country. He wished he could go back to fight on some island where his only thought was kill or be killed.

Alfie had almost phoned Mr Baxter to say he was unwell and wouldn't be able to go fishing as they'd arranged, but he hadn't wanted to disappoint him.

'We're hoping for fine weather for the wedding,' said Mr Baxter, throwing his freshly baited line over the side of the boat. 'So we can hold the reception in the back garden.'

Alfie had never known the ocean to be so glassy. It was as if it were under some kind of spell. This was the first time they'd gone out in the boat in the evening, and the sun was fat and hazy as it dropped lower in the pink-tinged sky.

'I don't know why she wants to rush off and marry him anyway,' said Peter grumpily, winding in his line. There was nothing left of his bait but a stringy white strand.

'Eddie is a decent bloke,' said Mr Baxter eventually. 'If Lorna wants to marry him, we need to respect that.'

'They've hardly been together very long,' grumbled Peter, piercing another piece of bait on his hook. He yelped and leapt to his feet, having accidentally stabbed the hook into his finger. Alfie stared at the blood dripping down Peter's hand and an image of Guadalcanal entered his mind before he had a chance to block it. It was of a Japanese soldier who had run towards him with a blade in his hand, screaming words Alfie didn't understand. Alfie had shot him in the chest three times before the boy had fallen to the ground inches from where Alfie lay. Alfie had climbed out of his makeshift stinking hole, walked up to the boy and pressed a finger into the congealed blood spurting from his belly. He'd then reached up to close the soldier's eyes, with his bloody finger leaving red streaks on the dead boy's face.

Because it had been a boy, not a man. A boy who had looked younger than Peter.

Alfie tried so hard not to think about all he had seen and done in Guadalcanal, but he had been that person. That savage.

A familiar chill gripped Alfie's body and he began to shake. He hadn't had a malaria relapse in months.

'Okay, son,' came Mr Baxter's voice. 'You're okay.'

Alfie thought Mr Baxter was talking to Peter, who had removed the hook and was sucking the blood off his finger, but he was kneeling down in front of Alfie's shaking body and squeezing his arm, giving him a look of fatherly concern that Alfie had never been gifted before.

The shaking was so pronounced that Mr Baxter had to assist Alfie up the stairs to their house, where Lorna's mother met them at the door.

'We'll settle him into Rick's room,' she said, taking Alfie's arm.

The boat trip home had been a blur, though Alfie remembered he had curled up on the bottom of the boat while Peter stared at him anxiously.

'Alright Alfie, you'll be alright now,' said Mrs Baxter, as she pulled back the blankets and helped him lie down in Rick's bed.

'He seemed fine,' said Mr Baxter, shaking his head. 'Absolutely fine.'

'You go sort the boat and get yourself cleaned up,' said Mrs Baxter. 'I'll take care of our Alfie.'

Alfie closed his eyes. 'I'm freezing,' he croaked through chattering teeth.

'I'll get the blanket off my bed,' came Peter's worried voice from the doorway.

'What about hospital?' Mr Baxter asked.

'No,' said Alfie without opening his eyes. 'I'll be okay soon. It's just a relapse.'

'What's going on?' Alfie opened his eyes at the sound of Lorna's voice. He didn't want her to see him this way.

'It's nothing,' he stammered.

'Malaria,' stated Mrs Baxter.

Lorna crouched beside him, her face so close he could reach up and touch her.

'You're an idiot,' she whispered, stroking a thumb gently across his cheek.

'I know,' he replied. 'Oh god, Lorrie, I know.'

⌒

The skies outside the window were dark when the chills began to subside and Alfie grew warm. He started to remove the blankets that had been heaped on top of him as his temperature continued to rise.

'Let me,' said Penny, coming into the room and helping to take the final blanket off, leaving just the sheet. She put a hand on his forehead and grimaced. 'You're burning up, Alfie.'

'This is just the start,' he muttered, knowing worse was to come.

It wasn't long before he felt sure he was going to die. His eyeballs burned and his head throbbed with an agonising ache. He was shaking again, not with cold, but with a fever that was doing its best to destroy him.

Alfie drifted into a fitful sleep, then woke to the feel of a cold cloth sweeping across his forehead. Cracking one eye open, he watched Lorna dip the cloth in a bowl and wring it out. She smiled gently as she wiped the cloth across his head again.

'Peter thinks it would be fun to try and cook an egg on your chest.'

Alfie tried to smile but his burning body wouldn't let him.

'Don't get married,' Alfie rasped, then he closed his eyes again.

He'd been in Silverstream hospital for almost a week.

'You've had a visitor,' said a nurse, coming to stand at the foot of his bed. 'She was sitting by your side for nearly an hour, but you were fast asleep.'

Alfie blinked, his eyelids heavy and hot. 'Who?' he asked.

'Not sure, she didn't give a name. Pretty though. American if that helps at all.'

Alfie sighed and ran a hand through his sweat-soaked hair. He needed a wash.

'Actually, come to think of it,' said the nurse. 'She had more of a Kiwi accent, but she was in an American uniform. Isn't that odd?'

Alfie glanced at the empty chair beside his bed.

'Well, hell's bells, he's finally back in the land of the living,' bellowed Jethro, striding down the ward. 'Welcome back, Alf.'

Jethro planted himself on the chair next to Alfie's bed and gave him an affectionate punch on the arm. 'Thought you'd gone and bought yourself a ticket back to the US of A for a while there.'

Alfie smiled. 'I should be so lucky.'

'Curtis will be here shortly. He's been worrying enough for both of us. Geez, that man is going to be a hopeless dad.'

'Did he tell you about his girl yet?' yelled Curtis from the door.

Jethro groaned. 'You said you wouldn't tell!'

'I changed my mind.' Curtis came to stand on the other side of the bed and gave Alfie an awkward pat on the top of his head. 'Thought you'd be sick of this place. Don't know why you insisted on coming back.'

'It's not like I had a choice,' said Alfie. 'Was Lorna just here?'

Jethro and Curtis exchanged a quick look.

'Not that I'm aware of,' said Curtis quickly. 'Now, this is where you ask Jethro about the Californian nurse he's seeing.'

Alfie shook his head. 'Someone was here – I thought it might have been Lorna.'

Jethro put a hand on Alfie's arm as if to stop him saying any more. 'Alf, she's getting married to that knucklehead whether we like it or not.'

'I know that,' snapped Alfie.

'The wedding's tomorrow,' said Curtis gently.

Alfie stared at him, trying to comprehend his words. 'What?'

'Furlough's over soon. The Kiwi boys are going back,' said Jethro. 'The mood around town is pretty low, I can tell you. They've brought the wedding forward.'

'Were you even going to tell me?' Alfie asked, his voice louder.

'Alf . . . bud . . . there's nothing you can do either way,' said Curtis.

Alfie shook his head. 'She can't be.'

'Why didn't you admit you liked her earlier?' said Curtis. 'You had a chance; you had plenty of chances 'cause it was obvious she was keen on you too. But you let her go, Alf. I don't understand why, but you did and it's too late.'

Alfie closed his eyes. 'Go away,' he muttered.

'You can't expect her to be your girl if you always treat her like she's nothing,' said Jethro.

Alfie's eyes flew open. 'Can you both just get out?'

With a sympathetic look, Jethro and Curtis left.

Chapter 31

LORNA

In less than three hours, Lorna was going to be someone's wife. Eddie was going to be her husband. They would be a married couple. Lorna didn't know why she had to keep telling herself these things. Why she had to keep convincing herself it was happening. Lorna had put herself on this path. She had said yes.

'It's okay to be nervous,' said Karen. She was standing behind Lorna's chair, pinning up her hair. 'Remember how I was on my wedding day?'

'I'm not nervous,' said Lorna flatly. 'I don't feel much of anything.'

Karen's hands stilled. 'Maybe that's a normal reaction too,' she said, without conviction.

Lorna picked up her hairbrush and started spinning it around, staring at it until her vision blurred. 'I went to see Alfie yesterday,' she muttered.

Karen hesitated for a second, then continued to insert another pin. 'How is he?' she asked lightly.

Lorna sighed and put down the brush. 'He was asleep.'

Karen moved to Lorna's side. 'Lorrie, look at me,' she said quietly.

Lorna looked up.

'If you still have feelings for Alfie, which I think you do, should you be marrying Eddie?'

Lorna tried to maintain eye contact with her friend but couldn't. She looked down and blinked rapidly. 'Does he know?' she asked, her voice cracking. 'Does he know my wedding is today?'

Karen picked up Lorna's hand and squeezed. 'Curtis and Jethro told him yesterday.'

Lorna felt a pain in her lower abdomen.

'They said he was upset,' said Karen. 'But he . . . you both . . .' Karen threw her hands in the air. 'You're marrying someone else, Lorrie. Don't you think it's a little late for this conversation?'

Both of the women startled at the sound of a loud knock on the door. 'Lorna, I need to speak with you,' came Eddie's muffled voice.

Karen strode across the room and cracked open the door. 'You can't see your bride until the ceremony,' she said firmly.

Eddie pushed the door wider. His eyes had a wild gleam. 'I have to talk with you, Lorna. Alone.'

Karen frowned at Lorna. 'I'll be in the kitchen with your mum.'

Eddie closed the door behind Karen and continued to face it, his hand on the door handle as if to compose himself.

'I'm not going back,' he whispered before turning her way. 'And I thought I could get married first and then tell you, but it isn't fair. On you or your family. I'll be a deserter. I'll bring shame on you all. And I can't . . . I can't do that.'

Lorna nodded slowly. 'It's not a surprise, Eddie. I appreciate you telling me now, before our wedding, but my family and I will support you regardless.'

She walked over to him and put her palms on his chest. He was a good man filled with conviction. An attribute Alfie was seemingly devoid of. Alfie was an American with no interest in a future with her. Lorna's future was in front of her.

'We'll work through it.'

Eddie shook his head angrily and pushed past her to cross the bedroom. 'I can't marry you,' he said, facing the window and crossing his arms. 'I've made up my mind.'

The past couple of weeks had been wretched. First there had been the cancelled wedding, then Gordon had left for Italy and Penny had refused to see anyone. Lorna's mother kept bursting into tears at random moments, and her father sat in his chair smoking his pipe and listening to the radio as if that was all there was left to do in the world. Peter was barely home, Lorna worked as many hours as she could, and everyone was miserable.

Lorna had stood at Eddie's side as he'd announced to her family that the wedding wasn't going ahead. While her father had been angry at first, it hadn't lasted long. Gordon, on the other hand, had almost come to blows with Eddie and had told him he was to have nothing to do with their family ever again. Lorna was surprised at Gordon's vehemence and wondered if perhaps he was more upset about the fact that Eddie wasn't going back to war than he was about the cancelled wedding.

Despite Gordon's strong feelings on the matter, Lorna doubted her brother had been the one to inform the authorities that Eddie had gone AWOL. Less than twenty-four hours after calling off the wedding, Eddie had been caught on a train at a small town in the Waikato, arrested and jailed.

Lorna didn't know what to do. How to behave, how to fill the hours when she wasn't driving trucks. How to fix the atmosphere of misery.

'What about a picnic?' said Karen, emitting a small groan as she sat down next to Lorna. Karen was finding the long hours she spent on her feet at the Allied Services' Club harder now that her pregnancy was advancing. 'The weather is lovely. It might be just the thing for everyone.'

They had met at their usual bench seat down by the waterfront during their lunch break. Lorna was trying to eat her egg sandwich but found she couldn't stomach it. She held it out for Chester and he gobbled it down eagerly. 'I'm not sure anyone is up for a picnic, Karnie.'

'Nonsense. It will be fun, come on.' Karen nudged Lorna with her shoulder. 'You can't keep wallowing like this, it isn't healthy.'

Lorna watched two young boys down at the water's edge. 'Do you think I should go and see him?'

Karen looked at her sharply. 'Who?'

'Eddie.'

'No.'

'But—'

'Lorrie, you are not to go and see that man. He's made his decision and now he has to live with it.' Lorna knew Karen had never been particularly enamoured of Eddie; now she was positively against him.

'He's standing up for his beliefs,' said Lorna. 'And he had reason to be upset. Other men should have gone in their place. If they had, Gordon would still be here.'

Karen sighed. 'Gordon went back because it was his duty to do so and that is extremely admirable. All those boys who went back are incredibly brave.'

Lorna felt tears prick her eyes. She hadn't cried after her failed wedding day, nor when she'd said goodbye to her brother. She didn't want to start crying now either. Not when she wasn't sure she would be able to stop.

'Maybe a picnic would be good for us all,' she said, taking a deep, shuddering breath.

'I'm sure of it,' Karen replied firmly.

It was a breezy, sunny morning and Lorna's mother smiled as she finished packing the picnic basket. Lorna hadn't realised how much she'd taken her mother's smile for granted until it had disappeared.

'This was a jolly good idea, Lorrie,' she said, giving her daughter a hug. 'Just the thing we needed to shake off our melancholy.'

Lorna hugged her mother back. 'It was Karnie's idea.'

'Well, thanks to both of you. Now, go and check your father put the picnic rug in the car, will you?'

Lorna jogged down the steps, the day warm and welcoming. Her father was putting his old cricket bat in the boot.

'Thought we might play a little beach cricket,' he said, glancing down the road to number 6 with a pained expression. They'd hoped Penny would come on the picnic too, but she was still keeping to herself.

A car turned into their road and roared up the steep hill to park behind their car. Lorna waved at Karen in the passenger seat and Curtis behind the wheel.

'Not sure how he managed to convince Karen's father to hand over his car for the day,' said her father under his breath.

Lorna laughed. 'I'm pretty sure it was because he offered to fill it with petrol.'

'Gasoline, you mean,' said Lorna's dad, grinning. They often joked about the Americans' vocabulary, 'gasoline' being a favourite.

Lorna wandered over to greet Karen and noticed two more people sitting in the back seat.

'I hope you don't mind,' said Karen cheerfully, though with a worried look on her face. 'Alfie got out of hospital yesterday, and Curtis invited him and Jethro along.'

Lorna tried to pretend it was nothing of consequence even as her heart thumped and she began to sweat.

'The more the merrier. Hi, Jethro,' she said, as he stepped out of the door closest to her. She then forced herself to smile at Alfie as he climbed out the other side. 'Hi, Alfie, it's good to see you're out of hospital.'

Alfie gave her the briefest of glances. 'Hi, Lorna,' he said quietly.

Her father strode over and shook Alfie's hand warmly. 'Good to see you up and about again, son.'

'I'm sorry to have inconvenienced you, sir,' said Alfie, his voice still oddly quiet. 'I hope I haven't put you off inviting me fishing again.'

Lorna's father laughed. 'Not at all.'

Alfie gave a ghost of a smile.

Jethro approached her father, holding up a metal can. 'Hope you don't mind, sir, but we took the liberty of borrowing some extra gasoline from the Marine stores and thought you might like it?'

Her father's eyes widened. He'd spent almost an hour the previous evening trying to work out how much petrol the picnic was going to use and where they could cut down usage to ensure they would make it through the month.

'That's very generous of you,' said her father. 'Let's hope no one stops me to inspect the tank.'

Since there was no rationing of petrol for the Americans, their petrol had been coloured as a way of making sure there was no cheating.

Karen sidled up close to Lorna. 'Sorry, I wanted to give you warning but there wasn't time,' she whispered.

'It's fine,' Lorna whispered back.

Alfie glanced at her again and she was reminded of when he'd been in Rick's bed, delirious, and had asked her not to get married. She wondered if he remembered saying those words, and what he'd meant by them.

Lorna's mother appeared at the top of the stairs and called down a greeting. Curtis and Jethro shouted 'Mom' and raced up the stairs to give her a hug before helping to carry things down to the car.

'Where's Peter?' Alfie asked.

'He's at the park again,' said Lorna's father, looking at his watch. 'I told him to be back by ten.'

'I'll jog down and get him if you like?' said Alfie. 'I need to get my fitness up again.'

'Thank you, Alfie,' said her mother, giving him a hug. 'He'll be pleased to see you.'

Lorna wondered if she should change out of her old cotton dress, which she'd put on for comfort and because she didn't have to worry about getting it dirty. Then she berated herself for thinking about changing simply because Alfie was going. She stomped back up to the house and busied herself cleaning up the kitchen and putting things away until she was called.

Climbing into the back seat next to Peter, with Milly, who was in the boot, leaning over the backrest and panting in Lorna's ear, Lorna decided she would pretend Alfie's presence was of no consequence. She would make sure her family enjoyed themselves and do her best to do the same.

'Alfie says he'll take me to watch a baseball game the Yanks are playing next week,' said Peter with a grin. 'You can come too, if you want?'

'Sounds fun,' said Lorna lightly. She caught her father's eye in his rear-view mirror and knew he was watching her for a reaction. She wondered how much he had picked up on. Not that there was anything to pick up on, Lorna told herself.

The drive around the harbour was pleasant, and when they arrived at Eastbourne her father stood on the beach with his hands on his hips and said proudly, 'I knew it would be sheltered from the wind here.'

'It's perfect,' her mother said, laying out the picnic rug.

They unloaded the cars, Lorna taking care to stay out of Alfie's way, then her father announced they should all go for a walk. They removed their shoes and paddled in the shallows as they made their way along the beach. Alfie was walking behind Lorna, chatting with her father, and she found it hard to concentrate on Karen's talk about the Eagles Club with Alfie's voice drifting towards her.

'You'd think she had already been to America,' said Karen, 'the way she carries on. She thinks she's an expert just because she has an aunt in Philadelphia.'

The Eagles Club had been set up for Kiwi women who were engaged or married to Americans. It was a place for them to come together and talk, to share their stories, and to learn from members of the American Red Cross about life in America. Karen had joked that they were learning about the three Cs: Cookery, Customs and the Constitution.

By the time they returned to their picnic spot, Lorna was hot and wished she'd brought her swimming costume. She watched jealously as Peter and the three Americans splashed around in the water, their voices loud as they shouted and flung themselves about. Milly was in the water too, swimming excitedly from one person to the next.

'Come on, let's go in,' said Karen, pushing hair off her sweaty face with irritation. 'We can't let the boys have all the fun.'

'I don't have a costume,' grumbled Lorna.

'Borrow mine. It was silly to think I'd fit it anymore anyway.'

'What will you swim in?'

Karen turned to Lorna's parents, who were enjoying a cup of tea beneath the shade of a tree. 'Would you be horrified if I swam in my frock? I have a skirt and blouse I can wear afterwards.'

'Of course not!' Lorna's mother said. 'Swimming is a wonderful idea.'

'What about your underwear?' Lorna asked.

'It'll just be damp, I don't mind.' said Karen. 'Come on, let's do it.'

Lorna desperately wanted to swim, but Karen's costume would be short and tight, and she'd feel exposed.

'I'm not sure.'

'Lorna, love, go for a swim,' called her father. 'It will do you the world of good.'

Lorna looked back at the sparkling water and felt a bead of sweat roll down her spine. 'Okay,' she announced, scrambling to her feet. 'Let's swim.'

Moments later, Lorna was diving into the water and sighing with relief as her body tingled with the sudden cold. It was bliss.

When she surfaced, she swam out until she couldn't touch the bottom and turned to see that Peter had swum out to join her.

'Isn't it great,' he said, treading water beside her.

'It is,' Lorna agreed. 'Though pretty cold.'

'Alfie just told me he can't swim,' said Peter. 'Can you believe it?'

Lorna glanced at Alfie, who was floating on his back closer to shore. 'How can he be a Marine and not know how to swim?' she asked, incredulous.

'He said he never had the chance to learn. I said you could teach him, since you taught me.'

Lorna laughed. 'There is no way I'm teaching Alfie to swim.'

Alfie stood up quickly. He was waist deep and water dripped from his shoulders.

'Did you just offer to teach me to swim, Lorna?' he asked in a teasing tone, raising his eyebrows in the cocky manner she'd once loathed but was now so thrilled to see she found she was grinning uncontrollably.

'Not a chance,' she called as she swam closer to Alfie. 'You'd be the worst student in the world.'

The warm expression on his face vanished and he began to walk backwards out of the water.

'You're right,' he said. 'It would never work.'

His rejection stung her worse than Eddie calling off the wedding.

Chapter 32

ALFIE

He'd done it again. Alfie thought he could joke around in the water, hassle Lorna about swimming lessons the way he used to always tease her. But then she'd swum too close with her wet hair and her full lips and those damn green eyes, not to mention a swimsuit that revealed the swell of her breasts, and his heart had started to hammer in his chest. He'd had to get away from her as fast as he could. He didn't have a choice.

'Would you like another sandwich, Alfie?' Mrs Baxter asked, holding out a container.

'Thanks Mom,' he said, thinking his own mother had never looked at him with such affection.

'You're freezing, Lorna,' said Karen, who was leaning against Curtis, his arm draped around her shoulders. 'Your lips are blue.'

Lorna had barely said a word since they'd gathered on the picnic rugs laid out in the sand dunes.

'There's a blanket in the car,' said Lorna's father, starting to rise to his feet.

'It's fine, Dad,' said Lorna quickly. 'I'm warming up.'

No, you're not, thought Alfie. Her hands were white where they cupped her mug of tea.

'I'll get it,' Alfie said, scrambling upright.

Lorna shot him a venomous look. 'I said I'm fine,' she snapped.

There was an uncomfortable silence as Alfie slowly sat back down. He felt sure the picnic would have been a happier affair if he hadn't come.

'There's cake!' said Lorna's mother gaily. She reached for a big round tin and pulled off the lid. 'It won't keep, so you'll have to force yourselves to eat extra-large slices.'

'I reckon I can manage that, Mom,' said Jethro. 'And if anyone else is struggling, I'll happily help out.'

Everyone laughed and Alfie tried to do the same.

Once the cake had been devoured, thanks to Peter, Curtis and Jethro having second helpings, Lorna's father retrieved a cricket bat and ball from his car, then split their group into two teams. Alfie was put into the same team as Lorna, Curtis and Mrs Baxter, and after a quick rundown on the rules of beach cricket, Alfie's team won the coin toss and chose to bat.

'Our star player should go first,' said Curtis, holding the bat out to Lorna.

Lorna shook her head. 'I'm too full of cake. You start.'

Curtis strode out to stand in front of their makeshift wicket — a thick piece of driftwood stuck in the sand.

'Get ready for a fast one,' called Peter, holding up the ball.

'I'm ready,' Curtis called back.

As the game got underway, Lorna's mum spied someone she knew further along the beach and went to chat, leaving Alfie and Lorna sitting on their own, waiting for their turn to bat. Lorna appeared entirely focused on the game, calling out and clapping, and Alfie felt the yawning space between them.

'I'm sorry about your wedding,' he blurted.

He thought she was going to ignore his comment, but then she spoke, her eyes still on the game. 'You asked me not to get married.'

Alfie stared at her profile. He remembered saying those words, Lorna crouching beside him while his body burned with fever, but he'd had no right.

'Did I?' he muttered.

Lorna glared at him now, her cheeks red. 'Conveniently, you were delirious at the time,' she said coldly.

'Out!' Karen shouted, knocking the driftwood to the ground with the ball in her hand as Curtis sprinted towards her, the bat outstretched.

Lorna leapt to her feet, brushing the sand from her dress.

'Curtis, what were you thinking trying to run? You hit the ball straight to Karnie,' she said, walking towards him and taking the bat.

Curtis shrugged. 'I guess I underestimated my wife's speed.'

Karen grinned. 'It pays not to underestimate me, Curtis,' she said, picking up the driftwood and twisting the end down hard into the sand.

Curtis grabbed her around the waist and planted a kiss on her neck, as Karen squealed with delight.

'Okay, Lorna,' called Jethro, preparing to bowl. 'I hope you're not underestimating me. I've been practising.'

Lorna smiled as she got herself into position. 'Show me what you've got,' she called.

Seconds later, she whacked the ball clean over the top of Jethro's head.

'How am I going to leave her?' slurred Curtis, leaning forward and putting his head on the table.

Eight hours earlier the 2nd Marine Division had been informed they would be shipping out in the next day or two, unlikely to return to New Zealand. There had been a mixed reaction at camp. Cheers at the news they were going back to fight, especially after all the training they had endured, and sadness that they would be leaving the country many had grown attached to. Most seemed pleased at the thought that this was, hopefully, the first step in their return home to America.

Alfie's reaction had been one of numb shock. He'd been desperate to get away, yet now he was going he couldn't imagine leaving. Mostly he couldn't bear the thought of never seeing Lorna or her family again.

Curtis had taken the news hard and wasted no time in trying to drink away his sorrows.

Alfie placed a hand on his friend's back. 'It'll be hard, Curt, but this war won't last forever. There's plenty here who've not seen their wives back home in well over a year.'

Curtis groaned, and his head remained on the table.

'Have you told Karnie yet?' Jethro asked.

'No,' came Curtis's muffled voice. 'I can't do it.'

'You'd better tell her soon or she'll hear it from someone else,' said Alfie.

Slowly Curtis lifted his head, picked up his Budweiser and drained the bottle. He threw it on the grass and staggered to his feet.

'I'm gonna go tell her now,' he said, swaying as he made his way towards their tent to presumably get changed out of his civvies.

Alfie chased after him and caught him as he fell face-first through the door of their hut. 'How about you sleep it off and we'll go into town tomorrow,' said Alfie, leading Curtis to his bed.

Curtis collapsed onto his mattress and curled up on his side. 'I don't wanna leave my wife and child, Alf. What if I die?' he mumbled. Then he was silent, having fallen into a drunken slumber.

Alfie stared at his friend for a few seconds, then he walked to the store and picked up the phone.

⌐

'I wasn't sure if ringing you was the right thing to do,' said Alfie. 'I just didn't want Karen to hear it from someone else.'

Lorna lowered her glass to the table between them and studied the small amount of wine left.

'It's fine,' she muttered.

Lorna had barely said a word to him since he'd arrived at the Cecil with Curtis half an hour earlier. The second Karen had spied her husband she'd burst into tears, and the couple had gone outside to have a quiet moment together, leaving Alfie to take Karen's empty seat at the corner table.

'How has she been?' Alfie asked.

'Not very well,' said Lorna. 'I was surprised she had any tears left. She's been crying all day.'

Alfie drained his beer. 'Would you like another?'

'Sure,' said Lorna. 'Thanks,' she added half-heartedly.

When Alfie returned with their drinks, Lorna was leaning back in her chair with her arms crossed and a determined expression.

'Is your plan to leave and never contact me again?' she asked, as Alfie sat down.

He held her gaze and found he was unable to speak. If he opened his mouth, he would tell her everything. He'd tell her he thought about her endlessly, he admired her, desired her, possibly even loved her.

'Because if that *is* your plan, and I suspect it is,' continued Lorna, 'I have to tell you it's a bloody awful one.' She picked up her glass and drank the entire contents in four or five big gulps.

'I'll have another please,' she said, sliding the empty glass towards him.

Alfie opened his mouth, then closed it again. If she wanted to get drunk, he had no right to stop her.

As Alfie stood at the bar, he noticed Lorna rise from her seat and head towards a couple of Marines sitting at a nearby table. She leant on the back of one of their chairs and laughed at something one of them said.

Furious, Alfie ordered a bourbon from Basil and knocked it back quickly before asking for another.

'Everything okay there, Alf?' asked Basil. 'I hope you're keepin' an eye on Lorna there, her father is a chum of mine.'

'Is he?' asked Alfie, surprised.

'Sure, we went to school together. You'd better go and rescue his daughter before I do.'

Alfie turned to see that Lorna was now perched on a Marine's knee. Something exploded in his chest, and he strode over, took Lorna by the arm and pulled her to her feet.

'Stop it,' he growled.

Lorna shook him off. 'As if you care,' she muttered.

Alfie reached for her hand, but she pulled it away.

'Come back to the table, please, Lorrie. We can talk.'

Lorna barked a bitter laugh. 'Whatever would we talk *about*, Alfie?'

'Stan,' Alfie shot back.

Lorna frowned, confused. 'Why do we need to talk about Stan?'

This time when he reached for her hand, she let him take it. 'If you come and sit down with me, I'll try to—'

'What's going on?' asked Karen, appearing with Curtis.

Lorna snatched her hand away from Alfie's and he felt as if a rope that had been keeping him tethered to her snapped.

'I need to go home,' said Lorna, making her way to the door.

Karen narrowed her eyes at Alfie. 'What did you do?'

Alfie was finding it hard to breathe watching Lorna disappear out the door.

'Alf,' said Curtis. 'If you're going after her, which you damn well should, you'd better go now.'

Alfie looked about wildly. The room had become hazy, out of focus.

'Do you want this to be the last time you see her?' Karen asked, putting a hand on Alfie's arm.

'No,' he replied.

Then he was running. Out the door, down the street towards where she was about to step onto a tram.

'Lorrie,' he called, his voice weak. 'Lorrie,' he tried again, louder this time.

She hesitated with one foot on the tram and turned towards him.

'Wait,' he called.

Lorna shook her head, tears pooling in her eyes.

'It's too late,' she called back, her voice cracking. She disappeared inside as the tram started to pull away.

Alfie chased after the tram and continued to chase it for another quarter mile until it slowed at the next stop. Leaping onboard, his chest heaving, he strode down the aisle to where Lorna was sitting. She looked up at him in shock.

'Lorrie, I need you to get off the tram with me,' he said. 'Please.'

'Why?' Lorna said, crossing her arms and staring straight ahead.

'Because I don't want this to be the last time we see each other.'

'I thought you'd be relieved,' Lorna muttered.

'You couldn't be further from the truth.'

Lorna brushed tears from her eyes, stood up and quickly left the tram, Alfie following behind her. She walked down the street, turned a corner onto a smaller lane, then rounded on him, her face in shadow.

'Okay, we're all alone now, Alfie, you can say whatever it is you want to say.'

Alfie didn't want to fight his feelings anymore. Not tonight, when he was alone with Lorna and it might be the last time he ever saw her.

'I don't have the right words,' he said quietly. 'All I can think about is this.' He stepped closer, slid both hands through her hair, cupped her head lightly and leant in to do what he had daydreamed about for so long. He kissed her on her full lips, groaning as she instantly responded. He continued to kiss her over and over again.

Chapter 33

LORNA

Of course, the infuriating man had to go and kiss her two days before he was set to leave New Zealand, possibly to be killed by the Japanese, highly likely never to return. It wasn't just a kiss either, it was multiple kisses. And it wasn't merely kissing, it was flying through the air with your arms outstretched. It was swimming underwater and the only thing keeping her from drowning was Alfie's lips, Alfie's breath, Alfie's body.

Eventually they'd pulled apart and Alfie had held Lorna's hand as he walked her back to the tram. He'd looked at her with eyes filled with love and passion before kissing her one final time. He'd said 'I'll phone you in the morning.' And she hadn't doubted him, not for a single second.

But he didn't call. All day she waited at home, hovering by the phone as her parents gave her strange looks. She didn't tell them that Alfie had kissed her, but she admitted it was Alfie who she was waiting to hear from.

They looked so pleased.

'I knew it,' her dad said, smiling.

'He's a wonderful man,' her mum said, giving Lorna a hug.

Karen broke the news to her that evening. She knocked on the door and Lorna ran to answer, sure it must be Alfie, convinced he would have a reasonable explanation for why he hadn't been in touch. Instead, Karen said, 'I'm sorry, Lorrie,' and Lorna could see from her expression that Alfie wasn't coming. He wasn't going to call.

'What happened?' Lorna asked.

Karen sighed. 'He's in the brig.'

'What?'

'Curtis asked if I'd come and see you. Alfie didn't go back to camp last night. He was picked up by Military Police down by the port this morning and put in the brig.'

'I don't understand,' said Lorna.

'Apparently he came back to the Cecil to find us, but we'd already left. He stayed for a couple of drinks with Basil and then . . .' Karen sighed again and ran a hand through her hair. 'He stayed for a few more. He was asked to leave when he started a fight with someone, and somehow he ended up sleeping in a warehouse down at the docks until the police found him.'

Lorna shook her head. 'It doesn't make any sense. Why would he do that? Has anyone seen him? Spoken to him?'

Karen glanced behind Lorna to the open living room door, where Lorna's parents were no doubt listening. 'Can we talk in your room, Lorrie?'

Frowning, Lorna led Karen into her bedroom and closed the door.

Karen sat on the bed and clasped her hands on her lap. Keeping her eyes down, she spoke again. 'Alfie asked Curtis to give you a message.'

'Okay,' said Lorna, hesitantly. The way Karen sat slumped, with her head down, made her sick with dread.

'I don't know what happened between you two, but Alfie said to say . . .' she paused. 'He said to say it wasn't going to work out between you and he was sorry.'

'He was sorry he kissed me?' spluttered Lorna.

Karen's head snapped up. 'Oh Lorrie, you kissed?'

'Yes, we kissed. And he said he'd call me this morning. I can't believe this. I thought . . . I was so sure . . . he . . .' Lorna stopped, a sharp pain in her chest.

The night that followed was never-ending. Lorna couldn't sleep, couldn't get comfortable. She kept replaying the previous evening over and over in her head. In the early hours of the morning, she threw on her dressing gown and crept out of the front door. She sat on the top step and watched the sky slowly transform from grey to a luminous blue.

The door behind her opened and her dad came to sit beside her. He didn't speak as he watched the sky too. Finally, he rose and placed a palm lightly on her head.

'Can I make you a cup of tea, love?' he asked quietly.

'Yes, please,' Lorna replied, closing her eyes against the sun as it peeked over the distant hills to shine on her face. She would write to Alfie before she left for work. She couldn't let this be the end.

Lorna wrote to say that she understood he was worried about starting a relationship with her when he was about to leave. She knew he had to focus on being a Marine, she respected his sense of duty. It was understandable to be afraid heading off to war again, but she was in love with him, she scribbled as she sat at her dressing table. She couldn't imagine loving anyone else. If he would just write back to let her know he cared for her too, then she would wait. She would wait until the end of the war when maybe they had a chance. A chance to build a life together.

The postman assured Lorna her letter would be delivered to camp within a few hours, and she did her best to focus on work for the rest of the day. It helped that she was kept busy, the departure of the Marines requiring much movement of goods.

After work, she raced home, but there was no word from Alfie.

Her parents flicked her sympathetic looks as they sat at the table for their evening meal. Peter, seemingly oblivious, talked about the American ships filling the harbour. He'd been down to the port with friends after school to watch as tanks and guns and amphibious boats were winched onto huge battleships. He'd been amazed, he said, at the amount of gear, at the piles of supplies being loaded onto the transport ships.

'They're taking everything,' he said. 'I don't think they have any intention of coming back.'

He went on to tell them about the troops marching to the port with their packs. Of the long lines of them walking up the gangways to board the ships as crowds of Wellingtonians gathered to see them off.

'You should have come down,' he said. 'It was quite the occasion.'

Lorna retired to bed early. She lay on her back and thought of Karen, who would have said her last goodbyes to Curtis. She thought of Jethro, and how she would miss his easygoing kindness. She thought of all the dances she had attended, of the milk bars and popcorn stands. She thought of the Cecil, the Allied Services' Club, of all the ways Wellington had changed since the arrival of the Marines. She fought to stay awake because although she was desperately tired, Lorna didn't want to fall asleep.

Because when she woke, Alfie would be gone.

PART FOUR

AMERICA

APRIL 1946

Chapter 34

KAREN

America was officially too big. How could anyone possibly consider all of this never-ending vastness one country? It was countries within countries, all of them joining together, one after the other, mile after mile after mile. *States,* Karen reminded herself, *they're states, not countries.*

She'd been in the United States of America for eight days. Eight long days of moving from San Francisco in the state of California, through the states of Nevada, Utah, Colorado, Nebraska, Iowa and Illinois. Changing trains at odd hours of the day or night in towns with strange names like Salt Lake City, Denver and Reno. She had spent not just hours, but *days,* on one train, then another, and another, with a two-year-old boy who was incapable of being still or quiet, except when (oh, blessed moments) he gave in to sleep. One minute Ricky was kicking the back of the seat in front with his pudgy little legs, shouting indecipherable words, the next he was passed out fast asleep in the aisle or across Karen's lap, and because she was too afraid to move for fear of waking him, she would try to sleep sitting up, her legs growing numb with his weight. Any sleep Ricky did manage was short and fitful. Karen had passed through every phase of exhaustion and was now simply a body that miraculously somehow kept functioning.

She hadn't been prepared for this part of the journey. Stupidly, Karen had assumed when she finally reached San Francisco harbour after two arduous weeks on board the *Monterey* that the worst was behind her. The sea voyage had been a nightmare from the minute they left the shelter of Wellington Harbour and the ship began to pitch and roll. Both Karen and Ricky had been seasick for the first few days, then Ricky had developed a tummy bug. They were in a tiny internal cabin without a window, and while the American Red Cross did their best to help the several hundred other war brides (many with young babies) by offering daily activities, care for the children, a playroom, lectures about America and movies in the evenings, Karen spent most of the time nursing her sick child, or chasing Ricky as he ran around the decks.

If it hadn't been for Tina in the room next to hers, Karen didn't know how she would have survived. Throwing herself overboard had crossed her mind more times than was healthy. Tina had twin boys a year older than Ricky, and they were boisterous too. Karen and Tina bonded over their 'terrors', as they called them, who spent hours playing amongst the lifeboats, ropes and pulleys, while Tina and Karen sat watching, talking, complaining, taking a moment to draw breath before a ship-hand told them off and they had to drag their 'terrors' away.

Tina was stopped by an official as they disembarked at San Francisco. He studied her paperwork and started to shake his head as he stabbed an accusing finger at a piece of paper. When Tina started crying – the first time Karen had seen her new friend show any sign of weakness – Karen had raced over to see if she could help.

'They won't let me in,' gasped Tina, her eyes red, her breathing laboured. 'Tony's waiting for me. He's right out there,' she said, pointing through a door to a man waving frantically and trying to get past a guard, who was pressing him back with a hand to his chest.

'Please,' she begged. 'These are his children.'

'This is ridiculous,' said Karen, facing the official. 'What is the problem?'

'No more than fifty percent,' the man said crisply. 'It says it right here,' he said, jabbing the form again.

'What!' Karen had said, raising her voice. 'You're not letting her in because she's half Māori? You can't do that!'

Ricky had thrown a tantrum then, probably in reaction to the tension. His face turned beetroot as he threw himself about, screeching. Karen had been approached and asked to leave by two men with holstered guns, and she still felt guilty that she'd given in and let them lead her away. She should never have left Tina and her boys behind like that. She hoped beyond hope that Tina had been allowed to stay, that she hadn't been denied the opportunity – no, the *right* – to be reunited with her husband in America.

Leaving the port, Karen had found a phone to call Curtis once she'd calmed Ricky down, and had only just managed to refrain from bursting into tears. It was the first time she'd heard his voice in almost a year and he sounded different than she remembered, louder and more American.

Curtis was expecting his wife and child to arrive in Nashville later today, but there had been further delays. They'd only left Chicago a couple of hours ago and Karen had been advised she would be unlikely to reach Nashville until early the following morning. What if Curtis gave up waiting? *Stop it*, Karen told herself. He'd waited this long, what were a few more hours?

Two and a half years, Karen thought. I haven't seen my husband for two and a half long years. Ricky had recently had his second birthday, and he had never met his father. Her son had spent all his life so far without a dad. Curtis wasn't there when Ricky was born after forty-three hours of labour. Curtis had missed watching his son learn to crawl, to walk, to eat, to run, to speak. Karen remembered the way Curtis had been fixated on food. He'd told her it was because he didn't have enough to eat as a child, but Ricky was provided with an endless supply of food and yet it seemed as if every hour he wanted something more.

Karen had thought briefly of Stan and Alfie while she'd been walking (and Ricky had been running) up and down the streets outside the train station in Chicago during their five-hour wait for a connecting train. She remembered the brothers had been from Chicago, and she tried to imagine what it would have been like to go from such a big, busy city to Wellington.

Ricky lay on his back in the dirty aisle of the train carriage, throwing his legs up and down in a steady beat in time to the rattle and lurch of the train, his head rolling from side to side, and his eyes glazed. He was as bored and sick of being cooped up on a train as a young boy could possibly be. Plus, he was dirty and no doubt stank, although Karen was so exhausted she'd lost all sense of smell. She probably smelt too, having not had a shower in three days.

Karen caught the eye of the man sitting across the aisle and quickly looked away. He'd already told Karen to control her child and put him in a seat, as if it was a straightforward, simple job that any good mother should be capable of achieving. Surely Karen had already demonstrated to him the futile nature of this task. If Karen was to attempt to lift Ricky off the floor, he would start to scream, just as he had done an hour earlier. He would scream and kick and slap Karen repeatedly on her breasts. Her breasts, which were sore from the bashings they had received from Ricky ever since he was born. He'd been a ferocious feeder and she had weaned him at eight months just to give her breasts a break, though of course this had produced disappointed comments from her mother.

At least Karen wasn't living with her parents anymore. One sliver of a silver lining.

Since her arrival in America, not one person had shown Karen any kindness. She had thought they would all be friendly and welcoming. She had thought they would act the way the Marines had done when they'd turned up in Wellington. But they were the opposite, especially once they heard Karen's accent. She'd learnt to say as little as possible, hoping that no one would single her out as different, yet somehow without her opening her mouth they knew she was a foreigner.

For a while, during the long stretch from Nebraska to Iowa, Ricky had befriended another little boy in the last carriage at the back of the train. They'd played happily together, rolling a stone across the floor to one another, and pointing at things from the window. Karen had been so pleased to see Ricky giggling and chatting with his new friend, and she'd tried several times to draw the boy's mother into conversation, but the woman visibly flinched every time Karen spoke to her. The others in the carriage stared at Karen and her child suspiciously, muttering under their breath, and one older man scowled and told Karen it was best for them all if she returned to her own carriage.

Karen had been undeterred and during a short stop in some town she already couldn't remember the name of, she'd invited Ricky's new friend and his mother to join her at the cafeteria. As they left the train, a stranger had grasped Karen by the arm and told her if she was going to have any chance of living in this country she had better stop fraternising with coloured people. He'd left a red mark on her arm, he'd gripped it so tightly.

When Karen returned to her carriage, Ricky on her hip slapping at her poor breasts and screaming that he wanted to play with his friend, the couple sitting in front of Karen stood up and pointedly moved to sit further away.

Karen felt completely alone. She wished more than anything in the whole entire world that Lorna was beside her.

The train pulled into the station in Nashville, Tennessee at 4.23 in the morning. Karen was ready at the door and threw their two suitcases onto the platform before climbing down with Ricky in her arms. It was warmer than she was expecting and her skin prickled with heat beneath her coat. The dimly lit platform was deserted.

Karen was unable to move, her body shaking with a terror she had held at bay all this time. Curtis wasn't here and she couldn't cope any longer. She simply couldn't survive another minute. Ricky was strangely still and silent as he perched on her hip, as if aware of his mother's state.

'Karnie!' Fast footsteps echoed behind her. Karen turned and started to shake even more. Her teeth were chattering as if she were freezing cold, but she was dripping with sweat.

'Curtis,' she croaked.

Her husband hadn't abandoned her. He was here, striding towards her with that familiar smile she'd missed so much.

'You made it!' called Curtis, breaking into a run.

A low moan escaped Karen's lips, and tears flooded her eyes. She *had* made it and it was hitting her now with agonising clarity. There was no going back.

Chapter 35

ALFIE

He could see Molly through the window. She was sitting straight-backed on a cushion with her legs stretched out in a V shape. Alfie wondered what changed in a human body as it grew. Few adults could sit in that position comfortably, or at all in Alfie's case.

Molly carefully poured water from a pitcher into a mug and slid the mug across the floor to the third in a row of five teddy bears lined up waiting to be served. She spoke to the teddy with a serious expression on her face, waited and then nodded as if satisfied with his answer.

Smiling, Alfie knocked lightly on the edge of the screen door and walked into the kitchen.

'Hallooo,' he called. 'Someone call for a taxi?'

'Me,' squealed Molly, scrambling off the floor and racing towards him. He lifted her off the ground and she wrapped her thin legs and arms around him.

'Hey Spider, had a good day?' Alfie asked.

Agatha came charging through the door, a basketful of washing in her arms.

'Alf, you're early! I was just getting the washing in.'

'Hey Aggie, she been good?'

Agatha placed the washing basket on the table, crossed her arms and narrowed her eyes. 'That little one has been nothing but an angel all day long. It's unnatural, that's what it is. If only just one of my boys had been half as well behaved.'

Alfie lowered Molly to the ground.

'Grab your things, honey,' he said softly.

'I packed already,' she said, running to her duffel bag, picking it up and hoisting it onto her shoulder.

'Course you did,' said Alfie. 'And since you're so organised, we've still got fifteen minutes till we can collect Mom. How about a milkshake?'

Molly widened her eyes. 'Yes please,' she said, walking quickly out of the open door.

'Thanks Aggie,' said Alfie. 'See you in the morning.'

Agatha took three fast steps towards him and squeezed his arm. 'You take care, Alf, alright?'

Alfie felt his throat tighten and nodded once before quickly following Molly down the path to his car. He took the bag from Molly's shoulder and threw it onto the back seat before opening the front passenger door.

'Jump in there, Spider.'

Molly slid onto the seat and shuffled across to the middle, then Alfie closed the door and walked around to his side. With a grin, he placed a hand on the top of the open window, threw his legs over the car door, and landed with his feet on the seat.

Molly giggled. 'Mommy told you to stop doing that. You'll ruin the leather.'

Alfie awkwardly manoeuvred his legs down beneath the steering wheel. 'Well, since it is my car and not hers, I get to make the rules.'

Turning the key, Alfie felt his Cadillac Series 62 convertible come to life. He'd spent far too much of his earnings from his time in the Marines on this car, but he didn't regret it for a second. Driving along Route 66 in his Caddy with the roof down was the only time he felt remotely close to normal.

Alice was a typist at a government office on East Madison. Alfie knew she loved her job, even if she felt guilty about leaving Molly in Agatha's care. Alfie was proud of his little sister and tried his best to help out. She'd fallen pregnant shortly after leaving school and the father had refused to accept responsibility. Unbelievably, it had been his mother who had suddenly and inexplicably stepped in to take charge. She'd given up drinking on the very day Alice had revealed her condition, and had used the money Alfie sent to enrol Alice in a typing class. She looked after baby Molly and encouraged Alice to take the job she was offered at a small accounting firm when she graduated top of her class. When the firm had asked if Alice would be willing to transfer to a new office they were opening up in Springfield, it had been her mother who had urged her to go.

When Alfie eventually returned to Chicago to visit his mother after the war, he discovered she had been replaced by someone else. Someone who opened the door of her small apartment, took one look at her son, and pulled him into her arms as if it was the most natural thing in the world. He'd stayed with her for a week and spent sleepless nights waiting anxiously for her to come home. She worked nights as a cleaner, and Alfie was convinced that it was all too good to be true and his mom would stumble through the door with gin on her breath and yell at him to get up and make something of himself, before passing out in bed.

The whole week he was there she never had a drop of alcohol. And she seemed to understand, in a way others didn't, that he wasn't whole. She never asked him about the war, about his time in hospital, about the months he'd spent on that island deep in the South Pacific called New Zealand. Occasionally they spoke of Stan, but Alfie could see the effort it took for his mom to remember her perfect son, for them both to face his permanent, horrendous absence.

Alice asked Alfie to come and live with her in Springfield. She had a spare room and would love some company in the house, especially at night. Not that she felt unsafe exactly, just a little on edge. So he'd bought his car and driven out of Chicago on Route 66, and a fraction of his core had begun to thaw.

$\sim$

'There's Mommy,' said Molly, pointing to Alice exiting the attractive building where she worked. Alice blew her daughter a kiss.

'How's my girl?' she asked, hopping into the car next to Molly and giving her a hug.

'Alfie jumped on his seat again and then he took me for a milkshake.'

Alice raised her eyebrows at her brother. 'Did he now?'

Smiling, Alfie drove them twenty minutes to their house and pulled into the driveway.

'I'll get the mower out tomorrow,' he said. The grass needed a mow again, even though he'd only cut it the previous week. Every living thing loved spring in Illinois, including – Alfie shook his head as he spotted the overturned trash can – racoons.

'You haven't forgotten about the meeting tonight, I hope,' said Alice, getting out of the car and watching Molly run up the path to the door. 'I'm not letting you come up with another excuse.'

'I haven't forgotten,' said Alfie. Sometimes Alice was more like the older sister, and he was the younger sibling needing to be looked after. He hoped she didn't see it that way. He hoped she still had some respect for her brother.

An hour later, they were sitting on the steps of the front porch, eating bowls of Alfie's chilli. He made it every Sunday and it lasted two nights. The first time he'd made it, Alice had announced it was the best meal she'd ever had in her life. Whether she was being completely honest or not didn't matter, it was enough for Alfie to look forward to cooking it each week.

'How was the date?' Alice asked, looking into her bowl rather than at her brother, presumably aware she was treading on dangerous ground.

Alfie shrugged. 'Not bad.'

Alice gave a short laugh. 'Well, that is high praise coming from you, Alf. Gosh, next you'll be proposing!' She glanced at Alfie and grimaced. 'Sorry,' she said quickly. 'It was just a joke.'

'I know,' said Alfie. 'I'm not going to lose my shit over it.'

Alice gave him a sad smile. 'Good.'

For a while they sat together in silence, watching Molly play on the tyre swing Alfie had hung from the big chestnut tree in the front yard.

'So you might go out with her again, you think?' Alice asked tentatively.

Alfie thought about Ruth. She had straight blonde hair down to her waist and brown eyes with thick dark eyelashes. She had a nice laugh, and she'd gushed over his car.

'I might,' Alfie said as brightly as he could. 'Stranger things have happened.'

Alice insisted on doing the dishes so Alfie could get ready. 'I don't have to do anything,' said Alfie, 'except put my shoes on.'

'What about putting on a new shirt? That one's got a hole in the hem.'

'I don't think I'll get kicked out for my shirt.'

'No one gets kicked out, Alfie. Please, will you get changed? For me?'

Alfie rolled his eyes and went to change his shirt. He was trying to stay calm, to not think about the next few hours, but he was finding it hard.

As he backed out of the driveway, Alice shouted good luck, and he waved at her sitting on the porch step brushing Molly's hair. It was such a small, unassuming scene, but he made sure to take a mental picture of them both, so he could keep coming back to it during the night.

Alfie hadn't slept properly in a long time. So long that he couldn't imagine there would ever be a time when he would sleep solidly through the night again.

The meeting was in a building across the road from the hospital. When Alfie walked through the main doors, he was greeted by a man sitting at a table in the foyer.

'Are you here for the meeting?'

Alfie nodded.

'First time?' the man asked.

Again, Alfie nodded.

'Welcome!' the man said warmly. 'If you just write your name on this tag, I'll show you where to go.'

With his name tag pinned to his shirt, Alfie followed the man up a flight of stairs and into a room where six other men sat in a circle. They nodded and said polite hellos, before shifting their chairs to allow Alfie to pull up a chair and join them.

'Should we get started then?' asked an older man who looked to be in charge. 'We'd love you to tell us a little about yourself, Alfie, since you're new. Perhaps you could tell us where you served?'

Alfie was expecting the question, yet it still made him feel sick.

'Pacific,' he croaked, then cleared his throat. 'I was at Guadalcanal and later at Tarawa.'

A young man beside him with a thick ginger beard nodded. 'A Marine, were you?'

Alfie nodded. 'I was, yes.'

'My brother was in the Marines,' the bearded man said. 'And at Tarawa like yourself. Said it was pure and utter hell.'

Alfie held himself still. 'That about sums it up,' he said.

'We're glad you're here, Alfie,' said another man in the circle.

Alfie tried to acknowledge him, but the room had become dark. It was as if he were in a long tunnel and he needed to find a way to the light he could faintly see at the end, but he didn't know how.

Chapter 36

KAREN

The heat was beastly. Karen hadn't known it was possible for the earth to be this hot and for humans to survive. It seemed as if every morning when she woke, the day was a fraction hotter than the one before. The worst part was that no one else seemed to be bothered. Even Ricky didn't complain. Then again, if Karen was able to run around half-naked for most of the day, jumping in and out of the creek, or lying about on the shaded porch, she probably wouldn't complain either.

Curtis had warned her in one of his letters. Said it would be a different climate to what she was used to in Wellington. Hotter in summer, colder in winter. But he should have been clearer. He should have explained that hot in Tennessee was like having fires rage all around you with no way to put them out.

Karen turned on the tap in the kitchen, cupped water into her hands and threw it over her face.

'Don't make me go, Curt,' she pleaded. 'Please.'

She heard her husband scrape back his chair and come to stand beside her. He didn't touch her or look at her, as they stared out of the window together.

'It might help,' he said quietly.

'Being in a roomful of people who hate me won't help, I promise you that,' Karen snapped, gripping the edge of the bench.

Curtis placed one of his big hairy hands on top of hers, and squeezed. 'Honey, they don't hate you. They just haven't figured you out yet.'

Karen sighed and pulled her hand away. It was too hot for any skin contact, even that of her husband.

'It's been two months. If they haven't figured me out by now, I don't think they ever will. Anyway, what's there to figure out? I can't change the fact that I'm not from around here and I don't like fried chicken.'

She was pleased when Curtis smiled. 'Still can't quite figure that one out myself.'

Karen let her head drop to his chest and groaned again. 'It wasn't supposed to be this hard,' she murmured.

'I know, honey, I know.'

Karen would have liked time to stop right then. For it to be just the two of them. But Ricky came barrelling in the door, and instantly Curtis was moving away, scooping up his son and throwing him in the air. They were both laughing and Karen should have found it adorable. She should have rejoiced that father and son had bonded so quickly and easily, but she was incapable of rejoicing over anything. All she felt, all day long, was a deep, aching emptiness.

She'd been warned during one of the talks given on board the *Monterey* that homesickness might occur. They'd been given suggestions on ways to alleviate their separation from the country they had left behind, but Karen hadn't been listening, because why would she ever get homesick when she was finally on her way to America. To the place she had dreamed of for so long.

There was so much Karen missed about her life back in New Zealand that once she started to list everything, she began to panic. All the things she had taken for granted or hadn't realised even mattered until they weren't there anymore. Karen thought endlessly about the sea, about the yawning absence of it. Karen hadn't gone a day in her life without the water being nearby. Even if she didn't actually lay her eyes on the sea, it was still always *there*. She felt it even if she couldn't see it.

Right now, Karen missed the Wellington winter. The biting wind that would tunnel down Lambton Quay and barrel into her like an overexcited dog snatching at her coat hem.

She missed how everyone was polite but not too friendly. They never stood too close or spoke too loud, demanding to know every single thing about her. They didn't all stare at her intently and tell her exactly everything she was doing wrong, and every word she mispronounced. They didn't try to offer a million suggestions on how she could improve.

Karen missed going for a walk for no reason, especially along the waterfront. She missed going to the movies and spending Sunday afternoons at Lorna's house. *God* she missed Lorna's house. She missed Lorna's mum and dad, and sitting by the fire playing cards, and climbing those stairs to Lorna's front door and knowing that her best friend was there, waiting for her.

Karen did her very best not to think about Lorna, because when she did, she wanted to run down their long dusty driveway, past the rows of cotton that Curtis was slowly removing to make way for more pasture for the cattle he was convinced were going to bring in more money. She wanted to keep running the seven miles to the nearest train station, which was being shut down because no one used it anymore. It didn't matter that if Karen tried to run that far in this heat she would collapse and die — that wasn't the point. She wanted to jump on the one train that came through each day and catch train after train after train. As many trains, as many agonising hours as it took to get back to San Francisco. Back on a ship that would take her home.

'Right, I'd better get back,' said Curtis, placing Ricky on the ground and reaching for his hat.

'Already?' said Karen, unable to hide the whine in her voice. 'Isn't it too hot for fencing?'

Curtis kissed her on the cheek. 'We're in the shade down at the creek. It's not too bad.' He paused at the door. 'See you tonight? For brisket?'

Karen forced a smile and a nod. 'I guess so.'

'That's my girl.' Curtis looked at his son. 'Be good for your mom.'

'Yes, Dad,' Ricky replied, adoration spread across his face.

They're happy, Karen told herself. *The least you could do is pretend to be the same.*

It had been the thought of air conditioning at Sammy's diner that had been the deciding factor in Karen going out. Otherwise, she would have feigned a headache and stayed home with the baby-sitter, even if it was bound to blacken her name further.

'Karnie, sweetie, you came!' Dot enveloped her in a sweaty hug and Karen held her breath until she was released. Dot, their neighbour, only bathed once a week, judging by her body odour. She was married to Don, and the couple were in their early thirties and childless. Karen presumed this wasn't by choice, that they would have liked children, but that something had prevented it. To make up for having no children to look after, they had decided to look after the neighbourhood. To get involved in everyone's business. They set up various committees, organised events and visited everyone in their small town on a weekly basis. Or *daily* in Karen's case, because she obviously needed more help than most.

'Did you water your tomatoes this morning, Karnie?'

'Yes I did, Dot.'

'Excellent. Well done now. And y'all remembered to shut the screens early like I said.'

'I did, there were hardly any bugs inside at all.'

'And how about our meeting tomorrow night? You coming along?' Dot spun and grabbed Curt by the arm as he was escaping towards the bar. 'Curtis, you know Karnie has a Women's Club meeting tomorrow night she can't miss.'

'I do, Dot, I'll be home early.'

Dot let him go, satisfied. 'You've got a good one there, Karnie, a real good one.'

What Dot meant was that she couldn't believe that a man as perfect as Curtis had turned up in Nashville, Tennessee with a war bride from some place no one had ever heard of.

Dot leant closer and Karen resisted the urge to step back. 'Brace yourself,' she murmured.

Karen stiffened. It could only mean Mrs Melville had entered the diner and was heading their way.

'Nice of you to decide to join in, Karen,' said the elderly woman by way of a greeting.

Karen didn't know how to respond. Mrs Melville's eldest son had been killed at Guadalcanal, and it was common knowledge that she had been strongly opposed to America's involvement in the Pacific. She felt, as many others did, that their boys shouldn't have been sent there at all. It was understandable that the Americans should go to the aid of those in Europe because it was closer and there was more of a connection. But to die on some small island in the middle of nowhere, well that was just plain wrong.

Mrs Melville didn't blame Karen as such, but she wasn't prepared to welcome her either.

'Are you taking Ricky to the baseball game in town next week, Karnie?' asked Dot.

'Oh, *god* no,' said Karen. 'He's far too young for that. I can hardly get him to stay still long enough to brush his teeth.'

Mrs Melville sniffed. 'Around here, we don't like to hear the Lord's name taken in vain. It would pay for you to remember that.'

Curtis chose that moment to appear at Karen's side with a bottle of Budweiser in each hand. Karen snatched one immediately and took several loud gulps, her eyes fixed on Mrs Melville's disapproving face.

'Aaah, that's better,' said Karen, wiping her mouth with the back of her hand. 'One good thing about America, you like your beer cold.'

Mrs Melville sniffed again and moved away.

'You're a braver woman than me,' said Dot with a grin.

'I think Alfie might be alive,' said Curtis quietly in her ear.

Karen spun to look at him. 'What?'

'I was chatting to Don's cousin at the bar just now. His brother is working up in Illinois and he said there's a Marine in his son's veteran meetings called Alfie. An Alfie who served in Guadalcanal and Tarawa.'

Karen took in Curtis's hopeful expression. She knew of his desperate desire to find his missing friend.

'It might not be,' she said, softly.

'Yes, but Alfie's from Chicago,' Curtis said excitedly, his voice rising. 'And Chicago is in Illinois.'

Karen hoped it was Alfie, but simultaneously worried that it was. Curtis hadn't been the only one trying to find out if Alfie had survived the war.

'Curt—' she started.

'That brisket smells delicious,' said Curtis, looking towards the large smoking barrel on the outside porch. 'I'm starving.'

The band that had been setting up in the corner chose that moment to strike up a tune, the four band members letting out a high-pitched hoot. Karen hadn't heard country music until a couple of weeks earlier, when she'd been here at Sammy's, feeling just as awkward. She couldn't decide if she liked the music or if she found it a little silly. Curtis reached for her beer and placed it on the tall table beside them. Then he took her hand and pulled her towards the dance floor.

'Come on, Karnie,' he said, putting a hand on her waist. 'We haven't danced together since we were in Wellington.'

Karen wasn't sure if she was going to start laughing or crying. It could have gone either way, so she was pleasantly surprised when laughter won out.

299

Chapter 37

ALFIE

The good thing about drinking most nights was that you barely woke with a hangover. Just a heaviness in the head and a bad taste in your mouth. Alfie left most of his drinking until he was sure Alice and Molly were asleep. Mainly to avoid another lecture from Alice, but also because he didn't want them to look at him with those expressions that made him want to crash his car. Molly's was even worse to encounter because how did a three-year-old know to make that kind of judgement? It wasn't like he was poorly behaved when he drank, or maudlin – at least, he didn't think he was either of those things. He just went quiet, disengaged himself.

One morning Alice told him he was turning into their mom. The mom from before. So he became careful after that. More discreet.

Alfie felt a light mist of rain and looked skyward to let the drops fall on his face. It felt good. *Notice the small things*, he reminded himself. The moon was still there, bright and full, but looking east to the horizon, he could see the sky growing lighter, a hint of mauve and yellow amongst the grey. When the sun rose, it would arc across the southern sky and eventually set in the west. This was the way Alfie had assumed the sun always moved, until his fourth day in New Zealand, when he'd realised that the door to their tent faced north, and yet it also faced the sun. He'd told Curtis of this sudden revelation and they'd both laughed, saying it was just another way the place had everything upside down.

The misty rain turned to thicker droplets and Alfie reached for the bottle of whisky lying on the ground beside him and scrambled to his feet. He examined the contents of the bottle and was pleased to see it was only just below half-full. Since seeing Ruth, he'd been drinking slightly less. Which surely meant she was good for him, that it had been the right decision to continue dating.

They'd been out three times in the past week, and each time they'd ended up in the back seat of Alfie's Caddy. Fooling around but not going too far, because Ruth was a respectable girl she said, she wasn't sleeping with him till he put a ring on her finger.

Alfie walked back through the cornfield, climbed the fence, crossed the road and turned onto their street. He had at least an hour until Alice appeared. He would have a shower, make coffee, prepare Molly's favourite oatmeal and be smiling and ready when she came running in to give him his morning hug.

'You working today?' Alice asked, taking another bite of toast.

'Yep, still working on Bob's roof. Though this rain might put us off.'

'Has he paid you yet?'

Alfie frowned. 'No, but he will.'

Alice hadn't come out and said it directly, but it was obvious she thought it was time Alfie found a proper job. She was always pointing out vacancies in the paper or talking about so-and-so who might have some work. Alfie preferred to do the odd job for people who needed help. Bob was a pensioner who lived alone with a huge lumbering Great Dane called Daisy. Alfie liked helping Bob, just as he'd liked fixing the chicken coop at Mrs Waller's house. The $30 payment he received from the Marines each week was enough to get by, and he was paying rent, buying groceries. He was doing the best he could.

'Forgot to tell you,' said Alice, dipping her head towards the wooden bowl at the end of the bench. 'Mail came for you yesterday. Different handwriting, but same sender address.'

Of course Alice would have examined the envelope. She was desperate to know why Alfie was suddenly receiving mail.

Alfie retrieved the envelope from where it poked out beneath the bowl. Alice was right, it wasn't Curt's messy handwriting. *Probably Karen*, he told himself, stuffing the letter into his pocket, and beginning to tidy up the breakfast dishes so Alice wouldn't ask questions.

'You never mentioned Curtis before,' said Alice, watching him. 'Just like you never talk about the Marines.'

'Yep,' said Alfie, still tidying. 'It's deliberate, obviously.'

'Why?'

''Cause I'm trying my best to forget all about that time.'

'But don't you talk about it at your meetings?'

Alfie shook his head. 'I listen to *them* talk about it. That's bad enough.'

'But Curtis was your friend, wasn't he?'

Alfie paused for a moment. Curtis was the best friend he'd ever had. 'I guess.'

'Are you going to open the letter?'

'Later,' said Alfie, then he went to call up the stairs. 'You all set there, Spider?'

'Coming!' Molly called.

Alfie reached for his keys.

He didn't last long at Bob's. They sat inside and drank coffee, played some cards, watched the rain grow heavier. 'Think we might have to leave it till tomorrow,' said Alfie, at last.

'Think we might, son,' Bob replied.

Alfie wished he hadn't called him son.

Before he left, Alfie gave Daisy a walk and filled her water bowl. He drove down Route 66 and thought about going all the way to Missouri, but decided he didn't want to use up the gas. He turned into a narrow lane and drove to the end. Parked. Stared at the rain on his windscreen. Eventually, Alfie pulled the envelope from his pocket.

When the ginger-bearded guy, Jake, had approached him at his third veterans' meeting and handed over an envelope, Alfie, for one heart-stopping moment, had thought it was from Lorna. He'd thought that somehow she'd tracked him down. Alfie hadn't wanted anyone to know where he was — it was the first thing he told his mom when she opened her door and hugged him and he cried so much his ribs hurt for days afterwards.

'I don't want anyone to find me,' he said, sobbing. 'I can't face them.'

The letter hadn't been from Lorna, but from Curtis. He'd found out that Alfie was attending the same meeting as the son of someone or other. Curtis was living outside of Nashville. Karen and their son Ricky were with him now, finally. Curtis was a farmer, just as he'd planned, and he loved it, but Karen was finding it tough settling into America. She was homesick, Curtis wrote. So homesick she wasn't herself.

Curtis had asked Alfie to write back. Just to let them know he was alright. Curtis had spent a long time wondering what had happened to his friend.

Alfie didn't write back. Not initially anyway. Eventually, after receiving his fifth letter, in which Curtis said that if he didn't hear from Alfie soon he'd have to head on up to Springfield to find him, Alfie sent a short reply.

Alfie wrote to say he was well. Living with his sister, dating a pretty girl, driving a nice car. He sent his regards to Karen and Ricky, said he'd look them up if he was ever down in their neck of the woods.

Alfie didn't hear back from Curtis after that. Nothing for almost three weeks, until this letter he was holding in his hands.

It was from Karen, and Alfie smiled the moment he read her first sentence.

Dear Alfie,

You are hands down the most self-centred, arrogant man on this planet. Like hell you'll look us up next time you're 'down in our neck of the woods'. You must come visit and that's the end of it. And don't you dare make any flimsy excuses. Curtis thought of you like a brother. Stop breaking his heart and come see him. We can't keep on like this — knowing you're out there and not being able to reach you. Please, Alfie. Come.

Love Karen

Chapter 38

KAREN

Curtis complained it was poor timing, Alfie arriving the day his first head of cattle was to be delivered. Curtis needed to stay at the farm and make sure everything went smoothly. Karen didn't mind going to pick Alfie up – it gave her something to do, plus she could see Curtis was nervous about seeing his friend again.

The train must have come in early, and Alfie was waiting outside the station. He gave a short wave and jumped in the passenger seat before Karen had even turned off the engine.

'Hi,' said Karen, surprised at how emotional she felt. 'You're actually alive then.'

'It appears so,' Alfie replied, swivelling to look at Ricky in the back seat.

'Hey there, little man.'

Ricky stared at him, open-mouthed. He was fascinated by all men and irritatingly better behaved whenever a male was present.

'Hello,' Ricky replied politely.

Alfie raised his eyebrows at Karen. 'Looks like his dad.'

'You're not the first to say that,' said Karen, not caring if she sounded bitter.

They looked at one another awkwardly until Karen leant over and gave him a brief hug. He responded stiffly and she quickly let go.

'I wasn't sure how I'd cope seeing you again, to be honest,' said Karen, concentrating on pulling back out onto the road. ''Cause I really hated you for a long time there.'

She glanced at him, and something about the way he sat braced, as if waiting for an axe to fall, made her hesitate.

'You look well,' she said, instead of launching into the speech she had planned. The one where she told him of all the damage he had caused.

Alfie took a long time to respond.

'You too,' he said eventually. 'Feels odd though,' he added. 'Seeing you here in America and hearing your accent. I'd forgotten . . .' his voice trailed off.

Karen had only ever seen Alfie in his Marine uniform, with his hair trimmed short and neat, and his shoes polished. He appeared smaller now, and less — she tried to find the word she was looking for — less confident maybe? His shirt could certainly do with an iron, and his hair was a mess, but then he had just spent all night on a train, and she knew what that was like.

'How was the trip?' she asked. 'Did you sleep at all?'

'Not really,' said Alfie. 'But it was fine. How's motherhood?'

Karen gripped the steering wheel tighter. 'Ricky's non-stop,' she said. 'And idolises his dad.'

'So it's tough then,' said Alfie. 'On you.'

Karen looked at him with surprise. 'Yes, but then so is moving to a new country.'

'I bet.' Alfie seemed about to say more, but didn't.

They drove for a while in silence.

'How's your sister?' asked Karen.

'Good. Great actually. And her daughter, Molly, she's great too.'

'Good.' Karen replied. It was odd, having to make conversation. Since Karen had arrived in Nashville, she'd barely needed to think of anything to say. She'd gotten used to everyone around her asking questions, talking fast, barely waiting for her to answer.

She pulled into their driveway and pointed at the newly built cattle yards.

'Curtis will be over there,' she said, honking her horn. 'He said to let him know when we'd arrived.'

Continuing on to the house, she parked and turned off the engine. Taking a deep breath, she faced Alfie, who was about to open his door.

'Alf,' she said softly.

He paused but didn't look her way.

'I haven't told Lorna yet . . . that you're alive. I'm not sure if . . . if it's a good idea.'

Alfie didn't move. He stared out of the window at the house, his hand on the door handle, like he expected someone to appear.

'Out!' Ricky screamed, kicking his legs up and down. 'Out,' he yelled again, pawing at the door.

Alfie jumped out and opened the rear door.

'Alright tiger,' he said calmly. 'No need for that.'

Curtis strode into the kitchen as Karen was trying to convince Ricky to eat his broccoli.

'He's upstairs,' she said. 'Having a shower.'

Curtis ruffled his son's hair and sat down at the table with a grunt.

'How is he?' he asked.

'Fine,' said Karen. 'As far as I can tell.'

At the sound of heavy footsteps on the stairs, Curtis rose to his feet. Alfie appeared in the doorway wearing a different shirt, his hair still wet.

'Hey Curt,' he said, stuffing his hands into the pockets of his jeans. 'Sorry it's been a while.'

Curtis took a step towards Alfie then stopped.

'Did you hit your head?' he asked, crossing his arms.

'Sorry?' Alfie asked, confused.

'Did you get amnesia or something? Is that why you straight-up forgot about me?'

Alfie looked down and shuffled his feet.

'No, Curt, I didn't hit my head. But I guess I did damage it — mentally, I mean.' He raised his head and Karen saw anguish in his eyes. 'I spent eight months in a psychiatric hospital, not really knowing if I wanted to be alive.'

'After Tarawa, you mean?' asked Curtis, his voice gentle now.

'Yeah, and the other places, I guess.'

Curtis unfolded his arms and looked from his wife to his son, blinking rapidly, then he launched himself across the room and threw his arms around Alfie.

'It's good to see you, bud,' he said, his voice wobbly.

Karen saw how tightly Alfie hugged Curtis in return.

Stepping away, Curtis wiped his eyes and smiled sheepishly. 'How about a beer?'

'Love one,' Alfie replied.

For a while they sat around the table, Curtis doing most of the talking. He told Alfie about the farm, his plans, his dreams. Alfie told them his mom had given up drinking, that he was doing the odd job here and there, that he enjoyed spending time with his niece. They'd drunk another two beers by the time Karen took Ricky upstairs for his bath.

When she came back down, they'd moved to the chairs on the porch, their feet up on the railing. Karen's shoulders lost some of their tension.

'I told Ricky you'd play a bit of catch before bed,' she said, sitting down on the top step and letting the exhaustion she'd been holding at bay all day wash through her.

Curtis leant forward and tapped her shoulder with a Budweiser. 'Drink?' he asked.

Karen took the bottle gratefully.

Ricky was in heaven as the three boys threw the ball to one another and Karen slowly sipped her beer. She knew she should go inside to prepare the meal, but the breeze was lovely, and she was the happiest she'd been all day. All week in fact.

'I've got something to show you, Alf,' said Curtis, jogging around the side of the house and returning seconds later. He held up the cricket bat he'd fashioned from a piece of wood.

'It's not much like the real thing, but I did my best. I've been trying to teach Ricky, but he keeps saying pitch instead of bowl.'

'And he shouts "home run" whenever he connects the ball and bat,' Karen called.

Alfie laughed as he took the bat and examined it. 'It's not a bad effort, Curt. A little heavy maybe.'

'Yeah, Ricky can hardly even hold it.'

Karen could see Alfie's mind had gone elsewhere. She wondered if he was thinking of the first time he'd played cricket. She wanted to mention how Lorna had bowled him out first ball and how everyone had found it hilarious. Everyone except Alfie. But she was afraid to bring up Wellington, or Lorna. Afraid it would make her instantly burst into tears.

Karen went to the kitchen and put the meatloaf in the oven. She fried the potato, set the table and called the men inside. After they'd eaten, Curtis took Ricky upstairs to read him a story and settle him into bed. It was the time of day Karen looked forward to the most.

Alfie sat at the kitchen table while Karen washed the dishes. He'd offered to help but she'd turned him down. Karen had lost track of the number of beers Alfie had drunk, and his eyes were glazed as he thumbed through a magazine. He hadn't said a word to her since Curtis had taken Ricky upstairs, and there was an uneasiness between them, as if they were waiting to see who would speak first.

'She's married,' Karen suddenly blurted. 'In case you were wondering.'

Alfie continued to thumb through the magazine as if he hadn't heard.

Karen tried again. 'Lorna got married just before I left New Zealand,' she said, raising her voice.

'I heard you the first time, Karnie,' said Alfie flatly.

Karen threw down her tea towel and sat down opposite. She clasped her hands on the table and waited. He closed the magazine and sat back, his head lowered.

'I think it was a mistake,' said Karen quietly. 'I think Lorna was just desperate to move out of home.'

'Why?' Alfie asked, still looking down.

'Because it was too hard. You do know Gordon and Rick were both killed, don't you?'

Alfie looked up sharply. 'What?' he croaked.

'Lorna's dad got a telegram a week after you boys left, saying Rick had been killed. It's why Curtis and I called our son Ricky, in memory. Penny received a telegram informing her of Gordon's death two months later. Lorna wrote to tell you, Alfie. Did you not get any of her letters? I know she wrote to you constantly.'

Alfie ran his hands through his hair and took a long, shuddering breath. 'I got her letters,' he whispered.

'So what? You didn't open them?'

Alfie took several seconds to respond, and when he did his voice was harsh. 'I read the first couple, but I got rid of the rest.'

Karen felt a white-hot anger rise in her belly. 'Jesus, Alfie, now I'm hating you again. Why would you do that?'

''Cause I wasn't going back. I wasn't ever going to see her again and it would have . . . it would have been too hard.'

'She waited so long to hear from you, Alfie. Why didn't you write — to Curtis, to Lorna, to anyone? They all cared about you, why didn't you once care about them?'

Alfie rose to his feet and gripped the edge of the table with shaking hands. 'I'm beat. Goodnight, Karnie.'

He walked out of the room, and she listened to his slow, steady footsteps on the stairs.

Chapter 39

ALFIE

When Alfie arrived downstairs in the morning, Curtis was already out on the farm and Karen was on the back porch watching Ricky throw stones.

'Morning,' he said.

She held up her mug. 'There's coffee on the stove.'

In the kitchen, Alfie poured himself a coffee and added a heaped teaspoon of sugar. He went back out to join her.

'Sorry I ran off last night,' he said, sitting beside her on the top step. 'I can be a bit of a bastard, as you know.'

Karen shrugged. 'Sorry to spring all that on you.'

Alfie took a long sip of coffee and looked across the fields of cotton shimmering in the heat. 'It's a bit hotter than Wellington.'

'I told Curtis last night I couldn't wait for winter, and he said I should be careful what I wish for,' said Karen. 'Apparently it's brutally cold instead of brutally hot, but I'd still take it right now.'

Alfie cleared his throat. 'Curtis mentioned you were finding it hard. Being away from New Zealand.'

Karen looked at him sharply. 'He did?'

'He's worried about you.'

Karen sighed. 'There is so much I miss, Alfie, and almost all of it I was never even aware of until it wasn't there anymore.'

'Such as?'

'Ice cream,' she stated. 'I miss our ice cream, and our bread, and our chocolate, and footpaths, and trees. Proper big trees with thick green leaves. I miss feijoas, even though it's not feijoa season, because they don't grow here – no one's even heard of them. And I miss Lorna, and going to Lorna's house, and walking along the waterfront. I miss the sea, Alfie. I never realised how much I would miss the sea.'

'I miss it too,' said Alfie carefully. It was the first time he'd allowed himself to talk about New Zealand.

'Remember how you used to go fishing with Lorna's dad?' said Karen with a laugh. 'God, he loved it. You had that entire family eating out of your hand.'

Alfie frowned. 'That's not . . .' He rose to his feet. 'Think I'll go and see what Curtis is up to,' he mumbled.

Karen leapt up and grabbed his arm. 'I was joking, Alf, I'm sorry. I just meant they all liked you.'

She fell against him then, crying, and he put his arms around her. 'I'm finding it hard to be nice at the moment,' she sobbed. 'To anyone. It's like I want the world to be as miserable as I am.'

'I know that feeling,' Alfie murmured.

'Why does it have to be this hard? Why can't I buck up? Curtis is probably regretting ever marrying me.'

'No, Karnie,' said Alfie. 'He's just as crazy about you as ever.'

Karen let him go and pulled a handkerchief from her pocket. 'How would you know?' she asked, sniffing and wiping her eyes.

'Because he told me last night.'

Karen's eyes glistened. 'Really?'

'Yes, really.'

'Thank goodness,' she breathed.

'How about I get us another coffee,' said Alfie.

Karen nodded. 'Thanks.'

When Alfie returned to the porch a moment later, he found Karen was standing beneath the giant oak tree giving Ricky a push in his swing. He joined her and they took turns pushing Ricky higher and higher as he squealed.

'Have you met anyone?' asked Karen suddenly. 'You live with your sister, so I assume you aren't married, but are you seeing someone?'

Alfie hesitated. 'I am, yes.'

'What's her name?'

'Ruth. We've only been dating for a couple of months.'

'But you like her? She makes you happy?'

'She makes me happier than I thought I could be.'

'That's good.'

'Hmm.'

'Alfie,' said Karen, punching him lightly on the arm with a smile. 'You're allowed to show some enthusiasm for the poor woman.'

Alfie smiled. 'Maybe I'm just too old.'

'Old!' said Karen. 'How old are you?'

'Twenty-two.'

'That's *young*, Alfie.'

'I feel ancient.'

'You don't look it.'

'On the outside, but on the inside . . .' he let his sentence go unfinished.

Ricky had grown tired of the swing and leapt off as it was mid-flight, landing with a loud smack on the ground. Alfie winced, but Ricky picked himself up and ran inside.

'I'm pregnant,' said Karen, staring after Ricky.

'Congratulations,' said Alfie, noting the lack of enthusiasm in her voice.

'Thank you.'

'Stan was in love with her,' blurted Alfie, surprising himself with his words.

Karen looked at him, confused. 'What?'

'Stan was in love with Lorna. He told me in a letter.'

Karen's eyes narrowed and she took some time before she spoke. 'No, I don't think so.'

'He said if circumstances had been different, he would have married her.'

Karen was still looking at him as if trying to process his words. 'Is that why you never dated Lorna?' she asked slowly. 'Because of Stan?'

Alfie stared out across the fields. 'It would have been dishonourable to . . .'

'Jesus, Alfie!' Karen pushed him in the chest and he stumbled backwards. 'That is the most ridiculous excuse I've ever heard. Stan wasn't keen on Lorna like that, he was . . . when he said "if circumstances had been different", he was referring to something else.'

'What?'

Karen bit her lip and lowered her voice. 'This is just between you and me, Alf. I haven't told anyone, and I never will.'

'Told them what?'

Karen took several seconds to speak again. 'Stan's friend, Derek, he was an unpleasant person, but he was the first Marine who asked me out and we dated for a short time. He told me once that Stan had made a pass at him. That he thought Stan was keen on him, in . . .' Karen appeared to search for the right word. 'In a romantic sense.'

Alfie shook his head. 'What are you trying to say?'

Karen glared. 'You know what I'm trying to say, Alfie.'

He thought about Stan's letter again. *She's the only one . . . if circumstances had been different.* 'But he wrote . . .'

'Whatever he wrote, you have misinterpreted it. I was there, Alfie. There was never any romance between Stan and Lorna. They were just . . . they liked each other's company. I never asked Lorna directly, but I got the impression she knew about Stan. She knew and it didn't bother her.'

Alfie turned and strode to the end of the porch. He gripped the railing, his heart beating so painfully he wondered if he was having a heart attack.

'Does this mean you still think about her? About Lorna?' Karen asked quietly.

Alfie's reply was instant, like a reflex.

'I never stop.'

PART FIVE

WELLINGTON, NEW ZEALAND

MARCH 1947

Chapter 40

LORNA

Ironing Patrick's shirts was her least favourite in a list of many jobs Lorna disliked yet was responsible for. It was up to Lorna to do all the washing, the cleaning, the shopping and the cooking, just as it was Lorna's responsibility to make sure Patrick had his every need met. Lorna knew this because he'd told her, outright, three months after their wedding day. He'd been disappointed when the marmalade had run out. She'd been meaning to buy more but she hadn't been to the shops yet because she was waiting to use the car — the car Patrick took to work each day. When she'd mentioned this fact — that she could only do the shopping on Thursday night when the shops stayed open late — he'd replied that Lorna needed to think ahead, to anticipate when something might run out before it did so.

'My wife needs to make sure my every need is met,' he'd said, nuzzling her neck and putting a hand on her bottom.

She'd pushed him away, furious. 'Don't!' she'd said, wanting to say a whole lot more.

He'd taken the car keys and left, probably back to the pub he'd just come from, and Lorna had needed to apologise the next morning – apologise with words, and with her body.

They had been married for over a year now and yet Lorna still felt she barely knew her husband. She couldn't seem to work out what would please him. It was a constant effort to get Patrick to smile, let alone laugh. Lorna had mentioned it once, how he hardly ever looked happy, and he'd replied that he was a serious man, as if it was something he was proud of and she should be too.

Lorna was so lonely when they were together in the house. He barely spoke, and seemed uninterested in having any conversations with her. When she expressed an opinion on something, anything, he pursed his lips and shook his head, as if she'd disappointed him.

Karen had been right, Lorna thought, running the iron over the collar of Patrick's Wednesday shirt – yes, he had a specific shirt for each day of the week. *Marrying him had been a mistake.*

Lorna knew it wasn't fair, but she occasionally found herself blaming her parents. They should have risen above their grief to see Patrick for who he was, instead of going along with the engagement and wedding as if it were of little consequence. Peter had tried, angrily telling Lorna she was making a mistake, but he'd been permanently angry ever since their brothers had been killed, and Lorna hadn't taken his words seriously.

The bitter truth was she only had herself to blame. Patrick had moved back to number 4 Ranui Road with his mother, Mrs Waters, at the end of the war. One day he'd fallen into step with

Lorna as she was going to catch the tram. He'd asked her on a date, and Lorna had been flattered by his attention, relieved to have someone to distract her from her grief. She'd been reminded of how much she'd been impressed by him at school, and he still had that same self-confidence, still spoke with such sureness, as if he was addressing a crowd. She'd welcomed his ability to take the lead, to make decisions for them both.

Ironing complete, Lorna turned her mind to how she might fill the hours in the day until Patrick arrived home at six, when he would sit in his armchair, turn on the radio, and Lorna would bring him his whisky so he could relax after a hard day's work as a bookkeeper, while she finished preparing their meal.

Sighing, Lorna put the ironing board away and wandered listlessly around the house she had disliked from the moment she'd laid eyes on it. Again, only herself to blame, though she doubted Patrick would have taken her opinion into account had she expressed one. He'd announced that the house was just what they were looking for. It was close enough for him to walk to work, a fact Lorna reminded him of a month after they moved in, when she realised he was taking the car to work each day; it was a new build so maintenance would be minimal; and it had three bedrooms, one for them and two for the children they would have. Patrick didn't mind that the house was ugly and sat in the shade of a hill. He didn't mind that nothing dried on the clothes line because the sun never shone in their small backyard where not a single tree or shrub had been planted.

Lorna had bought a couple of hydrangeas and planted them along the fence, but Patrick had been annoyed at her for spending money on something 'frivolous', especially as there had been no discussion on the matter. Lorna learnt she couldn't spend any money without checking with her husband first.

Lorna found herself standing in their gloomy hallway, staring at the front door, willing something to happen. For someone, anyone, to knock. With a cry of annoyance, Lorna tore off her housecoat and snatched at her cardigan hanging by the door. She slung her handbag over her shoulder, marched outside and strode down the street, stopping abruptly in the patch of sunlight at the corner. Closing her eyes, Lorna tipped her head up and let the sun warm her face. She wished Karen wasn't miles and miles away in America. She ached to see her friend, for them to go for a walk along the waterfront and talk.

The burst of energy that had driven Lorna from the house dissipated, to be replaced by a weariness that made her want to sit right where she was on the footpath and not move. Instead, she forced her tired body to move in the direction of home. Not the house she shared with her husband, but the house she had grown up in on Ranui Road.

Mrs Fogerty no longer lived on the corner, having passed away the previous year. Instead, there was a young couple with a baby. They'd moved there from Christchurch, and every time Lorna saw them, they were smiling. Today was no exception. As Lorna turned onto Ranui Road, Maggie was watering their garden, while baby Lily lay on a blanket beneath a magnolia tree. Maggie loved her garden, and according to Lorna's mother, spent countless hours tending to the ever-expanding flowerbeds.

Lorna waved at a smiling Maggie, and she waved back.

'How are you, Lorna?' she called. 'Have you time for a cuppa?'

'Not today I'm afraid,' said Lorna, attempting to match the cheeriness in Maggie's tone. 'Another time?'

'Just knock on the door,' said Maggie warmly.

Lorna made sure she kept the smile on her face until she was past Maggie's line of vision, then let it go. Maggie was only one year younger than Lorna and yet Lorna felt old enough to be her mother.

Number 5 was quiet, with the girls at school and Mrs Rowlson working. Her husband continued to work on merchant ships and was gone for long periods. It had been his idea for Mrs Rowlson to find some part-time work as a secretary while the girls were at school.

'My wife's a smart woman,' he'd told Lorna when they'd bumped into one another on the street. 'It's good for her to be out there using her brain.'

Though she tried not to, Lorna couldn't help but look across the street at number 6 as she went past. Penny had sold the house and moved to Hawke's Bay two months after Gordon's death. She couldn't stay, she'd told Lorna. She had to try to start again somewhere new.

A retired couple now lived in Penny and Gordon's house. Lorna rarely saw them and hoped it stayed that way.

It was far too quiet at number 9, with no Chester leaping and barking at the gate. Mr Bolton had come home from the Victory Day celebrations to find Chester lying by the gate, taking short, sharp, whimpering breaths. He'd phoned Lorna from the vet, being kind enough to ask her if she wanted to say goodbye. Her own dog Milly died the following week.

At the bottom of the steps leading up to her house, Lorna paused. She wondered if her mum would be dressed yet, if there would be any fresh milk. At least one of the front windows sat open, which was a good sign.

Lorna knocked and let herself in.

'Hello?' she called. 'It's me.' The hallway seemed even narrower and mustier than she remembered. 'Mum?'

Frowning, Lorna checked the living room, then made her way to the kitchen. It was tidy. No dirty dishes or mess on the bench. Lorna inhaled the smell of baking. Opening the pantry door, she lifted the lid of the biscuit tin and saw freshly baked Anzac biscuits. Her mum hadn't baked since Rick and Gordon had died.

Lorna replaced the lid, then walked over to the kitchen sink and looked out of the window. Her mum was crouched before a garden bed in her sunhat and gardening gloves. Lorna ran a hand down her face to compose herself, then headed for the back door.

'Hi Mum,' she called, approaching with a smile.

'Lorrie!' Her mum scrambled to her feet. 'What a lovely surprise.' She threw her arms around Lorna and squeezed her tightly. 'It's good to see you, love,' she murmured.

'You too,' said Lorna, tears pricking her eyes. She took a deep breath. 'You made Anzacs.'

'I did indeed.' She pulled off her gloves. 'Let's go have one with a cuppa, shall we?'

They sat in the shade of the front porch and Lorna found herself constantly glancing at her mum. She looked calmer and cheerier than Lorna had seen her in a long time.

'I see number seven sold,' said Lorna, sipping her tea. For years she'd harboured a daydream about buying the long-empty house and had been disappointed when she'd spotted the sold sign. Recently she'd been thinking of the house every day, imagining how it would be to have a place of her own that she could slowly restore. A garden she could nurture back to life. 'I always liked that place.'

'Yes, you did!' said her mum. 'When you were nine or ten, you told everyone you were going to live there one day.'

Lorna laughed bitterly. 'That didn't quite go to plan.'

Her mum reached over and put a hand on Lorna's arm. 'Lorrie, honey, I want nothing more than to see you happy.'

Lorna tried to force herself to say she was fine, but she couldn't. She couldn't pretend anymore.

'I know you do, Mum,' she whispered. 'I want to be happy too.'

'Your father thinks you should move back home.'

Lorna's heart thudded. 'He what?'

'We were so wrapped up in our grief that we let you marry that man, Lorrie. I'm sorry.'

Lorna slowly placed her teacup on the small table between them.

'I thought you liked Patrick,' she said. 'You're always so nice to him and . . . why have you never said anything like this before?'

Her mum sighed. 'We figured what was done was done, but he's changed you, Lorrie. You've lost your spark. Life's too short for you to be with him and miserable. If losing Rick and Gordon has taught us anything, surely it's that.'

Lorna thought of her brothers again. Of their bodies lying in graves thousands of miles away from home.

'I miss them,' she murmured. 'I miss our life before the war.'

Her mum didn't respond, but her expression was enough. Lorna sought to change the subject so the despair on her mum's face would disappear.

'Dad's car is here,' she said, dipping her head towards the road. 'Did he walk to work again?'

'He did,' her mum replied. 'He'll have to get his shoes resoled soon if he keeps it up.'

Lorna's dad had taken to walking the four miles to work, except when it was wet and cold. It took him over an hour each way, but he said it was good for him and helped to clear his head.

'Can I borrow the car, do you think?' asked Lorna. 'I need to get a few things.'

'Of course!' said her mum. 'What about going for a drive first? It's a lovely day. I could come with you. We could go over to Eastbourne or . . . oh I forgot, I can't, I have a committee meeting in an hour.'

Her mum had joined the local residents' committee a few weeks earlier. Lorna was pleased she was getting involved with things again.

'Actually,' her mum paused and gave Lorna a strange look. 'I had a letter from Karen yesterday.'

'Did you? You're lucky, I haven't heard from her in a while.' Lorna knew her friend was busy, but she wished Karen would write more frequently — once a fortnight simply wasn't enough.

'She had some news,' said her mum.

'Not bad news, I hope?'

'No, no . . . it's good news. Karen just felt that perhaps your father and I might like to decide, well, if it was something we should share with you or just, well, let it be.'

'Okay, now I'm lost. What are you talking about?'

Her mum bit her lip and studied Lorna. 'Alfie is alive.'

Lorna held herself very still. 'What?' she breathed.

'He went to visit Karen a few weeks ago, and Curtis thought it was best they didn't tell us, but Karen said it didn't feel right, saying nothing.'

No one had heard from Alfie in three years. He'd never replied to her letters, never made contact with anyone. Lorna had convinced herself Alfie had been killed during the war because the alternative — that he was alive and had simply left her and his time in New Zealand behind him — was too hard to accept.

'He's alive,' said Lorna, saying the words to try to convince herself.

Tears filled her mum's eyes. 'Karen said he didn't want to talk about what happened when he left New Zealand. Apparently, after the war, he spent time in a psychiatric hospital.'

Lorna didn't know how to respond. She should be pleased that Alfie was alive, but she didn't feel pleased. She felt . . . what did she feel? Agitated? Annoyed? She got to her feet.

'Well, that's good news, isn't it? Dad must have been pleased. Have you told Peter? Peter rather idolised Alfie, didn't he?'

Her mum stood and tried to reach for her, but she stepped away.

'Lorna, honey.'

Lorna didn't want her mum looking at her that way.

'It's fine, Mum. Like you say, it's good news.' She glanced at her watch. 'I should go.' She retrieved her mug. 'Thanks for the tea.'

'What about taking the car?' her mum said, following her inside.

In the kitchen, Lorna placed her mug on the bench and gazed out of the window at the woodshed. The woodshed where Alfie had gone to get firewood to light the fire that he said he wasn't lighting for her benefit, but he was. He was, and they both knew it.

Alfie being alive didn't change anything, she realised. She was never going to see him again. Her life was going to carry on just as it was.

'I'll make do with what I have, Mum,' she said, firmly. 'There's nothing that can't wait.'

Chapter 41

ALFIE

'A letter arrived for you,' said Alice, pointing to the envelope stuck to the fridge.

Alfie finished his mouthful of pie. 'Thanks,' he said.

'It's another one from Mrs Baxter in New Zealand,' Alice continued. 'How did you know her again?'

Alfie focused on his knife and fork. 'She's a mom who used to invite me 'round for 'tea', as they called it, which as it turned out didn't mean drinking tea but having dinner, which is confusing because you could also be invited to places for tea, where you actually drink a cup of tea.'

Alfie wasn't sure why he was rambling.

'How interesting,' said Alice, looking alert. 'What else?'

'What do you mean?'

'Well, you spent quite a long time in New Zealand and yet you never talk about it. What else was different? Did you like it there? Were the people friendly?'

'That's a lot of questions.'

Alice held her palms up and shrugged. 'I've got nowhere to be.'

It was a Wednesday night and Molly had already gone to bed by the time Alfie arrived home. Alice had kept the leftover chicken pie warm in the oven, and she was keeping Alfie company at the table, having eaten with Molly earlier.

'Well, it was different in lots of ways,' said Alfie. 'Everything was closed on Sundays, for a start.'

'Everything?' Alice exclaimed.

'Yessir,' Alfie nodded. 'And they drove on the other side of the road, which took some getting used to. Also – and this upset the boys – all the bars closed at six.'

'You're kidding me.'

'So there wasn't a whole lot to do in the evenings, though they put on some dances, and there was the cinema, which they called the movies or the flicks. There were quite a few things they said differently.'

'So did you like it there?' asked Alice.

'Yeah,' Alfie said, clearing his throat. 'I liked it there. It's a beautiful country, and the people – they're quite a reserved bunch, but friendly – they went out of their way to make sure the Marines were looked after, that's for sure.'

'Do you miss it at all?' Alice asked.

'I miss the sea,' said Alfie quickly.

'I've never seen the ocean.'

'Never?' said Alfie. 'Well, I'll have to take you and Molly to the coast sometime.' Alfie paused. 'Mr Baxter used to take me out fishing, with their youngest boy, Peter. I enjoyed those fishing trips. We caught snapper.'

'Snapper?'

'It's a type of fish. Tasty it was, really good.'

'Sounds like you spent quite a bit of time with the family.'

Alfie nodded.

'How old was Peter?'

'I think he was around fifteen when I first met him. He loved his sport – they all do in that country. Peter played rugby, and he was good at it too.'

'What on earth is rugby?'

'It's sort of like American football, but different. They loved horse racing too. We enjoyed going to the track and placing bets.'

'So if Peter was the youngest, who else was there in the family?'

Till now, Alfie had been pleased with how he'd been able to talk about New Zealand. He'd enjoyed reminiscing, even though it made his chest ache. But now he wanted to stop.

Shovelling the last of his pie into his mouth, he stood and rinsed his plate in the sink. Alice was watching him, waiting for an answer, but he hoped that if he acted as if the conversation was over, it would be.

'Alf?'

Alfie filled his glass from the tap and took several gulps.

'Who else was there in the family?' asked Alice firmly.

Alfie faced her. 'Two older brothers who were both killed during the war, and a sister,' he added.

'Oh, how awful!' said Alice.

Alfie nodded. 'Think I'll give Ruth a call, see if she wants a visitor.'

Alice studied him. 'You okay?'

'Sure, I'm fine.' Alfie grabbed the envelope off the fridge and headed towards the door.

'Alf?'

He paused in the doorway and turned. 'Yep?'

'How old was the daughter?'

Alfie shrugged. 'Not sure, nineteen, I think.' He left quickly, taking the stairs two at a time. It wasn't until he was standing in his bedroom that he realised he hadn't phoned Ruth. Rather than risk going back downstairs, he closed his door, sat on his bed and turned the envelope over and over in his hands.

Finally, he ripped it open and skimmed Mrs Baxter's words. Yet again, there was no mention of Lorna and he sagged with disappointment. What was he expecting anyway?

It was the third letter he'd received from Lorna's mum in the past three months and he had yet to write back. He'd tried a couple of times and ended up throwing his attempts in the trash. Karen must have given them his address, and it had been a shock when the first letter arrived from Mrs Baxter. She'd written to say she was pleased to hear Alfie had survived, that she remembered him fondly and hoped he was settling into a new life after the war, though she appreciated it wouldn't be easy. She said Karen had mentioned he'd been in hospital and she hoped he was recovering well. It had been a polite, kind letter, telling him so little.

In her second letter, which he received a few weeks later, she wrote that the weather had been so cold that it had briefly snowed, and that she had been to visit Penny, who was now living in the Hawke's Bay and training to be a dental nurse. The letter had been two pages long and yet she hadn't mentioned Gordon or Rick or Peter or Lorna. It was like she was holding back from telling Alfie anything of importance — perhaps it was her way of making a point, of punishing him for disappearing.

The most recent letter was less than a page long and it was more direct than the previous two. Mrs Baxter said she was disappointed she hadn't heard back from Alfie, that she was finding it hard with no children at home. There were so few signs the Americans had ever been in New Zealand. *I miss those times,* she wrote. *Remember when you and your friends came for Christmas and you brought a gramophone? I haven't laughed or danced like that since.*

Alfie still had nightmares about Tarawa. About being in the Higgins boat with Curtis and Jethro, and being stuck on the reef. They'd been warned the tide hadn't risen as hoped, but they were still ordered to approach the beach. Everyone had assumed the aerial bombardment the Airforce had inflicted on the Japanese earlier would have caused enough damage to ensure the Marines would be able to make it to shore without the enemy causing trouble.

Instead they had been sitting ducks. Trapped in their boats as bullets rained down. Their only chance of survival was to jump out and try to wade over the reef to the shore, with more and more bullets coming at them from every direction. Alfie had never been so scared in all his life, and when he'd looked at Jethro beside him, tears were running down his cheeks and his hands were shaking so hard he couldn't hold his rifle. It kept slipping into the water, and Alfie would snatch it up and hand it back. Alfie couldn't bear the petrified look on Jethro's face, so he tried to keep his eyes trained on Curtis a little way in front of them. Then he saw Curtis take a bullet and fall forward into the water, and Alfie had turned to Jethro to tell him that Curtis had been hit, but at that very second Jethro was hit in the face by a bullet. A bullet went right into his eye and his face was exploding with blood and skin and bone, and Alfie was screaming. He was screaming and no one was listening because it was impossible to hear any of their screams above the constant barrage of gunfire.

Alfie's next memory is of being on the beach, of crouching up against a sandy bank and looking back towards the ships anchored further out and all the bodies floating in the water, drifting towards shore, piling up like logs of driftwood on the sand.

'Later, we were sent to gather up as many bodies as we could find. We laid them in lines so they could be identified.' The men sitting in the circle bowed their heads as Alfie continued. 'We identified Jethro, but Curt . . . Curtis wasn't there, so I asked around and eventually I found out that he'd survived. He'd been taken to the ship's hospital and sent home with the wounded.'

'So you lost your two best buddies,' said Ethan, sitting opposite. 'On your first day at Tarawa.'

Alfie nodded. 'I went numb after that. Just kept going until the end. It was after . . . when I got back to America, I guess I fell apart.'

Everyone in the room was quiet, and Alfie didn't feel judged. He felt their silence was a sign of respect. They honoured him for being there and for having the courage to talk about it. Everyone had a different story to share and yet in some ways their stories were all the same. They had gone into the war as one person and emerged as someone else. Someone they were still trying to understand.

'Thanks for sharing with us, Alf,' said their co-ordinator, Bill. 'I know this process hasn't been easy for you, and I hope that it helps you to find a way forward in your life and in your relationships.'

Ethan rolled his eyes, and Alfie tried to keep a serious face. Bill meant well, but he was an earnest type who liked to spout what he thought were deep, philosophical thoughts, but were 'cringe-inducing dribble' according to Ethan.

'Speaking of relationships,' Ethan said loudly as he winked at Alfie. 'What's this I hear about an engagement?'

'Are you getting married, Alf?' asked the man sitting beside him.

Alfie opened his mouth to respond but Ethan cut him off. 'Ruth had to ask *him* in the end. Said she wasn't gonna sit around waiting any longer.'

Everyone began to congratulate Alfie, and he smiled and said thanks.

'You'll all be invited to the wedding,' he said, knowing he'd be in trouble for not running it past Ruth first.

After the meeting, Alfie drove home, parked in the driveway and turned off the engine. There were no lights on in the house, which meant Alice must have gone to bed. She'd been surprised when he told her he was getting married, and less excited than he had anticipated.

As quietly as he could, Alfie let himself into the house. He took a beer from the fridge and sat at the table. It was his first touch of alcohol in over a month, and the first sip tasted glorious. Alfie let his mind flash back to Camp Mackay. To lying on the grass drinking Budweiser and playing cards with his friends. He pictured Jethro's laughing face and imagined the sea breeze, the warm afternoon sun and the hills rising behind them. It was the first time he'd been able to picture Jethro whole. Until now, his only memory of his friend had been seeing his face blown apart.

Alfie had received his first letter from Lorna a few days after Jethro's death. He was sitting in a tent with a couple of strangers listening to gunfire and watching swarms of insects gather at the tent flap. He read her words saying that she was in love with him, that she would wait, that they could build a life together when the war was over, and they meant nothing. He felt nothing. With his mind and heart blessedly numb, he held a lighter to the letter and watched Lorna's words disappear.

Chapter 42

LORNA

By September, Lorna was no longer sharing a bed with Patrick, instead sleeping in the small single bed in a spare room – the room Patrick had insisted on calling 'the nursery' from the day they'd moved into the house, and now referred to as 'the other room' in a quiet venomous tone. Ever since she started sleeping in the spare room, she made sure she was out of bed, showered and dressed before Patrick appeared, otherwise she felt uneasy, more vulnerable.

Patrick was always angry now, in a silent, brooding way until something set him off. Then he would shout and become violent, mostly after he'd had too much to drink. He didn't often raise a hand to Lorna, though it did happen, usually on the occasions when she was brave enough to shout back. He would smack her across the head with the heel of his hand, or shove her into a wall. Once, he pushed her so hard she fell and cut her cheek on the edge of the table. When her dad had stopped by to visit the next day, he'd expressed concern at the bruise and cut on her cheek. Patrick had laughed, saying how Lorna had walked into a door in the night when she'd gotten up to use the bathroom and how the bang had woken him from his sleep.

'She's lucky it wasn't worse,' he'd said, laughing again.

Lorna's dad hadn't laughed, nor had he looked convinced with Patrick's story. As he was leaving, he hugged Lorna tightly and asked her again to come and visit soon. She hadn't been home to see her parents in months.

This morning, Lorna noticed Patrick was in a brighter mood. He thanked her when she placed his cup of tea before him, and again when she gave him his boiled eggs and toast. When she sat across from him and nibbled her toast, he smiled and said she looked lovely in her new blouse. It had been a gift from Penny on her birthday.

'Thank you,' Lorna replied, pleased he was being nice, but anxious it wouldn't last.

'I wondered if we might go to a movie tomorrow night?' asked Patrick, smiling.

Lorna tried to hide her shock. 'Okay.'

'Perhaps I could pick you up from work?' said Patrick. 'We could get a meal somewhere first. What time will you be finished?'

Lorna didn't know what to make of this person sitting opposite. He simply couldn't be the same husband who had told Lorna it was disgraceful that she had found a job behind his back. She had no respect for him or their marriage, he'd yelled. The day Lorna told Patrick about her new job was the day Patrick showed his angry side, and it had shocked her to her core, but she'd held firm, prepared to pay the price.

Lorna caught the tram into the city with a lightness of spirit she hadn't felt in a long time. Now Patrick had finally turned a corner and accepted her working, perhaps things would improve and she wouldn't have to broach the topic of separation again. She'd tried once. Told him she was unhappy and wanted a divorce. He'd gripped her arm painfully and hissed. Hadn't even said a word, and hadn't needed to, because it was clear from the expression on his face that a divorce was out of the question.

Penny was the one who had planted the seed about getting a job. She'd written to Lorna, telling her how much she was enjoying being a dental nurse. *I love the routine,* wrote Penny. *The expectation that I am needed somewhere. I don't earn much, but it's rewarding being paid and appreciated. Maybe you should look to work too?*

Lorna had cried after reading Penny's words, remembering how rewarding she had found driving trucks for the Americans. Yes, she'd worked long hours, but it had given her such a sense of purpose. Since marrying Patrick she'd felt worthless.

The next day, as if it were a good omen, Lorna had bumped into an old school friend, Sally, who mentioned she was working as a research assistant at Victoria University while studying there part-time.

'The pay is pitiful, but I love it,' Sally said enthusiastically. 'I remember you were one of the clever ones, Lorna. Didn't you get top of the class in mathematics?'

'Yes,' Lorna had replied, a lump in her throat. 'I'd love to go to university, but I didn't finish school.'

'Oh, neither did I,' exclaimed Sally. 'They're making exceptions because of the war. You should look into it.'

Lorna had thought about it constantly, but she hadn't looked into it because she knew Patrick wanted her at home, where wives were supposed to be. Sally was married, sure, but she was an exception.

Then a week later, Sally phoned Lorna's mother to ask for Lorna's number, then phoned Lorna to tell her there was a research assistant position in the mathematics department. She'd taken the liberty of speaking to the supervisor on Lorna's behalf, and they were keen to hear from her.

Lorna again dismissed the idea. It wasn't until she met her mum in town for afternoon tea a week later that she reconsidered, when her mum insisted, quite stridently, she apply.

It was worth it, Lorna said to herself, getting off the tram and starting the steep walk up to the university. For all the trouble her job had caused, she knew it was worth it because she loved every second she spent on campus. And finally Patrick was coming around. Maybe they could make their marriage work after all.

❦

Patrick was waiting for Lorna on the corner outside the mathematics department, a cigarette in hand. As she approached, he squinted as if assessing her, before the serious look disappeared and he smiled.

'Hello', he said, leaning in to kiss her on the cheek. 'Good day?'

Patrick had never asked her about work before.

'Yes, thank you,' Lorna replied. 'Where are we going?'

'The Green Parrot,' Patrick replied as they climbed into the car.

Lorna's stomach clenched painfully. She hadn't been to the Green Parrot since the Marines had been in town. She remembered being there with Stan when the earthquake had hit, then later with Curtis, Karen and Alfie. It still came as a jolt, knowing Alfie was alive. That he was living a life miles and miles away without her.

'Sounds lovely,' Lorna heard herself say, though the words felt as if they were coming from someone else.

Patrick was a gentleman, pulling out Lorna's chair, offering to switch sides when Lorna commented on the draft coming through the door. He was calm and relaxed and became quite animated as he talked about them taking a holiday to the South Island.

'We could visit your brother,' he said.

Lorna missed Peter and loved the idea of going to see him, but she knew how much Peter disliked her husband. Though maybe if they spent more time together, he would start to warm to Patrick.

Normally Patrick didn't like them to order dessert, but he insisted they share the pavlova, knowing how much Lorna liked it.

As they drove home, Patrick placed a hand lightly on Lorna's knee and squeezed gently. 'Any chance I might be able to convince you to come back to our bed tonight?' he asked, his voice hesitant, yet hopeful.

Lorna placed her hand on top of his. 'I'd like that,' she said.

'You never know,' said Patrick, his forehead creased in concentration as he sped up. 'Tonight might finally be the night.'

Goosebumps rose on the back of Lorna's neck, and she had to fight hard to control her breath. She had a dreadful suspicion that Patrick hadn't simply woken up that morning and decided to be nice to his wife. He had an ulterior motive — to lure his wife to bed with the aim of finally getting her pregnant.

Four days later, Lorna moved back home to live with her parents. She waited until Patrick had left for church, using the excuse of a stomach ache so she wouldn't have to accompany him, then she phoned her father, who was waiting for her call. She packed a suitcase and her dad arrived with a few empty boxes, which they filled with shoes, clothes, books and photographs.

Her mum had baked a lemon cake, and as soon as they'd unloaded the car and her mum had helped to hang Lorna's clothes in her closet, they sat on the front porch and had a slice of cake with tea. As much as Lorna's parents tried to act relaxed, she knew they were tense. It wouldn't be long before Patrick read the letter Lorna had left, and she was sure the first thing he would do would be to drive over to demand she go back.

Sure enough, ten minutes later, Patrick's car appeared and roared up the hill. As he climbed out of the car, her dad rose to his feet.

'You two head inside,' he said, his eyes fixed on Patrick. 'I'll handle this.'

'Dad, it's my problem,' said Lorna, her body shaking.

'You don't have to deal with him any longer, Lorrie,' her dad replied, his eyes dropping to the cut on her lip from Patrick's most recent outburst. 'It's our turn.'

'That's right,' said her mum, taking Lorna's arm. 'Come on inside with me.'

Lorna caught Patrick's eye as he started up the steps, and she felt afraid. For herself and for her parents. She followed her mum inside, and they went to stand in front of the fireplace as if, even though it wasn't lit, it would provide comfort and warmth.

'I'm here to speak with my wife,' Lorna heard Patrick say. She looked towards the front bay windows and could just see the grey hair on the back of her father's head.

'I don't think that is a good idea right now,' her dad replied.

'It's not up for discussion.'

Lorna's breathing sped up. When Patrick spoke low, emphasising each word, it didn't bode well. She made to move towards the door, not wanting her dad to witness the anger she knew was about to burst out of Patrick, but her mother stopped her.

'No,' her mum said, simply. 'Not anymore.'

Tears filled Lorna's eyes. 'What about Dad?' she whispered.

'He can handle Patrick.'

They both startled as they heard a crash. Glancing at the window, Lorna could no longer see her dad, but she could hear him well enough. She'd never heard her father so furious.

'You are not going to see my daughter, today or any other day. You are not going to speak to her, and you are not going to turn up here or at her work. You are never to lay a hand on her again.'

There was another crash, followed by a grunting sound. Lorna raced to the front door and swung it open to see Patrick doubled over, the chair Lorna had been sitting on moments earlier on its side. Her dad stood glowering beside Patrick and immediately stepped in front of Lorna as if to protect her.

'I want you off my property,' he growled.

Her mum pushed past Lorna, and as Patrick straightened she gripped him by the shirt.

'Lorna wants a divorce,' she said, leaning closer, 'and I suggest you agree, otherwise I'll be talking to everyone I know about the type of man you are, and they will tell their friends and family and so on, until everyone in Wellington looks at you the way I'm looking at you now.'

Then she let him go and stepped back. 'Goodbye, Patrick,' she said calmly.

Patrick didn't speak. He didn't look at any of them as he walked down the steps, got in his car and drove away.

Lorna looked at her dad, who was rubbing at his red knuckles and smiling, and her mum, who was watching Patrick's car disappear around the corner with her hands on her hips. Then Lorna started laughing.

'That was incredible,' she gasped. 'You're both amazing.'

Then her dad put his arms around her, and she began to cry instead.

Chapter 43

ALFIE

Karen and Curtis came to visit Alfie shortly after he wrote to tell them of his engagement. Karen was adamant she wanted to meet Ruth before the wedding day. Curtis's neighbour, Dot, had offered to look after Ricky, insisting that Curtis and Karen have a nice weekend away before the baby was born. Alfie was excited for their visit, counting down the days till they arrived.

When he saw them stepping off the train, he had to work hard not to cry. The three of them chatted non-stop for the next hour as Alfie took them for a drive to show them around – with Karen and Curtis both exclaiming often over Alfie's car.

At Alice's house, they settled at a long table under the pergola in the backyard.

'I still can't believe you made this,' said Curtis, running his hand along the smooth wooden tabletop. 'No wonder you're so busy with your new business.'

Alfie had taught himself a number of skills doing odd jobs for people in the neighbourhood. He'd spent a few weeks working with an older man, Roger, who was a semi-retired furniture maker but needed Alfie's help to make a large wooden table for his grandson. He'd taught Alfie about dovetail joints, bevels and saws, and had kept Alfie on as an apprentice.

Roger had been the one to encourage Alfie to start his own furniture-making business, and though Alfie was still using Roger's workshop, he was hoping to be able to afford one of his own soon.

'I might have to employ someone to help me out at this rate,' said Alfie, taking a sip of his beer. 'But I'm reluctant.'

'Why?' asked Karen, resting a hand on her heavily pregnant stomach.

Alfie considered his answer. 'I guess I prefer working on my own.'

Alice arrived home with Molly, and the way everyone was so happy to meet each other made Alfie feel emotional again. He retrieved more chairs from inside and they sat around talking as the sun dropped lower in the sky.

'Well, I can see why you like living here, bud,' said Curtis, leaning back in his chair and closing his eyes. 'It reminds me of New Zealand in some way.'

'I was thinking the same thing,' said Karen. 'Something about the light, and the rich green of the grass. No scent of the sea though,' she added wistfully.

Curtis put his arm around her, and she leant her head on his shoulder. 'We'll go back there one day, honey. I promise.'

'Alfie said it's been a challenge coming to America,' said Alice, sympathetically. 'Are you settling in better now?'

Karen nodded. 'It's getting easier. I'm starting to realise that what I took for people being nosy and giving advice all the time was actually just them showing they cared.'

Ruth's car pulled into the driveway and Alfie went to greet her.

'Sorry I'm late,' she said, her lips warm and soft on his as they kissed. 'I got into a heated discussion with Mr Milne again.'

Ruth was a legal secretary who seemed to know more about law than her boss and wasn't afraid to tell him that. Alfie admired her passion for work, her drive.

Alfie took Ruth's hand and led her over to introduce her to Karen and Curtis.

Ruth slipped into the empty chair next to Karen, and they began to chat as if they'd known each other for years. Alfie went back into the house to check on the chilli he had prepared, and Alice helped him carry out plates and cutlery. As the sun dropped lower, they ate and they laughed, and Alfie made sure he noticed and appreciated every moment.

When it grew dark, Molly reluctantly went to bed, and Alice insisted on doing the dishes, leaving the others to relax in the living room.

'Have you set a date for the wedding?' Karen asked from the settee she was sharing with Curtis.

'Not yet,' Ruth replied. 'But we're thinking in the spring, April sometime.'

'Did you hear Penny is getting married?' said Curtis.

Alfie shook his head. 'No, but I heard she was dating again.'

'Who is Penny?' Ruth asked.

When Alfie didn't answer, Karen responded. 'She was married to Lorna's older brother, but he was killed in Italy during the war. I'm pleased she's found someone after losing Gordon. Lorna's happy for her too.'

'Who's Lorna?' said Ruth.

Karen looked at Alfie and waited, but again he stayed quiet.

'She's my best friend,' said Karen quietly. 'I'm surprised Alfie hasn't mentioned her, or her family.'

'You remember,' said Alfie, smiling at Ruth. 'I told you about that nice family. The dad took me fishing.'

'Oh yes, with the young boy who played that sport . . . what was it called?'

'Rugby,' Curtis and Alfie said in unison.

'No, the other one, the boring one you said goes on all day.'

'Cricket,' said Karen, laughing. 'And it's not that boring. Alfie just didn't like it because Lorna was better than him. Remember when she bowled you out? Gosh, you were mad, Alf.'

Curtis was laughing now too. 'You couldn't handle being shown up by a girl.'

'She wasn't just any girl, that's why,' Alfie snapped.

Ruth had been smiling along during the conversation, but now her smile disappeared. Karen and Curtis looked about awkwardly, and Alfie wished he could take back his words.

'Were you keen on her, then?' asked Ruth, never one to avoid a topic.

Alfie hesitated. 'I guess,' he replied. 'Though initially we didn't get on well at all.'

'He broke her heart,' said Karen, an edge to her voice.

'Karnie,' said Curtis, giving his wife a warning look.

'Sorry,' Karen muttered.

'So, what happened to this Lorna? Presumably she got over my Alfie?'

Alfie felt a flash of irritation at Ruth calling him hers, as if she owned him.

'She married,' said Karen. 'But it didn't work out. Lorrie's moved back home and is in the process of getting a divorce.'

'A divorce?' said Alfie, his heart pounding.

Karen fixed him with one of her intimidating glares. 'Patrick wasn't a nice man, Alfie. He couldn't control his anger.'

Alfie knew what she was telling him. He knew, and his chest began to burn.

Ruth gasped loudly. 'Oh my goodness,' she said, her eyes wide as she clapped her hand over her mouth. 'The poor thing! Are you saying her husband beat her?'

⁓

Alfie sold his car the day before he told Ruth. He knew if he sold the car first, there was no going back. A man down in St Louis paid a good price, but not before he told Alfie he was a fool.

'I wouldn't care how much I needed the cash, I wouldn't be parting with this girl,' he said, patting the bonnet. Alfie had to look away as the man got into the car and drove off.

'So you're really doing it then,' Alice said that night, staring out the window at the empty space in the driveway.

'I guess so.'

'Have you spoken to Ruth yet?'

'Tomorrow.'

Alice turned to look at him. 'Good luck,' she said grimly, then she walked past him and went upstairs to bed. He knew she didn't understand.

⁓

'You're going back to New Zealand?' exclaimed Ruth. 'What on earth for?'

'Because I can't move on until I've seen Lorna and her family.'

'Is this because you feel guilty you haven't written to them? Come on, Alfie, that's ridiculous. Write to them now, tell them you're sorry but you've been busy rebuilding your life. They'll understand. Why do you feel like you owe them anything?'

'Because I do. I owe them more than they'll ever know.'

'What about us? You want me to just sit around and wait for you? We're supposed to be getting married in three months, or have you forgotten? Why didn't you discuss this with me before selling your car? I could have loaned you the money to go to New Zealand, or better yet, I could have talked you out of going.'

'I'm sorry.'

'What makes you think they want to see you? You're not that special, Alfie, trust me.'

'Thanks,' said Alfie sarcastically.

Ruth threw her hands in the air and let out a cry of frustration.

'Can't you see how this looks? It looks like you're running away so you don't have to marry me. Is that what's happening here, Alfie? Are you breaking up with me?'

Alfie wanted to shake his head and ask for forgiveness. To tell her he'd had a moment of insanity. Of course he wanted to marry her, she was wonderful. He wouldn't go to New Zealand, he would stay there and get married, have children, buy another car.

Alfie opened his mouth, but he couldn't do it. He couldn't say the words.

Chapter 44

LORNA

Lorna's mum told her about Alfie the second she walked in the front door.

'He's here,' she said from the kitchen doorway. 'In Wellington.'

'Who?' Lorna replied, closing the door and hanging up her handbag and hat.

'Alfie.'

Lorna stared at her mother. 'What's he doing here?' she asked sharply.

'Visiting,' her mum called as she disappeared back into the kitchen.

Lorna didn't know whether to follow her mother to find out more, or go to her room and try to do something that would distract her. She'd heard from Karen that Alfie had called off his engagement several months ago, but there had been no mention of Alfie coming to New Zealand. Curiosity sent her towards the kitchen.

'How do you know he's in Wellington?' She asked her mum's back as she scrubbed carrots in the sink.

'He phoned a couple of hours ago. I invited him over for tea,' her mum paused. 'He'll be here soon.'

'Soon!' Lorna exclaimed, her heart pounding.

It had been almost four years since she'd seen Alfie. Since he'd kissed her, then left and never made contact again.

'It would have been nice if you'd checked with me. I don't want to see him, Mum.'

Her mum kept scrubbing.

'Mum, did you hear me?'

'I heard,' her mum replied, not turning around. 'But *I* want to see him, Lorrie. And so does your father.'

Lorna put her hands on her hips.

'I'll go out then,' she stated.

'If you have to.'

Lorna had never heard her mother be so short with her.

'I wrote to him constantly for a year, Mum, and he never replied. Not to you, not to me, not to anyone.'

Lorna's mum stopped scrubbing and slowly turned to face her.

'We don't know what that young man has been through, but he's come all the way back to New Zealand, and I am going to welcome him into our home and make sure he knows that whatever it is he suffered was worth it, because if it hadn't been for those boys – all our boys – sacrificing their lives, who knows what kind of life we would be living right now.' A single tear rolled down her cheek and she used the back of her hand to wipe it away.

Lorna took a deep breath and let it out slowly.

'I'll get changed and come help with tea,' she said quietly.

When he knocked, Lorna was sitting in the living room attempting to read the paper. Her father leapt to his feet and went to open the door.

'Alfie, old chap,' she heard her dad say.

'Hello, sir,' came Alfie's voice.

Lorna closed her eyes. He sounded just the same. Hearing his American accent was a sudden reminder to Lorna of a time in her life she'd all but buried.

'Alfie!' Lorna heard her mum exclaim as she walked quickly down the hallway from the kitchen. 'It's wonderful to see you.'

'You too, Mom.'

Rising to her feet, Lorna waited.

'Come in, come in,' her dad said.

Lorna held her breath as Alfie entered the living room. It was him. He was there, right in front of her, wearing a blue shirt and jeans and with longer hair than she remembered. For some reason, Lorna had thought he would turn up in his Marine uniform, but of course that was silly of her.

'Hello, Alfie,' she said, clasping her shaking hands in front of her.

He looked at her with an intensity that made her heart leap.

'Hello, Lorna,' he said, striding towards her and holding out a hand. She knew she should shake his hand and pretend like seeing him wasn't splitting her in two, but she couldn't. Instead, she stared at his hand and her vision blurred.

Alfie's hand dropped and he took a step back.

'How about a beer?' said Lorna's dad brightly.

'That'd be swell,' Alfie said, turning towards her parents.

'Excuse me,' whispered Lorna, then she brushed past Alfie, fumbled for her handbag and escaped out of the front door. As she raced down the stairs, no one called after her and no one followed. Reaching the footpath, Lorna started running. She kept running until she was out of breath.

Chapter 45

ALFIE

Every cell in his body screamed at him to run after her, but Alfie let Lorna go. He still couldn't quite believe that he had been standing that close to her again. He was struggling to come to terms with the fact that he was back in New Zealand, in her house, with her parents, who had shown him love and support, made him feel valued, made him want to be a better person. They had shown him what family was, and what it stood for. So he didn't run after Lorna, because Mr and Mrs Baxter had lost two sons in the war and they were standing there, smiling apologetically. Alfie owed it to them to stay.

'Sorry about Lorrie,' Mrs Baxter said. 'It's been tough for her recently.'

Alfie shook his head. 'I'm the one who's sorry. For a great number of things.'

'Take a seat,' Mr Baxter said, waving to the armchair Alfie remembered sitting in the first time he came to visit. Instinctively, he looked around for Milly, but she had been an old dog when he'd met her, and was no doubt gone. It felt strange to be there, without her racing up to him to say hello.

For a while, they talked. Alfie told them about catching the train out to Paekākāriki that morning and how strange it had been to see there was nothing left: no sign of the camps, no indication the Americans had ever been there. He told them about his long journey out. How it had taken him two months just to find a transport ship. He wasn't the only American on board, he said. There had been quite a few Americans wanting to return to New Zealand.

'They have very fond memories of their time here, as do I.'

Mrs Baxter talked about her new volunteer role at the hospital, and Mr Baxter told Alfie about going fishing with Peter the previous weekend when he'd been up for a visit.

'You should have seen the size of the snapper Peter hauled in,' he said. 'I could take you out? If that fits with your plans?'

'What are your plans, Alfie?' asked Mrs Baxter kindly.

Alfie rubbed a hand over his chin. 'Honestly? I don't know, Mom. I'm a little lost.'

'That's okay, son,' Mr Baxter said gently. 'You'll figure it out.'

Lorna arrived back home as Alfie was leaving. He'd said his goodbyes and was walking down the steps when he spotted her turning onto Ranui Road, her shadow stretching long and narrow behind her. He walked down the hill towards her.

'Can we talk?' he asked as he drew close.

She studied him with narrowed eyes. 'Is there any point?'

'Yes, I think so.'

Lorna shrugged. 'We can walk to the park, I suppose.'

He fell into step beside her and before he could begin to tell her what he wanted to say, she spoke.

'Did you get my letters?'

Alfie hesitated. 'Yes.'

'Did you read them?'

'A couple.'

Lorna scoffed and Alfie felt a twinge in his chest.

'What did you do with the letters you didn't read?'

'I burnt them, threw them in the river, buried them in the mud,' he said tersely. He was doing it again. Why did he always behave like this with Lorna?

'Do you enjoy hurting me?' asked Lorna.

Alfie wanted to take her by the shoulders and shake her. Instead, he kept his arms stiffly by his side.

'I couldn't read your letters, Lorna — it was like being tortured from the inside out. I knew I wasn't going to see you again, mainly because I was convinced I was going to die. Every hour I was there, I thought, this is it. And I wanted to die, so many times I wanted it all to be over.'

Lorna took a long time to respond.

'I kept trying to convince myself you were dead and that's why you hadn't written,' she said. 'When I found out you were alive, I . . .' she stopped.

They'd reached the corner of the park where they'd played cricket on Christmas day.

'I'm sorry about your brothers, Lorna,' Alfie said. 'Real sorry.'

Lorna was looking towards the area of the park where they had played cricket too.

'Everyone fell apart,' she said softly. 'Mum, Dad, Peter, Penny.'

Alfie wanted to wrap his arms around her. 'What about you?'

'Me? I helped Penny pack up her house and move away. I found Peter a job and somewhere to stay down south so he could escape, because he said it was the only thing he could think to do. I cooked and cleaned for Mum, and tried to keep an eye on Dad. He disappeared all the time. For hours at a time. I still don't know where he went. I was afraid to ask.'

'Sounds like you kept the family going,' said Alfie. 'You didn't have a chance to fall apart yourself.'

Lorna laughed bitterly. 'No, instead I thought getting married would be a good idea. I thought it would make everyone happy.'

'Did it?' asked Alfie.

Lorna kept staring into the distance without answering. 'I hear you were engaged?' she said eventually.

'Yes.'

'Were you happy?'

'I'm not sure I know how to be happy. Not properly. Not since Tarawa.'

Lorna stepped over the low railing and walked across the grass. She slowed near the middle, lay down on her back, put her hands beneath her head and looked up at the indigo sky.

Alfie hesitated before doing the same, leaving a small gap between them.

'I get the feeling you've done this before,' he said, feeling the cool damp of the grass through the back of his shirt.

'Ever since we lost Rick and Gordon,' Lorna replied. 'It seems to help.'

Alfie wanted to reach out and clasp her hand. He wanted to tell her what he had come all this way to say.

'Will you tell me about Jethro?' Lorna said. 'About what happened to you?'

He closed his eyes. Took a long, deep breath and let it out. Then Alfie talked about Jethro, and Tarawa, and the months of fighting that followed in Saipan and Okinawa. He told her of his loneliness, his terror, his time spent in hospital when he lost all hope, his mum and sister and Molly. He told her about his car and selling it in order to get back to New Zealand. He told her about Ruth and how he had wanted it to work, but he had realised it couldn't.

Lorna barely said a word. She asked a few questions, made the odd noise to show she was listening, and when he'd finally said everything he needed to say, apart from the one important thing he wanted to say but didn't know how to, he fell silent.

'Thank you for telling me,' said Lorna, turning her head to look at him at last.

He could barely make her out in the darkness. 'Your folks told me you're working at the university getting to use that incredible brain of yours.'

'Does it bother you?'

'Why on earth would it bother me? You were always the smartest person I ever met. Would be a shame to waste it.'

Lorna made a strange growling noise. 'That was not my husband's view.'

'Tell me about him,' Alfie said gently.

Lorna immediately looked away. 'We should never have married.'

Alfie waited.

'He made me feel worthless,' whispered Lorna. 'And I let him.'

'He didn't deserve you,' said Alfie, wishing Lorna would look at him again.

She scrambled to her feet.

'I should get home,' she said, beginning to walk away.

'Did you love him?' called Alfie, getting to his feet.

She spun back, her face contorted in anger and pain. 'The only man I ever loved was you, Alfie.'

He reached for her, but she backed away. 'Leave me alone. Please. I don't want to see you again.'

For the second time in the space of a few hours, Alfie let her go.

Chapter 46

LORNA

Alfie phoned the morning after his visit. He spoke to Lorna's dad, informing him he'd decided to catch the ferry to the South Island. He asked for Peter's number so he could get in touch.

Lorna took the news calmly and continued getting ready for work, telling herself over and over it was a relief. That it was what she wanted.

Her mum looked crestfallen. 'Did he say if he'll come and see us again?'

Her dad shook his head. 'No, but I'm sure he will, love.'

Lorna knew it was her fault. 'Sorry,' she murmured.

Her dad squeezed her shoulder. 'Nothing to be sorry for, Lorrie.'

The day passed in a blur, and Lorna was pleased to have the distraction of work. She was halfway down the hill to catch the tram home when she heard footsteps behind her and turned to see Patrick. She froze at the expression on his face.

'Thought I wouldn't find out, did you?' he snarled.

It was the first time Lorna had seen him since he'd come to her parents' house on the day she moved out. The sight of him made her tremble and she was grateful for the handful of people walking past.

'What do you want, Patrick?' she asked.

'I want my wife to come back home where she belongs.'

Though Patrick's voice was raised, no one turned to look. He grasped her by the elbow, and she shook him off.

'I know,' he hissed, leaning closer. 'I know that American is here, so don't try to make excuses.'

Lorna frowned. 'Have you been spying on me?'

'You are still my wife, Lorna.'

'Because you won't finalise the divorce like you promised.' A sudden thought came to her. 'How do you know who Alfie is, anyway? You've never met him.'

Patrick rolled his eyes. 'You think I'm stupid?'

Lorna shook her head, confused. She had no photograph of Alfie anywhere. It had been one of the things her mother was upset about after Alfie left – that they had no photo to remember him by. And Lorna had certainly never spoken of him when Patrick was around, though her parents had once or twice.

Patrick gave one of the condescending smiles she hated.

'My mother still lives on your road, remember? She knows all about the Americans who used to be in and out of your house. Mother found it disgraceful, the way your family all talked about Alfie as if he was a member of the family, the way you all carried on having a good time while your brothers were overseas giving up their lives.'

Lorna felt herself start to sway.

'I can't believe I ever married you,' she whispered, lightheaded.

'Well, you did,' said Patrick, pulling a switchblade from his pocket, flicking it open and yanking her close to hide the knife between them. 'And it's time for you to come home.'

Chapter 47

ALFIE

He'd taken only a handful of steps up the gangway before he stopped. Running away wasn't the answer. Alfie had come all the way back to New Zealand for one thing, and he wasn't even prepared to stay and fight for it. He didn't want to be like his father, someone who ran away when things became too difficult, too much for him to handle. He wanted to be like his brother, Stan. A man who took on the burdens and responsibilities of others, who showed care and kindness, even when battling troubles of his own. Stan had died never being able to express who he was. Never having a chance to fall in love, openly and completely, and be loved in return.

Alfie apologised to the couple standing behind him as he turned and made his way past the passengers boarding the ferry. Then he walked purposefully towards the tram that would take him to Ranui Road.

‘This isn't like her. She always comes home after work, and if she does make plans and won't be here for tea, she lets us know.’ Mrs Baxter's hands were gripped together, her fingers moving about in agitation. ‘I'm sorry to ask, Alfie, but I'm worried. Did you say something to Lorna last night that might have . . . that might have upset her?’

Alfie had arrived a few hours earlier and been welcomed warmly by Lorna's parents. They hadn't asked why he had changed his mind about going to the South Island, or why he had turned up at their house unannounced. It was almost as if they'd been expecting him.

Alfie put down his knife and fork and took a deep breath.

‘We talked and . . . I'm sorry . . . she was a little upset.’

‘She seemed fine this morning,’ Mr Baxter said, his forehead creased. ‘Perhaps I should go and have a look for her.’

Alfie pushed back his chair. ‘I'll come with you, sir.’

‘What about your meal?’ Mrs Baxter asked.

Alfie and Mr Baxter looked at one another.

‘We'll finish it when we get back,’ said Mr Baxter. ‘Keep it warm for us, would you, love?’

They made their way quickly down to the car. Mr Baxter scrambled into the driver's seat, then paused, his hand on the keys in the ignition.

‘It's not my place to ask, son, I know that. But I'm going to ask now because after that business with Patrick I'm not going to let any man hurt my girl again, you understand?’

Alfie looked Mr Baxter in the eye. ‘Yes, sir.’

'Did you come back for her, Alfie?' Mr Baxter asked. 'Just a yes or no answer is all I need.'

Alfie thought of his brother. Of the words in Stan's letter. *If circumstances had been different, I would have married her.* Circumstances had brought Alfie here. Alfie was here for one reason.

'Yes, sir,' Alfie said firmly. 'I came back for Lorna.'

Mr Baxter nodded once, satisfied, and started the engine.

As they drove down Ranui Road, Alfie saw an older woman standing on her front porch smoking. It was the same woman he'd seen the night before when he'd met Lorna and they'd walked to the park together.

Alfie bit his lip. 'Patrick's mother lives on this street, doesn't she?'

Mr Baxter nodded. 'Number four, next to Gordon and Penny's old place. Awful woman. Like mother, like son, I'd say.'

'I saw her last night,' said Alfie. 'She was outside smoking and scowled at me as I walked past.'

Mr Baxter swore as he swung out of their road. 'She would have phoned Patrick. She would have told him you were here.'

'She doesn't know me,' Alfie replied, gripping the dashboard as Mr Baxter shot around another corner.

'Of course she does, everyone on the street knows you, Alfie,' said Mr Baxter grimly. 'You're the American that captured Lorna's heart, and everyone knew it, including Patrick. I saw the way he reacted when anyone mentioned your name.'

Dread flooded Alfie's body.

'I knew that wouldn't be the end of it, goddammit,' said Mr Baxter, banging the steering wheel. 'I bloody well knew it!'

Chapter 48

LORNA

Patrick didn't take her into the house. Instead he parked in the driveway, unlocked the garage, and swung open one of the two large wooden doors. He marched around to her side of the car, and hissed at Lorna to get into the garage. She quickly did as he asked, aware of the knife in his hand, and stood silently in the far corner beside the lawnmower as Patrick stepped outside.

'You can stay in here until you decide you're ready to come back into our house and be my wife,' Patrick snarled, closing the door with a bang, sliding the bolt across, and locking her in.

She stood in the darkness for a few seconds then fell to her knees and crawled towards the double doors. With her ear to the wood, she listened, but she couldn't hear a sound. Breathing fast, Lorna stood and pushed her shoulder hard against one door, then the other, but neither door budged.

Lorna thought about screaming in the hope that someone would hear her, but the most likely person to hear would be

Patrick, and she didn't want him to come back. She was scared about Patrick coming back.

With a sob, Lorna sat with her back against a door. She curled her legs up and wrapped her arms around her knees.

'Dad,' Lorna whispered, tears dripping onto her trousers. 'Dad, I'm here.'

Lorna had grown uncomfortable sitting on the concrete floor and was walking around in slow circles in the dark, trying to stay calm, trying to stop the panic from overwhelming her. How long was Patrick going to leave her here? She heard a car pull up outside, then the slam of one car door, followed by another. There were rapid footsteps and then someone hammered on the door of the house. Lorna heard her father's voice.

'Patrick, open this goddamn door!'

'Dad!' Lorna yelled, banging on the wooden door. 'Dad, I'm in here!'

'Lorrie!' Then footsteps came towards her, and he was outside the garage calling to her. 'Lorrie, are you okay?'

'I'm okay, Dad, but he's locked me in and he—' She heard someone run back towards the house.

'No!' she shouted. 'Dad, he has a knife, he's dangerous, don't go in there.'

'It's alright, love, I'm right here,' said her dad, his voice close. 'I'm going to get you out.'

Lorna heard the rattle of the padlock, then a grunt as he tried to open the door.

'Lorrie, I'll be right back,' he called.

Lorna was so afraid she couldn't breathe. 'Dad, don't go,' she gasped.

'I'm just running to the car for some tools.'

'What about Patrick?'

'Don't worry. Alfie won't let him get to you.'

Lorna froze, both hands on the door. 'Alfie,' she breathed.

'I'll be right back,' called her dad, his voice already fainter as he moved away.

Lorna closed her eyes. Alfie had come back. Alfie was here.

Her body shaking, Lorna waited. Her dad was taking too long; why was it so quiet out there?

'Dad?' she called hesitantly.

Lorna heard a police siren. It was faint at first, then it grew louder and louder until it was right outside. When the siren suddenly went silent, Lorna heard voices, then footsteps coming towards her. She heard someone put a key into the padlock, snap it open, and slide the bolt across. The door swung out, and he was standing there, lit by the glow of headlights from the police car.

'Alfie?' she whispered.

He scanned her body. 'Are you hurt?' he demanded. 'Did he hurt you?'

Lorna shook her head.

'What the hell were you thinking, Lorrie, getting married to that man?' he growled.

Lorna took a step back. 'What are you doing here?' she said crossly.

'I came for you,' he snapped back.

Her father brushed past Alfie and threw his arms around her. 'Lorrie, love, are you alright?'

'I'm fine,' Lorna said, her voice muffled against his shoulder. 'Where's Patrick?'

'The police have taken him into custody.' He pulled back and brushed a strand of hair from her face. 'They need to talk to you, love, is that okay?'

Lorna nodded, ignoring Alfie, who was still standing in the same spot. With her father's arm over her shoulder, she went to speak with the police.

Later, her father drove her home. Alfie had left while she was talking to a police officer. She overheard him telling her father he'd check in on them in the morning, but he didn't say anything to Lorna. He just disappeared.

Lorna's mum sat beside her, gently stroking her hair until she fell asleep, and when she woke suddenly in the night, her dad was asleep in an armchair nearby. He must have carried the chair in from the living room while she slept.

In the morning, Lorna woke to find her room empty. She put on her dressing gown and went into the kitchen, where both her parents were sitting at the table nursing cups of tea.

'Morning,' she said, pulling out a chair. 'That was a fairly interesting night.'

'I called the university,' said her mum. 'Told them you weren't well and would be staying home.'

'You didn't need to do that, I'm fine.' Lorna wasn't really fine. She was exhausted and fragile.

'A rest day will do you good,' said her dad.

'I'll get you some tea,' said her mum, standing.

Moments later she placed two mugs filled with tea in front of Lorna, and Lorna looked at her, confused.

'He's waiting out front,' her mum said softly.

Lorna didn't ask who. She stood, picked up the mugs and carried them outside.

Alfie was sitting on the top step, and she handed him one of the mugs before sitting down beside him.

'I thought you didn't like tea,' she said.

'It's growing on me.' Alfie took a sip and grimaced. 'Slowly,' he added.

Neither of them were looking at each other.

'How are you?' asked Alfie.

Lorna shrugged. 'I'm fine. A bit shaken.' She glanced at his profile and saw a lump on his cheek from clenching his jaw.

'I could have killed him, Lorrie,' he said. 'I wanted to, for a second there—'

'But you didn't,' Lorna interjected.

Alfie shook his head. 'No, I didn't.'

'He had a knife,' said Lorna.

Alfie gave a short barking laugh. 'After everything I've seen, that pathetic thing didn't scare me for a second.'

'It scared me,' Lorna whispered.

He looked at her at last. 'I'm sorry, Lorna. I'm sorry for so much, but mostly I'm sorry I didn't tell you I loved you. I should have told you when we first kissed. No, well before then.'

Lorna held herself rigid. She wanted to believe him so much her heart ached.

'But you didn't, Alfie. You left and . . . and moved on. You say you loved me and yet you were prepared to hurt me, savagely. You destroyed my letters, cut me out of your life and I still don't understand *why.*' Lorna's voice cracked. 'How can you do that to someone you love?'

Alfie closed his eyes. 'Because of my brother,' he said softly, then his eyes fluttered open. 'Stan wrote in a letter that he would have married you if circumstances had been different, and I became obsessed with it, Lorrie. I was determined not to fall for you because I was convinced you would have been his if he hadn't gotten himself killed. I thought he was in love with you. You deserved him, not me.'

'No,' Lorna said. 'We would never have married. We didn't . . . it wasn't like that with Stan. I cared for him, but I didn't feel . . .'

Alfie's face twisted in anguish. 'He was the person I looked up to more than anyone else in the world. I loved him, but I never told him, never even showed him. I thought if there was one thing I could do, it would be to honour his intentions, but I . . .' Alfie put his head in his hands. 'I was a goddamn idiot.'

Lorna reached out a shaking hand and placed it on the back of his head.

'Alfie,' she murmured, her thumb brushing his neck. 'Did you really mean it? That you love me?'

Alfie's hands dropped from his face and he gazed at her, incredulous.

'Why do you think I came back here? I love you desperately, Lorrie. I *ache* for you. I've spent every day since I left New Zealand with this hole in here—' Alfie banged his chest with his fist, '—because I'm not with you.'

'Are you going back?' Lorna asked. 'To America? Because if you are, I can't go with you, Alfie. I can't leave Mum and Dad.'

Alfie shook his head, tears glistening in his eyes.

'I'm not going anywhere,' he said. 'I'm staying here, with you. If you'll have me?'

Lorna slid her hand from the back of his neck to his chest. She felt him shudder as she pressed her palm against his heart, thumping hard and fast like her own.

'I'll have you,' she said, smiling softly. 'Though you'll need to learn the rules of rugby if you want to stay in this country. As for your cricket skills—'

The rest of her sentence was cut short as Alfie huffed out a quiet laugh, took her face in his hands and pressed his lips to hers.

AUTHOR NOTE

On numerous occasions, while researching my previous novel, *The Songbirds of Florence*, I came across accounts of New Zealand soldiers fighting in the Middle East during WWII who were anxious about the increasing threat of a Japanese invasion on their home country. With most young, able-bodied men fighting overseas, New Zealand was vulnerable and practically defenceless, and the Kiwi men were desperate to get home to defend their country.

It therefore came as a bitter blow to members of the New Zealand Second Division Army, many of whom by this stage had been fighting overseas for a long time, to discover they would not be returning home, but that instead, Roosevelt (after discussions with Churchill) would be sending American troops to New Zealand to set up bases from which they would defend the Pacific region.

During the following months, anger and resentment grew amongst the NZ soldiers as they heard about the wealthy, charming American boys back in New Zealand wooing their girls. Many a Dear John letter was received by the Kiwi boys based overseas as a result.

There is a well-known saying coined during that time which New Zealanders are still familiar with today: the US soldiers were 'overpaid, over-sexed and over here'.

For the Americans, life in New Zealand was unlike anything they had known and while most came to embrace the different lifestyle and developed a lifelong bond with the country, some couldn't wait to leave this relatively poor, conservative nation deep in the South Pacific.

The US soldiers were based in many areas throughout New Zealand, but it is in Wellington where perhaps their presence was felt most strongly and where the US Marines in particular have left a lasting legacy.

While little is left of the camps based out near Paekākāriki, thanks to the wonderful Kāpiti US Marines Trust, there are a number of significant historical sites in the area, including the site of Camp Mackay and the excellent display in the Paekākāriki Station Museum. I highly recommend a day visiting these places and learning more about a fascinating time in our past.

While I have done my best to be historically accurate, this is a work of fiction, and on occasion I have chosen to veer from the actual timeline of events.

Firstly, the earthquake experienced while Lorna and Stan were at the Green Parrot (this restaurant spant still exists today) happened only ten days after the Marines arrived in Wellington, but since I wanted more time to develop the relationship between these two characters, I have the earthquake happening two weeks later.

Secondly, I needed furlough to end for the Kiwi soldiers while the US Marines were still in Wellington. I therefore have the New Zealand soldiers leaving in November 1943 when in actual fact they left well over a month later.

Other inaccuracies, should you find them, are entirely my own and I apologise for any inadvertent errors.

In case you are wondering, Ranui Road, where Lorna and her family live, is a fictional street and does not exist, though in my mind it certainly does! I imagine it to be somewhere in the Kilbirnie/Lyall Bay area, on the lower slopes leading up to Mount Albert. I spent several years living in the eastern suburbs of Wellington (my two oldest children were born in Wellington) and have many fond memories of my time spent in this special city.

ACKNOWLEDGEMENTS

Thank you to the incredible Moa Press team and everyone at Hachette Aotearoa New Zealand. With particular thanks to Kate Stephenson, Dom Visini, Melanee Winder, Sacha Beguely, Cyanne Alwanger, Angela Radford, Abby Irwin-Jones, Emma Dorph, Suzy Maddox, Sharon Galey, Nicola Faisandier, Angie Williams, Alison Shucksmith and Maiko Lenting-Lu. Special mention to the wonderful Tania Mackenzie-Cooke.

Once again, I must single out Kate Stephenson from the above list of talented individuals. Kate, I thank my lucky stars that this is the third book we have worked on together and I am beyond grateful for your expertise, guidance and support.

Thank you also to the team at Hachette Australia, who have encouraged Australians to take a punt on this Kiwi author.

To Theresa Crewdson, whose grandmother, unbeknownst to me, was not only called Lorna but who nearly married an American soldier she met in Wellington during WWII (can you believe it?). Theresa, we were fated to work on this book together! Thanks for your wonderful copyediting and eagle eye for detail (and dates). I'm slightly embarrassed at the extent of my grammatical errors, but will endeavour to improve.

Thanks also to my wonderful proofreader, Stacey Clair, and to Christa Moffitt for designing a fabulous cover.

To everyone involved in the Kāpiti US Marines Trust, thank you for everything you have done and continue to do to preserve the history of the US Marines who were based in this area. Special thanks to Steve La Hood for showing me around all the sites and sharing your time and stories with me, and thank you to Dave Johnson for opening up the Paekākāriki Station Museum especially so that I could look around.

Thank you to Rachel and Laura at The Booklover Bookshop, and to the many customers and colleagues I have come to know in the book world. Your support means the world.

To my dear, precious family, friends, and fellow authors who deserve to be mentioned individually, but I'm paranoid I will miss someone out! Thank you a million times over for your love and encouragement.

To my readers, many of whom, when they asked me what I was writing next, revealed their own stories about the Americans based in New Zealand in the 1940s. Thank you for sharing your memories with me, and for your incredible support of my writing. Speaking of support, a huge, heartfelt shout out to librarians and booksellers — my books would be nowhere and nothing without you.

Finally, to my husband, Mike, and our children Grace, Sophie and George. Thank you for being truly outstanding and for your unwavering belief in me, especially on those days I am filled with self-doubt. This topsy-turvy writing journey is infinitely better with the four of you by my side.

The American Boys is Olivia's third historical fiction novel. Her first two books, *The Girl from London* and *The Songbirds of Florence*, were both number one New Zealand bestsellers. She is the author of two contemporary novels, *A Way Back to Happy* and *A Bumpy Year*. Olivia lives with her family in Auckland, New Zealand, and runs her own business, The Booklover Bookshop, an independent bookstore in the seaside suburb of Milford. To find out more about Olivia and for book club notes, go to oliviaspooner.com.

A heart-wrenching story of love, loss and the resilience of the human spirit.

London, 1940. Ruth volunteers as an escort helping to evacuate children from war-torn England to Australia and New Zealand. Her three-month voyage is fraught — their passage is perilous, and the children anxious and homesick. Nine-year-old Fergus is more troubled than most and Ruth forms an unexpected bond with the boy — and with a fellow volunteer, the infuriatingly laidback Bobby.

Tragedy strikes on their return voyage, when the *Rangitane* is attacked by German raiders. As the ship goes down, the surviving passengers are taken as prisoners of war. To the rest of the world, they are missing, presumed dead.

New Zealand, 2005. Hazel boards a plane to London, eager to explore Europe. Sitting next to her is a man named Joe. On her lap is a treasured book from her grandfather, Fergus. A book that will finally reveal Ruth's story.

A sweeping, captivating, inspiring WWII story.

In 1942, a group of young women arrive in Cairo, Egypt. The Tuis, named after the beautiful New Zealand songbird, are the first women from their country to serve overseas.

Addy joined the Tuis for the adventure. Vivacious and outgoing, she is the life of the party, with an unforgettable voice. Margot is quiet and withdrawn, grieving the young husband she lost to the war. Despite their differences, the girls become fast friends.

When the Tuis are relocated to Italy to set up clubs at grand venues in Florence, Bari and Rome, Addy and Margot are enchanted by the culture. But despite the exhilarating and romantic nature of being abroad in the company of soldiers, dark shadows loom.

And as their illusion of peace is shattered with news of a devastating attack, Margot and Addy will find their endurance pushed to the limit, as they discover the true meaning of courage, sacrifice and sisterhood amidst the brutal reality of WWII.

Read on for an extract from

THE
SONGBIRDS
of
FLORENCE

MARGOT

She entered the trattoria and sat at a small inside table, her back against the cool stone wall. It was a welcome reprieve from the midday heat.

A waiter approached. '*Buongiorno,*' he said, with the slightly flirtatious expression Margot had come to associate with so many Italian men.

'*Buongiorno,*' she replied, continuing in fluent Italian, 'what is the dish of the day?'

The man blinked in surprise, no doubt having assumed she was yet another English or American tourist. They were swarming all over Tuscany at present, with a number of them currently ensconced at the tables beneath the awning out the front.

'Where are you from?' the waiter asked, glancing at Margot's hand. It happened often, that quick, less-than-subtle check for a wedding band. Margot sometimes considered wearing a ring but decided against it: a small yet not insignificant act of defiance.

Margot hesitated before answering, 'New Zealand.'

The man's eyes widened, then he turned his head and shouted towards the kitchen, 'Nonna! This beautiful lady is here all the way from New Zealand.'

There was an answering cry, and seconds later a short, grey-haired woman in a yellow-and-blue apron bustled through the swinging doors. Her eyes filled with tears as she gripped Margot's shoulders and kissed first one cheek then the other. 'We are grateful, so grateful to your Kiwi boys.'

Margot struggled to maintain her composure. '*Grazie*,' she murmured.

The woman studied her face for a moment then dragged a chair closer. She eased herself onto it with a sigh, then leant forward and gripped one of Margot's hands. 'You lost someone here, no?' she asked, in stilted English. 'A husband maybe?'

Margot didn't want to talk about the war. She didn't want to remember what had happened in this tiny village on the outskirts of Florence all those years ago. But it was the reason she was here. The reason she had finally plucked up the courage to come. 'Not a husband,' she said softly in Italian. 'But someone I loved.'

The woman barked at her grandson, who immediately hurried over to the bar.

'He was seven years old when the Nazis came,' the elderly woman whispered. 'He didn't cry once while we hid in the cellar, not once in those long ten days until' – she stopped and took a deep breath – 'until your brave boys saved us. Then he cried for hours.' She wiped at the tears on her cheek then pointed at a woman sweeping past with an armload of dirty plates. Her long shiny black hair was tied back with a scarf. 'His sister, Aria. She was ten years old and she cried every day. Those Nazis killed her father, they beat her *nonno*, they destroyed our home, but' – the woman squeezed Margot's hand – 'we survived, yes?'

Margot nodded, her throat tight. She'd visited the wine cellar that morning: the dark, underground room where, in July 1944, hundreds of citizens of San Michele a Torri had hidden while Nazis occupied the villa overhead. For ten days, with only wine to quench their thirst and a small amount of bread and sugar, they listened to the constant barrage of gunfire and bombing as the Kiwis fought to expel the Germans.

'We didn't know who would open the cellar doors,' the woman said, a wobble in her voice. 'Would it be the Nazis, who had taken our food, our homes, our loved ones, or would we finally be freed?'

Her grandson returned with a bottle of Vin Santo and three small wine glasses. He poured in silence. 'We toast,' said the woman, lifting her glass. 'We toast the bravery of your boys, who came from the other side of the world to help us.'

With a shaking hand, Margot raised her own glass. 'Thank you,' she croaked. 'Thank you for remembering them.'

They downed their drinks, and the woman heaved herself to her feet, patting Margot on the back. 'You eat my fine food, yes?'

'Yes,' Margot replied, forcing a smile.

With the restaurant busy, Margot was left in peace to devour her pasta with a simple peppery sauce, followed by a delicious plate of thinly sliced roasted veal. She took her time, making her way through two glasses of the local white wine and watching the other diners. It didn't bother her sitting at a table alone. She was used to it by now.

When she finally rose to leave, the grandson refused to let Margot pay for her meal. If she insisted, he would be in big trouble, he said, dipping his head towards the kitchen. Margot thanked him warmly and stepped back out into the brightness of the day. Glancing at her watch and deciding she had a little more time before she needed to return to Florence, she wandered past the shops and houses rebuilt after the war and down a chalky track between rows of grapevines to a pond at the bottom of a steep hill. With the sun warming her back, she stared up at the village and thought of all the men she had met during the war years. The ones who had made it home, and those who now lay in cemeteries across Italy and the Middle East. The New Zealanders who'd been a part of the 2nd Division Army twenty years ago would be remembered for many more years to come — and rightly so — but Margot had a feeling her own role in the war would be forgotten, was already fading from history. The women she had worked alongside would become a footnote, a surprising anecdote one or two people might bring up at the dinner table. Some days Margot thought they'd sacrificed every ounce of themselves during the years they'd spent in Cairo, Bari, Rome and Florence; at other times she wondered if their contribution to the war effort had been of any value at all. Not that Margot would ever regret boarding the ship from Wellington to Egypt. The experience had changed her in ways she could never have imagined. For a start, she would never have met Addy.

Checking her watch again, Margot strode back up the hill and climbed into the little Fiat she had hired for the day. She opened her window to release the stuffy air and left it open as she drove down the narrow, winding road. Addy would understand Margot's conflicting thoughts. They had been through so much together since those overwhelming early days in Egypt.

Margot's heart grew lighter as she admired the fields of bright yellow mustard flowers covering the Tuscan hills. She thought of the evening ahead and grinned. Oh, how she had missed her friend. She couldn't wait to finally see Addy again.